THE SILENT MEN

by

Richard H. Dickinson

RUGGED LAND | 276 CANAL STREET · FIFTH FLOOR · NEW YORK CITY · NY 10013 · USA

RuggedLand

Published by Rugged Land, LLC

276 CANAL STREET • FIFTH FLOOR • NEW YORK CITY • NY 10013 • USA

RUGGED LAND and colophon are trademarks of Rugged Land, LLC.
Library of Congress Control Number: 2002091881

Publisher's Cataloging-in-Publication
(Provided by Quality Books, Inc.)
Dickinson, Richard H.
The silent men / by Richard H. Dickinson. -- 1st ed.
p. cm.
ISBN 1-590-71004-5
1. Vietnamese Conflict, 1961-1975--Fiction.
2. African Americans--Fiction. 3. Snipers--Vietnam--
Fiction. I. Title.
PS3604.I455S55 2002   813'.6
QBI33-520

Book Design by
HSU+ASSOCIATES

RUGGED LAND WEBSITE ADDRESS:WWW.RUGGEDLAND.COM

OCTOBER 2002
1   3   5   7   9   10   8   6   4   2
First Edition

DEDICATION

To the silent men of both sides.

ONE

05:09

9 Klicks East of Chau Doc
Kien Phong, Vietnam

The sniper typified a predator: sinuous and quick, remorseless. Nothing about him was gentle except his movement, footfalls so soft he floated in the fog, appearing and fading in the mist like an apparition. His face was black, more visible in the silvery cloud than the pallid skin of a Caucasian, but the terrain was green and deep, and he safely found its ragged shadows. Seeking the thickest vegetation, he sloughed through silently, deftly lifting the stalks and vines, replacing them to their original form, his passage barely discernible to the spotter who followed, ten feet in trail.

Few ventured into the Mekong dawn, when fog diffused across the delta like the discharge of a million smoke grenades. At Firebase Christine, the soldiers snapped alert before sunrise, spooked by the heavy mist, isolated in their bunkers by vapors so thick they touched their eyes to make sure they were open. Even the Americans heard the murmurs of the *Ma Tham Vong*, the Whispering Death Ghost, urging them to join the lifeless. The in-country GI became an animist, like his VC enemy and his ARVN ally, for in those hours of absolute aloneness, there was no limit to what a man might believe.

Forward of the perimeter wire, terrified in their listening posts, the South Vietnamese sentries knew the spirits were alive. There were dead men about, the ghosts of two lost Viet Cong battalions, slaughtered months before by American artillery and napalm. The Vietnamese now called this corner of the delta the Swamp of Silent Men. For them, the fog held the mingled souls of men slain in combat—men doomed to wander where they died, turned away from entry into the Other World. The ARVN troops heard their music and mournful whispers and felt the touch of the frustrated demons that drifted among them. It was unusual for a night to pass without someone in a forward bunker firing his claymore, blasting a swirl of fog to smithereens because of phantoms scampering through the concertina. Only snipers dared to stalk before dawn.

Jackson Monroe thought little of the Silent Men or of the men who feared them. He embraced the fog and used it to tactical advantage, for it provided concealment when he needed to travel. But it was a limited asset for the hunt. The mist hid his approach, but it also cloaked his quarry. Monroe welcomed the fog not for hiding, but for listening. He heard his prey before it heard him. Sound travels in water more distinctly than in air, giving an upper hand to the most stealthy, and Monroe had evolved into one of the most silent men in the delta, as subdued as the soft flutter of bats or the water dripping from banana leaves. He taped his gear, padded his ammo, and drank all of his water at once, so nothing sloshed in a half-filled canteen. He would have preferred to work alone, for sniper teams were only as muted as their noisiest member, and few glided through the underbrush with such lethal silence as Monroe.

Behind, Monroe's spotter followed. Tobias Patterson calmly wrestled his PRC-25 radio through the densest thickets, making subtle noises in the struggle to keep pace. Both men were expert marksmen, but Patterson had more missions under his belt. Patterson intuited Monroe's inexperience in his cockiness, for Monroe led where too few spotters could follow, not with a radio on his back. Patterson would have broken an easier trail, with a more measured pace, and would have considered the man behind him. A proficient sniper didn't need thick foliage to remain undetected. But they were in the shit now and any plaintive whispers would carry more distinctly than the rustle of his radio against the undergrowth. So Patterson followed carefully, straining his eyes in the darkness and listening acutely in an effort to stay within ten yards of his partner. If Monroe faded into the shadows and left him, Patterson knew he would not be able to follow Monroe's invisible trail, and being lost in the Thap Muoi Wilderness was the same as being dead.

They followed the edge of a drying canal that served adjacent rice paddies, now abandoned by farmers killed by Viet Cong tax collectors or American bombs. In the hazy landscape the canal was a familiar avenue of elephant grass and "come-along" vines, thick with mosquitoes and stagnant water that covered the unforgiving Mekong mud.

Monroe retrieved his watch and compass, cupping his hand over the luminous dials. With few terrain features among a massive grid of rice paddies, nipa palms, and a dizzying network of waterways, delta navigation was difficult. And in the fog, even existing landmarks vanished. Dead reckoning was rigorous, too, because it was impossible to judge distance by counting steps in booby-trapped areas of operations that mandated zigzag routes, if walking was possible at all. Monroe judged distance by time; one hour meant three quarters of a klick. They had left Fire Support Base Christine at 1703 hours the previous day, and Monroe knew he was near the target location—a virgin VC supply trail spotted by gunship Huey pilots from the 9th Infantry Division.

Monroe remained motionless, listening. The quietest time of day was just before sunrise, and Monroe thought he could tune in anything: water percolating through the roots of banyan trees, blood sucked through a mosquito's proboscis, photosynthesis. But Monroe heard only Patterson, breathing hard as he struggled to haul his gear through another tangle of undergrowth. They could glimpse each other now in the translucent dawn, and Monroe motioned for Patterson to freeze. After a minute of silence, Monroe diligently checked for trip wires, slowly exhaled, then climbed up the canal bank. Prone at the top of the berm, he listened again, and hearing nothing, slithered into the native bamboo, the shoots still young and pliable, which had grown between the paddy and the canal. Carefully, he moved ahead and pushed aside the undergrowth. The bamboo gave way to the abandoned rice paddy. While the fog prevented him from seeing more than a few feet in front of him, he saw the stubble of past cultivation rotting under the growth of fresh weeds and shoots of wild rice. The blanket of mist still hovered above the surface, but it thinned rapidly in the rising sun. In an hour he would have a thousand yards visibility, every inch within his field of fire. Monroe crawled back into the copse of bamboo and waited for Patterson.

Patterson followed Monroe's trail, assiduously concealing every trace of their passage. Their point of exit, where they left the canal, was a sniper team's vulnerability, the telltale spot most noticeable to anyone tracking them. Patterson crept backward, restoring each blade of grass and broken leaf as he passed over it. By the time he reached Monroe, minimal trace of their inlet was visible, as if they had dropped from the sky. Meticulously and without words, the two men built their hide. They traveled light. Monroe carried the bolt-action, single-shot Remington Model 700-40, plus eighty precious rounds of the highest-quality, "match-grade" 173-grain, boat-tailed, 7.62mm M-118 full-metal-jacketed ammo. Patterson carried an M-14 and ten twenty-round magazines. Regular grunts were burdened with a hundred pounds of gear, but a sniper's pack contained little more than two days' worth of rations and two canteens, plus a first-aid kit. White sniper teams carried camouflage face paint, but like Monroe, Patterson was black and both men viewed the cammo as a white man's burden. Monroe packed a Redfield AccuRange 3x-9x scope, and Patterson a 20x spotter's scope. Snipers didn't carry letters from home, or books or Bibles or good luck charms.

They laid their packs on the ground, covered them with reeds and stalks of grass to obscure their man-made shape. They disguised their human features by stuffing tufts of foliage in their clothes and hats. Dug in with their backs against the berm of the canal, they eliminated their silhouettes against the sky, and then lay on their stomachs to prevent casting shadows when the sun burned off the fog. Each man moved methodically, said nothing, and listened as he settled into the landscape.

As the undercast thinned enough to reveal a row of palm trees a few hundred yards distant, Monroe placed his rifle on his pack before him and removed the lens covers from the scope, set at low power to maximize the field of view. He dug a small hole and placed his left elbow into it. Then, with his left hand gripping the forestock to support the heavy barrel, Monroe grasped the small of the stock firmly with his right hand and pulled it tight into the pocket of his shoulder. All snipers were right-handed, for the cheek-plate was on the left side of the Monte Carlo stock, and Monroe placed his cheek firmly against the thumb of his right hand where it crossed over the top of the stock. This welded his head, hands, and rifle into a single unit, ready to absorb the recoil without losing alignment. Monroe settled the crosshairs on a single nipa palm on the far edge of the clearing. He moved his head rearward a fraction of an inch, until his right eye was two inches from the scope itself. The focus was clean, with no shadows in the sight picture. Monroe relaxed and closed his eyes. When he opened them, the scope's reticle remained squarely on the palm tree. He had found his natural point of aim, and he would be able to maintain his firing position with a minimum of muscle strain or tension. When the time came to take a shot, there would be no trembling from exhausted or cramped muscles. He could now remain motionless for hours.

Beside Monroe, Patterson prepared his own equipment. His task was simpler. Though no less of a marksman, the spotter's purpose was to support the sniper, to help identify the target, to monitor the results of his partner's shot, and if need be to protect his sniper in the aftermath. Patterson's M-14 lay next to him, accessible but not shouldered. Equipped only with iron sights, he carried the semiautomatic M-14 rifle in case their position was compromised and they had to lay down a blanket of fire to buy time for escape. The M-14's open sights were better than Monroe's long rifle for firing on running targets, which tended to pass too quickly through the narrow field of view of the high-powered sniper's scope. The spotter's primary tool was the 20-power M-49 spotter's scope, twice as powerful as the AccuRange mounted on Monroe's rifle. With it, Patterson would estimate wind speed by viewing fluctuations in the ever-present heat mirages. And if the first shot missed, the spotter's scope could identify the point of impact of the miss. The spotter could then quickly adjust the sniper's fire for a second shot. Patterson put his eye to the scope and found a comfortable position. Like Monroe, he did not know when he might move again.

The sun rose higher. As its rays penetrated the mists at increasing angles, rainbows marched across the field, the Silent Men retreating on parade. Then came harsher shadows, as the crickets limbered up their rasps, and dragonflies sortied below the rising ceiling just above the black-mouthed geckos who croaked for another torrid day in the delta. With each increase in visibility, the sniper team scanned the field before them. After another hour, the last mists would dissolve, and the sun would reveal a barren paddy with unrestricted fields of fire.

As the distant tree line came into view, Monroe focused on the raised trail along a dike above the fallow paddies. The path ran perpendicular to his line of sight, partially hidden under the overhanging tree branches. Monroe estimated the range to the trail at six hundred yards. Peering into the shadows among the trees, he settled in for another day's vigil, his fortieth since earning his sniper qualifications. On those missions, he was credited with seventeen kills.

Patterson hated waiting. As the sun rose, so did the temperature, and the beads of perspiration on the back of his neck attracted shimmering clouds of gnats seeking moisture and mosquitoes hunting blood. Sweat trickled off the ends of his hair, drowning the tiny insects in the folds of his skin. Patterson did not move, for he found the physical discomforts of his profession more bearable than the mental ones. He had been in-country for eleven months, six more than Monroe. With one hundred missions behind him and forty-five confirmed kills as a sniper, this was his tenth mission as Monroe's spotter.

Patterson was a short timer and he knew that his internal countdown made his hands fractionally unsteady. He'd lost precise control of his breathing. He had handed over the Remington and would never ask for its return—three or four more missions, and he'd be headed back to The World.

Now he lay in weeds, trickling sweat and losing blood to the swarms of mosquitoes, watching heat mirages dip and flutter and tilt in the lens of his spotting scope. He wished desperately for a target, if only to justify communicating with Monroe, who lay hypnotically still, with only an occasional flair of his nostrils indicating he was alive. Patterson envied his partner's silent tolerance of misery, though he wondered if the price a man paid for that kind of fortitude was an equal indifference to pleasure. In the time he'd known him, Monroe never joked and he had no vocabulary for casual banter, even inside the relative security of base camp. Patterson was everyone's friend, while Monroe had none. They were partnered together solely because they were both black, but in Patterson's estimation, Monroe was as cold as a white man; he had no soul.

Their hunting had been bad, just two kills in their ten missions together. Neither of those targets was worth the bullets that killed them, thought Patterson—a couple of horse-playing gooks foolish enough to fuck around on a trail in broad daylight. Snipers prided themselves on important quarry, and it bothered Patterson that Monroe announced their presence in the AO by expending ammo on lesser targets. Nevertheless, large-scale enemy activity was down and the brass credited the sniper teams. Patterson didn't think their two kills had anything to do with Charlie's disappearance.

The Americans were not the only force to arm sharpshooters with long-range rifles and telescopic sights. But most VC snipers were local cadre with decrepit weapons who took potshots at passing traffic, rarely hitting anyone. Often, passing American targets didn't even know they'd been shot at. Still, Charlie did have some skilled marksmen, NVA-trained men with icy nerves and animal instincts every bit as dangerous as Patterson or Monroe. And one of them was in their AO now, picking off Americans, fourteen in the previous eight weeks. His attacks were scattered miles apart, and he never took two shots from the same hide. Even with additional targets in his sights, he never got greedy, leaving the survivors to spread rumors of the enemy sniper who never missed.

Division was anxious. Sudden death was bad for morale, and rumor even worse. The sniper, some grunts said, was an American, gone over to the enemy. Or gone nuts. ARVN troops called him a phantom. The commanders wrote off the ignorant and superstitious but they could not ignore the impact of the sniper's unexpected bullets. A convoy of supplies running from Division HQ in Dong Tam to FSB Christine sat duck because one shot took out the lead driver, causing a deuce and a half full of ammo to careen into a rice paddy. There was no explosion, but the other drivers cowered in their cabs for six hours before the lieutenant in command tore ass and got them rolling again.

For Division HQ, the convoy was the last straw. Reasoning that the most effective weapon against a sniper is another sniper, they dispatched sixteen division sniper teams across the delta. Monroe and Patterson competed with the other teams to hunt the man down.

Movement on the trail. Monroe and Patterson focused their eyes through the lenses of their scopes, not sure what they had seen, only sure that something had stirred. They calmed their breathing, focused their eyes wide, scanned the trail, watched shadows in the trees, and waited for whatever had moved to move again.

A dog stepped into the sunlight, sniffing deliberately, as if cognizant of the danger of an exposed position. A mixed breed with protruding ribs that heaved with each breath, he panted in the heat.

"Crosswind," whispered Patterson to remind Monroe that the dog would not smell them, as long as it stayed on the trail. Trained dogs were dangerous, and Charlie used them effectively to clear his passage. Monroe leveled the crosshairs on the animal and briefly considered killing it. But he knew that the real target would follow. Monroe kept his finger off the trigger as the dog trotted along the path, stopping once to mark a clump of growth before moving on. At last, the dog reentered the bush, five hundred yards downwind.

Monroe tightened his grip on the Remington and steadied his sight picture, focused where the dog had first appeared. "Get ready," he whispered. "Charlie won't be far behind."

As with the dog, Monroe sensed movement before he identified the pajama-clad figure emerging from the trees. He swung the muzzle to his left and focused the AccuRange for a better look. Patterson, too, adjusted the focus on his wide scope and the face of the figure came into view. "It's a kid," muttered Patterson.

"Weapon?"

"AK-47."

"What's he carrying?" asked Monroe.

"Elephant intestines." Patterson used the slang for the bolts of rolled cloth the VC carried across their backs. "Probably rice." The weight pulled the boy forward and down so that he could not raise his head to fire his weapon without first dropping the load.

"He looks to be about ten years old," whispered Patterson. His first kill, a boy with rotten teeth and Ho Chi Minh sandals, flashed in his mind. That boy carried rice bags too. Patterson shot him in the ear because he also carried an AK-47. Patterson turned in his kill sheet that day and did not think about the mission for six months, until one day, the rotten-tooth boy began waking him up, sitting on his cot every morning, staring at him until Patterson was fully conscious and the nightmare faded away.

Monroe centered the crosshair on the target's chest and fingered the trigger.

"Monroe. It's a little kid." There was urgency in Patterson's voice.

Monroe paused. "No shot."

The kid had a weapon and they were in a free fire zone. The kill would have been legal, and most snipers would take it. Monroe took his finger off the trigger.

"You got kids, Patterson?"

Patterson glanced at his partner, surprised by the familiarity. Monroe had never before asked a personal question of him. "Three."

Monroe seemed not to have heard, but continued tracking the target with his scope.

As the boy approached the edge of the clearing, where the trail turned back into the jungle, he stopped. He dropped the roll to the ground and placed his rifle on top. He withdrew a handkerchief from his pocket and wiped his face and brow, then drank from his canteen.

After replacing the canteen in his pack, the boy opened another pouch and withdrew a folded sheet of paper. He opened it. He looked behind him, then ahead, then at the paper in his hands, studying it by the light of the afternoon sun. He turned and stared across the abandoned rice field, directly into the lens of Patterson's spotting scope.

Patterson cursed. "*Dinka dau,* motherfucker."

"Map," said Monroe, his finger back on the Remington's trigger. "He won't be able to see any landmarks once he goes back into the jungle."

Intel offered two-day passes for every useful map recovered by snipers. Battles were won or lost with maps. The boy soldier wandered away from his gear as he studied the document, not realizing that it was his death warrant. *Dinka dau,* thought Patterson again. *Crazy.*

"Wind still four knots," said Patterson, all business, resigned to the boy's death. He watched as Monroe reached for the windage knob on the Remington and turned it a click.

The youngster refolded the map and stuffed it into his pocket. He turned and stepped off the raised trail, hopping into the mud below, directly facing the men who were about to kill him.

Through his more powerful scope, Patterson was the first to realize that the target was female. She pulled down her pajama pants and squatted.

"Aw, Christ," Patterson groaned. "It's a girl, Monroe! I guess she don't want to piss in the middle of the fucking trail."

"Head shot," announced Monroe. He closed his mind to the fact that his crosshairs centered on the face of a girl, or that she was in a helpless position. He focused on the fact that the body would have cover below the berm, out of sight of any VC following her path, which would make his recovery of the map less dangerous. And the body was still. Any shot taken at a moving target over five hundred yards introduced too many variables to be a guaranteed one-shot, one-kill opportunity. He took up the slack in the trigger, partially exhaled, then held the remaining breath and waited for the trigger to release at exactly four and one half pounds of pull. He was ready for the recoil when it came.

A sniper instinctively knows when a shot is on target, and Monroe felt the satisfying kick at precisely the right moment: between breaths and heartbeats. The heavy barrel, nearly as thick at the muzzle as at the breach, spit the bullet so smoothly that Monroe felt it travel the length of the bore. The bolt-action rifle fires with a higher muzzle velocity than an automatic because no exhaust gas is diverted to blow back the bolt. The aerodynamic round flew the six hundred yards to the target in just under two seconds.

Two seconds, however, was sufficient time for the girl to stand and begin pulling up her black pajama bottoms. The bullet, aimed originally at her head, plowed instead into her abdomen. The weighty round drove straight through the soft tissue of her torso, exiting cleanly through her back. The impact lifted her into the air, and the pulsating action of cavitation, in the wake of the bullet, ruptured every mesenteric blood vessel below her diaphragm. Expanding gasses pushed the mixture of blood and tissue up though her digestive track, so that a crimson spout of vomit arched from her mouth as she pitched backward against the ground.

"Hit," verified Patterson. It was SOP for the spotter to call hits and misses, but Patterson made it clear by the tone of his voice that the shot was a disaster. "You gut-shot her."

Furious, Monroe jacked another brass shell into the smoking chamber and slammed the bolt forward. It was one thing to kill a woman. But to shoot her in the stomach—the worst way to die—was the act of a sadist.

The victim lay faceup, arms at her sides, motionless against the embankment. Patterson could see that her eyes were closed and blood had gushed from her mouth, soaking her face and chin and chest. "Don't shoot," he said. "She's dead."

"You sure?"

"If she ain't, she ain't suffering none."

Monroe could see how she lay, face to the sun, and recalled what his First Shirt had once told him about corpses on the battlefield: dead men lie faceup; the wounded roll over to protect themselves. Undoubtedly, the bullet had scrambled her internal organs. She was dead of shock and blood loss, if nothing else. Monroe took his finger off the trigger. Every shot risked exposure and there was no need to take another.

They lay still for fifteen minutes, not speaking, listening for sounds behind them and watching for movement on the trail. The sun began its descent. The temperature eased by a degree. The killing ground remained silent as the birds and insects waited with the snipers for any threat to show itself.

Nothing appeared on the trail or in the trees beyond it, and Monroe heard no sounds from the abandoned canal behind them. He suspected that she walked alone, thus the necessity of her carrying the map, and why she thought little of relieving herself so brazenly. Monroe doubted that anyone had spotted the muzzle flash. Still, if there had been others, and if they were VC, they were already maneuvering to outflank them. It was time to move out.

They gathered their gear and low-crawled through the thickets and coarse grass, parallel to the body below the trail. As before, Patterson restored the trampled weeds, obscuring the traces of their passage. One hundred yards upwind, they stopped and scoped the terrain.

Nothing stirred, save the birds that returned to the paddy after fleeing from the Remington's crack to feed on field mice and kernels of wild rice. The girl lay where she fell, still facing the sun, lower now on the horizon.

In order to be credited a kill, snipers were required to search their victims for items of military intelligence and to recover the enemy weapon. Monroe would collect the map, of course, but the score meant more to him, another number to put up on the board for the other snipers to see. It pained Patterson to see Monroe make the same mistake he had made with the rotten-tooth boy, when his own score meant something to him. Some snipers claimed not to count, but every man did.

Monroe handed the Remington to Patterson. "If anybody comes, don't shoot unless they spot me."

Patterson settled into position while Monroe crawled ahead, taking only the M-14. He turned toward the field and slid on his belly into the rice paddy. He employed the sniper's crawl, a motion undetectable from even a few feet away. But at that pace, it would take days to cover the entire distance to his victim. And if he waited until dark, VC trail traffic would begin.

When he had covered enough distance to disguise his point of entry, Monroe breathed deeply, and quietly rose to his full height. He started to jog, slowly, but steadily, avoiding turns and stumbles. The only thing more noticeable on open ground than a runner is an erratic runner. Monroe had already bet his life that the trail was unwatched by anyone but Patterson; there was no point in second guessing himself by zigzagging.

Two minutes passed as Monroe labored across the field. Although his pace was restrained, and all snipers were physically well conditioned, the heat and his fear conspired to exhaust him. Twenty yards away from the girl, he sank to the ground, closed his eyes, tuned in to the surroundings, and calmed his panting. He looked back, but could see nothing in the now distant undergrowth where Patterson watched from his hide. Monroe gave Patterson a careful thumbs-up, then began his final crawl to the girl.

He reached the embankment, fifteen feet from the body. He could see her clearly now, the blood drying on her face, flies feasting. It wasn't the first kill he'd seen up close. But this was his youngest, a sparrow of a woman, and even in death her face bespoke innocence. Monroe looked away. Overhead, he spotted a vulture drifting on the rising thermals from the sweltering land, keying on the battlefield's lone body below. He concentrated on his training and swept the kill zone.

Above the body, still resting on the trail where she had placed them, lay her rifle and pack and saddlebags. Monroe reached over his head and slowly tugged the gear toward him, catching it as it came over the edge of the embankment. He did not see the dog resting on the trail.

Her AK-47 was worthless, more dangerous to the shooter than the target. The butt was cracked and there was no magazine, but Monroe would carry it home. Intel counted recovered rifles to be the same as an actual body. He did not waste time inspecting the rest of the gear, but dragged it with him as he turned to the body.

He could see now that the front of her pajamas were soaked with blood, already stiff and turning black in the sun. But the clothes were different than the black pajamas worn by the others he had killed; these were pressed and clean, except for the blood, as if they had never been worn before. The woman's hands were soft and well manicured, and she wore canvas shoes on her feet. Monroe had never seen a VC with any footwear other than rubber flip-flops. *You ain't no village mama-san.*

He did not touch her, but reached into her pocket for the map, nearly gagging as his hand felt through the blood that had pooled there, now coagulated to the consistency of jelly. The map and another piece of paper protected in an envelope were there, along with a single stick of Juicy Fruit gum. The snarl of the flies grew louder, vicious in the ambient silence. As he turned to leave, he glanced at the young woman's face.

Her eyes were open and focused, black as the bore of his Remington, watching him.

Monroe recoiled, tripping over the girl's saddlebags as he fumbled for the M-14. Alerted by the noise, the dog sprang from the bush, barking viciously, the ragged fur on its back standing on end.

Monroe grabbed the saddlebags and held them to his throat as the dog leapt. The animal sank his fangs into the armlike sack, ripping it open and spewing its contents in an arc across the field. Monroe rolled to his right, clawing his web gear for his K-Bar knife. The dog's next bite would be for his jugular.

The dog's head disintegrated. A mist of bone and brain burst skyward as a bullet ripped through his snout. The dull smack of the bullet's impact was followed a moment later by the sound of the Remington, like thunder after lightning. The dog lay twitching, nerve impulses still discharging with no brain to guide them.

Only habit and training compelled Monroe to remain at the scene long enough to retrieve his weapon. His right hand pulled the M-14 from a shallow mud puddle. He clutched the saddlebags and AK-47 in his left hand as he bolted away, head up, knees pumping, high-stepping through the mud. If the dog alerted nearby VC soldiers, he would soon be racing bullets.

He covered three hundred yards at a dead run, then collapsed into the muck. He was beyond the effective range of AK-47 fire from the trail; anything that hit him now would be dumb luck. He crawled a few feet, sobbing with relief and exhaustion, listening for the rattle of gunfire behind him and the sizzle of incoming rounds. But he heard nothing but his own gasping, and after a moment of rest he stumbled on, his legs rubbery with fatigue. Three hundred yards away, Patterson held tight, watching Monroe's exaggerated efforts through his spotter's scope.

Monroe staggered back to his feet, lumbering on in slow motion. At last the undergrowth rushed up to envelop him, as Monroe pitched headfirst into its embrace. He lay on his back for an eternity, too spent to conceal himself. The field remained silent and empty. The shadows grew long as the sun faded to the color of urine. He had to press on, and he wondered where the hell was Patterson.

"What the fuck happened out there?" Patterson came into view.

"The girl was bleeding out. Still alive."

"Christ."

"Where the hell did the dog come from?" gasped Monroe.

"He came back a long time ago. Nothing I could do to warn you. I figured you saw him."

"Not until he bit." Monroe threw the saddlebags to the ground and reached for his pack. "She must be dead now," he hoped out loud. They could not risk a mercy kill.

Patterson swung the PRC-25 radio onto his back. It didn't get much worse, a gut-shot girl left to bleed out. "Let's *di di*. It'll be dark in an hour."

"I thought you couldn't shoot anymore," said Monroe, calming down as he prepared his gear. Patterson's bullet hit a small airborne target at six hundred yards with dozens of variables—a remarkable head shot.

"I can shoot dogs." Patterson handed the Remington to Monroe and took back the M-14. "You shoot the people." His face was blank, his eyes focused on the terrain.

Monroe strapped the woman's saddlebag to his pack.

"Fuck the rice," said Patterson. "Leave that shit here."

"It ain't rice." Monroe reached into the torn sack and withdrew a small cardboard box.

"What the fuck she doing with that?"

"Four boxes," said Monroe. "Two hundred rounds of 7.62 match-grade ammo. Gooks probably stole it from the division armory. They're killing us with our own fuckin' bullets." His voice found its confidence again and the kill began its slow fade into the righteous death compartment in his mind.

"We gotta move." Somewhere close was a VC sniper waiting for his ammunition. "You got the map?"

Monroe reached into his pocket and waved a bloodstained envelope. "She wasn't reading just a map. Maybe Intel can read it and figure out where the fuck she was going."

"Let's go," said Patterson.

Monroe took the lead, crawling double-time into the abandoned canal. They moved briskly now, less careful to cover their trail, determined to put as much distance between themselves and the body as possible. After twenty minutes, Monroe moderated the pace. By nightfall, they moved slowly, checking for trip wires, covering their trail. Monroe pointed to a thicket of roots and weeds and vines in darkest shadow. They would wait there till midnight, and return to Christine's perimeter in the fog. The Silent Men would be thick tonight, with one more soul in the air.

T W O

Fire Support Base Christine
Kien Phong

P atterson made no effort to contact Christine's RTO. They hunkered down in deep foliage outside the firebase to wait for daylight. Leaving Christine in the dark was dangerous; entering it was suicide. Patterson took first watch while Monroe slept, his first in forty-eight hours.

Fire Support Base Christine sat on a barren knob of ground two feet higher than the surrounding delta. A small piece of relatively dry real estate in the middle of swamp, it was the farthest outpost from Dong Tam—headquarters of the 9th Infantry Division—and deep in the VC-dominated Base Area 470. Viewed from an approaching Huey, it had the appearance of a billiard rack with a watchtower at each corner. Christine served as a support station to dispatch troops into the hairy AO that was Charlie's supply trail from Cambodia into the delta. The stay-at-home ARVN soldiers and GI advisers were tasked with providing artillery fire from six 105mm howitzers whenever ops were underway. But the MACV rules for engagement paralyzed Christine's effectiveness. Grunts in the field could not fire into Cambodia even if fired on. And the artillery had to be targeted inside the Vietnamese side of the border. Breaking ROE meant a certain court-martial for ARVN and GI alike and Charlie took full advantage of Cambodia's neutrality. With the thousands of entry points along the amorphous demarcation, thick cover to protect him, and the decided advantage of operating primarily at night, Charlie lost few men to Christine's WWII–era Howitzers.

The troops at Christine, isolated and vulnerable, obsessively prepared for the inevitable—Charlie in the wire. They filled C-ration tins with pebbles and dangled them on the concertina surrounding Christine's perimeter. If Charlie attempted to infiltrate, he'd send them clattering to the ground. Claymore mines waited in the tangle foot ready to blow away anything that moved, or anything that was imagined to move, by the jittery troops in their bunkers. M-60 machine gun pits ringed the perimeter just inside the wire. Spaced forty yards from one to the other, the pits were divided by additional two-man foxholes.

The fog lifted at 0800. Patterson broke squelch and alerted the RTO. They exchanged passwords. A moment later, an ARVN private opened the northeast gate. The snipers broke cover and fast-timed it inside the perimeter. Passing the machine guns, and then the six Howitzer pits, they made their way into the deepest and most protected ring of Christine's onion. A sandbagged tactical operations center for radio operations and command personnel formed the epicenter. One hundred ARVN infantry and a few dozen artillerymen bunkered in around it, half sleeping, half on guard duty. American advisers were among them, and many Mekong GIs bivouacked at Christine at one time or another while on operations. The snipers found a tent, stowed their gear, and crashed on adjacent cots.

Monroe woke at 1207, the ten-man quarters an oven. He sat on the edge of his cot and blew a film of sweat off his upper lip. The other beds, occupied at night by the US advisers, supported rucksacks and web gear with grenades and ammo pouches attached. M-16s and bandoleers of ammo hung on the poles. Patterson snored quietly, facedown beside Monroe, his T-shirt soaked through. Beads of sweat clung to his hair. Monroe checked his boots for centipedes before he pulled them on, then reached under the cot for his Remington. He was hungry, but his rifle was dirty and the food could wait. He stepped outside.

Shielding his eyes against the midday sun, he scanned the horizon. To the west he saw a thousand yards of rice paddies crisscrossed by dikes, tended by Vietnamese women in conical hats, bent at the waist, water to their knees. To the east was the Bassac River, a branch of the Mekong, an ocean of mud and Cambodian sewage sliding southerly en route to the South China Sea. An irrigation canal joined the river along Christine's southern edge, its deep black water and slippery banks made even more impassable with the addition of sharpened stakes and claymores. Beyond the canal, where the border between land and river blurred, lay ground too wet to cultivate, but dry enough for a jungle of mangroves and vines. More wire surrounded the flank, and additional minefields stretched along the other approaches, where the trails and dikes led right up to the southern gate. Interlocking fields of fire extended as far as he could see, but Monroe took little comfort in them. An army could approach along the river at night, through the mangroves, and if Charlie could move as slowly and quietly as Monroe did, he could put five hundred men in black pajamas through the wire before anyone knew what hit them.

Monroe turned his attention inside the camp, searching for a patch of shade. He saw only the circle of gun pits, each thirty feet across, with the 105mm Howitzers in the center, surrounded by a wall of sandbags sufficient to stop shrapnel or incoming small arms fire. High-explosive shells were stacked inside the walls, and sandbagged corridors led to the fortified ammo bunker, stuffed with five hundred additional HE shells, plus specialty rounds like Willie Peter, smoke, and beehives. Christine had wooden observation towers at its triangular points, like reinforced tree houses—an appearance as intimidating as the tiger-striped ARVN soldiers manning them.

The tactical operations center was a hovel of sandbags with a log roof covered with old ammo boxes filled with yet more sand. The cover would stop incoming shrapnel, but mostly it protected the RTOs, forward observers, and plotting technicians from the concussions of the Howitzers.

The TOC was a hot, dark, crowded, noisy place during a fire mission, but the guns had been quiet for several days. Whenever snipers moved into an AO, Charlie laid low. A few kills were all it took to rattle the local VC.

Other firebases strung up volleyball nets during lulls, but Christine was not that kind of place. The gun pits, command bunkers, and sleeping hooches barely left space for the latrine, and the ever-present mud was so slippery it was difficult to walk. Because Christine's knoll was the only land above sea level for miles, it served as a graveyard for previous generations of farmers. Only here could a grave be dug more than a foot deep without hitting water. During the last monsoon, the boots of 150 men had churned the soil into mud as deep as their knees, which was better than the waist-deep water everywhere else. But the bones of the dead had a habit of rising to the surface. The ARVNs said the fog was thicker around Christine than in other parts of the delta because of the wandering souls of the uprooted skeletons. The Silent Men, they added, kept the enemy away. But the ground hardened during the January dry season and the baked earth threw up an ashy dust. The Americans hoped there were still enough ghosts around to keep Charlie at bay.

Christine was populated by ARVN artillerymen and G-2 Recondos sent there to protect them. They were as filthy as the corpse-filled dirt they lived in. Sleepless and half deaf from the guns, unmotivated and perpetually terrified, they were exhausted and brutal men. They had no respect for themselves or for each other or for the authority of officers or for the dead, whose bones they tossed into the canals. Many Recondos were petty criminals, recruited from Vietnamese prisons and offered a shot at freedom and a snazzy set of tiger-striped fatigues in exchange for their time at Christine. Even if there had been room for a volleyball net, they would have laughed at the idea.

One general-purpose tent, twenty by forty feet, was set up with a wooden floor and the side flaps raised to allow air circulation. The Americans called the tent the "dance floor," and it was the only available shade at Christine. A knot of ARVN soldiers gathered at one corner of the hooch, listening to American rock and roll on radio AFN—the Armed Forces Network. Their conversation turned to muttering as Monroe approached, the lethal Remington conspicuous in his left hand. Snipers unnerved them, for they imagined that Monroe thought of himself as a hunter and his quarry as animals, and his quarry looked just like they did. And Monroe was a black man, *do moi ro*. The ARVN wanted no black advisers, nor Chinese, nor Montagnard, nor Cambodian. They wanted purebreds, like themselves, and purebred Americans were white.

Monroe spread his cleaning gear on his poncho liner between his legs and began disassembling his weapon.

An American adviser stepped onto the dance floor. The Army had run out of Special Forces units to man every outpost and firebase, and now filled the requirements for advisers from the ranks of combat units. Courage and combat savvy were the primary criteria for selection, although it was not unheard of for commanders to occasionally "volunteer" a troublemaker in order to get him out of the commander's unit. The GI squatted on his haunches and watched Monroe work. Monroe did not look up, though he noticed that the man had a skull tattooed on his left arm and the sleeves of his fatigue shirt had been removed at the shoulder.

"Musta been good hunting last night."

"Yeah."

"The captain sent your Intel up to Division on the morning log bird. Pretty heavy shit, all that ammo. How many of them magic bullets was that gook carrying?"

"Couple hundred," said Monroe.

The soldier nodded. An eight-month veteran in-country, he had paid his dues as an infantryman, and had been assigned duty as an adviser after his second Purple Heart. He was callous and crude, no Green Beret, but he knew what an enemy sniper could do with 200 rounds of match-grade ammo.

"Must be a trip." He waited for a reaction, got none. "Out there alone.

Seeing some gook's face before you waste him."

Monroe ignored him and soaked a swab with Hoppe's #9 powder solvent. He knew what was coming next.

"I've killed beaucoup gooks, man. Them're some mean motherfuckers and I could dig lookin' one in the eyes and puttin' a bullet between 'em. Real personal-like." The man added, "I hate these raggedy-ass ARVN, and these fucking guns are making me deaf."

"You ain't got what it takes, Sylvester."

Startled, the adviser turned to find Patterson behind him. Patterson stepped lightly onto the dance floor and stretched, then squatted Vietnamese-style. To blacks, all white men were weak sisters named Sylvester. But Patterson's demeanor was friendly, and the man took no offense. He offered Patterson his hand and led him through an elaborate ritual of knuckles and palms passed against each other, fingers grasped and released. He conducted the dap with pride, for he had learned it in the jungle from black boonie rats where everything was shared, and the dap wasn't just for blue boys.

"I can shoot a rifle pretty fucking good," said Sylvester.

"You talk too much," Monroe challenged.

"And you ain't got the personality for the job," added Patterson. "You can't be worrying about what it's like to kill a man personal-like. That shit'll fuck you up." Patterson knew what he was talking about.

"And snipers ain't deaf," said Monroe, ending the conversation.

The two snipers glanced at each other and grinned. The white man caught the telepathy and realized he was not a part of this conversation. He rose— "Killing with a fucking telescope ain't nothing"—and walked away.

"That boy would make a good sniper if he can shoot good as he shakes hands," said Patterson.

Monroe almost laughed as he ran a swab down the bore of his rifle. It was the closest Patterson had seen Monroe come to camaraderie. The two snipers had become partners when Monroe's previous teammate, a new boy named

Sadowski, disappeared somewhere in the Thap Muoi Wilderness. Monroe never explained what had happened when he had returned alone, stating only that they had separated in the swamp and lost each other's trail. Division sent SAR teams out for five straight days, though nobody was surprised when he didn't return. The other snipers knew Monroe was hard to follow, like a shadow. *The nigger musta slinked away from him,* they said. *Just left the poor bastard out there wondering where the fuck he went.* Monroe, saying nothing, held firm and let them think whatever they wanted.

Many snipers were Southern crackers who grew up hating niggers, learning their craft early shooting squirrels for the sheer satisfaction of killing living targets. The idea of a black sniper would have been hilarious to them if it were not for the fact that Monroe could outshoot every one of them. All were solitary and unsociable men, with the confidence and steady nerves of youth and eyes that communicated more than their mouths, whether on a mission or on R&R. Their quietude was disconcerting to grunts their age, most of whom felt compelled to fill the silence of the world with gunfire, music, or the sound of their own voices. Even Patterson, as easygoing as any sniper in the division, felt disjoined from the other snipers, though he recognized that they ignored him by the same measure that they ignored each other.

It was Monroe they truly ostracized, and who enraged them by not noticing. Monroe was from Philadelphia, a *Yankee* nigger, handsome and smart, who looked down on the hayseeds and hillbillies. With square, glossy teeth, mahogany skin, and tightly curled hair, Monroe exuded disdain, provoking the insecurities of the poor white trash, further infuriating them. He didn't know his place. So when faced with the task of assigning a new partner, the CO assigned Monroe to hunt with Tobias Patterson, the only man who would work with him, the only other Negro sniper in the division. "Why all the white boys hate you?" asked Patterson.

"I'm smarter than they are. Nothing like a smart nigger, to piss off the Man."

"Then you must be one smart motherfucker."

Monroe grinned, and Patterson smiled, quietly sucking in little breaths that passed for laughs among snipers. Patterson knew he was stupid; his acknowledgment of his limitations was his most endearing quality . . . He muttered, "If you so smart, Monroe, what you wandering around for in this crazy fuckin' fog? You ain't no ghetto trash like the rest of us."

"I'm trash, just like you, Patterson. A brother don't stop being trash just because he got a high school fuckin' diploma."

Patterson persisted. "Still, you ain't a moron. Snipers is a volunteer assignment. Why'd you volunteer for this shit, when you coulda been a REMF?"

"Why'd you?"

"I don't know," said Patterson with a shrug and a grin that revealed a gold front tooth, the most valuable thing he would probably ever own. "My captain saw I could shoot. I don't remember signing no papers."

Monroe wondered how a man so dull-witted could function so well on the battlefield. Patterson could shoot vultures out of the sky, and decipher a map like a cartographer, yet in three weeks someone would have to tell him when to catch the freedom bird back to The World because he couldn't read his own orders.

Patterson smiled at his ignorance, accepting whatever came along, not even imagining that he might be able to do anything about it. Monroe suffered the curse of all intelligent men: the arrogant conviction that he could control his own fate. It galled him that a man as dense as Patterson had achieved the same level of success without the slightest effort.

"I signed everything I could get my hands on," said Monroe. "I submitted 1049s for every MOS in the army: door gunner, AirCav, K-9, cook, demolition, NCO Academy, tanks, artillery, clerk-typist, MPs, everything. I wasn't going be a grunt anymore, humping the swamp every day, my feet rotting off, carrying all that shit and living like an animal. That shit is for dumb motherfuckers who can't do anything else. I even volunteered for

Officer Candidate School. And pilot training. Snipers is what I got."

Patterson burst into laughter. "Officer! Shit, Monroe, you blacker 'n fucking shoe polish. No white man gonna salute no nigger officer. ARVNs neither."

"Fuck 'em," said Monroe. "Sylvester can salute with his honky ass, for all I care."

"Snipers!"

Monroe glanced into the sun. The silhouette of Master Sergeant Wolfe stood before him. Wolfe was a lifer, a twenty-year Masterblaster who ran the show at Christine, notwithstanding the ARVN commander or the American officer to whom he reported. He looked the part of a military adviser, a proper soldier, square and powerful. Even his uniform seemed crisp, despite the filth in which he lived and the air that sagged with humidity. "Log bird's inbound. Division wants you to report ASAP."

"What for?" asked Monroe.

"Didn't say. Gather up your gear." Wolfe appreciated having snipers attached to his command, even if he didn't like the sullen bastards themselves. These two had been with them for three weeks and seemed to have single-handedly pacified the entire AO, scaring the bejeezus out of everyone within ten miles. Christine had not fired their guns in days.

The Remington was clean. Monroe expertly reassembled it, while Patterson gathered up the cleaning equipment. Wolfe waited patiently, staring at a contingent of ARVN, lounging by their Howitzer, who stared back with insolent sneers. They were a vicious pack, filthy as dogs, comparing necklaces of VC ears and homemade tattoos. They were professional killers—Wolfe had taught them that well enough—but they were not professional soldiers.

The snipers were ready. "Look sharp," said Wolfe, not for Division, but for the ARVN troops. He wanted them to see what real soldiers looked like.

T⚏REE

Chau Doc, Vietnam

The Nung guards lounged with malevolent grace outside the concrete-block wall that surrounded the apartment building. The wall was topped with barbed wire and shards of glass to deter thieves and beggars, but it provided no protection from VC surveillance. Which is why the residents had informed their contacts within the local cadre of the American major who had rented an apartment in the building. The mercenary Nung were his bodyguards.

Dac studied their dark faces, moving the crosshairs of the telescopic sight from one to the other. Though of different builds, one squat as a mortar, the other lithe, they possessed the identical eyes of men who had never known security or comfort. With a reputation for savage ferocity and unconditional loyalty, Nung tribesmen were recruited by the CIA for covert missions and personal security. Each man carried an M-16, but it was their secondary weapons that interested Dac. They wore K-Bar knives suspended upside down from the shoulder straps of their web gear, ready to slash a throat simply as part of the act of drawing it from its scabbard. Dac lowered the crosshair to a pistol strapped to the squat man's hip. The pearl-handled grip of the 9mm Browning was clearly not US Army issue. Only CIA customized side arms and Dac found it remarkable that they would advertise themselves so blatantly.

The NLF, the political arm of Charlie's forces in South Vietnam, had known of the Army major for months prior to his rental of the apartment. A bear of a man, he was the kind of American loved by the Vietnamese—full of laughter, money, and boisterous camaraderie. Most Vietnamese found the Americans as inscrutable as the GIs found their ARVN allies and NVA/ VC enemies. But they enjoyed the company of any man who treated them with unself-conscious respect and expressed himself in unambiguous ways. Recognized as a spy hiding in plain sight, his behavior baffled the NLF, who debated whether to kill him or cultivate him as a counterintelligence source. The major settled the matter himself, however, by falling in love. The object of his affection was a young woman, seemingly no one of consequence, who kept the books at a local Texaco distributorship. The apartment was for her.

Dac lay in a drainage ditch alongside Route 91, the only road to Chau Doc from Saigon. During the rainy season, the culvert filled with water to the level of the flooded Bassac River that formed the border for both sides of the highway, but now only six brackish inches of water remained. Monsoons were still months away and the rice paddies on both sides of the road were thirsty and ready for harvest. Dac had been in the ditch since midnight, having crept a mile through the paddies, enfiladed behind the elevated highway. The Nung, too, had been there all night, vigilant outside the wrought iron gate. They remained purposeful and alert even as the fog-burning sun appeared on the horizon. Dac estimated the range at five hundred meters. Dead calm. The first vehicles of the day passed above him as he checked his watch: 0740.

Dac plucked a round from his shirt pocket and delicately jacked it into the chamber, savoring the incredibly smooth action of the bolt. He marveled that Americans could mass-produce weapons of such quality and he thanked his ancestors for providing the opportunity to make it his own. As if in a trance, he closed the bolt quietly and offered a prayer with a nod—a ritual he began the first day he fired a round as a sniper.

In 1966, the leader of the local cadre, now dead, handed Dac a 7.62mm Mosin Nagant. The gun had undoubtedly killed a thousand Germans in Leningrad or Stalingrad, but it was Russian surplus now, junk given to their

North Vietnamese allies. The burned-out barrel had a three-meter kick to the left at seven hundred yards. The gun's optics were scratched and cloudy, barely better than its iron sights. An amateur gunsmith, or perhaps a poor marksman who believed that a soft trigger would reduce excessive tension in his arm, had modified the trigger housing to a hair touch, causing the rifle to fire unexpectedly. Dac wondered how he had managed to kill twenty-six people with it.

Dac's American Remington was shorter and lighter, despite its massive barrel, thick and true. He balanced the gun carefully in his lap, then removed his glasses by slipping them over his head. He cursed his eyesight, so critical to his profession, for spectacles were a constant burden to keep clean in the jungle, or anywhere else in Vietnam, with the drenching rain or blowing dust. He wore a black kerchief around his neck that he used now to clean the lenses. Sweat beaded across his forehead and into his receding hairline; he was no young man, his thirty-four years exaggerated by the malarial pallor common to all men who fought in the delta. He wiped his face with the bandana and slipped the glasses back onto his head.

Dac positioned the butt plate against his frail shoulder and placed his cheek against the walnut stock. At just over five feet, Dac was small even by Vietnamese standards, but the gun fit him nearly as well as it would an American. With one eye closed, he squinted into the nine-power scope and focused the crosshairs again. He sat now, immobile, sinking deeper into his trance, elbows on his knees with a sling wrapped tightly around his left forearm to strap his arm, shoulder, and weapon into a single, solid unit. He closed his eyes to contemplate for a moment the audacity of his business, before setting the crosshair one final time on one of the Nung. He would not move again until the target appeared.

The apartment building sat on the outskirts of Chau Doc, where urban landscape gave way to endless rice paddies. Though below road level, nothing interrupted Dac's line of sight as he aimed slightly upward across the heavy-tipped sprouts of rice. The sun rose another degree behind him, effectively blinding the Nungs despite their aviator sunglasses.

The girl was a fool, but Dac nevertheless regretted the pain she would suffer. Neither communist nor capitalist, she was just a woman in love, and Dac knew the value of love. No doubt, she was truly devoted to the major, or she would not have betrayed him the way she did. The NLF had approached her with an offer: *Tell us his secrets. Make him valuable to us and we will not kill him.* So she asked him about operational issues and passed the information on to the cadre. But the major, too sly for his own good, surmised her ruse and fed her false intelligence. Perhaps it had been his plan from the beginning. Twice, cadre patrols acting upon the girl's intelligence were ambushed and wiped out.

Dac wanted to check his watch. With the rising sun, farmers would be in the fields soon. He knew the major never left the apartment later than 0800, so he resisted taking his eye from the scope. *Checking the watch will not change the time. He will come when he comes.* As if on cue, the Nung turned toward the interior of the compound, reacting to a whistle that floated faintly across the paddies. The smaller guard jogged quickly to an alley behind the concrete wall and signaled, a flick of the wrist with fingers pointed toward the ground. *Come now.* A black Ford appeared and turned the corner toward the gate. The car would block Dac's line of sight. *How could we not consider the car? Did we think the man would walk to the Special Forces compound?* He cursed the cadre, but accepted the intelligence failure as his own. He could have done his own recon. He took his finger off the trigger as the car stopped directly in front of the gate.

He could tell by the sudden activity that the major was approaching. Briefly, he got a look at the man as he passed through the gate, smiling, joking with the Nung. Dac then heard their laughter roll across the paddies through the moist morning air. A man so happy did not deserve to live, thought Dac, for he understood nothing. His red American nose was the size of a clown's, and

Dac centered the crosshair for a head shot. But the target passed through his field of vision in an instant, quickly ducking in through the rear driver's-side door of the car. The small Nung closed the major's door, skipped around the bumper, and climbed into the front passenger seat, the subtle thump of the closing door audible. With a final check, the other guard surveilled the street behind and in front of the car's path before following the major into the rear door behind the driver.

Dac released his finger from the trigger, again cursing the American Ford. But as Dac watched the final guard enter the car, he realized that another of his silent prayers had been answered. The major would have slid across the backseat to allow the second Nung to climb in after him. He was sitting behind the front passenger, the side of the car closest to Dac's culvert. Although hidden behind the wide roof support—a design feature never intended by the Ford engineers to contribute to the security of rear passengers targeted for assassination—the target was a tall man. His head would be inches away from the top of the car's ceiling. Dac centered the crosshair on a spot on the gleaming sheet metal. The world fell silent with the tranquility that always descended upon him whenever his finger squeezed the trigger. He emptied his mind of everything except the lub-dub beat of his heart, sensing the infinitesimal rise and fall of the crosshairs with each steady stroke. The trigger resistance was smooth and steady—an autonomic action between heartbeats, as if someone had looped a tight rubber band around his finger and pulled. The hammer fell exactly as he anticipated, the firing pin igniting an explosion that generated eighteen tons per square inch of pressure inside the chamber, enough to force the bullet through the barrel at supersonic speed. The report was deafening inside the culvert, but muted to those above ground. A pinpoint glimmer of muzzle flash winked from the ditch. Dac knew instinctively the shot was true.

The bullet punched straight through the thin steel, making less noise than a can opener. The head liner muffled the impact further. The major pitched forward without a sound. The bullet struck him in the occipital lobe, slicing off the back bottom of his skull like a spoon removing the end of a hard-boiled egg. The impact caused a surge of pressure that rammed the brain forward, crushing it within the cranium, before it bounced back and spewed out the back of his head. The swelling induced by the trauma would ultimately kill him, but the major was already a vegetable by the time he slumped forward against the front passenger seat. The blood in the air alerted the driver that they were under attack. The sedan fishtailed as it bolted away. Through his scope Dac saw the red splatter on the rear window. He allowed himself a quick prayer before efficiently breaking down his weapon and stuffing it into a canvas laundry bag marked "US Army." A Chau Doc taxi parked above the culvert and honked twice. Dac scrambled in. Another sedan passed, the Vietnamese driver glancing with mild curiosity at the taxi stopping for a fare in the middle of a thousand acres of rice paddies. Fifteen minutes later, Dac was riding through the unruly traffic of Chau Doc, exhausted yet committed to his next assignment.

FOUR

9th Infantry Division Headquarters
Dong Tam, Vietnam

The trip to division headquarters took twenty-five minutes by air. The helicopter turned east with the river's current, crossed over a wasteland of swamps until the main channel of the Mekong came into view, and joined a gaggle of aircraft following the river downstream. The pilot leveled the UH-1 at two thousand feet, where the air was cooler, almost chilly. Monroe and Patterson fell asleep immediately, indifferent to the view. They had seen the delta and the river and rice paddies before; they always looked the same.

Ninety klicks downriver, the division headquarters loomed in the haze as an irregular cluster of buildings, a square mile of corrugated steel and concrete and canvas and dust. For every soldier actually humping the boonies, there were ten REMFs, ten thousand of them at the 9th Infantry Division Headquarters in Dong Tam, hard against the Mekong River south of Saigon. They were exhausted and irritable men, fed up with mud, dust, and heat, marking their tour one day at a time until their DEROS arrived and they could go home. REMFs envied the men in the field while being simultaneously grateful that they were spared the horrors of combat. These men staffed the hospitals, flight lines, maintenance shops, and POL dumps. There were detachments of communications technicians and intelligence teams, MPs, and the worst REMF job of all, Graves Registration, where the KIAs were embalmed and sewn back together for the trip home. When not out hunting, the division sniper teams quartered here as well.

The pilot imagined the men he carried must be important, for he had been diverted from the division airstrip to land directly at the HQ pad, a twenty-four-foot square of PSP at the general's doorstep. Monroe sensed the change in vibrations as the pilot rolled off the power. He roused Patterson. They watched the BX pass beneath them, and a row of tropicalized hooches with sheet metal roofs, surrounded by waist-high walls of sandbags. The aircraft flared, careful to avoid the two flagpoles planted foolishly close to the pad. One flag was American, the other Vietnamese. The chopper settled into the cloud of dust that hovered above the delta during the dry season when the sunshine itself seemed filthy. The cargo compartment filled with wind and muggy air and the smell of excrement burning in drums of JP4.

At the LZ, an officer faced away from the tumult of wind and debris as the helicopter landed, but Monroe recognized him nevertheless. Captain Anderson commanded all snipers assigned to the division. Directed by the commanding general to create the division's first experimental sniper platoon, Anderson soon learned that snipers were the most effective operatives—both tactically and psychologically—in the delta. He quickly recommended full deployment of snipers at battalion level, with division sniper schools to teach tactics and marksmanship.

Anderson had learned his trade with the Marines near the DMZ and acquisitioned Marine weapons and instituted Marine administrative procedures. He doled out his teams to units that used them effectively and pulled his men from commands that didn't. He had sent Monroe and Patterson to Firebase Christine three weeks before, as part of the effort to hunt down the enemy sniper who had wrought such havoc. The snipers rarely saw their commander, except when there was trouble or when a sniper was wounded. A brisk and unfriendly man, Anderson was nevertheless a conscientious leader who took care of his troops.

Patterson and Monroe exchanged wary glances. Although pleased to see their commander, they knew he was not there to welcome them home.

Anderson approached the chopper as the snipers jumped off. A mustang, commissioned from the ranks, Anderson disdained the formalities of command demanded by West Pointers. The men exchanged casual salutes. "Snipers!" yelled Anderson over the unwinding turbine. "Follow me!"

Anderson led the way into Division headquarters, a dusty compound surrounded by a six-foot berm of sandbags that enclosed the DTOC plus the separate buildings of Division Intelligence and the 9th Division general's own command section. All three buildings were low-slung Quonsets, metal-sided, with roofs covered in sandbags to absorb any direct hit from a harassing mortar round. The officers' latrine occupied a spot equidistant from all three buildings. The enlisted men had to hoof to a far corner of the compound, under the radio tower that bristled with a massive cluster of antennas.

The only entrance into the DTOC was through a gap in the earthworks, guarded by two sentries twenty-four hours every day. A guard saluted perfectly as Anderson passed through. Monroe glanced at the man's polished boots. *REMF*, he thought. He ignored the guard and followed Anderson inside.

Patterson returned the guard's salute, checked their gear, and walked behind Monroe and Anderson into the DTOC control center. Installed in a space that might have held ten men comfortably, twenty enlisted men sat at desks, monitoring various radio frequencies, recording situation reports, and passing messages. The room was stiflingly hot from the bright lights and the heat generated by too many men in a confined space. Cigarette smoke hung against the ceiling. A wall-sized tactical map of the Mekong Delta hung against one wall, unit locations plotted in grease pencil that melted in the heat and dribbled downward in little black rivers. The officer in charge chatted with another captain and pointed at a spot on the chart, a location upriver where the Mekong crossed the Cambodian border.

Anderson led them into a tight conference room separated from the DTOC by an incongruous wall of glass. Three men stood around a large table in the center of the room. The mission briefing had begun without them, and a colonel used a collapsible pointer to indicate terrain features on a small chart spread on the center of the table. As the snipers entered, Colonel Steven Lyons looked up and motioned for them to approach the table.

"Gentlemen," he began, formally taking control, "we have our snipers."

The two other officers shuffled sideways to make room around the table, more room than was necessary. Monroe wasn't sure if their deference resulted from respect for his skills, contempt for his rank, or revulsion of his color. Any way he looked at it, commissioned officers unnerved Monroe. Few of them went anywhere near the AOs they ordered swept and cleared. And for snipers, officers meant missions in support of company or battalion operations where massed groups of men invited enemy ambushes and mortar attacks. Officers got men killed.

Colonel Lyons continued, using the pointer as he spoke: "In the last two weeks enemy sniper attacks have decreased dramatically. Until today, we were prepared to credit our own sniper teams for suppressing Charlie's ability to travel or gather intelligence about our movements. Now, however, we believe that the reason for this sniper's sudden hiatus is more fundamental that that. Basically, we think he's low on ammunition." Lyons nodded toward Monroe and Patterson. "Within the last twenty-four hours, these snipers recovered approximately 150 rounds of American made, match-grade 7.62mm ammunition from a VC courier on a footpath about nine and half klicks east of Chau Doc, here." He pointed at the map on the wall. "It seems clear that the courier was delivering this ammunition to the sniper who has been causing so much trouble."

"American ammo means American rifles." All eyes shot to Terry Ingram. Another full colonel, he outranked Lyons by virtue of his seniority and position, G-3, Director of Ops. He chewed a cigar and pushed the words through his teeth with a no-nonsense growl. His skull could have been molded in a helmet, smooth and round with his scalp showing through the stubble of his hair. Monroe noted that Ingram wore crossed rifles on his collar. Infantry. Across his cheek and into his pale scalp ran a scar, too deep and jagged to have come from anything but shrapnel, and too old to have originated in Vietnam. Ingram had seen plenty of combat, something that could not be said of Colonel Lyons, the division G-2 Director of Intelligence, who now withered under Ingram's stare.

"That would explain the remarkable accuracy," said Lyons. "And Captain Anderson has lost a couple of teams in the last few months. Charlie could have recovered the weapons."

Anderson kept his mouth shut, but Monroe saw his commander's eyes glance his way.

Ingram spoke instead. "Don't blame men who have been killed in action, Colonel."

Lyons felt the smirks of the other men in the room and his face flushed. This was not the first time that Ingram had rebuked him in public. The two men despised each other.

Humiliated, Lyons continued his briefing. "In addition to the ammunition, our snipers were able to recover a crude map and a letter, written in Vietnamese and French, that appears to be from a sniper to the courier. The courier was a woman with a romantic connection of some kind to the sniper, probably his wife. She was going to visit him for reasons beyond simply delivering the ammunition. Based upon information in this letter, we think we know where they were going to meet."

"Colonel," said Ingram, "what, exactly, does this letter say? We've heard your suspicions, your theories, your deductions, your reading of tarot cards and chicken guts before, and it usually turns out to be a load of crap. We've all heard the rumors about something brewing, but how do I know you aren't sending my men out on another wild goose chase?"

Lyons held firm, withdrew a bloodstained piece of paper from his briefing book, and without breaking eye contact with Ingram handed the letter to the third field grade officer in the room. "Major Tam," he asked, "would you be so kind as to translate this for the Colonel?"

Chief of Intelligence for the ARVN 9th Infantry Division, Tam was responsible for military intelligence gathering throughout the delta by the local South Vietnamese militia, the Regional Popular Forces. While green and skittish in combat, the Ruff Puffs occasionally provided good Intel, "operating" as they did along the periphery of government-controlled areas on the outskirts of places like Firebase Christine. Although Tam considered himself a professional officer and was committed to the allied cause, the Americans regarded the Popular Forces as a joke, more effective in disseminating information about GI troop movements to the VC than the other way around. Many Ruff Puffs were VC counterintelligence operatives. Tam and Lyons worked together frequently, and like many naive men, their familiarity led them to believe that they understood one another despite the cultural chasm between them.

Tam read slowly, *"My love, Do you remember the poems we read to each other in Paris? They seemed important then. I wish I could write a poem for you now, but my efforts are foolish in the face of our struggle. That I should value your love more than our Cause is my greatest weakness.*

"My cadre is suffering because of my emptiness. Bring me your love and your strength. Join us here for a historic meeting. It will not be long now. Dress like a peasant and stay on paths away from the roadblocks. You will be safe once you cross the canal. The final hike is less than an hour—I will be waiting for you."

Tam returned the letter to Lyons. A quiet moment passed as the men kept their eyes on the table.

Ingram broke the silence. "So we shot this poor bastard's wife and took his ammo. Now what?"

Lyons countered. "We also recovered a map, Colonel. And now we're going to shoot him, too."

The G-2 placed the tip of his pointer on the map. Snipers were excellent map readers, but this one was different from those Monroe normally carried.

He saw no place names, no written notations of any kind. The map was sanitized, devoid of latitude and longitude, without even the grid squares required for calling in artillery. The few contour lines simply indicated terrain. North was not marked, but a major river flowed nearby, which could only be the Mekong or the Bassac. Three klicks south of the clearing was a metropolitan area.

Patterson nudged Monroe, and mouthed, "Cambodia."

Lyons stared down Patterson, moved the pointer to the small city. "Chau Doc, South Vietnam. The map recovered by the snipers indicates the area of greatest interest to us. Up here." He drew the pointer northward across a waterway so straight that it was obviously a canal, and stopped at a clearing. "This open area north of the city consists mainly of rice paddies, a virtual no-man's-land. It is bordered on the south by the Vinh Te Canal, and by dense jungle on the north."

Lyons nodded to Tam, who continued. "At the edge of the jungle is a group of small dwellings, including a plantation home from before the war, plus outbuildings that predate the house. According to the letter recovered from the dead woman, her destination would be 'less than an hour' from the canal. This settlement is the only human habitation that fits those criteria."

Ingram ignored Tam and looked directly at Lyons. "Colonel, are you telling me that you want to send my men into Cambodia, a neutral country, to assassinate some gook sniper with an American rifle?"

Lyons almost smiled. He had anticipated this challenge from Ingram, and he was ready with an answer that he knew would startle them all. "No, Colonel. There's more to it than that. Much more." He withdrew a photograph from his briefing folder and dropped it onto the table. The image was old and poorly focused, a photo of a man in an NVA uniform reviewing troops. "General Tuan Le of North Vietnam, during a state visit to Moscow ten years ago. He was a colonel then, part of Ho Chi Minh's entourage. Today, General Le is the highest-ranking member of the North Vietnamese

Army who ever leaves North Vietnam. He is responsible for distribution of material along the entire length of the Ho Chi Minh Trail.

"We have been receiving increasingly precise intelligence reports that the VC and the NVA are planning some sort of general offensive in South Vietnam. We also know that General Tuan Le is somewhere in Cambodia at this time, and meeting with members of the local VC cadres. The letter intercepted by our snipers makes reference to a 'historic meeting' which she has been invited to attend. We don't know who this woman was, but based upon the snipers' description of her overall appearance and health, we suspect that she was a relatively influential member of the VC infrastructure. Therefore, based upon analysis of all available intelligence data, we believe that General Le will conduct a high-level meeting tomorrow with unknown members of the local VC cadre at the location we just specified. The mission is to take out General Le and any other high-ranking targets of opportunity."

For once, Ingram had nothing to say.

Lyons continued. "At the confluence of the Vinh Te Canal and the Bassac River is an ARVN firebase. Christine, as it is designated, is occupied by two hundred Regional Forces troops plus a full complement of Special Forces advisers. Their mission is to provide fire support for allied units operation in this AO, plus watch the river traffic and monitor infiltration across the border. They routinely conduct patrols on both sides of the canal. Tonight, we propose to send a patrol across the canal and to the north along the river, away from the clearing." The G-2 drew his pointer along the western and southern shore of the river. "The patrol will consist of two additional men." He nodded toward Patterson and Monroe. "After crossing the canal, the snipers will peel off into the underbrush as the patrol moves away. After they determine that they have successfully detached themselves from the patrol without being detected, they will proceed to the firing point, here." He pointed to a spot north of the canal, five kilometers from the Special Forces destination. "There is a narrow tree line which will provide adequate concealment. You will have a clear field of fire across the clearing. We estimate the shot will be eight hundred yards."

"What's the timetable?" asked Ingram. He glanced at his watch and Monroe saw that his eyes were bloodshot.

"Immediate departure. If the snipers are to be in position in time for the meeting tomorrow, they have to be back at Firebase Christine before dark. We have a chopper standing by for departure immediately following this briefing."

Captain Anderson spoke up. "What backup do my men have? Artillery? Air support? Evacuation?"

The G-2 directed his response to Anderson, looking away from the snipers as if they were not there. "None," he said. "Your boys go in with their weapons only. They make the hit and E&E back to the Special Forces camp. The patrol will wait eighteen hours after separation to escort them back to Christine. Your boys will be back here in twenty-four hours."

"And if something goes wrong?"

"They're on their own." Lyons broke eye contact as he inched away from the table. He handed the map to Anderson. "Have them memorize it. Now you better get going."

An awkward moment passed as Anderson considered the mission. His snipers had participated in special operations before but he had always received ample time to select his team, review the situation, evaluate the risks, and devise appropriate tactics. Assassinations were always tricky and this one had been laid on without his input. He didn't like the mission and he didn't like being left out.

Ingram cut him off before he could begin. "Move 'em out, Captain."

Anderson shepherded his men out of the room and closed the door, leaving Ingram and Lyons alone.

"Cambodia is off limits," said Ingram. "This mission is illegal."

"As long as the snipers stay close to the canal, they will still be inside Vietnamese territory."

"Right. Whether you walk across the border and cut the man's throat, or whether you fire a bullet across the border, it's still a court-martial."

"Colonel, our special ops teams conduct cross-border missions all the time. Besides, who's going to complain? The NVA aren't supposed to be in Cambodia any more than we are. No one at MACV has any problem with the legality of these missions."

"Then I suggest you get some of your own spooks to do this job."

Hypocrite, thought Lyons. *He complains to Intel about enemy infiltration, but he wants someone else to do his dirty work to stop it.* "Colonel, your snipers know the AO and are best equipped and trained for a long-range assassination. This man will be heavily guarded, which is not a scenario suited to a SOG operation. Our boys are more of the throat-cutter variety."

"I'll take this to the Old Man, but he'll never approve it."

"I've already briefed him."

You little prick, thought Ingram. *Someday you are going to go over my head and you won't have MACV to protect you.* Ingram bit down on his cigar and leveled a dreadful stare at Lyons.

"This is a MACV operation," said Lyons. "There isn't much any of us can do about it, sir."

Anderson walked his snipers from the building. The UH-1 sat quietly on the tiny headquarters pad; it was the first time in Monroe's six months in Vietnam that he had approached a helicopter without being deafened by the turbine or blinded by debris blowing in the rotor-wash. The pilots were in their seats, running through the preflight checklist, while the crew chief walked around the aircraft, checking the fuselage for damage or evidence of fluid leaks: oil, fuel, or hydraulics.

"Monroe," said Anderson, "what do you think? What support do you need?"

"Our backs will be against the canal, sir. They could flank us easy, and I am not much of a swimmer."

"They can't flank what they can't see, Monroe. Take the shot and fade away. Just be quick about it. Any delay in getting out of there, and they'll pin you in against the water."

Patterson spoke up quietly, almost apologetically. "Captain, I got three weeks before my DEROS." Patterson stared at the floor, his lower lip quivering.

"What are you saying, Patterson? You want me to assign someone else?"

"Sir, it's better I do this one myself," Monroe protested. "Patterson's too jumpy for a job like this." The two snipers locked eyes.

"Shut up, Monroe. You aren't as good as you think you are." Anderson turned to Patterson. "If you don't think you can handle this mission, I'll assign someone else to work with Monroe. But the two of you together are the best I've got."

Patterson breathed deeply, almost hyperventilating. The mission was dangerous, and officially there would be no shame in refusing to go. But the other snipers would know that he had turned it down and someone else would go in his place. *So what?* he thought. *In three weeks I'll be back in The World. I'll never see these crackers again.* Patterson knew what the smart decision was, and he knew what Monroe would do if the situation were reversed. But knowing what to do and actually doing it were two different things. Patterson smiled at the irony. *I finally know the smart answer, and I still do the stupid thing.* "I'll go."

Monroe shook his head. "You got even less brains than I thought. The captain is offering you the chance to sit inside and answer a fucking phone, man."

"That's when the Reaper comes, when a brother lays back too soon. I can't start half-stepping now, 'cause just when you start being careful, the Freaky Flukey comes along and plays the Joke on you. I seen it happen. I seen it a hundred fuckin' times."

"That's bullshit. I don't see these half-steppin' REMFs going home in body bags."

"I ain't no REMF."

"That's enough," said Anderson. "Get on board."

Colonel Lyons emerged from the DTOC and jogged slowly to the pad. "Just wanted to wish you luck," he announced.

Monroe noticed that Lyons's boots were shiny and that they zippered up the side. He could not imagine what function the zipper served, other than to facilitate putting them on and taking them off. It wasn't something people worried about in the boonies, where you wore your boots day and night. Lyons also wore a 9mm Browning automatic on his hip. Monroe wondered why he would pack a weapon issued only to Christians in Action, the CIA. He wondered why REMFs carried weapons at all.

Monroe said nothing and climbed onto the chopper deck. He sat on the aluminum floor next to Patterson, each man holding his rifle between his knees, muzzle pointed upward.

"Well, gentlemen, all I need now are your dog tags." Lyons held out his hand. If they didn't make it back, there would be nothing to identify them as American soldiers. Monroe smirked as he lifted the tags from around his neck and handed them to Lyons. *What's Charlie gonna think? That I'm some black Cambodian out taking a stroll with my high-powered Remington?*

Lyons passed two boxes of C-rats to the snipers, then rapped the fuselage by the pilot's seat and gave the man a thumbs-up. "When's the last time you men had anything to eat?"

Monroe already had the first spoonful of food in his mouth as the chopper lifted off. He looked out and saw Anderson standing next to Lyons. The men on the ground leaned against the turbulence of the rotor blades as another man joined them. Even as the pilot lowered the chopper's nose and built up airspeed, Monroe could see a star on the officer's collar. He nudged Patterson and pointed him out.

Patterson nodded. "That's the Old Man," he said, his mouth full of spaghetti. "General Vandermeer. You go on a mission to kill a general, makes all the other generals nervous."

Monroe had heard of the division commander, but few grunts ever saw him. Vandermeer's reputation had filtered through the ranks to the lowest private. It was rumored that he had passed up a meeting with Bob Hope to fly his own chopper into a hot LZ, but Monroe didn't believe it. The only commissioned officer he'd ever seen anywhere near combat was Anderson, and even he spent most of his time pushing paper at Division. Monroe closed his fist except for his index finger, which he pointed at Vandermeer, like a pistol. "Keep your head down, General." He jerked his hand back, as if in recoil from a shot. "Hit."

Patterson put his hand on Monroe's arm and pushed it down. "He's the Man, brother. Don't fuck with him."

Vandermeer saw the gesture. He stared at Monroe for a moment, then raised his hand to his forehead. Monroe had never before seen an officer initiate the courtesy required of enlisted men, and he wondered what kind of man would salute anyone he didn't have to. Vandermeer held the salute until their eyes locked, and Monroe looked away.

FI▼E

14:12

Fire Support Base Christine

They returned to FSB Christine along the main channel of the Bassac, retracing their downstream trip to Division HQ. The river was filled with oceangoing cargo vessels on their way to Phnom Penh, and sampans moving downstream with cargoes of rice or enemy ammunition. The helicopter turned north over the swamps of Thap Muoi, an uninhabitable landscape dominated by water, war, and fear. A few hamlets did exist inland, where the terrain was marginally higher and drier and stable enough to support civilization. The villes were surrounded by rice paddies in turn surrounded by mud dikes drained by canals, the land a patchwork of waterways, bordered by hedgerows of nipa palms and wild banana trees. At intervals along the river, firebases supported combat operations with their umbrellas of artillery.

The war had interrupted aeons of maintenance that built the intricate system, and many dikes had been breached, hemorrhaging their water. Acres of paddies had gone wild, choked now with weeds and wild rice and berries. Throughout the region were groves of forest, much of it defoliated by herbicides. Still, there were jungles enough to hide whole regiments of VC, and open fields of fire that had to be crossed or landed in if anyone wanted to root them out. The pilot kept his chopper centered over the river, out of small arms range, and Monroe was glad of it. He knew he was looking at the best sniper country in the world.

A pale sun hovered above the horizon, blinding the pilots as the UH-1 approached Firebase Christine. As the chopper slowed, Monroe looked over the pilot's shoulder, and through the stress cracks in the Plexiglas windshield he could see the outskirts of Chau Doc to the west. The city's suburbs gave way quickly to rice paddies and then swamp, isolating Firebase Christine amid the jungle that bordered the river. There, hard against the muddy banks of the Bassac, was the LZ, a sandbar. The pilot's lips moved against his microphone as he reduced airspeed, descending in a rapid 360-degree spiral; the less time within small arms range the better. With jungle so dark and close, any LZ watcher with an AK-47 could put a bullet through the windshield or into the turbine. The chopper landed firmly, Monroe and Patterson un-assed in darkness, and the skids picked back up in seconds.

On the LZ stood Master Sergeant Wolfe, wearing a soft cap with no visible rank. His eyes cut to the Remington in Monroe's left hand. He knew nothing of the mission he had been instructed to support, but he was accustomed to operating on a need-to-know-basis, unconcerned by anything except his own orders. "Welcome back, snipers. Thought we'd seen the last of you. The patrol is standing by, plus two advisers."

"Let's get off this sandbar," said Patterson.

In front of the command post, a row of men squatted in the dirt, flat-footed, talking quietly in Vietnamese. They wore tiger stripes, but no boots, and each had an M-1 carbine. The men rose to their feet as Wolfe led the snipers into the compound. Two uniformed Americans stood nearby. Patterson recognized the grunt with the fancy handshake. "Sylvester's taking us out tonight," he muttered.

Monroe glanced at the GI and said nothing.

To his men Wolfe said simply, "These are the snipers. Same boys as before."

Patterson swung his PCR-25 off his back. "What channel is your command net?"

Wolfe told him. "We'll provide a guide for you. Ever work with Regional

Forces before?"

"We never work with anybody," said Monroe, "No guides either. And never no worthless Ruff Puffs."

The advisers exchanged grim smiles. "The guide's a Kit Carson Scout. Trustworthy. The others ain't worth a shit."

"No guides," Monroe reiterated. The fact that a guide had been selected made him wonder if the mission was already compromised, especially a Kit Carson Scout, VC turncoats that knew every weed of their AOs. Most scouts were loyal to the Americans, but you never knew for sure. "We know the AO. No guides."

"Fine," said Wolfe. "Saddle up."

They moved through the perimeter wire and into the darkness, walking single file along a trail through bamboo and single-canopy jungle and clumps of elephant grass along the river's edge. The night was calm and humid, silent but for the quiet march of bare feet. However ragged they may have been at soldiering, the ARVN on this patrol could move through the forest like elves. They carried no equipment other than their loaded carbines, not even water, eliminating the constant jiggle of extra ammo or dog tags or the rubbing of web gear against their skin. The trail was rough, but they knew where they were going and how to get there. Even in darkness the patrol moved fast.

They turned away from the water. The trees gave way to rice paddies. Bats passed silently among the stars as the men crossed the open fields by compass, north, toward the canal. Monroe felt the ground rise under him, then turn dry. He crested a berm. Ahead was open water; tiny waves lapped against the banks and the faint smell of sewage wafted in the air.

Monroe moved carefully down a steep embankment until his feet entered the water. An adviser grabbed his arm. "Wait," he whispered. Monroe smelled Dexedrine on his breath, uppers passed out by the medics to keep men alert at night. High or not, Sylvester seemed to know what he was doing.

Two boats waited in the darkness, fifteen-foot sampans that could carry ten men each. Nothing more than long canoes, they plied the waterways during the day with rice or other goods, powered by shrimp-tailed Evinrudes. At night, they were subject to curfew, though there were plenty of sampans about at any hour. Operated by entrepreneurs who sold their services to anyone who would pay, tonight they had arrived on time, ready to collect some greenbacks.

The patrol boarded in silence, though even the lightest splashing of water carried in the muggy air. "OK," whispered Sylvester, pushing Monroe toward the craft when it was his turn to board. The Americans sat in the center of each boat, the Vietnamese paddling fore and aft. They crossed the canal in less than a minute.

One adviser took point and moved inland through brambles and bamboo shoots until they came to a trail. Sylvester, with the snipers, pulled them aside while the rest of the band moved on. He whispered in the darkness. "Here's your trail. It parallels the canal but don't use it; booby traps. Follow it west two klicks, then north three and a half to four klicks to your final firing point. You got the canal along the south side of the trail and open terrain to the north, mostly rice paddies and minefields. Stay off the dikes," he cautioned. Sylvester paused for a moment and listened as the patrol inexplicably bunched up in the darkness, accordion-like, before spreading out again in single file. "We'll take these gomers on down the road a ways and return in a couple hours and cross back over. Gotta tuck 'em in before the spirits come out. I'll wait here for you until tomorrow noon and take you back. If you ain't back by then, I'm gone."

As the last of the ARVN troops moved past, the snipers crossed the trail and squatted in the bushes, listening to the patrol's fading footfalls and waiting for the natural sounds of the night to resume. They lay dog for fifteen minutes. Monroe stared into the darkness, ears cocked for the slightest sound, sniffing the air for the scent of enemy trail watchers. Every hair on his body became an antenna, tuned to the frequency of other humans. In the jungle, a man relied upon his hearing for warnings of danger, and upon his vision for navigation. Satisfied that there were no unusual sounds in the air, Monroe turned his attention to the terrain. It was amazing what a man could see at night, as long as he looked to the side, never directly at anything. The human eye had evolved in response to sunlight shining through the pupil onto the back of the retina. The edges of the retina, in constant shadow, had evolved accordingly. Snipers were trained to use their peripheral vision at night, and to resist the urge to focus. Without a moon or stars or any human light in sight, Monroe could nevertheless make out the contour of a tree line and open fields to the northwest. He touched Patterson on the arm. Sylvester never heard them leave.

The rice paddies were fallow and dry, but not yet overgrown, having only recently been deserted. In darkness, the snipers' only concealment, they crawled steadily through the paddies until reaching an irrigation ditch. The ditch was muddy and difficult, but the banks hid them and the water was quiet. The snipers had eight hours to reach the firing point.

The stars came out at midnight, as heavy cirrus from distant afternoon thunderstorms evaporated or blew away in the stratosphere. Monroe raised his head above the embankment to get his bearings. Whenever the skies cleared, fog soon followed as the ground radiated the day's heat into space, cooling the air enough to condense the moisture it contained. Monroe could find his way in the dark, but if the fog came in before they established their position, they could pass their objective and never know. It was one thing to dead reckon in fog to an ambush site on a trail, where the targets moved through a kill zone five hundred yards wide, but it was something else to find a stationary hooch and be at just the right angle to put a bullet through a doorway.

But the stars shed more light than he needed, almost more than he wanted. He could see the jungle tree line across the rice paddies, and deep in its shadow something man-made, a hint of a shape, a straight line. He glanced across to his own tree line and estimated where the hide should be, seven hundred yards farther. Now, if the fog rolled in and the target faded from view, he could dead reckon to the spot.

The fog did arrive, thin wisps at first, floating at knee height over the paddies. The snipers crawled from the drainage ditch and lay on the bank listening, allowing the water to drain quietly from their fatigues and trickle back into the earth. Nearly blind in the dark and fog, Monroe's hands lightly searched for trip wires and booby traps as he crawled into the undergrowth. When he could feel the bushes all around him, he stopped. Patterson moved up behind and they lay there, waiting for dawn and listening.

Dense shallow fog swirled above their heads like wreaths of smoke. As the first streaks of sunlight filtered through the mist, Monroe realized he had failed to find the deepest cover. He had seen ambushes set up in the dead of night blown at sunrise when daylight revealed men sitting in plain view of anyone walking a nearby trail, and he saw now that the real tree line grew ten yards beyond the clump of banana trees where he and Patterson lay. Worse, Charlie had been there to pick the fruit, his footprints everywhere, fresh and crisp. Ominously, the tracks were not made by the sandaled feet of local VC, but by the hard-core soldiers of the North Vietnamese Army, uniformed professionals who wore combat boots.

Monroe crawled forward, while Patterson sterilized their back trail, erecting every stalk of grass they crushed in passing. Below the treetops, vines, shrubs, flowers, and ferns choked one another for air and light. Mahogany saplings twisted between larger trees, presenting any who might try to pass among them with a writhing wall of foliage, impenetrable.

Monroe rolled onto his back and snaked faceup under the leafy skirt of forest, entering another world where a million plants coalesced into a single living tangle. Patterson wriggled into the jungle behind Monroe until both men were locked in the dark embrace of undergrowth.

Monroe placed the barrel of his Remington in the crotch of a small tree, careful to ensure that the muzzle did not protrude beyond the veil of foliage in front of him. The scope encompassed a field of view of only two degrees, narrow enough to peek easily through the tiny gaps between the leaves. Patterson checked the radio net, listening to confirm traffic, not saying a word. He then set up the spotting scope, moving slowly and deliberately, virtually imprisoned among the limbs. Unable to sit, unable to stand, both men hunkered into the most comfortable position they could find. They would not be able to wait in a relaxed, hypnotic state. But the fog was thin today, the sun rising fast. With luck, the target would show himself early, and they might be out soon.

They waited. In the distance, the incongruous shape of a mountain resolved in the early light. Monroe had never seen it before, but he knew from studying his maps of the Mekong Delta that the only mountain within fifty miles was ten klicks deep into Cambodia.

The fog broke by 0800, a sign that the temperature would soon reach a hundred degrees. Patterson worked, reading the mirages in his spotting scope to estimate the wind. As he scrolled the focus knob, however, it was not the mirage that attracted his attention. He nudged Monroe, who merely nodded, his own rifle scope already zeroed in on the pagoda.

The shrine could not have been larger than a single room, topped with a bell-shaped dome of concrete, gone green with mildew and moss. Some tint of gaudy color still streaked its walls, but the temple was now in ruin, more from neglect than war. The arched entrance had no door, but the interior was too dark to determine if a Buddha statue still sat inside. The pagoda was the central feature of the settlement, impossible to ignore. *What else did Intel miss*, wondered Monroe.

He scanned the other buildings. Near the pagoda stood a concrete house, painted white to reflect the sun and furnished with wide French windows to catch the breeze. A veranda surrounded the structure, which had a roof of red tile—the kind of place a general might spend a day. Behind the building at the tree line, a second structure nestled in the shade. Less substantial than the first, it appeared sturdy enough, constructed of wood with a metal roof, not unlike the tropicalized barracks at Division. Something about the building bothered Monroe.

"Antenna," whispered Patterson. "In the trees."

Monroe refocused his scope until the tree line swam into view. He spotted it then, a black filament among the crooked limbs of the tree line, too straight and too thin to be anything other than man-made. The adrenaline level in Monroe's bloodstream crept higher. Such an antenna could only lead to sophisticated communications equipment, gear required to communicate with Hanoi. Intel might have missed the pagoda, but they were right about one thing: somebody of consequence had moved into the neighborhood.

A uniformed soldier stepped from the communications building into the morning sun. The movement riveted the snipers, who evaluated him reflexively: healthy, well fed, khaki fatigues, pith helmet, side arm. His clean clothes indicated he had recently arrived in the area. Patterson, with the more powerful scope, could make out the red collar insignia and three stars of a captain, unusual in a combat zone, where most unit leaders removed their rank. Monroe pegged him as an administrator, an NVA REMF, probably an all-around bird dog for somebody important. *Follow Steppin Fetchit*, thought Monroe, *and shoot whoever he salutes.*

In the shade of the main house veranda, two soldiers stood on either side of the door. They snapped to attention as the captain approached, the sound of their hands slapping their AK-47s faintly audible in the early-morning air. Monroe noted their professionalism and felt a twinge of anxiety. He sensed that these men were much more dangerous and difficult to kill than the pajama-clad peasants he had wasted so far.

By the pagoda, an NCO gathered his men, his commands carrying distinctly as his troops formed into three squads. The sergeant barked orders and the troops jogged into position with proficient aloofness, bored with the routine choreography of the morning patrol. One squad checked the tree line to the east, another the tree line to the west. The third squad moved between them, into Monroe's line of fire, ten men abreast to sweep the half mile of open field between the veranda where the captain waited for his commander and the tree line where the snipers waited for him, too. Behind the squad of soldiers walked another man, dressed not in the NVA khaki but in black pajamas. He walked more slowly, his eyes on the ground, occasionally kneeling to inspect a plant or a footprint before moving on. Patterson spotted him first, attracted by his unique uniform, but it was the man's rifle that riveted Patterson's attention.

"Sniper," he whispered, "in the black pajamas. Check his weapon."

Monroe swung his scope. The man carried his rifle in the crook of his arm, as if tracking quail. But the gun was a Remington, with a Redfield AccuRange 3x-9x scope mounted upon it. There could be no doubt that this was the man hunted by every sniper in the division. As Monroe studied him, however, he found it hard to believe that such an unimposing man could have killed so many Americans so skillfully. American snipers were well-muscled and highly conditioned young athletes with perfect vision and hearing. Yet the man in Monroe's crosshair was frail, almost emaciated, with thick glasses held to his head by an elastic strap and the receding hairline of a man older than thirty. Nothing about him bespoke danger, except the rifle. Whether he got his NVA general or not, thought Monroe, he would not leave without killing the man in the black pajamas.

Dac meandered behind the screen of soldiers. None of them knew what they were looking for, only to observe anything "unusual" like a sniper hidden in the grass. A patrol like this would only find a sniper by stepping on one, and if a soldier came close, he would be dead long before he could shoulder his weapon. Dac left such gross discoveries to the squad in front of him, and made minor adjustments to his gait to make sure that there were enough men in front of him to cut off his own vulnerable lines of fire. He searched for less obvious clues: a trail of crushed grass or an unusual footprint. But the field was empty, as it had been the day before and the day before that, crisscrossed by nothing but the footprints of the NVA soldiers.

Dac came to the drainage ditch, where he paused each day, an obvious avenue for anyone who wanted to approach unseen. The shallow water covered any footprints that might otherwise be visible, so Dac focused on the banks. He looked for indications of passage, broken stalks of grass or a trail of wet ground. Something caught his attention. On the far side of the ditch a spot of earth seemed darker, moist, and a footprint was clearly visible. Dac knelt to examine the mark and saw the pattern of the NVA beta boots, left by the soldier ahead of him a moment before. *His passage must have disturbed the underlying moisture in the soil*, thought Dac, *or released drops of dew.* He saw the soldier now, several yards ahead of him, moving to the tree line at the end of the field. A barely discernable trail marked the soldier's route. Dac followed after him, uneasy about something he could not define.

Neither sniper spoke as the NVA patrol moved slowly toward them, spread on line across the abandoned rice paddies. Monroe could hear the enemy soldiers occasionally call to each other, singsong voices carried on the moist air. But he noted that their level of discipline diminished as the distance to their leaders increased. The morning sun was in the enemy's eyes, and they squinted and stared at the ground, confident that today's sweep would be uneventful as that of the day before.

The squad spread out, thirty feet apart as they approached five hundred yards from the snipers. They marched closer, closing the distance to three hundred yards, and Patterson reached for his M-14. At this range with open sights, Patterson could drop a dozen men with a dozen shots, and Monroe could drill the communist star on every pith helmet as fast as he could work the bolt. Both men caressed their triggers, but neither fired. One shot would announce their presence, and the hunters would become the hunted.

Monroe focused the crosshairs on the face of a young man who stared for a moment directly into the lens. Squinting into the sun, he drew back his lips to expose teeth already stained black by betel nut, despite his obvious teenage youth. The boy looked down at his feet and continued on. At one hundred yards, it was clear the squad would sweep the field all the way to the tree line. The betel-nut boy kept coming directly toward them. He stopped at the drainage ditch, as if awaiting instructions. There were voices, and the boy passed along a command. To the left and right of him, his comrades began the long hike back to the pagoda. He looked up, directly into Monroe's eyes. Although the boy saw nothing but foliage, Monroe flushed with sweat; at fifteen yards, he did not need the scope on his rifle to see the look of interest in the soldier's eyes as he jumped across the ditch.

Don't look! Monroe remembered his training and cast his eyes away. The whites of a human eye are beacons, attracting insects and animals and other human beings. Primal, instinctive organs, they will lock onto any eyes that look back at them. The willpower to look away must overcome the instinctive urge to stare, as well as the rational imperative to keep your enemy in sight. Monroe stared at his hands and trembled, his ears primed for the sound of the boy's rifle being lowered, the sound of his hands in the leaves, or a cry of alarm. In an instant, his sweat glands disgorged whatever volume of fluid had not already been sweated out. He could only wait, terrified that the enemy soldier would see him, smell him, or hear his body vibrating with fear.

A banana had ripened since the last patrol, and the boy picked it. As he turned to retrace his steps, the young soldier was startled to find himself facing Dac, who had come up behind him. Instinctively, the soldier hid the banana behind his back. Like most NVA, he scorned the *Bung*, the Viet Cong swamp fighters. The boy's comrades joked about the creepy old man with the fancy American gun.

"Did you break this trail?" asked Dac.

"What trail?"

The boy knew nothing, Dac realized. *If there had been a trail, this Tonkinese nitwit followed it without knowing it.* "Check the tree line."

"Check it yourself, comrade." The boy's courage returned. He spoke with disdain and pointed to the others, already heading back. "I have other orders to follow." He jogged away to catch up with his squad.

Dac stood alone, staring at the blank curtain of undergrowth, nine hundred yards from the residence where General Le waited. *No one could make that shot,* he thought. *I am becoming an old woman.* He turned his back to the trees and followed the patrol back to the settlement.

Monroe heard Patterson exhale a long, quiet sigh as Dac's footfalls lightly receded across the field. When Dac was one hundred yards away, Monroe replaced his eye to the rifle scope, considering the shot, but he couldn't calm his breathing or keep the sight picture from bouncing wildly with each stroke of his pulse.

The NVA patrols, their morning security detail complete, retreated quickly back to the compound. Dac remained in sight, taking up a position at one end of the veranda where he scanned the jungle with binoculars. Monroe warned himself to keep track of the enemy sniper's position. The smell of rice and fish mingled with what remained of the ground fog, now virtually dissipated by the rising sun. Monroe hoped the target would show himself as soon as possible, while the sun was behind him. As long as it shone in their eyes, the enemy would be blind to any muzzle blast that might escape the tree line. And as the sun rose, so did the temperature, increasing the thermals and decreasing the air density, both of which would elevate the mark of the bullet. A few extra degrees of heat were enough to cause the powder in the cartridge to burn faster, propelling the bullet with more velocity, raising the trajectory. In ballistics, wind had the most impact, but temperature was trickiest to gauge.

On the porch, the NVA captain snapped to attention. If there was a general inside the building, Monroe knew, he was about to step through the door. He focused the scope on the opening, though his heart still beat too strongly to hold the crosshairs steady. He made the effort to breathe deeper, to quiet the furious churning inside him.

The general made his appearance abruptly, throwing open the door and stepping briskly onto the shaded veranda. The man wore a uniform similar to the captain's, except with epaulets trimmed with golden braid. He was taller than the captain, and much older, but Monroe did not focus on his face. It did not matter what he looked like, and it would have been an indulgence to look him over. Monroe centered the crosshairs on the man's throat. The Remington was zeroed at five hundred yards; Monroe estimated the distance at nine hundred. . . If he aimed at the head, the bullet would impact the chest. Nothing fancy. Monroe wanted to take the shot and get out of there. He waited for Patterson to judge the wind.

"Calm," Patterson said, as if on cue.

Monroe exhaled slowly, then took up the slack on the trigger. The conditions were perfect: no wind, no mist, no mirages to confuse the sight picture. His pulse returned to normal, slow and steady. Monroe held his breath for the split second of dead calm between heartbeats when not even his blood moved, to gently allow for a pull of the trigger. The uniform disappeared. The general's aide stepped into the line of fire, his back to the snipers. He saluted crisply.

"Get outta the way, motherfucker."

Patterson had never heard Monroe speak unnecessarily, even at a whisper, and he guessed Monroe was nervous. "Chill," he whispered. "Keep your breathin' steady." He checked for the enemy sniper. Still there.

The general returned the salute. The aide gestured skyward, and handed the general a pair of binoculars. He remained by the general's side, unaware that a sniper now considered sending a single bullet through both of them.

The general put the binoculars to his eyes and scanned the horizon above the tree line where Monroe waited.

Patterson heard it first.

"Chopper. Inbound." The forward motion of an oncoming helicopter compressed the sound waves, creating the distinctive thumping recognized by every infantryman in Vietnam. An outbound chopper, no matter how close, merely whirred. Patterson had intuitively learned the telltale sounds. "He's low, too. Moving fast. Coming up behind us."

"If he comes across the canal, those fuckers are gonna scatter." The thought crossed Monroe's mind that perhaps Intel had sent a team in by helicopter to take out the general and that the snipers were merely backup. He could hear it now and knew it was a Huey. It would be carrying cargo or troops. It came closer.

But the NVA troops made no effort to hide. The general continued searching for the helicopter with his binoculars. The beat of the rotors filled the air with noise as it crossed the Vinh Te Canal, low enough that the downdraft rustled the foliage in the tree line where the snipers waited. The pilot flared abruptly and the nose pitched up. There was no incoming fire from the general's troops as the general himself calmly watched the aircraft's approach, a few yards from the hedgerow where the snipers watched and waited.

Despite the deep flare, the UH-1 landed gently, softly touching its tail skid before settling down in the abandoned paddy, incongruously sleek, clean, and gleaming. It bore ARVN markings, though neither Patterson nor Monroe recognized the distinctive insignia of the 9th ARVN Marine Division. There was no assault team on board; the chopper was empty except for the crew: two pilots and two door gunners who manned M-60s port and starboard. The pilot disengaged the rotor, but did not cut the power. The turbine wound down to idle speed, while the rotor blades turned ever more slowly until the sound of the sweep of each blade through its arc became separate and distinct from the last.

"What the fuck is going on?" grumbled Monroe. The Huey was not in the line of fire, but close to it. Monroe refocused the crosshair on the target and considered a shot across the nose of the aircraft.

"Hold your fire," urged Patterson. He grabbed the handset of the radio and whispered urgently, thankful for the Huey's ambient noise. "Reliable Two, this is Batman. We have an unidentified ARVN UH-1 just landed in the target area. Do we continue the mission? Advise."

The left side door of the chopper swung open and the pilot dismounted. Through his scope, Monroe immediately spotted the black star on the collar of the man's tailored flight suit. He wore aviator glasses with reflective lenses, and the wings of a pilot. This ARVN general, whoever he was, flew his own helicopter. In his left hand, he carried a briefcase. The general glanced up at the sky, then stared blankly for a moment at their jungle hide. Abruptly, he turned and walked around the nose of the aircraft, exposing himself to the NVA and turning his back to the snipers.

"Who is this fucker?" said Monroe.

"Reliable Two," muttered Patterson into the radio handset. "Pilot of unknown aircraft is an ARVN general officer. Expedite instructions."

"Batman, we're still checking with G-2. Stand by."

Patterson clicked the transmit key twice to acknowledge Reliable Two's transmission. To Monroe he said, "Nobody knows shit. Or they ain't telling us." Whenever Division directed you to wait, it was bad news.

Patterson's spotting scope was powerful enough to read the name tag on the general's flight suit, but he had been so surprised by the star on the man's collar that he had failed to do so. If he had, he would not have recognized the name, for few men in the field had any reason to follow the progress of rising stars in their own army, not to mention that of their Vietnamese allies. But General Cho was a man well known to the division G-2, and any reporter in Vietnam could have told Monroe that this ARVN commander demanded respect. He had started the war as a helicopter pilot, but due to his reputation for cunning and connections in high places, he had risen through the ranks like a missile to become the commander of the ARVN 9th Marine Division. His willingness to fight and his disdain for casualties brought him to the attention of the Americans; his flamboyance brought him to the attention of the press, who called him the Tiger.

The snipers watched as General Cho marched the 850 yards to the whitewashed house where the NVA waited. Patterson checked again for instructions. None came. Monroe noted that the door gunners remained with their weapons, vigilant, only fifty yards away. The turbine noise would cover the sound of his shot, but fifty yards was too close for comfort. He pointed to the helicopter and Patterson understood: if the shit hit the fan, it was his job to take out the chopper.

Cho stopped a few yards short of his NVA counterpart. The two men exchanged salutes. The snipers, watching through their scopes, turned and stared at each other.

"Something is going down," said Patterson. He reached for the handset, and wondered if Colonel Lyons, the G-2, already knew what he was going to tell them.

The NVA general turned to his aide and spoke over his shoulder. The captain motioned toward the veranda, where a table had been set up in the shade. A white tablecloth covered the table and a pitcher of water was set in the center. The enlisted guards held the chairs while the generals took their seats.

"This is the meeting they were talking about," said Monroe. "G-2 was right for a change. I'm gonna take both these gomers."

"Wait," cautioned Patterson, emphatic. He was on the radio, still holding. "Get me G-2," he said. "Patch me in to G-2 right now, and don't tell me to stand by. Over." Rarely did anyone follow proper radio procedure to the letter, but Patterson now used the word "over" to emphasize his impatience. The RTO would get the point.

"Roger, Batman. Stand by." All RTOs took pride in sounding bored, regardless of how imperative the communications. The relay operator at the Special Forces camp knew his business, but Patterson needed guidance fast and the man at the other end of the radio net was too cool, and too slow.

"Fucking peckerwood," he groused, glancing at Monroe to ensure he wasn't about to do anything stupid.

General Cho placed the briefcase on his lap and opened it, withdrawing a large map, which he unfolded and spread out across the table. Both men leaned forward as Cho pointed from place to place, drawing his finger across the paper. While the generals talked, the captain paced the veranda, keeping a vigilant eye on his soldiers, who had taken up positions surrounding the building. Patterson saw the man's mouth move as he muttered something to the sniper in black pajamas. If the sniper responded, he did so without moving his lips or removing the binoculars from his eyes.

Monroe swung the Remington back to the officers at the table on the veranda, still talking like old friends. If he fired now, he could take out one man, but the other would take refuge in the building before he could get off a second shot. And there was still the sniper to deal with. He resolved to wait until the meeting ended, when the ARVN general would strut back to his aircraft, in the middle of the rice paddy with nowhere to hide. He would take out General Le first, then the sniper, hopefully getting off both shots before the first struck its target. Finally, he would shoot the ARVN general. Ten seconds after the first shot, they would be headed for the drainage ditch.

The generals rose to their feet and shook hands. Eager to conclude their business, they did not exchange pleasantries, for the skies were American; anything might fly over. Through his scope, Monroe watched the ARVN general turn, to begin the long walk back to his UH-1.

Monroe settled the crosshair on General Le. With the sun higher in the sky now, the general was in the shade, but the scope cut through the glare and presented a clean image. The air was still calm and not yet superheated—an easy shot with no variables except the drop, and that was the most predictable because gravity never changed. Monroe was confident despite having to push the envelope of his range. Only now did he notice the features of the face of his target, and as with all previous kills, he found them unremarkable. Through the scope, one Vietnamese face looked like another. Asian. Flat noses, flat eyes. This one older than most, and more aware. There was a mind at work behind the eyes; even in the People's Army dullards didn't become generals.

Patterson noticed Monroe take up the slack in the trigger and thought to protest. The situation was not as briefed; he stood by for instructions; a shot now would eliminate any chance that the mission could be quietly aborted. A solitary thought of his daughters infiltrated his mind before he forced it out. *Concentrate. A man dies when he starts being careful.* He'd seen it a hundred times. Patterson put his eye to the spotter's scope. "Wind calm," he said.

The bullet exited the muzzle at supersonic velocity. It passed across the nose of the ARVN helicopter before the sonic shock wave struck it. Even then, the crew noticed nothing, deafened by their headsets and the whine of the turbine.

The bullet cruised for just over two seconds, dropping ballistically at the same rate as an apple falling from its tree. It traveled an inch above the tabletop and impacted the NVA general just below his sternum. The impact lifted him out of his chair, and turned every organ in his abdominal cavity to paste. His diaphragm spasmed and the general, coughing his lungs out through his nose, was dead before hitting the ground.

"Hit," said Patterson.

Monroe had already jacked in another cartridge and swung the barrel an inch to the right. The sniper was gone. "Where the fuck is he?" he cursed.

"Shit," said Patterson, scanning the veranda with the spotter's scope.

The violence of the impact had thrown the general to the ground with such force that his feet kicked upward, upsetting the table and tossing the map into the air. The guards froze, perplexed as if their commander's rib cage had burst open of its own volition. The sound of the gunshot came later, vaguely audible, mixed with the distant drone of the helicopter turbine.

The NVA troops reacted then, grabbing their weapons and shouting, pointing in all directions as they scrambled to protect their already dead commander. Soldiers ringed the veranda in defensive positions, weapons aimed outward but at no specific target, for the muzzle blast had been hidden in the foliage, half a mile across the rice paddies through shimmering heat mirages that now started to quiver in the air. A medic appeared and the guards dragged the general into the building, but Monroe knew the man was dead. Nobody went down that hard and lived to tell about it.

General Cho sensed the bullet as it passed by him like a meteorite, and vaguely heard the gunshot. Behind him was chaos, and Cho realized he would be the next target and that he had nowhere to hide. He began a zigzag race through the rice paddy, with the helicopter still four hundred yards away.

An evasive target at four hundred yards would not be easy, but Monroe had a plan. "I'll let him run. He's old. I'll shoot when the fucker slows down."

There was no time to move their position, as doctrine recommended, nor time to remain in place. There was one more shot to take and if not taken soon, the enemy would recover and sweep the area. For now, the enemy troops were too stunned to move. They lay on their stomachs, frozen with indecision, afraid to stand, unsure of where to attack, knowing only that another anonymous bullet could come from nowhere to kill the first man to show some initiative.

"Let him go," said Patterson. "They's looking for us now. If you shoot, the sniper'll spot us for sure. We got what we came for. Soon as that bird is gone we can slide right out of here."

Patterson took his eye from his scope and glanced through the vines at his partner. Monroe's eyes were calm and flat, the pupils huge to absorb data and light, so open that Patterson imagined he could see his partner's thoughts forming deep inside his head. Patterson had seen the same intensity in the faces of other snipers who moved about the battlefield with predatory poise, a sense of control amid the confusion. He knew that Monroe would kill the ARVN general. Snipers were more than executioners; they were judges, too. While ordinary infantrymen did their work amid havoc and terror, snipers made reasoned decisions about the targets they shot. Some they spared, some they executed. This judging had undone Patterson, who could not bring himself to condemn men no better or worse than himself. He had presumed that Monroe killed without moral reflection, for he could not imagine executing someone any other way. So it was with some surprise that Patterson recognized the zeal on his partner's face.

But Monroe didn't care about Cho. Monroe cursed himself for not targeting the sniper first. The man had undoubtedly spotted the muzzle blast with his binoculars, reacting even before the first round struck its target. *He's hunting us now.* But Monroe doubted that any man could compete with him at nine hundred yards, especially a sniper as frail and blind as the little man in the black pajamas, even if he did have the Remington. Although the sniper's range had been increasing, all of his previous kills had been at seven hundred yards or less, and Monroe had obsessively checked enemy sniper after-action reports. *He'll have to close the range, and he'll have to do it fast. He'll show himself. And then I'll kill him.* There was a debt to repay, for Monroe knew whose weapon the enemy carried.

Patterson did not need his scope to see the door gunner looking about, scanning the tree line. The copilot's mouth moved as he craned his neck to look back toward the settlement, and Patterson guessed he was on the radio to someone inside the enemy camp. The engine RPMs began to rise and the rotor engaged. The copilot eased in more throttle until the blades spun at three hundred RPM, enough to take off with the addition of pitch. The copilot waited then, fighting the shuddering machine to keep it on the ground while General Cho closed the distance between himself and his helicopter. Patterson kept the sights of his M-14 steady on the door gunner, where the danger lay, for the M-60 machine gun could rip the forest apart and the gunner was looking hard for them.

On their feet now, the NVA charged after General Cho, urged forward by a foolish NCO who ran behind them waving his pistol. The initial shock was over. Patterson watched one group peel off in a flanking movement to his left, while the others closed the distance across the paddies at a dead run, bobbing and weaving. If they got within three hundred yards, the snipers would be within range of the enemy AK-47s. There would be no stealthy escape then, only a mad dash across open ground. Patterson scanned the target area for the sniper, but could not find him. He knew that Black Pajamas was already scoping the tree line, waiting for Monroe's next shot.

Cho jogged and heaved, slowing considerably. He had covered two hundred yards at a dead run in sweltering heat across rough ground wearing heavy boots that now felt like they were made of lead. Monroe could see his cheeks blowing with exhaustion, and the sweat draining down his mottled face. His eyes bulged with fear. *Your number's up,* thought Monroe. *If I don't kill you, you're gonna have a fucking heart attack.* At four hundred yards, Monroe centered the crosshair on General Cho's chest and slowly squeezed the trigger.

Cho went down as if he'd run into a clothesline. The bullet impacted at the base of his throat, ripping out his esophagus, which went flipping through the air like a bloody snake. The troops behind him dropped to the ground, again frozen with confusion, still too far from the tree line to see a muzzle flash. As before, the sound of Monroe's shot reached them after Cho had exploded in a spray of blood. The bullet came out of nowhere.

The helicopter crew was closer to their hide, however, and the door gunner alert. He spotted the flash, deep in the trees, and instantly pressed the trigger of his M-60 as he swung it toward the snipers, sending bullets streaking into the leaves. The gunner fired only a single burst before Patterson put one bullet through his helmet. The man spun around and collapsed to his knees before falling backward from the open helicopter, dangling in his harness.

The pilot yanked on the collective and twisted in more throttle. Already light on the skids, the Huey jerked into the air, but yawed to the left, nose down and pointed directly into the iron sights of Patterson's M-14. The pilot was still talking on the radio when Patterson fired a round through the Plexiglas windshield and down his throat. Dying, the pilot kicked the rudder and the aircraft rolled over, the blades plowing into the ground, snapping shorter and shorter with each rotation until the Jesus nut at the top of the mast buried itself sideways in the rice paddy and two hundred gallons of JP4 drained into the still screaming turbine. The fuel erupted in an orange whoosh, quiet by the standards of combat, that sucked the air inward, then exhaled it skyward in an oily black fireball.

Amid the carnage, the snipers never saw the gentle flash from the door of the pagoda, 850 yards away.

The paddies remained motionless. The NVA lay facedown, six hundred yards from the snipers' hide, leaderless and afraid.

Patterson grabbed the radio and untangled himself from the prison of limbs. He lowered himself to the ground and prepared to crawl under the hedge—the same way they had crawled in. They would need thirty seconds to slither through the open weeds to the drainage ditch, and he reckoned that the soldiers would need that much time to regain their courage. The escape route was open. "C'mon," he said. "We're gone."

But Monroe did not follow. Crouched over and bewildered, he stared at Patterson with a look of puzzlement and pain. "I'm hit," he muttered, his voice calm, slightly plaintive, with a trace of embarrassment. Abruptly, Monroe sank to his knees. He grabbed his head, his right hand slipping on the thick blood that oozed from his scalp. "Oh, shit." Pain overwhelmed him. Disoriented and fragile, he collapsed face first into the thicket.

"Get up, m'fucker. We gotta go." Patterson reached through the tangle of foliage and grasped Monroe by the collar of his shirt. Monroe tried to move and he pushed himself toward his partner, but his legs remained rubbery and the trees began to spin. Patterson heaved, and Monroe felt himself being hauled through the undergrowth like a plow, broken branches digging at his wound, until they lay on the edge of the tree line, under the lowest cover. There was no time for treatment.

Twenty yards of open ground lay between them and the drainage ditch. Patterson knew he had to get them across the ditch while the NVA still lay prone—maybe fifteen more seconds. He knew, too, that somewhere beyond the enemy soldiers a sniper scoped the terrain. He was less concerned about the gun than he was about the 9x telescopic sight, for if the sniper in black pajamas spotted their point of entry into the ditch, he could guide the squads of NVA to easily outflank them. So they would have to crawl, find low cover, and slip away while the enemy still believed they were in the trees. And he'd have to drag Monroe.

As Patterson broke cover, however, he looked back to grab Monroe and realized that his thirty seconds were long gone. An enemy soldier behind them popped to his feet, rabbit-like, and ran forward a few yards before diving to the ground. Immediately, another soldier followed in similar fashion, and then another, darting through the weeds like field mice. And Patterson had not forgotten the flankers still moving through the trees to his left. With five hundred yards still between them and the enemy, he could still slither quickly to the ditch before the approaching soldiers got close enough to spot him. But he could not move quickly and also drag Monroe.

Slowly, Patterson leveled his M-14, placing the muzzle against Monroe's forehead. Compared to what the gooks did to captured snipers, murder would be an act of mercy. Monroe felt the warm steel and smelled the burnt carbon in the bore, and opened his eyes. He thought of his mother, fleetingly, his first thought of her in weeks. "Do it," he gasped, and he started to cry.

As Patterson took up the slack in the trigger, an insistent buzz penetrated the silence. An odd familiar sound, Patterson recognized the ringer on the PRC-25. He swung the muzzle of his rifle away from Monroe and grabbed the handset.

"Reliable, this is Batman! We have one serious WIA, and we need a medevac now! Over!"

"Batman, this is Reliable Two. Abort your mission. I repeat: abort your mission. How copy? Over."

"Mission accomplished! We require immediate medevac and a gunship. Copy!"

The reply did not come immediately, and Patterson knew the colonels were dithering. He was ready to key the handset again when Division finally responded. "Batman, confirm you copy mission abort, over." The voice was calm, steady. Patterson recognized it as Lyons. "Batman, your mission is to abort, over."

"Listen, you motherfucker, we already shot every general in sight. And if you don't get us out of here, I'm gonna shoot you next. You copy?"

Monroe still lay under the branches of the foliage, conscious but unable to move, his limbs like lead. The bleeding barely slowed, now covering his face and darkening the collar of his shirt, dripping from his ear and chin. Head wounds were always dangerous, but Monroe willed himself to move, to roll onto his stomach and crawl. But as he sat up the world turned over, and nausea welled up in his stomach. *Move! Move your ass!* But his blood pressure was falling, and he knew he fluttered on the edge of shock. He was swimming, the air like water; his hearing began to short circuit. Monroe's eyesight tunneled; blackness crowded the periphery of his vision. The center of his field of view, however, remained sharp. He saw the enemy soldiers maneuvering closer and understood that they would soon be upon them. *Patterson should have shot me.*

Monroe felt the sling of his Remington still looped tightly around his left arm. He rolled onto his side, his knees drawn up in the fetal position. The urge to vomit returned but he could keep the dizziness at bay as long as he did not lift his head. Prone, Monroe placed his eye behind the scope. He pulled the cheek plate against his bloody face and lay upon it like a pillow.

He watched the NVA captain pop to his feet, then drop to the ground before he could get a bead on him. Monroe marked the spot where the officer had gone down and waited. At three hundred yards, the shot would be simple; Monroe reminded himself to aim low. Another soldier sprang to his feet, then another, and by turns the enemy advanced toward the tree line, avid as hounds, though never exposing themselves for more than a couple of seconds at a time. Monroe waited, fighting the urge to vomit and the buzzing in his ears, the reticle of his scope trained directly above the spot where the target had dropped for cover. The captain rose up then, his turn to advance again, and Monroe squeezed the trigger. The bullet struck the man in the nose, and his head disintegrated like a shattered pumpkin. The soldier next in turn did not move.

Monroe's gunshot carried across the radio, as if to emphasize Patterson's threat. A moment of silent consternation carried across the airwaves.

"Batman, this is Reliable Two. Your orders are to escape and evade. We have no aircraft available at this time. Reliable Two out."

They were dead, already listed as MIA. If Patterson had any further communications, Division did not want to hear it. Patterson simply stared at the handset, too shocked to be furious.

"Hit," he said, quietly, looking at Monroe and seeing him now unconscious. He grabbed his M-14 and prepared to run, hopeful that Monroe's shot would keep the NVA pinned down long enough for him to make the ditch. A bullet whined through the leaves, inches from his head. He ducked instinctively, then heard the deep boom of a Remington. The enemy sniper, he realized, had their range.

"Batman, this is Reliable Six, airborne at this time approaching your position. Do you have smoke? Over."

This voice from Division was different, older, less cool. Patterson knew that "Reliable Six" was the call sign for the division commander, but he never imagined that General Otis Vandermeer would make his own radio calls. He understood only that Division had returned to the air, trying to help this time.

"Reliable Six, where are you?" responded Patterson.

"We're over the river, turning up the Vinh Te Canal. Throw smoke when you hear us, over."

"Roger, Reliable. We have smoke. Be advised, the LZ is hot. Land as close to the tree line as you can, over."

"Negative, negative." Vandermeer imagined the scenario: the chopper would become a target as soon as it approached the trees. They would be over the Cambodian border, and if things went badly, it would be difficult for the Army to explain how one of their generals was killed or captured in a firefight in a neutral country during a rescue flight for a mission that did not officially exist. "Disengage and get to the canal. We'll pluck you from the water. Over."

In the distance, Patterson could hear the wop-wop of an incoming helicopter. Ahead of him, the NVA approached the wreckage of General Cho's helicopter, which was within the effective range of an AK-47. As soon as Patterson tossed his smoke grenade, bullets would be swarming through the trees. Monroe's eyes were open again, but he barely held the Remington and made no effort to fire it.

"Roger, copy, Reliable Six. We are moving now. I'll throw smoke when you're closer. This is our last transmission. Out."

Patterson threw down the radio and his pack. He stuffed the smoke grenades in Monroe's pack, turned his back to the closing enemy, and reached back and grabbed Monroe by the shoulder straps of his rucksack. Pushing himself while pulling Monroe into the undergrowth that stood between them and the canal, he bulled forward, thrashing, pushing aside tree limbs when he could and crushing them when he had to, indifferent to the movement of the foliage that might betray his position. The game of stealth and deception was over;

now came a race, flat out.

With each lunge through the bushes, Patterson yanked Monroe's body behind him. The Remington remained strapped around Monroe's left arm, snagging constantly on the undergrowth, as Patterson desperately dragged him through the bamboo.

Reliable Six banked left and descended to within a few feet of the water. On both banks, trees rose above the helicopter blades, but the canal was wide and the chopper hurtled downstream, nose down at full pitch.

General Vandermeer's Command and Control ship was a Huey, identical to the one flown by General Cho. Rated at 1100 horsepower, the gas turbine could safely drive the aircraft at a sustained speed of 120 knots. Redlined, it might push 150, and the tachometer was pegged as the division commander's helicopter roared down the canal, a rooster tail of spray in its wake.

Vandermeer sat behind the pilots, in a jump seat facing forward. Several radios lay on the deck around him, the coiled handset cords tangled. Normally, he monitored them all, but he threw down the last handset and pointed through the windshield to a column of oily smoke in the distance, rising from Cho's downed bird. He wore an aviator helmet and visor, the commo line plugged into the overhead console. "They'll be near that smoke," he said,

Patterson's ears were tuned to the sounds of the helicopter, but it was the metallic pop of AK-47s that he heard first, and the sounds of the rounds flicking through the leaves. Each lunge brought him closer to the canal, through the choking thickets that grew along the sunny edges of the tree line. He moved faster, hauling Monroe mercilessly through the broken undergrowth in his wake.

Patterson found himself in a clearing with tall palms and evergreens overhead. The AK-47s cracked behind him, but intermittently and wild. His pursuers would be crashing into the shrubbery soon, and Patterson wondered who would arrive first: Reliable Six, or the NVA.

He heard the distinctive beating of a Huey and the pitch told him it was moving fast. Patterson dropped Monroe and reached into his pack. The smoke grenades were there, one green, one red. He pulled the pin on the green one and tossed it into the vegetation along the bank of the canal. The chopper was almost upon them.

The smoke grenade hissed, then popped, and thick green smoke spewed forth, climbing upward through the vegetation and leaking through the treetops and into the air above. The pilot yanked on the cyclic and reduced pitch; the tail dipped low, almost touching the water.

The NVA, too, heard the aircraft, and the smoke alerted them to its position. Although the Huey was beyond the trees, they raised their weapons and fired at the sound of its approach.

The pilot maneuvered the aircraft as close to the shoreline as he dared. He hovered there, inches above the surface, jockeying first the cyclic, then the pedals, admiring his own airmanship even as the first enemy tracers passed across the nose. Quiet, relentless, they seemed always to Doppler in slowly, then accelerate past at astonishing velocity, unless they hit something.

As Patterson reached for Monroe, the tree beside him exploded. Bullets flew passed him, lacerating the air. The crack of AK-47s came from his left and he realized the NVA flankers had found him. Passing through the woods under the tallest trees, they had been moving to cut him off.

Patterson jumped for cover, spinning to bring his M-14 to bear. He saw muzzle blasts only, but the incoming rounds began chewing through the trees closer with each moment. Voices began yelling, Vietnamese, high pitched and excited. Patterson heard the others crashing through the brush behind him, following the trail he had broken. Toward the canal, he caught a glimpse of the helicopter through the trees, hovering perfectly still, beating the foliage with its downdraft and almost drowning the sounds from the gunfire.

Patterson turned his selector switch to full automatic and spotted a single muzzle blast through the trees. He aimed low and pulled the trigger, walking the rounds up and down and through the position where the muzzle blast had been. The deep-throated roar of the M-14 overwhelmed the other sounds of combat as the heavy bullets ripped apart everything in their path. Magazine empty, Patterson threw down the weapon. The only sound was the screaming of a dead man whose single remaining functional organ seemed to be his vocal cords, the rest of him shredded in Patterson's fusillade.

With his final reserves of strength, Patterson grabbed Monroe by his shirt and hoisted him into a bear hug. The Remington fell from Monroe's grip, but instinct compelled Patterson to grasp it, too, as if the weapon itself afforded some measure of protection. He charged into the tangle of undergrowth that stood between them and the canal. Monroe was dead weight in his arms, a human battering ram as they crashed ahead. Behind him, the NVA recovered quickly. More rounds passed him, whipping through the weeds and bamboo. Patterson's foot sank beneath him into mud and water. He began to fall, and with a final scream of effort he heaved Monroe forward. Monroe crashed through the remaining thicket into daylight, landing with a splash in the filthy water of the Vinh Te Canal.

"There!" yelled Vandermeer, pointing.

Revived by the water, Monroe splashed feebly, vomiting water and blood. Patterson struggled in the mud behind him.

The door gunner loosed a long burst into the jungle, a few feet above the snipers' heads. Green tracers answered, and the aircrew heard the tap of rounds impacting the fuselage.

Patterson waded into the rotor wash that churned the stagnant canal into whitewater, and he knew he could go no farther. Before him, barely twenty feet from the shore, floated a Huey suspended in a perfect hover. The water reflected the sonic shock generated by each swoop of the blades and Patterson braced himself against the flying water. A solid wall of noise engulfed him, as if the sound waves alone kept the helicopter in the air. He could see the underside of the chopper, chipped by debris kicked up by uncounted landings on dry land, though now the skids touched water. The pilot eased closer as the forty-foot blades cut a perfect disk out of the smaller trees along the shore, filling the air with twigs and leaves and pulverized cellulose.

The gunner climbed onto the landing skid, now below the surface of the water. As he extended his hand for Monroe, a man stepped up to the machine gun. Patterson saw the black stars embroidered on his collar and realized that the division commander had come personally to take him home. With one last dose of adrenaline, Patterson shoved Monroe a final time toward the helicopter. Monroe raised his hand and the gunner grasped it. And then Patterson felt the skid.

"Go!" yelled Patterson, as he held the skid more firmly and looped one leg over the top. The Remington dangled below him, one arm still through the sling.

A wild spray of rounds from an AK-47 swept the UH-1, punching through the thin skin as if it were paper, each round a distinct puncture-pop, including one that hit the door gunner in the hip. He recoiled first, then collapsed, his blood looping through the flight deck in a brief arc. Cursing in anger more than pain, he pitched onto the skids of the helicopter before his harness arrested his fall.

In the tumult, the machine gun opened up, the throaty rumble of its heavy rounds adding to the cacophony of noise and confusion as spent brass bounced off the men hanging on the skids and fell hissing into the canal. Vandermeer leaned into the weapon, hanging out over the water and bouncing with the recoil like a puppet dancing in the downwash.

"Go! Go! Go!" screamed the gunner, himself hanging from the skid with one arm, the other latched onto Monroe like a vise.

Above the noise, they could hear the puncture sounds of bullets piercing the fuselage. Patterson made himself small, as did the crew, all except Vandermeer, who stood untethered in the door with his finger frozen on the trigger of the

M-60, which fired nonstop, chewing away the wooded shore, dismembering trees and humans in a hurricane of flying bark, bone, and lead.

The pilot pulled pitch and the Huey lifted its skids from the water. The airship groaned and the slap of the rotor blades grew louder and slower as they bit more deeply into the air. The nose dropped and the bird moved sluggishly forward, bullets still impacting, searching for a fuel line or a turbine blade or a crew member. The M-60 still roared, never pausing, miraculous that the gun had not simply come apart in the general's hands, the barrel glowing like a branding iron. Finally, the chopper heeled away, exposing its underside to the enemy, who fired at but missed the men clinging underneath.

The pilot flew low along the canal bank gathering speed, for the damaged aircraft was now too weak to climb and dangerously unbalanced with three men hanging on the starboard skid. Patterson held on grimly while Vandermeer hauled the weakening gunner onto the flight deck. As Monroe swung below the struggling helicopter, he could feel the gunner's grip loosen. He looked above him and saw apology in the man's face. Three hundred yards from the spot where the gunner had grasped him, their hands broke free. Dropping weight, the aircraft started to right itself and began to climb.

S¦X

**Vinh Te Canal
Kien Phong**

Vandermeer hauled the gunner and then Patterson onto the chopper's cargo deck, and soon the aircraft resumed level flight.

"Are you hit?" yelled Vandermeer as Patterson collapsed onto the floor. Even as he asked the question, he tore open his own first-aid kit and applied a field dressing to the gunner's bleeding hip. The danger over, the gunner now gritted his teeth in agony.

"No." Patterson breathed in hot aluminum and engine exhaust and hydraulic fluid mixed with sweat and blood and spent shell casings from the door guns. It was the way slicks always smelled. Going in, it made men sick; coming out, it was perfume. A wave of guilt swept over him and he turned to see if he could spot Monroe in the water.

Vandermeer directed Patterson to keep pressure on the gunner's wound, while he moved forward to the cockpit. He yelled above the sound of the rotor blades and the whistling of air through the bullet holes in the fuselage. "Captain, turn this ship around! We left a man in the water!"

"No can do, sir! We're losing hydraulic fluid and the turbine is rough. If it took a bullet, the whole engine could disintegrate and blow right out the exhaust. We should put her down!"

"Negative! Turn around! Now!" Vandermeer turned away from the cockpit and grabbed his radio from the command console above his head.

The pilot exchanged a glance with his copilot and gently twisted in more throttle while carefully pulling the cyclic and pushing the directional control pedals. The Huey banked right in a lazy arc to minimize the stress on the engine, but as they passed though ninety degrees of turn the engine coughed. A turbine blade clattered through the exhaust and the power dropped to 50 percent. The turbine whine changed pitch, more shrill, and the aircraft lost altitude. The pilot rolled off power and leveled out, then allowed the plane to coast as long as possible, slowly losing altitude, but gaining airspeed. Too focused and worried to display nervousness, they crossed the canal and continued east, gliding over the barren rice paddies, ready to pull pitch and auto-rotate if the turbine failed completely. Ten feet above the ground, the pilot finally twisted in a hint of throttle. The engine took it and held its altitude. Reliable Six lumbered for home, its skids barely clearing the wild grass that grew along the dikes of the abandoned paddies. There was no conversation. Even Vandermeer knew that there would be no going back for Monroe.

Reliable Six approached the helipad behind the 3rd Surgical Hospital in a billow of dust, small vortices of condensed water vapor swirling off the tips of the rotor blades. Vandermeer had made the inbound call himself, and the stretcher bearers stood waiting as the Huey touched down on the red cross emblazoned on the PSP pad. He signaled for them to move forward as the pilot rolled the throttle to idle, then jumped from the cockpit to help unload the gunner himself.

At the edge of the action, inconspicuous in an olive-drab T-shirt, a reporter from the division press corps held a camera to his eye. For a brief moment, Vandermeer stood poised on the helicopter's skid, barking orders and looking directly into the camera's eye. The shutter blinked.

The general reached across the gunner to help lift him from the aircraft to the stretcher. His shirt pressed against the man's bloody hip. More blood, already black and congealed in the tropical heat, pooled on the floor where Vandermeer placed his forearm for balance. Smeared with blood, he passed the gunner to a T-shirted private. The photographer triggered the shutter again and the press sergeant knew he had another cover photo for the *Stars and Stripes*.

Patterson remained in the aircraft, not knowing what to do. He cradled the battered Remington in his arms and stared at his feet.

As the stretcher was carried away, Vandermeer found himself alone. No high-ranking member of the medical staff came to greet him, for Division policy forbade it. If there were wounded men in the hospital, Vandermeer wanted every available doctor with them, not out saluting the brass. The helicopter crew busied themselves with systems checks, running through checklists and inspecting damage, all the while keeping the turbine going, fearful that if they shut it down it might not start again. As Vandermeer turned to climb back aboard his helicopter, the press sergeant jogged to the aircraft. "I got some great shots, General. They'll make the paper for sure."

"Give me the film, Sarge. I'll deliver it for you."

The sergeant popped the back of his camera and handed the roll to his commander. "Don't let the developers fuck it up, General. Those shots will win my Pulitzer, and your next star." He smiled.

Vandermeer ignored him and dropped the film in his pocket and turned to the pilot. "Get me back to HQ, Captain. Just keep this crate flying for two more minutes."

The pilot nodded grimly as Vandermeer climbed back on board. Carefully, the captain eased in the power. The chopper struggled into the air, shuddering with each sweep of the blades. The pilot eyed the gauges carefully, noting that the RPMs struggled to reach five thousand. The foot pedals were mushy and he knew the hydraulics were almost shot. He slowly pulled pitch and twisted in more throttle, hoping to coax enough altitude out of her so that they would have time to auto-rotate if everything fell apart.

Vandermeer deposited himself in a webbed seat in the rear of the Huey and stared angrily at the ground. He withdrew the canister of film from his pocket and dropped it on the bloody floor, where he crushed it with his foot before kicking it out the door. Only then did he realize that Patterson was still with him. The two men stared at each other, separated by too much rank to say anything.

SE✝EN

10:28

9th Infantry Division Headquarters
Dong Tam

At the helipad, a committee of two scanned the horizon. One wore a uniform, the other did not, and the soldier ignored the civilian, listening instead for the approach of Vandermeer's helicopter. Reliable Six had reported inbound upon leaving the field hospital, and would be coming into view at any moment.

Colonel Ron Boettcher had been in Vietnam ten months. He had been the general's chief of staff for three years, since the day Vandermeer returned from his first tour in Vietnam and pinned on his first star. Through Vandermeer's successive assignments, from division commander in Germany to staff slots in the Pentagon, Boettcher had enjoyed the trappings of rank vicariously, following Vandermeer with the devotion typical of staff officers, most of whom regarded their proximity to power as opportunities for visibility and promotions of their own. But the colonel was no lapdog; when something needed doing, he invoked Vandermeer's authority and his own pit-bull determination in order to get it done.

The civilian was a war correspondent.

"I heard," said the reporter, "that the adventures of General Vandermeer have become pretty standard fare in the *Stars and Stripes*."

"This division has a top-notch press corps," Boettcher replied.

"I'm looking forward to meeting him." Dan Brady slung his camera onto his other shoulder and wiped his brow. After three years in Vietnam, he was accustomed to the heat, but no amount of acclimatization could control his sweating. He marveled at Boettcher, who stood as stiff as a flagpole and betrayed not a hint of moisture.

"You're wasting your time here. We have better things to do than deal with the press." Colonel Boettcher did not like reporters, even those like Brady with combat experience and a reputation for honesty. He had no use for civilians who poked about like inspectors general, getting underfoot and requiring attention that could be better spent on the battlefield. Boettcher had become expert at deflecting their questions and foiling their attempts to get to Vandermeer. The whole thing had become a game to Boettcher, a game he detested. He would have preferred to simply toss the bastards in the stockade, but such efficacious solutions were no longer tolerated by the higher-highers in Saigon. By order of the President, simple possession of a press card authorized privileges for food and transportation and lodging that even military officers were denied. Boettcher, therefore, was obligated to humor men he considered dilettantes. But the colonel kept his thoughts to himself, and focused his vigilance into the haze above the trees.

Brady smiled to try to lighten the atmosphere. "Yeah, I've heard you guys don't put out the welcome mat the way they do elsewhere. I respect that. I was a Marine in Korea. Took a bullet at the Chosin Reservoir. Ever hear of it?"

Brady knew there was no military officer alive who didn't know about the sacrifices made at Chosin. His Purple Heart was a more effective calling card than his press credentials. He stared back respectfully when Boettcher turned to look him in the eye for the first time.

"I'm not here to get in your way," Brady continued. "But nobody has really ever heard of Vandermeer outside of the Army. I see UPI dispatches all the time from military reporters from every division except this one."

"You'll get your story. But I want see it before you file it."

The correspondent turned to look at Boettcher to see if there was anything in his expression to indicate that he was joking. He saw a face frozen except for the eyes. They were moving, scanning, absorbing; their animation was unrelated to everything else about him.

The reporter laughed. "What are you afraid of, Colonel? I always print the truth. Nothing but."

"I checked you out, Mr. Brady. You don't print anything. Not since the *New York Times* fired you."

Brady was impressed with Boettcher's Intel. He'd been freelancing for a year, eating in Army mess halls and making ends meet with hometown news releases about local football heroes who missed their girlfriends and their '57 Chevy. None of the networks would touch anything from him, not since the *Times* had been forced to retract his story about a band of American deserters living a clandestine high life in Saigon. When the story broke, his sources came forward in full uniform, expressing bafflement at Brady's accusations. None of them were so much as AWOL.

"I was set up," said Brady.

"I guess none of us can be too careful, can we?"

The conversation was interrupted by the approaching throb of chopper blades, and Boettcher squinted to the southeast.

Brady pointed, more easterly than Boettcher had expected. "Four o'clock, low, just above the tree line. That bird's in trouble."

Boettcher spotted the helicopter then, trailing a thin plume of smoke.

"I've been in-country for a long time," said Brady. "I know a thing or two about helicopters."

Reliable Six reached an altitude of five hundred feet before the pilot began his descent to the division HQ pad, coasting in under minimum power to decrease the need for torque control. Vandermeer sat expressionless in his jump seat, displaying not a hint of the nervousness felt by the pilots as they wrestled with the increasingly flaccid controls. A good crew could always coax an extra mile out of a dead ship, and the general's crew was the best in the division—handpicked by Colonel Boettcher. So while the pilots struggled to set the aircraft down in one piece, Vandermeer pondered the sniper mission that had ended with one MIA and near catastrophe. *What the hell happened out there?* He knew that he would get no answers from G-2. Intel always covered their tracks, especially when things went wrong. Vandermeer had always felt that his own Intel chief, Colonel Lyons, was more responsive to the puppet masters in Saigon than to him, passing information up channel and planning missions without consulting Ops. MACV had laid on this mission over his misgivings. *I should have objected,* he thought, but it had seemed a small battle at the time, not worth squandering political ammunition. Now there were people who would have to answer some tough questions, and one of those people was himself.

He turned his attention to the sandbagged city below him. Normally, the sight of the division base camp filled him with pride, an impregnable beehive of military activity that he had built from a pitiful hovel of tents. He preferred the bird's-eye view of his command because it offered the best vantage point for evaluating the compound's security and fields of fire. The defensive perimeter was constantly expanding, miles of strong points and razor wire. The base was a maze of roads and sandbags, Quonset huts and screened barracks, motor pools and maintenance yards, a paved swamp of OD green and dust the color of dried blood, sealed under a steamy blanket of air laced with trapped diesel fumes and sewage from the latrines. The 9th Infantry Division was a fighting unit, 100 percent functional, devoid of the whitewashed rocks or ice cream parlors so common at other division headquarters. Vandermeer saw it as purposeful and pure, beautiful.

Reliable Six came in slow over rows of barracks, then flared gently over the helipad, keeping the nose level. Despite the pilot's airmanship, the tail skid hit the ground, kicking the cockpit down. The aircraft touched down firmly, twisting slightly clockwise before finally settling on its skids. The pilot chopped the power immediately and slumped in his seat, exhausted from wrestling the deteriorating aircraft the last mile to the division pad.

Vandermeer hopped out and jogged through the dust thrown up in the windstorm under the decelerating rotor blades. The officers greeted each other with salutes.

"Welcome back, General. Status reports have been coming in all morning. Pretty quiet, so far."

Tell that to the people who were on that helicopter, thought Vandermeer, noting that both Boettcher and the civilian were staring at the bullet holes and shattered windshield of Reliable Six. He said nothing in front of the stranger, obviously a reporter, who extended his hand.

"Dan Brady," said the civilian. "Looks like things might not be as quiet as Colonel Boettcher would have me believe." He nodded toward the aircraft.

"Welcome to the delta, Brady." Vandermeer placed his hand on Brady's shoulder and guided him toward the headquarters compound, away from the helipad. "We flew a little too close to a suspected VC position. It's not suspected anymore. It's confirmed."

Boettcher and Vandermeer laughed heartily. As Brady followed them toward the HQ building, he glanced over his shoulder at the helicopter, where the pilots counted bullet holes. He saw an inch of blood pooled against the lip of the flight deck and noted the stains on Vandermeer's uniform. *Someone died in there.* Patterson stepped slowly from the cargo floor onto the ground, attracting Brady's attention. This soldier was no crew member; he wore fatigues too filthy to have spent the day in the air and he carried a high-powered rifle with a scope. Brady noted casually that the man was black, and wondered why this sniper was flying with the division commander. Patterson glanced up briefly, meeting Brady's eye. Brady prided himself on his ability to judge a man's mood, but Patterson revealed nothing. The newsman sensed only loneliness as Patterson trudged away.

"What's the scuttlebutt in Saigon?" asked Vandermeer, reclaiming Brady's attention. "We don't get too many visitors." The general walked swiftly now, all business, and Brady had to hustle to keep up.

"That's one of the reasons I'm here, sir. Nobody seems to know much about you guys. Central Highland gets all the press."

"They can have it. Lots of casualties there."

"I thought the folks back home might like to know how you've kept casualties so low in this division, especially in light of the fact that your enemy body counts compare favorably with other divisions."

"It's an ARVN war down here. We're the second string; don't see as much action as in the rest of the country, so our casualties are lower."

"Modesty is an uncommon quality among most division commanders," said Brady. "Even false modesty. But I would imagine that the heavy ARVN presence here makes this a very political assignment."

"I'm a soldier," said Vandermeer. "I go where my government sends me and I leave the politics to the politicians." He wished to God that were true. "What else have you heard?"

"That you are a candidate for another star. That you're going places. That you are glamorous and mysterious and that you don't give interviews."

"Well," responded Vandermeer, "you're right about that last one. I don't give interviews, and my staff will not provide you with a dog and pony show. You can tag along with the troops as long as you stay out from underfoot and don't go anywhere without a press escort. I'll assign a man to you."

"That won't be necessary, General."

Vandermeer stopped abruptly and looked Brady in the eye. "Civilians don't go anywhere in my command without protection. It's for your own safety, and so I won't have to write up any accident reports about you." Having made his point, Vandermeer turned to Boettcher and ordered, "Colonel, see to it that Mr. Brady gets an escort, then join me in my office."

Vandermeer turned to leave, but Brady asked a parting question. "General, how did you get so much blood on your uniform?"

Vandermeer looked down at his shirt, now stiff with the door gunner's blood, and thought for a moment. "War is a bloody business."

"I saw a lot of it on the floor of your helicopter. Any chance I might interview the man who spilled it?"

"Sorry, Brady. It's hard enough when one of my boys loses a leg to a booby trap without some reporter sticking a microphone in his face asking how he feels about it."

"Don't patronize me," said Brady, indignant, but the general had already entered the DTOC. A guard stepped in front of the doorway, blocking access to anyone without a security badge.

Boettcher placed his hand upon Brady's chest. "Come with me. We'll get you an escort."

Vandermeer growled at the first man he faced as he entered the Ops center. "Where's Lyons?"

"Intel briefing in the conference room, sir." The sergeant pointed to the same glass office where Lyons had conducted the initial mission brief. The door was closed.

Vandermeer could hear angry voices inside. The yelling ceased and the room sprang to attention as the general stepped through the door. He studied the two men before him: Colonel Ingram, his own chief of operations; and Colonel Lyons, division G-2, Military Intelligence. Lyons stood at rigid attention, like a plebe at West Point; Ingram was proper, but relaxed. He and Vandermeer had worked together a long time.

"What happened?"

No one responded, though all eyes focused on Lyons.

"I want an answer," said Vandermeer. His voice was very quiet, but gravelly. His gray eyes turned black and his lips disappeared, drawn back as if ready to strike. He smelled of cordite and dried blood, and if he had been a dog Colonel Ingram would have shot him on the spot.

"We think we killed General Cho," said Ingram.

"What?" Vandermeer looked directly at Lyons, the fury on his face now mixed with puzzlement.

"General," the colonel stammered, "the sniper shot him without authority. We directed him to abort the mission and he fired anyway."

"What was Cho doing there?"

"We don't know. We can't even be sure it was him, except that he seems to have disappeared."

Vandermeer addressed Ingram. "Terry, we left a man in the canal. See if you can round up a SAR mission. My pilot can fly it; he knows the spot. And check with the Navy. Maybe they can send a boat in there."

As Ingram exited, Lyons said, "Only a handful of people know what happened out there, sir. Intel at MACV is working on the cover story at this time. I'm certain that they will issue a statement indicating that General Cho died in combat against the VC. We'll classify the incident and keep the surviving sniper under wraps."

"I don't give a damn what they tell the press," said Vandermeer. He stepped forward until he was nose to nose with Lyons. "I'm ashamed to be your commander. You left my men out there to die."

"That's not true, sir."

"I was on the net, Colonel. I heard your command to abort, and the E&E. What was that bullshit about no aircraft available? I had a dozen birds within a mile of mine. I did the job myself, but any one of them was available for the job!"

"General," said Lyons, "this was a covert mission, approved by the highest levels at MACV. You were briefed. There were to be no complications."

"Complications! Is that what you call the situation we have now? Let me tell you something, Colonel: if you and the rest of those covert lunatics in MACV are going to pull your political strings to override my decisions, you better make sure your missions go off without a hitch. Don't ever conduct another illegal operation in my AO again, or I'll have you walking point!"

Vandermeer stormed from the room, slamming the door behind him.

Boettcher pushed through the PIO office door with Brady in tow, and SP-4 Olivetti sprang to loose attention.

"Speak to me, sir." Tall, cocky, and smart, SP-4 Olivetti had been selected to work at Division PIO because Boettcher wanted reporters who could handle themselves around men of superior rank, military or civilian, in a way that conveyed neither obsequiousness nor awe. The Division Public Information Office staff worked in the field, unsupervised. They had to be men who could think on their feet and get the job done without getting in the way or pissing anyone off.

"Have you met Mr. Brady?" asked Boettcher, irritated by Olivetti's familiarity in front of a civilian.

"No, sir." Olivetti glanced toward the civilian behind Boettcher and nodded.

"Well, you have now. Mr. Brady was one of the best correspondents in Vietnam. Take care of him, but don't let him out of your sight. If he causes trouble, I want to know about it."

"I'll shoot him on the spot, sir."

Ordinarily, Boettcher appreciated Olivetti's deadpan humor, but he saw nothing funny about being upstaged with a reporter looking on. He placed his fists on Olivetti's desk and leaned forward. "Can the bullshit, Specialist. Get this man a story. Get him a room and get him a girl if he wants one. He is not to go anywhere near the WIAs or the field hospital. Treat him with a mixture of respect and indifference."

"I understand, Colonel." Olivetti wiped the smile from his face.

Boettcher turned to Brady. "Any questions?"

"I want to interview the Old Man," said Brady.

"Sorry, Brady. The general has no desire to become a household name in an unpopular war. There is no upside for us."

"He could be another MacArthur."

"Or the 'Delta Butcher.' Isn't that what the press named the last division commander here?"

"No, I think the press merely reported what the peasants called him."

"Well, when the peasants start calling him 'MacArthur,' you'll get an interview."

Both men were smiling, but Brady felt the animosity, the barely concealed contempt that had surrounded him from the moment he had arrived at division headquarters. Brady had interviewed hundreds of men in every division in the US Army, each pathetically eager to express his contempt for the war or the Army or the press or for the draft dodgers back home. But the men of 9th Infantry Division were unlike any of them. The division was a throwback to a different era, when leaders placed their individual stamp upon their armies and commanded personal loyalties. The 9th Infantry didn't behave like a well-oiled cog in the modern Army engine; it was its own machine, and it belonged to Vandermeer. This, Brady realized, was the story he would write.

"I'll tell you what," said Brady. "Give me an hour with Vandermeer and I'll be back in Saigon for happy hour. Otherwise, I'll be all over this goddamn delta, in a crappy mood, talking to every pissed-off grunt I can lay my hands on. What are you afraid of? I've got nothing against Vandermeer, so if you ask me, the only upside you've got is to let me talk to him."

Boettcher considered Brady's proposition. The war in the delta was uglier than anywhere else in Vietnam because the dense population almost guaranteed that civilians were involved in every operation. Scenes involving crying babies and pleading mama-sans had become de rigueur for the evening news and daily newspapers back home, and Boettcher had no doubt that Brady would find plenty of material. It mattered not whether the hell of war was foisted upon civilians by the VC or the NVA or the ARVN or the local militias or by troops of the US 9th Infantry Division. The American troops were the most disciplined of them all, but the "Delta Butcher" had learned that such distinctions made little difference to the folks back home.

"Wait here," said Boettcher. "Let me see what I can do."

Boettcher knocked twice on the door to Vandermeer's office and stepped inside when the general ordered, "Enter!"

"Brady is with Olivetti, sir."

"Good. Get him out of here as soon as possible." Vandermeer unbuttoned his uniform. "I need a clean shirt."

Boettcher opened a closet door, where he fetched a shirt and pants from among a dozen starched sets of fatigues. "General, I think the quickest way to get Brady out of our hair would be for you to give him an hour of your time. Otherwise, he threatened to poke around looking for trouble. To tell you the truth, I don't think the man wants to nuke us. He just wants back in the ball game."

Vandermeer nodded, distracted by thoughts of the sniper still in Cambodia. The general trusted Boettcher's judgment when it came to practical matters; the man was Machiavelli in fatigues. Yet there was something missing in Boettcher's makeup, a hollowness that made the difference between a shrewd man and a wise one. Through the years, Boettcher's counsel had served Vandermeer well, especially as the general became a player in the political game of high military rank. Though he remained leery of Boettcher, he knew when to listen to him. And when not to. The issue of Brady was straightforward, however, and Vandermeer shared Boettcher's sense that Brady was not a dangerous snoop like so many of the holier-than-thou youngsters who passed themselves off as reporters.

"Fine. Send him in." Vandermeer popped the starch out of his fresh shirt. "By the way, I just ripped Lyons a new asshole for leaving those snipers. I shouldn't have done that."

"He had it coming, sir. We don't hang our people out to dry."

"Bullshit. That's exactly what we did. I let it happen"—venom still in Vandermeer's voice. "But that's not the point. You should never humiliate weak men. They don't get over it. Transfer Lyons out of here ASAP. I don't trust him or the skunk he works for at MACV. He'll fuck us if he can."

"I'll get right on it, sir. But don't discuss this with Brady."

"I'm not an idiot, Colonel."

"No sir, you are not. But you're not a very good liar either."

The men exchanged glances and Vandermeer surrendered a forlorn smirk. "That's why I keep you around, Ron."

Brady had visited the offices of almost every division commander in Vietnam. Most of them were comfortable copies of what a general might expect back home: air conditioning, carpeting, paneled walls, and large mahogany desks. Vandermeer, however, worked in a space that captains at MACV would have found unacceptable. Except for the two-star flag in the corner opposite the Stars and Stripes, nothing in the office suggested that an officer of any rank worked there—a concrete floor supported a standard-issue metal desk. The brutal heat inside the Quonset building was unmitigated by any air conditioning. An old fan circled above, which only stirred the fetid Mekong air trapped inside. The single window framed the DTOC across the compound, with the officers' latrine on its left. There were no pictures on the wall or family photos on his desk.

"I love what you've done with the place," joked Brady.

"I'll have my decorator contact you." Vandermeer offered Brady a gray metal chair.

Brady appreciated the tone and set about taking Vandermeer into his confidence. "General, I know you don't like interviews, but how about a personal piece: your hometown, career, family. Nothing operational."

Vandermeer didn't bite; Intel began interrogations with captured VC using this same approach. *Where you from, soldier? Any family? Too bad, an Arclight raid is planned for just those coordinates. Give us something and we'll change the op.* "You don't care about my personal life or why I joined the Army. I'm your ticket out of humping all over IV Corps, stringing for backwater news. What do you really want to know?"

Brady paused to frame his question, impressed that Vandermeer gave enough of a shit to understand his situation. The fact he even mentioned it implied a level of cooperation. It also hinted at a quid pro quo, and Brady was prepared to deliver it. "General, I need to ask some serious questions. But I'll do everything I can to ensure that you and this division are portrayed favorably."

"Shoot."

"From everything I've heard about you, sir, you are a highly regarded major general, a man on the way up. But you're commanding the 9th Infantry Division in the delta. Why?"

Vandermeer's face turned hard. "Brady, that's just the kind of question that makes the press unwelcome around here. You've implied that there is some dark secret that the public needs to know, as if command of this division is somehow unworthy."

"Maybe if this division were a little friendlier toward the press, it would have a more high-profile reputation."

"I asked for this assignment specifically," said Vandermeer. "I was offered the Americal Division up north, but turned it down."

"Really?" Brady held firm. "I would have thought that a man with your reputation would want to be where the action is."

"There's plenty of action for everyone, but I wanted to be where I could do the most good."

Brady knew a lot of high-ranking officers, and the one thing they all seemed to have in common was an intense desire to be at the center of attention. In war, that meant the battlefield. For the most part, Brady didn't question their commitment to Duty, Honor, and Country, but the Army was built on competition. Rank and glory were the prizes, and these men fought each other for them as intensely as they battled the enemy. Nobody stepped aside to "do the most good" unless ordered to for a specific career ticket punch. And Brady had heard enough about Vandermeer to know that his star was still rising.

"What do you think you can accomplish here in the delta, General? This isn't the place for a man with ambition. Why would you turn your back on the Americal? Every general in the army wants that assignment."

Vandermeer smiled. "There are a dozen major generals in Vietnam," he said, "and every one of them wants to become a three-star. Most of my peers think that high body counts and a long list of battlefield victories get them there. I don't."

"You think bringing in the rice crop and chasing Charlie will get you the attention you deserve? So far, it's gotten you nothing but anonymity, while your colleagues are becoming better known with each battle."

"Better known for what, Brady? The way the press reports our victories, I'll settle for bringing in the harvest." Vandermeer stood and walked to the door. "Let's go topside."

He led Brady past Boettcher's adjoining office, where he spotted his adjutant talking earnestly with Colonel Lyons.

"The general has lost confidence in your ability to carry out your duties as this division G-2 and has directed me to see that you are reassigned to another command where you might be more valued."

Lyons caught the Old Man's eye as he walked by. Stunned that Vandermeer would delegate his dismissal to a staff officer, Lyons found no suitable response other than to don a mask of contempt and wait for the follow-up. The two men stared at each other until Lyons realized that Boettcher had nothing else to say. So he forced himself to smile and said, "I'd like nothing better than to leave this outfit, Colonel, but neither you nor I nor General

Vandermeer have anything to say about it. MACV sent me here and they are determined to keep me here, especially in light of this fiasco with General Cho. If you and your general want to get into a pissing contest with G-2 at MACV, you're in for a battle you can't win."

"Colonel, we both know that this mission was conceived and instigated by MACV and initiated over the objections of General Vandermeer."

"He's been singing that song since the minute the shit hit the fan," Lyons took over the conversation. "But I think the lady doth protest too much. And let me set something else straight for you, sir. I conceived the mission and I am responsible for its success. And make no mistake: the mission was a tactical success. We got the man we were after. In addition, we confirmed that there is an enemy sniper using American weapons and we almost got him, too."

"Of course, you also got General Cho," Boettcher shot back. "Have you confirmed it was him?"

"We've debriefed the surviving sniper, Patterson. The man has limited intelligence, but he has great recall. He described Cho perfectly. MACV is rounding up Cho's staff now. I'm confident that we will confirm that American snipers under the ultimate command of General Otis Vandermeer have assassinated the most popular and most competent general in the Army of Vietnam, despite orders to abort their mission." Lyons's implication was clear: MACV would place the blame solely on Vandermeer if necessary to clear themselves.

"What the hell was he doing in Cambodia, meeting with the NVA?"

"Cho was never in Cambodia. Officially, he was shot down during a routine reconnaissance mission and died in combat. His body has not been recovered. The announcement will be made tomorrow."

Boettcher grimaced. "This is the kind of bullshit that drives fighting men nuts. Will MACV follow up with some sort of written instructions to make sure we all get the story straight?" He stared at Lyons to see how the colonel would react to his reference to "fighting men."

Lyons did not flinch. "I'm giving you the story right now, one REMF to another. You know there won't be anything in writing."

"I want it in writing. We are not going to be left holding the bag if this story gets out."

"Don't be naive. You will be left holding the bag, which is precisely the reason I expect everyone in this command to abide by the official story. I'm especially concerned that Vandermeer keep Colonel Ingram under control, for he is a man who cannot be trusted to keep a secret."

Boettcher almost smiled. "He's a man who cannot be trusted to tell a lie, Colonel. I have that problem with him myself."

Lyons was a man who smiled easily, though he found few things funny. He gave Boettcher a grin that revealed too much of his gums. "Colonel, I've always appreciated your devotion to Vandermeer as well as your practical nature. I think we have some things in common. We can help each other."

The chief of staff changed course. *Now you're talking.* G-2 always had something up their sleeve, some negotiating gambit, and Boettcher was determined to wring it out of Lyons. He knew exactly what he wanted. "What did you have in mind?"

"It must never be revealed that Cho was assassinated by Americans, especially in a neutral country. The political repercussions are obvious. Equally devastating would be any revelation that Cho was working with the enemy. We require your help to ensure that any source of information contrary to the official story be squelched. We are particularly concerned about three sources of leaks. First, the sniper Patterson must be kept under wraps until his DEROS. I've already directed him not to speak of this to anyone, but I don't think he grasps the whole concept of national security. If he starts talking when he's back home, no one will give one shit, especially when two colonels and a two-star stand against him and his Vet benefits. Second, the missing sniper should remain missing. More than likely he is already dead. But we don't want any rescued hero to come back from the dead and start giving the grunts the skinny about what the hell happened to him. Bad for morale and just the kind of crap that leaks to the press. Third, I want that reporter, Brady, out of here ASAP. I understand he has already asked about this mission?"

"He met the Old Man at the helipad. Asked how he got so much blood on his uniform."

"Christ."

"We can handle Patterson and Brady. But Ingram and General Vandermeer are going to move heaven and earth to get that missing sniper back."

"See to it that they don't find him."

Boettcher paused, but had already made up his mind. "All right, Colonel. I'll do what I can to take care of this problem for you, but let me tell you what I want in return."

Vandermeer and Brady stepped into the sunshine, where the dust-laden air was somehow hotter even than the sweltering offices inside the Quonset. A watchtower had been constructed just inside the sandbags, and Vandermeer led Brady up the ladder to the observation platform, where a sentry leaned against a sandbag parapet listening to AFV rock and roll on a tiny transistor radio. The guard flipped off the music and snapped to attention.

"At ease," ordered Vandermeer with a disapproving look at the radio. "You staying alert up here?"

"Yes, sir," popped the kid, the first words he'd ever said to a general.

"Charlie's always waiting, son," Vandermeer told him. "I'm relying on you to keep my ass alive. Anything going on out there?"

"No, sir."

Though barely twenty feet above the ground, they still had a panoramic view across the Mekong, filled with the unending boat traffic that plied the channel. To the north, beyond the base perimeter of razor wire and minefields, rice paddies ran off into the haze as far as they could see. From horizon to horizon, a checkerboard of dikes nurtured the blessing and the curse of South Vietnam. A Midwesterner, the general knew little about growing rice, but he was no stranger to farming.

"Brady, take a look!"

"I've seen rice paddies before."

"Good thing you're a reporter, Brady, because you aren't much of a poet. There is more than beauty in this view; there's meaning. You asked me why I became a soldier. There's your answer."

Brady leaned forward.

"There are a million farmers out there," explained Vandermeer. "Theirs is the primary and most noble of professions, preeminent even over the profession of arms, which is second. Without food, there is nothing, and even defense is irrelevant. As a soldier, I protect the foundations of civilization, and as far as I'm concerned, that means protecting the food. That's why I volunteered for the delta."

"I've been around a long time, General. I know all about the delta, the 'rice basket of Asia' and all that. I even wrote an article about it a couple of years ago. Nobody bothered to read it. The economics of the war might be important, but it's pretty boring stuff."

"Yep," Vandermeer agreed. "I'm probably the most boring general in Vietnam."

Brady smiled, until he saw that Vandermeer was dead serious.

A highly decorated veteran of two wars, Otis Vandermeer coveted glory no less than his peers. But he had learned lessons from the previous transitions to peacetime that the others had failed to grasp. Despite the presumptions of the civilian press to end the war by discrediting the warriors, he knew that the Pentagon would remain staffed by professionals, just like himself, veterans with Purple Hearts and Silver Stars who did their duty and ignored the sensational journalism of idealistic war correspondents. These were the men Vandermeer courted, not the politicians who read civilian newspapers.

"I've never seen a headline with the word 'boring' in it," said Brady, and both men laughed.

"Let me tell you something," said the general. "You know those silly hometown news releases you do? You'll never earn a Pulitzer doing those things, but I respect those articles a hell of a lot more than most of the bullshit that I see in the newspapers. Do us all a favor and keep writing them. I don't need any column inches in the *New York Times*, but it means everything to kids like this unmotivated draftee with his unkempt uniform and unauthorized transistor radio to know that folks in Davenport, Iowa, have an interest in where he is and what he's doing." He turned to the sentry. "Where you from, son?"

"Davenport, sir."

Brady was as stunned as the soldier. "You know all your men?"

"No. I have ten thousand men under my command. But I never forget a name or a face. And I swear, Brady, that if you write one bad word about any of them, somebody in the 9ᵗʰ Infantry Division will get you."

Brady glanced at the boy and knew that Vandermeer's comments would be all over the barracks by nightfall.

Vandermeer stepped onto the top rung of the ladder. "I'll send Olivetti to fetch you. I suggest you interview this man while you wait." He turned to the soldier. "Private, what's a soldier's preeminent responsibility?"

"Protect the food, sir."

Vandermeer smiled as he descended the ladder.

An hour after his interview with Brady, Vandermeer sat at his desk and opened a file drawer to his right. In the back, he found a bottle of whiskey and two small glasses. Into one, he poured a finger of booze. He offered none to Boettcher, who did not drink.

"Brady got his interview," said the general. "Now let's get him back to Saigon."

"Olivetti's taking care of that."

"Good."

"In the meantime, we need to discuss General Cho," said Boettcher. "MACV is going to announce that he was killed in action and they expect us to make sure nobody says otherwise. "

"Lyons threatened us?"

"They've got us over a barrel, sir. This could not have happened at a worse time, with your promotion before Congress."

"Westy already told me that he'll recommend confirmation."

"Not if this gets out. He'll disavow any knowledge and leave us holding the bag. He can't blame his own Intel shop."

Of course Boettcher was right; the buck would stop with Vandermeer. It had been Saigon's mission from the beginning, but the spooks kept their fingerprints off everything, legal or otherwise. MACV had undoubtedly already hid behind a hundred degrees of separation from the assassination, and the higher highers would not take kindly to any revelations to the contrary. Vandermeer would keep the secret, or it would be the end of his career.

Boettcher took the liberty of refilling Vandermeer's glass. "But there is some good news. Lyons needs us, and he's willing to pull some strings at MACV for us."

"I thought I told you to reassign that prick!"

"MACV assigned him, General." Boettcher let it sink in. "We get the promotion and the assignment we want: Superintendent of the U. S. Military Academy. Congratulations, General."

Vandermeer spun slowly in his chair until his back faced Boettcher. The single Army assignment he had coveted since he was himself a cadet had been traded in a political knife fight in exchange for a promise to conceal a lie. He would keep the Army's secrets in any event, but an assignment of such solemn responsibility should never have been bartered for the very antithesis of its mandate. The bourbon tasted bitter.

"What's the status on the snipers?" Vandermeer stared at the wall, refusing to engage Boettcher directly.

"According to Colonel Ingram, the MIA is Monroe, PFC Jackson Monroe."

Boettcher produced a personnel file and laid it on Vandermeer's desk. "I picked up Monroe's folder on my way back from the hospital. His name rang a bell." As Vandermeer leafed through the documents in the folder, Boettcher summarized the cogent information: "Monroe has a number of volunteer assignments pending . . ."

Vandermeer cut him off. "He's missing in action. Let's get him back before we worry about his next assignment."

"I spoke with Colonel Ingram. He's got a crew ready to initiate a search, but there is an element of risk. You barely got out of there in one piece and Charlie was likely to see where you left Monroe. They'll anticipate a search and rescue and any rescue ship will run into an ambush. Ingram is trying to get air support, but he's not having much luck. Air Force doesn't want to waste the aircraft on one man."

"I've seen them waste an Arclight raid on one sampan."

Boettcher said nothing, knowing that his point was made.

Vandermeer continued, "Since when have we avoided risks in recovering our own people? We can get one hundred volunteers in twenty seconds."

"That's not the issue, sir."

"Then what's the problem?"

"Colonel Lyons is concerned that a high-profile rescue attempt for a man who could testify to an illegal mission may not be in our best interests. Especially with Brady around. There is an argument to be made for leaving him where he is."

"This is the deal we made?"

"He's probably dead, sir." Boettcher knew it had was dangerous to challenge Vandermeer's unwavering commitment to bring his men home alive, and he had told himself to argue only with the facts. It galled him that he had to resort to rationalization, a defensive measure.

"I will not sacrifice this man to save Lyons, for Christ's sake!"

"Then consider your own career, sir. If Monroe talks, or if any reporter finds out, you won't get that next star."

"And if I let him die, I won't deserve the stars I have!"

Boettcher knew when to stop. Ingram would launch the SAR mission and they'd probably get shot up. They'd deal with it. "Whatever you say, sir. I'll take care of it."

Vandermeer's demeanor softened, appreciating Boettcher's loyalty, no matter how misguided. "One more thing, Ron. Monroe's partner, the one who made it back with me—Patterson—he earned a Silver Star out there today. See that he gets it. And a Bronze Star for Monroe."

"The mission was classified, sir. There won't be any awards for them."

"Then make something up."

"Intel will have to approve it. Colonel Lyons."

Vandermeer snorted. "Good. Make him choke on it."

Boettcher made sure that the slight discomfort in his tone was discernible. "And what about Brady?"

"What about him? He has his interview. Get him back to Saigon, so he can be there when MACV announces that General Cho died with his boots on."

E!GHT

**9th Infantry Division Headquarters
Dong Tam**

Patterson made his way back to the barracks slowly, trudging through the dust between rows of GP tents and flimsy warehouses of corrugated tin. There was surprisingly little activity, given the time of day. A squad of soldiers as tired and filthy as he was passed him on their way to their own quarters at the opposite end of the division base camp. Patterson moved aside for them to pass. They walked by with little interest, too tired even to glance at his weapon, which usually attracted attention wherever it went. Patterson walked on.

His bunk was one of twenty in the sniper hooch, a wood-frame and wire-screened building forty feet long and twenty feet wide, surrounded by a berm of sandbags. The heat inside was stifling, despite the open ceiling and screened ventilation just below the eaves, which seemed to do little except allow the dust to filter in. Dusty beams of sunlight crisscrossed the room, shining through shrapnel holes in the metal roof, legacies of nightly mortar attacks that sent everyone scrambling into the bunkers outside the doorways. Patterson's bunk was as he had left it, save for the skim of dust. Next to it, someone had placed a filthy pack on Monroe's cot. The room was unoccupied, except for Revelle, who reclined on the bunk beyond Monroe's, trying to sleep. He tossed in the heat, his olive-drab T-shirt black with sweat.

Patterson laid his rifle upon his bunk and sat next to it. He was required to check in with the CQ, to let the CO know he was back, but he could not take his eyes off the pack on Monroe's bunk. Deliberately, he picked up the pack and walked to the doorway, where he hurled it into the dusty space between barracks.

Patterson returned to his bunk. The sleeping sniper now awoke, leaning on one elbow, wondering what the fuck. Nineteen years old, he had a physique that defied the debilitation of war. Every muscle seemed drawn upon his body, copied meticulously from an anatomical chart. "What's your problem, Patterson?"

Patterson unlaced his boots and said nothing.

"Go get my pack," said Revelle, quietly, sitting up on his bunk. He yawned, his eyes red and tiny, like those of the rats he learned to kill as a child with his .22 single-shot Ruger in the county dump outside Gatlinburg, Tennessee.

Still Patterson said nothing.

"Where's Monroe? C'mon, Patterson, where the fuck is Monroe?"

Patterson remained silent, staring into Revelle's bloodshot eyes. "MIA," he whispered, breaking his gaze.

Revelle did not move for a moment, then muttered, "Better him than you, man." He shuffled out the door to retrieve his pack, which he tossed again onto Monroe's bunk. "That boy was just a little too cool for his own good, Patterson. And my pack is staying right there until that smart-ass comes back to move it himself." He stood across Monroe's bunk from Patterson, daring him to object. "You ain't too bright, Patterson, and that's good. I never liked niggers much, but I like you fine. Just keep your hands off my stuff."

Patterson lay down on his bunk. In other units, such confrontations would lead to raised voices or fistfights, but snipers rarely argued with anyone. Killing people made them arrogant or humble, and in either case any violence short of murder seemed trivial.

Patterson did not understand white people. Revelle claimed to like him, but he had done nothing to warrant his affection, no more than Monroe had to earn his antipathy. Even among themselves, white men were cold, jockeying for some leg up on one another that baffled him. *I'm dumb*, he thought. *They like me 'cause I ain't got no advantage over them.* Friendships between whites were merely alliances, nothing deeper. He wondered if they truly loved anyone—even their wives. Patterson thought of his own wife and three daughters and felt simultaneously desolate and comforted. *I'm comin' home, babe.* In two weeks he'd leave these crackers behind. He wondered if Monroe had anyone waiting for him back in The World. Probably not.

Captain Anderson knocked on the door frame as he stepped into the hooch. A skilled marksman with the toll of twenty-eight confirmed kills etched across his face, Anderson earned his command through hard work, attention to detail, technical savvy, and administrative skill. As tough and solitary as any of his men, he was also committed to their well-being, despite a permanent case of the ass. Neither popular nor unpopular, he was too brisk and businesslike to win unqualified devotion from men who were themselves indifferent to human relationships. He reported directly to Colonel Ingram.

Anderson assigned his sharpshooters to various missions as requested by unit commanders, special ops, or MI. When the kill sheets dwindled to a trickle, Anderson figured Charlie was laying low and recalled his teams. They rested up in the compound until it was time for the next foray. The teams were always on the move, and rarely were there more than a few snipers in the barracks at any one time.

"Room, Atten-hut!"

Revelle snapped to his feet, while Patterson struggled from his bunk into a sloppy position of attention.

"At ease," said Anderson. He glanced at Revelle and ordered him to dress before settling his eyes on Patterson. "Colonel Lyons wants you to report to him on the double."

"Yes, sir," mumbled Patterson, his eyes on the floor.

Anderson spotted the Remington on Patterson's bunk and picked it up.

"I'm sorry about Monroe. They're setting up a SAR now. If he's alive, they'll find him."

Patterson said nothing, having learned that it was best to respond to officers only when they asked questions. To statements, he simply listened.

Anderson grabbed Revelle's pack from Monroe's bunk and threw it on the floor. "Monroe is alive until I say otherwise. You got that, Revelle?"

Revelle nodded.

"Now get some rest and chow. Orders will be coming down tonight." Anderson escorted Patterson into the sunlight. "Effective immediately, you're the CQ. No more missions for you." Captain Anderson strode away, Monroe's rifle in his hands.

NINE

9th Infantry Division Headquarters
Dong Tam

B rady watched Vandermeer climb down the observation tower ladder. During his days with the *Times*, generals would have invited him to attend briefings, or spend an afternoon inspecting the troops. Throughout Vietnam, commanders complained among themselves about how the press expected a parade everywhere they went, and then they would provide one. At II Corps, a division commander spent a million dollars in ammunition for a live fire demonstration featuring a combined arms assault, artillery prep, and air support, all for Brady. The newsman was surprised by how little he missed those dog and pony shows. After his canning, he found that he liked hanging with the grunts, away from the trappings and all of the bullshit. Vandermeer treated him like a hack, but that was what he was now and he couldn't blame him for it. He pawned him off on Olivetti. But Brady suspected that Vandermeer would treat Walter Cronkite the exact same way.

Olivetti found Brady chatting up the kid on the observation platform. The two men, one old enough to have fathered the other, laughed like old friends. But Colonel Boettcher's instructions were fresh in Olivetti's mind when he took charge of the newsman.

"Follow me, Slick. I'll get us some food and take you downtown to find you a bed and a little poontang for the night."

Brady responded, "Forget downtown. I'll grab a cot in the barracks."

"No can do, sir."

"I always bunk with the troops."

Olivetti shrugged and smiled. "Not here, sir. We never let civilians stay on post, especially with the base on alert. There's a decent hotel in town. You'll be more comfortable there if anything happens."

"What alert?"

"We're always on alert for something. ARVN troops are going home for the gook holiday. So we pick up the slack."

"I don't see you or any other REMF digging any foxholes."

Olivetti turned serious, for no man with combat experience, no matter how brief, considered himself a REMF. And Olivetti had paid his dues. Six months in the free fire zones along the Bassac River, where the dead simply disappeared into the mud, had taught him a thing or two about incoming and booby traps and pacification of villages. He remembered the looks of hatred in the eyes of the civilians he had ostensibly rescued. He buttered up the chain and landed in Boettcher's PIO, happy to have nothing to do with the Vietnamese: Viet Cong, civilian, or ARVN. They all scared the shit out of him. "The perimeter guard has been doubled. And I carry my weapon and steel pot wherever I go. And I ain't no REMF."

"Me neither." Brady proffered his press credentials. "This mean anything around here?"

Olivetti read the card:

> The bearer of this card should be accorded full cooperation and assistance to assure the successful completion of his mission. Bearer is authorized rations and quarters on a reimbursable basis. Upon presentation of this card, bearer is entitled to air, water, and ground transportation under a priority of three (3).

Olivetti shrugged. "Sorry, man. Just following orders. We got no room at the inn for members of the press."

"What's with you people? I'm not the fucking enemy! I've probably killed more gooks than most men in this division."

"And we appreciate it."

The nearest mess hall was a wooden building with screened windows near the ceiling to keep out the insects and to provide ventilation. Although sandbags surrounded the walls, the tin roof would do little to stop a mortar round, as evidenced by the shrapnel holes. But there had been no incoming for several weeks, and even then Charlie had not come close to penetrating the perimeter. If it got hairy again, the troops figured they were as safe under the chow hall's heavy picnic tables as anywhere else and they were not about to pass up hot food for anything short of an Arclight raid.

"Old Man eats here himself," said Olivetti, "just to make sure we get good chow and plenty of it."

Brady looked sideways at Olivetti, and considered the possibility that the soldier was truly the rube he pretended to be. Olivetti fished a pack of Winstons from his shirt pocket and offered one to him. As he lit the cigarette, Brady said loudly over his empty tray, "What's the real story with Vandermeer? Why isn't he up north? I heard he got in trouble with MACV, and he's been put out to pasture down here." A trick from his journalist grab bag, throw out a rumor and see if anyone bit. No one even looked up.

Olivetti grinned and expelled a chestful of smoke. "What have you got against the Old Man?"

"Not a thing."

The condescending twinkle disappeared from Olivetti's eyes. "So why look for trouble?" he asked. There was a warning in his tone.

But Brady could not imagine that any reporter, even a PIO hack like Olivetti, would ask such a question. "It's what I do, Olivetti. It's my contribution to ending the war."

"Colonel Boettcher says you want to end the war by losing it."

"I've seen a lot of wars, son, and win or lose, I've yet to see one worth fighting."

Olivetti scrounged a jeep from the motor pool for the short trip to My Tho. Security was high and only Olivetti's blanket travel authorization persuaded the MP at the gate to let him through. Although My Tho was as peaceful a town as there was in the delta, Olivetti did not like to be outside the perimeter after dark.

At they approached the second security gate, they passed through several rows of concertina wire and under the muzzle of an M-60 tank, loaded with a beehive round aimed straight down the main street of Dong Tam. Whatever town had been there before the war was gone. Only hovels existed now, constructed of cardboard and crushed beer cans, that lined both sides of the road for a hundred yards. Beyond the shanties were the ubiquitous rice paddies, tended by farmers who had owned the land long before the war and who had no use for their destitute countrymen who polluted the fields and stole their crop.

The shantytown residents were refugees, survivors from villages now destroyed, who lived on the streets and subsisted on the charity of Americans who passed through in heavily guarded convoys. The only street through town was crowded with children, savvy and violent orphans adept in the art of begging and deft enough to snatch a watch from a man's wrist faster than it could tick off a second. Called the "dust of life" by the Vietnamese, the kids cried, "Hey you, Number One!" "You give me, GI!" "OK Salem!" The GIs tossed them money or candy; guilt was a uniquely American notion. The richest person in town was a young girl with a missing leg who hopped about hawking cigarettes to GIs in the back of passing deuce and a halfs, cigarettes that other GIs had tossed to her for free. The soldiers called her "Pogo" and asked her for blow jobs, then tossed money at her and laughed, pretending to be hard motherfuckers who had seen plenty of worse horrors. Most of them had. It was only a matter of time, thought Olivetti, before Charlie paid her twenty bucks to toss a grenade into the back of a packed troop carrier.

Olivetti accelerated through the gate, scattering the loitering children. The jeep roared through the gauntlet of shacks, leaving a rooster tail of dust. A few adults, mostly old folks, glared sullenly from the dark interiors of their squalid homes. The young men were gone, dead or in the army, and the women worked the bars in the bigger cities, where prostitution paid a living wage. Garbage and human excrement filled the street, reeking in the broiling sun until the next vehicle ground it into the dirt.

At the end of town, an old man stood by the side of the road. Unlike the children, he did not beg, but instead proffered a gift, which he held out to the Americans as they passed. The man's eyes were downcast and his face expressionless, despite his betel-nut smile. "Jesus Christ," gasped Brady as he snapped his head back to look behind him at the man who now stood in their dusty trail, his hands still outstretched. "What the hell was that?"

"Dead baby."

Brady returned face-forward, somewhat embarrassed by revealing his shock. *I've seen dead babies by the truckload. Nothing special about one more.*

"The old guy's nuts," explained Olivetti. "Stands out there every day, rain or shine, handing them out. Nobody knows where he gets them."

"And we call ourselves human."

"Are you kidding? Only a human being would do something like that," Olivetti laughed.

The trip to My Tho was only a few miles down the highway. At one time, Dong Tam had been a suburb of the city, but the war had destroyed everything between the division HQ and My Tho's "metropolitan" area. The highway had never been paved, and was now rutted by military traffic. Sycamore trees had grown up along the way, although there was still plenty of room for two vehicles to pass one another. Olivetti had the road to himself for My Tho had the good fortune of being off-limits to most GIs day or night and few delta civilians had any reason to go there. He barreled down the center of the highway, wondering which clump of sycamore concealed the sniper that would put a round through the windshield. He drove hunched down, his eyes barely over the dashboard.

Brady smiled. "I've been driving around this country for three years. Nobody's shot me yet."

T⌐EN

My Tho
Dinh Tuong, Vietnam

My Tho was a riverside town and a provincial capital, the avenues bordered by shady parks surrounded by stucco villas with tile roofs and flower gardens. The windows in the upper stories remained shuttered to keep out the sun, and louvered to let in the breeze. At dusk, people stepped onto tiny balconies to view the sunset over the river. Below, in traffic, Olivetti and Brady drove slowly past, peeking through wrought iron gates into the courtyards where banyan trees shaded the buildings and fountains babbled in peaceful contrast to the fetid gutters in the streets. The city echoed the days of French colonialism, the faded pastel colors more Mediterranean than Asian. In the center of the Mekong Delta surrounded by war, the relatively untouched city seemed even more displaced than it was. My Tho was beyond European; it was the Land of Oz.

It was a city in denial, a community without violence in a country at war. Perhaps because few American soldiers were permitted there, the communists and capitalists of My Tho managed to live together without killing each other. Nevertheless, the truly wealthy members of society had fled the war, abandoning their mansions along the river. But war was good business for some, at least until the economy completely collapsed, and the mansions had been converted to hotels, full of civilian wheeler-dealers from America and Japan and Australia and India and Singapore and Europe and Israel, all negotiating with their Vietnamese counterparts for rubber or rice or plywood or auto parts or whiskey or lingerie. Antique stores opened along the waterfront and restaurants did a brisk business catering to the merchants. Were it not for the bullet holes in the walls and the battalions of whores in fishnet stockings, no one would have guessed that My Tho was a city full of murderers and malevolent orphans.

The streets were clotted with bicycles. Two-cycle Lambrettas added their oily exhaust to the palpable smog of diesel fuel and kerosene, and the odors from the open sewers. The jeep dwarfed the other vehicles on the road, and Olivetti had little difficulty pushing his way through the sweltering chaos until they found a hotel that appeared well maintained and seemed somehow to have retained a hint of French colonial ambiance. Brady carried little baggage, only his rucksack with notebooks, pens, a change of clothes, flashlight, toilet paper, poncho, water purification tabs, cash, a pair of cameras, and a revolver. He plucked it from the back of the jeep and said, "It's been fun, Olivetti. I don't suppose there's any point in my coming back tomorrow."

Olivetti shrugged his shoulders. "I could show you the volleyball court."

"Tell that arrogant boss of yours that next time I'll be back with Westmoreland himself. He'll think twice before he tosses me off base again." Despite his irritation, Brady spoke with a smile. There was something about Olivetti's bullshit that Brady found appealing.

Olivetti hit the gas and pulled away, tires spinning.

Brady made his way to the registration desk. The sweltering lobby was deserted except for the Margouilla lizards that scurried away as Brady approached. He tapped the bell gently, twice, the pathetic ring loud enough to break the early-evening silence. Eventually a man appeared, obviously the owner, dressed in distressed khakis, a soiled linen shirt, and flip-flops. He shoved the registration book indifferently at Brady while giving the reporter a methodical once-over.

Brady scribbled the address for the *Times* office in Saigon. He still had friends at the bureau office, and the *Times* address was a measure of protection. "Pretty quiet." Even if there had been no other customers, the place should have been crawling with girls. Their absence alerted him, warning him like the way the pigeons disappeared in Saigon twenty-four hours before a typhoon. Like the birds, the whores somehow knew where not to be and when not to be there. The man said nothing. Brady persisted, "Speak English?"

The man shook his head slowly, disdain in his eyes. Brady noted the peculiar scars on the man's face, not smallpox, but tiny splatters of skin. White phosphorous bombs were among the most horrible American weapons, melting their victims as much as burning them, leaving unrecognizable lumps of cooked meat in their wake. A few stray droplets had left the man with a face nobody would forget.

"Bao chi," said Brady, identifying himself as a reporter. The man responded with stony indifference. "Beer," said Brady.

Every hotelier in Vietnam understood the word "beer" and whether they had a bar or not, the front desk maintained a six-pack on ice. If they couldn't get Budweiser on the black market, they stocked locally brewed Ba me Ba, piss in a green bottle, as much formaldehyde as it was beer, a feature that allegedly kept it colder than anything else available. In Vietnam, a man would drink jet fuel if it had an ice cube in it.

The owner placed a key on the counter and a bottle of beer. "Ten dollars."

For a man that spoke no English, thought Brady, his pronunciation was damn good.

The room was austere, sweltering despite the electric fan that moved the air across the bed with some authority. Brady killed the beer quickly, before the heat got to it. The bed had a futon, which was good, since there was not a firm mattress left anywhere in Vietnam. Brady undressed and lay naked for a moment, pondering his plans for the next day while the fan cooled him as well as it could. *Might as well go home.* The delta was too hot, and he had what he needed to run a decent piece on Vandermeer. The general might be an arrogant bastard, but he had style and seemed to care about his men and about his mission. Brady knew he could put something together, something inspirational, that would paint a fascinating picture of the man. News magazines all over the United States screamed for new copy, anything to fill a page. Vandermeer was a legitimate subject and an unknown quantity, something the news peddlers would pay for. Brady planned to rebuild his resume one article at a time, starting with the commander of the 9th Infantry Division. The newsman closed his eyes as the sun set.

A career of sleeping in dangerous places had taught Brady to slumber lightly, and the sound of keys in the hallway alerted him instantly. He reached for his trousers, but the door to his room opened before he could slip them on. Vietnamese police, notorious "QCs," advanced in cadence. Though barely five feet tall, their tailored uniforms and reflective glasses lent them an air as intimidating as that of any Alabama state trooper. The QCs enforced local laws, and checked ID cards, looking for draft dodgers or ARVN deserters. They rarely had any legitimate business with Americans, but shakedowns were not uncommon and more than a few victims had resisted at the cost of their lives. They pulled their nightsticks as they approached, acting in concert as if on some inaudible command. Brady could ascertain no rank insignia—two of the men seemed as identical as twins until one of them, apparently in charge, removed his sunglasses and tucked them into his shirt pocket.

"On your feet." The policeman's English was perfect.

Brady obeyed. "What did I do?" he asked, as they handcuffed him. This was no shakedown; it was an outright arrest. "I have money! What did I do?" Still no answer.

They shoved the naked newsman into the hallway, pushed him down the stairs and into the lobby. "My clothes," pleaded Brady, more concerned about his cash and weapon than for his modesty. He glanced toward the desk clerk, who shuffled papers quietly, carefully ignoring the proceedings around him.

The policeman wasted no time with explanations, but shoved Brady through the back door of the hotel, into a darkened alley. Brady landed face first in the dirt. The first punch caught him by surprise, and he rolled onto his belly, curled into the fetal position. His hands still behind him, he could not protect his head, and he knew he had no chance to escape. Panic grabbed him.

"*Bao chi!*" yelled Brady. "Reporter!" the reflexive cry rehearsed by every war correspondent in Vietnam for the day he might need to explain himself in a hurry. "*Bao chi!*" The American press corps assumed that the Viet Cong regarded them as an ally in the war, if only because the American military regarded them as the enemy. Although no journalist had ever verified that the term "*Bao chi!*" had caused any enemy soldier to spare his life, Brady nevertheless clung to the hope that the enemy understood the value of good press and prayed that there was some reason why these QCs had come for him. So he screamed "*Bao chi!*" again and again, louder each time.

But the blows continued, focused on his head and his genitals. Brady closed his eyes and tried to remember the prayers he had recited in Sunday school.

"*Dung lai!*"

Brady recognized the Vietnamese command to stop. He turned his head toward the sound, but a fist smashed into his face and drove his head into the ground.

"*Dung lai!*" The command was more emphatic now.

This time, the blows ceased. His head spinning, Brady looked up through swollen eyes as the senior policeman stood over him

"Thank God," he mumbled, split lipped. Brady never knew what hit him, however, when the policeman raised his nightstick and clubbed him behind the ear.

ELEVEN

Vinh Te Canal
Kien Phong

Though barely ten feet above the water, Vandermeer's helicopter had accelerated to forty knots when the gunner surrendered his grip on Monroe. He slapped hard upon the canal's surface, rolling over once before going under. The impact forced the air from his lungs and Monroe's involuntary gasp refilled them with water. But he was close to shore, and though half drowned, the water invigorated him and he succeeded in grabbing on to overhanging limbs from the mangrove trees that choked the muddy banks. He pulled himself under their protective canopy and lay silently, half submerged in mud. His stomach, pumped full of adrenaline and the rancid water of the canal, contracted. Monroe vomited repeatedly, as sick from fear as from anything else, for he was lucid now and aware that he was alone in Indian country.

Minutes passed. Faintly, he heard footsteps, then movement above him. Monroe reached slowly down to his boot and withdrew the K-Bar knife from the scabbard strapped to his leg. Troops moved along a trail beside the canal, but they moved too fast to be searching for anyone. Most of the NVA had never seen Vandermeer's helicopter, firing only at the sound of the rotor blades through the canopy of trees. Though they glimpsed Monroe and Patterson clinging to the skids as the aircraft peeled away, Vandermeer's final barrage had kept their heads down. Consumed with their own injured and blinded by the thick undergrowth, they were unaware of Monroe's fall, two hundred yards downstream. Several squads passed by, then nothing.

For an hour Monroe lay still, struggling to cope while straining to hear the sound of a helicopter, anything American. But there were no more sounds, hardly even the rippling of water against his body as the incoming tide backed up the canals and rendered them stagnant. He heard only the metronomic plop of blood dripping into the water. The pain in his skull increased, a talon squeezing, touching his brain with each beat of his heart. Monroe clenched his teeth to fight the increasing pressure; his breaths grew increasingly shallow until dizziness overcame him. Neither pain nor terror can keep a man conscious when too much blood is lost, and Monroe passed out gently in the mud. His pulse steadied and his body diverted its energies to clotting his head wound.

The tide ebbed and the water in the canals began to flow again toward the sea. Some conscious portion of him felt the movement and urged him awake. An hour passed while Monroe floated between sleep and wakefulness, until the talon of pain jolted his eyes open and he heard his own cry. He groaned again quietly, gasping for breath, remembering where he was.

The bleeding had stopped; he sensed it intuitively. But the pain in his temple remained, sharp, like the point of a bayonet jabbing with each pulse. The silence continued, except for the occasional ripple of water as it flowed past the branches that surrounded him. Through the canopy of leaves Monroe could see the sky, torrid with the setting sun. If anyone had searched for him by day he had not heard it in his stupor. At night, there would be no rescue attempt. He doubted there would be one in any case.

Slowly, Monroe became lucid enough to look around, to study his hide. Only as the last rays of the setting sun filtered through the branches did he notice the *ghe* secured to the branches and hidden by them, ten feet from where he lay. It could only be VC, hidden from American surveillance under the same indifferent canopy of leaves that now protected him. There could be dozens, a hundred, of the canoe-like sampans stowed along the canal. He heard the muffled sound of oars. Tropical sunsets came startlingly fast, and with the wave of darkness, the canal filled with boats. Through the branches, Monroe could make out the silhouettes of men and weapons. Other small *ghes* crossed the canal as the blackness thickened, and Monroe realized that significant troop movements were under way. And soon they would be coming for the boat next to him.

Monroe pulled himself from the ooze, climbing the steep bank slowly to allow the water to drain silently from his clothes. He pulled himself up the embankment by grasping the overhanging boughs, careful not to bend them with his weight. In five minutes he covered fifteen feet, slowed by the raging pain as much as by careful stealth. At the crest of the embankment was a trail; he remembered the footfalls of unknown men earlier in the day. Monroe waited, listening for traffic and fighting the pain. He was bleeding again.

Trail crossings were always treacherous, and had to be made quickly. Moreover, the trail was dry but Monroe was wet; any drop of water would clump the soil and darken it. The faster he moved, the less water he would spread behind him. Hearing nothing, Monroe stumbled to his feet and staggered across. Dizziness immediately overwhelmed him and he crashed headfirst into the dusty foliage on the opposite side of the path. He lay for a moment to regain his equilibrium before crawling into the black jungle, fearful that someone had heard him. His back trail left a snail-like slime, a wet furrow through dry brush. Fighting panic, he prayed for the fog to come early and thick, for the night to be pitch-black. Nausea returned and his head seemed to burst with each pulse, each breath, each movement. He curled into a ball, shaking with pain and dry heaves until unconsciousness claimed him again.

He awoke at midnight, in fog so thick he was not sure if he had gone blind from the pain. Monroe knew little about concussions, but he guessed that he had one. He touched his temple—a crusty finger-sized scab had formed over the bullet's graze, though the throbbing still took his breath away. There was no battlefield first aid for a concussion, but Monroe reasoned that mere consciousness was a good omen.

He lay in black silence. Not even bats fluttered in search of insects, for the fog lay on everything, smothering movement. He heard only water lapping at the canal banks.

Monroe began crawling, still too dizzy to stand, moving parallel to the trail. The path led to his rally point, where he and Patterson had detached themselves from the patrol the night before. He did not know what he would find there, but whatever it was, it would be better than what waited for him where he was. He crawled for hours, excruciatingly slow. Monroe realized that for once he was not the most silent thing in the jungle. In a still evening, any movement reverberated. Even his ragged breaths seemed amplified by the fog, broadcast to anyone within twenty yards.

Charlie doesn't like the fog, he told himself. But he heard voices, whispered commands of NVA soldiers too close for comfort. They were all around him, too many to be real. The Silent Men played with him, laughing at his fear, amused by their own clever tricks as they swooped among the trees rustling leaves like zephyrs.

TWELVE

S omewhere within the rabbit warren where six thousand of My Tho's Vietnamese lived, a stream of water trickled down the center of an eroded alley. Originating in the filthy Mekong, it now carried a heady concoction of urine, garbage, soap scum, and oil—all of the ingredients that gave Vietnamese cities the distinctive odor that Americans found so appalling. The sound of the running water was loud because Brady's face lay in it, along with the rest of his nude body. He jerked his head with a cough and a sputter. Slowly, his senses returned.

With a groan of disgust, he rolled out of the pool that had formed around him. His hands remained cuffed behind him. The movement caused his head to ache and he groaned again, this time in pain.

Lined by high walls of concrete block topped with broken glass, the only light in the alley came from the moon, full and high, which provided adequate illumination to see down its center, but not into its corners. It shone through a thin veil of fog that drifted in from the river. Brady struggled to sit against the alley wall, but the exertion caused his head to swim. So he lay on his side and tried to collect his thoughts.

"Good morning."

Brady's eyes opened and he peered into the darkness hiding the opposite wall. He could feel his heart thumping in his chest, blood rushing in his ears.

He heard a metallic click, the unmistakable sound of a Zippo lighter being flipped open. A splash of flame ignited the tip of a cigarette, illuminating a bespectacled Asian face he did not recognize. Brady exhaled deeply and coughed again, too miserable to be afraid, resigned, almost indifferent, to what the man might have in store for him. "Who are you?"

A sigh escaped from the shadows. "I saved your life, Mr. Brady." Brady said nothing, and the stranger felt compelled to explain. "I sent the police to collect you, but they misunderstood my intentions. Fortunately, I was able to stop them before they killed you."

"What do you want?"

"I want you to do your job, *bao chi*."

"What do you know about my job?"

Brady's wallet flew out of the darkness and landed beside him. Brady strained to open it, his hands still locked behind him. Only his press credentials remained inside. He said nothing, and thought to put it in his back pocket until he remembered that he had no clothes. "You got my clothes over there, too?"

"I have something more important than your clothes. Information."

Still lying on his side, Brady took a deep breath and exhaled, placing his throbbing head on the ground. He realized then that he was going to survive, that this man really had saved him, for nobody gave information to a journalist without wanting something in return. He wanted to laugh, but the relief came out as tears. He stifled a sob, but his body quaked and he gasped in silent weeping.

A plastic card landed in the puddle next to him. Brady heard a quiet click, and the beam of a flashlight cut across the alley and illuminated a military ID card. Unable to pick it up, Brady moved his face close to it. He could tell by the color that the card was ARVN, but he did not recognize the photo. "Is this supposed to mean something to me?"

"Do you recognize the name and rank?" The flashlight came closer.

Brady squinted carefully and did not attempt to conceal his surprise when he read the name, written in English.

"You interviewed this man once."

"I remember him."

"You should. It was your interview which made General Cho a national hero."

"So?"

The flashlight turned off, the alley plunged again into moonlit dimness. The voice continued, a whisper in the dark. "General Cho is dead. It was announced today in Saigon that he died heroically in combat against the Viet Cong."

Brady knew the question expected of him. "So what's his ID card doing here in My Tho?"

"An excellent question, Mr. Brady." The tone of voice was lighter. "Listen carefully."

Brady groaned as he struggled to sit up. He wondered if any bones had been broken. His testicles, he could tell, were swollen. His ribs seemed to move independently from each other. He worried about internal injuries, and he could still taste blood on his lips. "I'm listening," he gasped.

"General Cho was assassinated by an American sniper from the 9th Infantry Division. He was killed in Cambodia while he was meeting with the North Vietnamese to discuss a peaceful end to the war."

Brady attempted to take a deep breath, but bent over could not. His body ached, and the pain was an exhausting burden. He wanted to sleep but he knew that if he closed his eyes now, this man might kill him. "How do you know this?"

"I was there," he said. "The American sniper shot my commander, then he killed General Cho."

"Why are you telling me this?"

The flashlight snapped on again and veered into Brady's eyes. The voice turned harsh. "We believe it is in our interest to inform the American public that their own army is involved in the murder of allied generals who would seek to end this war. You informed the hotel manager of your profession, and we've since confirmed that you have a reputation as an impartial journalist. I am confident that you will verify what I have told you and you will report what you know to be the truth."

It's bullshit, thought Brady. People fed him stories every day, wild tales of entire American battalions gone AWOL to Laos, secret hospitals full of GIs with incurable strains of venereal diseases, a nuclear weapon detonated in the South China Sea. *Check it out,* they told him. *You're a reporter; check it out.*

He did check them out. And they were bullshit. There were no blockbuster stories, just grinding little affairs that accumulated into one gigantic atrocity. Someday, he knew, something big would break the war wide open, but this story wasn't it. Big stories didn't fall into your lap, and whenever someone insisted they were telling you something because you were a good journalist, you knew it was a setup. He'd been there before. And he'd taken the bait.

"How can I get started?" asked Brady. He had to ask. You check out everything, even when you know it's crap.

The man killed the light and his voice spoke again, disembodied in the darkness. "I can only tell you what I am authorized to tell you. You will have to verify this through your own sources, as any good newsman would. But I can tell you this: General Cho was killed by a single shot to the throat. The sniper was wounded. He was rescued by an American helicopter with the markings of the 9th Infantry Division. The helicopter was damaged by ground fire, but did not crash."

"How do you know the sniper was wounded?"

Because I am the one who shot him, thought Dac. "We followed his blood trail to the canal. We have offered a reward for this man, for he is evil. He shot a pregnant woman, and killed her dog. She died slowly, what you call gut-shot. She lived long enough to tell us that the animal who shot her was a black American soldier. And the man who shot

General Cho was black. I saw him."

"Half the US Army is black." An image flashed in Brady's memory: Vandermeer's helicopter, shot to pieces, and a black man walking away. A man with a high-powered rifle and a sniper's scope.

"I've told you all I can. Keep the general's identification card. It may be useful to you." The soldier stepped into the moonlight. "There is one more thing."

There always is, thought Brady.

"I want the name of the sniper."

"Yeah, I'll check it out. But if what you're telling me is true, the identity of the man who pulled the trigger is really incidental."

Dac knelt down, his face close enough that Brady could smell the fish on his breath. "I am handing you the story of a career, Mr. Brady. You will provide me with this name or we will put a price on your head as well." Dac threw his cigarette butt into the water still trickling down the alley. It winked out with a hiss. He turned to walk away, and added, "What sort of man shoots pregnant women?"

Brady lay back in the alley, more weak now from relief than from exhaustion or pain. Exultation had already come and gone. He became aware of the ache in his ribs, but he did not call for help. No one helped anyone in this corner of My Tho, not even an American with NVA protection. He stumbled to his feet, naked, his cuffed hands clutching his only possessions: his press credentials and Cho's ID card. The alley led to other alleys, but eventually the maze would open onto a main road where MPs patrolled. Brady shuffled along, memorizing everything he could remember from the story he had just heard. He told himself again that the story was bullshit, but he could not shake the image from his mind of the black soldier with the big Remington walking away from Vandermeer's helicopter. The man didn't appear to be wounded. But this fact reminded Brady of another reality in a reporter's life: when it came to the truth, nobody ever got it right the first time.

THIR╤EEN

05:30

**9th Infantry Division Headquarters
Dong Tam**

O fficers packed the conference room so tightly that the lower-ranking members of Vandermeer's staff stood in the hallway and took notes, their necks craned through the door in order to follow the proceedings. A pall of cigar and cigarette smoke drifted against the ceiling. The air conditioner, one of few that Vandermeer authorized, struggled noisily to wring the humidity from the atmosphere, but with little success. Everyone sweated.

Vandermeer arrived precisely at 0530 and the staff popped to attention. "At ease, gentlemen. Let's get this over with quickly," he ordered. "It's going to be a busy day." The general took his seat in the leather chair reserved for him as the division G-3 stepped onto the raised stage at the end of the room.

Colonel Ingram, a capable operations officer and one of the general's favorites, looked the part of an infantry colonel, though not at all like a recruiting poster. Crew cut and pewter eyed, with a beak nose and a partial bridge to replace five teeth lost in Korea, he was in tune with his commander's aggressive attitude, both in combat and in staff meetings. His troops knew him for the shrapnel scar that ran from his scalp to his jowl, and in a society where scars mattered, it carried as much weight as his Silver Star. When Ingram talked, people listened, and his briefings were succinct because he never had to say anything twice.

"Gentlemen, in the last twenty-four hours, NVA and VC troops attacked US installations in Ban Me Thuot, Kontum, Hoi An, Da Nang, and Pleiku with mortars, rockets, and small arms. MACV has placed all US forces on full alert. As you know, tomorrow is Tet, the Vietnamese new year, and a significant percentage of ARVN troops are on leave, including those from our own 9th ARVN Division at My Tho. I doubt that many of them will report for duty in time for any action." Ingram withdrew a collapsible pointer from his shirt pocket and pointed to an area on a huge chart that covered the wall behind him. The chart depicted the areas of IV Corps and III Corps that comprised the 9th Infantry Division's AO. Various aspects of the chart had been crudely modified with grease pencils or crayons. The Mekong River, which rose and fell with each monsoon, created new channels and island and geographical features faster than any cartographer could keep up with them, leaving the charts in a constant state of revision. Human forces were at work changing the face of the delta as well, *x*-ing out numerous villages, labeled "uninhabited," victims of B-52 Arclight strikes or resettlement.

"Fortunately, most of the action so far seems to be up north. The delta has been unusually quiet for the last several weeks. However, we have received increasing intelligence reports of NVA troops crossing the Cambodian border under cover of darkness at various points along the Vinh Te Canal, near Chau Doc, and massing in forested areas throughout our AO. All US facilities have been alerted and are at full readiness. Given the depleted ARVN ranks due to Tet absences, however, we are very concerned about the security of isolated ARVN firebases and outposts throughout the AO. Certain installations, due to their vulnerability of strategic importance, have been reinforced with elements of various 9th Infantry units, including some HQ personnel."

"Firebase Christine," Ingram continued, "is an ARVN 105 battery protected by one company of infantry, plus a team of American advisers. The firebase is situated on a very low knoll adjacent to the Mekong River, surrounded by dikes and rice paddies. It is typical of a dozen firebases throughout the AO, and we consider them all vulnerable to attack. We have made the following tactical preparations:

"First, we have placed several of our division snipers with starlight scopes under the direct command of the senior American adviser at Christine, as well as at other remote firebases. They will be able to spot any sappers who might try to penetrate the wire by stealth prior to an assault, and pick them off.

"Second, we have prepared a warning order for the Air Force at Bin Thuy, requesting one AC-47 gunship to fly a combat air patrol mission all night to assist whatever firebase may need it."

Ingram stood at parade rest for a moment, awaiting questions. No one spoke for several seconds, though the level of tension in the room increased. Men calculated their own requirements and assumed responsibilities without discussion. Finally, Vandermeer spoke.

"Establish a strategic reserve at Can Tho Airfield. If Charlie attacks the base, the reserve can defend the aircraft. If Charlie attacks elsewhere, the reserve will already be in position for airlift to wherever we might need them." Ingram nodded. Alpha Company, 3/47th was already en route.

"I would agree with your precautions, General, but it appears that the worst may already be over."

Heads turned, surprised that Colonel Lyons, the division G-2, Intelligence, would interject a comment in a conversation between the division commander and the director of operations.

Expressionless, Vandermeer turned toward him. "If Colonel Ingram has nothing more, we'll proceed with Intel."

Ingram snapped to attention, then yielded the floor. Lyons stepped to the podium. A student of history, Lyons believed in the efficacy of military intelligence, that the key to success on the battlefield lay not so much in violence as it did in simply outsmarting the enemy. He studiously idolized the Duke of Marlborough, who never lost a battle, and who once persuaded his adversary to surrender his entire army without a fight after a series of brilliant tactical maneuvers had left his enemy hopelessly enveloped. Lyons felt frustrated, however, in Vandermeer's coterie, which seemed to have little use for tricky tactics and battlefield statistics. Still stunned by Vandermeer's tongue-lashing the day before, Lyons felt cornered by hard, bellicose men who advocated brute force and wholesale slaughter, and who believed that the best way to minimize American casualties was to maximize the enemy's. *West Pointers*, he thought contemptuously. *They still act like warriors. Duty, Honor, Country; the creed of Neanderthals. Combat won't win wars anymore, gentlemen. You need hearts and minds, not KIAs. And hearts and minds is where I come in.*

"General, MACV announced yesterday that ARVN General Nguyen Cho was killed while in combat with NVA forces near Chau Doc when ground fire downed his helicopter. Rescue attempts were unsuccessful, but in our efforts to recover his body we did capture enemy documents which indicate that we are up against the 261A Main Force Battalion, and elements of the 332 Sapper Company." Lyons glanced at Vandermeer to gauge his reaction to the charade. Vandermeer said nothing, but Lyons could see in the general's face that he did not take the same perverse pleasure in rewriting history that the spooks in Military Intelligence did. Vandermeer had once told Lyons that the truth was hard enough to determine, even without MI changing it.

"G-2 does not believe that these units present sufficient enemy strength to seriously threaten our defenses. Moreover, the attacks in the central highlands seem to be related to a weak offensive in conjunction with the siege at Khe Sanh and do not have any relationship with the exaggerated reports of NVA present in our AO. In fact, those attacks have already been repulsed with minimum damage and no further attacks have occurred. Therefore, we are of the opinion that the so-called Tet offensive has already been launched and defeated."

"Colonel," began Ingram, "if you pinpointed General Cho's body somewhere within our AO, and he was shot down by elements of the 261A Main Force Battalion, and the 332 Sapper Company, then who the hell are the sons of bitches who've been crossing the canal all night near Chau Doc?" A number of snickers could be heard from the other combat veterans in the room.

Lyons leveled a condescending stare at Ingram. "Smugglers, mostly. And maybe a few NVA or VC heading to town for some beer and some hookers. They aren't much different than American boys in that respect, Colonel."

"American boys would be raising hell all night long. My sources are telling me that Chau Doc is quiet as a morgue right now, locked down tight. I guess Charlie must be a quiet drunk. Must have hired every whore in town, too. In fact, I think the closest available pussy is in Manila right now." The snickering turned to outright laughter and Lyons felt his ears turn hot.

Though not smiling, Vandermeer made no effort to restrain his men or to hide his contempt for Lyons's threat assessment. "Colonel, if you don't mind, I think I'll keep the division on full alert. And I would suggest that you get somebody up to Chau Doc and find out what the hell is going on. In fact, maybe you should make the trip yourself."

Lyons thought to protest, to explain that his contribution was in ideas; there were others better qualified than he to execute them. Determined to punish him for the perceived fiasco with the snipers, Vandermeer made his vindictiveness clear. *He takes war personally*, thought Lyons. He saw, however, that there would be no further discussion. He said "Yes, sir," and meekly took his seat.

"Next."

An Air Force sergeant, attached to the division HQ staff, provided a weather briefing. The dry season had fallen upon them, a dense Himalayan high-pressure area dominated the weather. Ocean air crept inland at low levels, but trapped by the subsiding air above, it could not rise. Without lift, there could be no rain, so for the next twenty-four hours, the delta would remain under a stagnant pool of moist air that would condense into fog by midnight and evaporate by noon. Night visibility would be marginal for gunship missions, since the fog would rise to the treetops, forming a dense layer of stratus. The fog, however, would be thicker than ever under the jungle canopy, and surface visibility would be zero. And the full moon would make conditions above the fog CAVU—clear and visibility unlimited.

"Charlie will wait for the fog to set in before he attacks," volunteered Colonel Ingram.

"Yes," agreed Vandermeer. "Unless we find him first."

Other briefings followed. The S-4 discussed the division supply situation, and by the time the S-5, Civil Affairs, stepped to the stage, the men started checking their watches.

Major Robert Blenheim, a small man who, barely five feet six inches, had spent enough years as a security policeman to develop a presence of authority despite his unintimidating size, was another of Vandermeer's favorites.

"What have you got, Bob?"

"General," answered Blenheim, "I have a report from the Security Police that two MPs picked up our visitor, Mr. Brady the reporter, downtown this morning after curfew. Stark naked."

With full attention now, Blenheim continued, "The intrepid reporter was discovered wandering alone and nude in My Tho at approximately 0500 hours. When asked to explain the circumstances of his predicament, Mr. Brady refused all comment and demanded to be taken to the nearest US medical facility." There were grins and quizzical looks around the room, as if in anticipation of a punch line. "Upon further questioning by the MPs, Mr. Brady revealed that he had been beaten by a group of civilians and was in need of medical attention due to extremely swollen testicles. His hands were cuffed behind him and he carried only his wallet, which he refused to surrender." An explosion of laughter rocked the conference room. Men reared back and guffawed, acting more like patrons at a comedy club than men preparing for war. Even Vandermeer betrayed a puzzled grin. He glanced at Boettcher, who shrugged his shoulders in ignorance.

"Mr. Brady," said Blenheim, quieting his audience, "was delivered to the local field hospital, where bolt cutters were employed to remove the handcuffs. The cause of the attack upon Mr. Brady is unknown, since Mr. Brady refused to comment." Blenheim's deadpan delivery wavered as he wrapped up his report: "Mr. Brady was last seen wearing a blanket and sitting gingerly on a small inner tube. Gentlemen, this concludes my report." Blenheim took his seat amid cheers and applause. He received a pat on the back from Colonel Ingram.

Vandermeer leaned toward Boettcher and muttered, "Ron, check this out with Olivetti. If he had anything to do with this, put him on report."

The room came to attention as Vandermeer stood. He scanned the room and focused his eye one by one on every member of his staff, as if each were the only person in the room, before heading to his office.

FOUR⊤EEN

Khet Prey Veng, Cambodia

W hile Vandermeer conducted his morning briefing, Monroe awoke in the fog. The world was pale: ivory light everywhere, but no source. Dawn. The air was dense, the animals restless. Monroe sniffed and listened, but divined nothing. His head ached intensely, throbbing where the bullet had creased his temple, now thinly scabbed over, but oozing a thin dribble of pus. He staggered to his feet and managed to remain standing by leaning against a tree. Gently, he stepped away, moving from tree to tree, quiet. The brush was not as thick as it had seemed in the dark and Monroe was glad to be moving, lest he be caught in the open when the sun broke through. He moved in the direction of the deepest forest, choosing the thickest vegetation whenever a choice was to be made. He stopped frequently to rest, and even more frequently to listen.

The sun rose and the fog thinned. He found himself in dense undergrowth. The sun hung high overhead but the shadows concealed the direction from which it had risen. The canal, he knew, lay to the east toward the sun, and Firebase Christine farther east of that. The rally point was north. He moved out slowly.

Soon he heard noises, the sound of men on the march behind him. Monroe froze in his tracks. The trail, he realized, was only yards away, packed now with a platoon of soldiers also heading north. Another platoon marched by, eighty men now between him and the rally point, each loaded with combat gear and extra ammo. Every fifth man wore a chest pack with B-40 rocket rounds. The American adviser from Firebase Christine had promised to wait until midnight, but that was six hours ago. If anyone was waiting for him still, they would not be waiting for long.

A third platoon moved through. Someone muttered a quiet command and the men halted on the trail. Monroe watched as an NCO passed among them, issuing commands in Vietnamese, guttural grunts and hisses. The men slinked silently to the ground and hunkered under the shrubbery along the trail. Fully camouflaged with grass and foliage strapped to their bodies, they disappeared into the landscape. The NVA ate cold rations in silence, the smell of *nuc mam* obvious. Monroe marveled at their stupidity: good soldiers who excelled at stealth and camouflage, only to advertise their position with seasoning foul enough to turn a man's stomach at a hundred yards. But it was enough to remind him that he had not eaten for two days, and the pain in his stomach had begun to rival the pain in his head. The soldiers lay back to rest. One man remained alert, slowly patrolling the trail where his comrades slept.

The calm was thick and disquieting. Surrounded by sleeping soldiers, Monroe could smell their fish-scented perspiration and hear their steady breathing. Too close to the enemy to risk movement, Monroe waited throughout the day, sweating as the sun slowly traversed the sky. Still suffering from the disorientation of his concussion, now exacerbated by dehydration, he carefully lay down and delicately covered himself with leaves. He dared not sleep, but lay awake gripping his knife, waiting in terror for a sudden cry of discovery.

Every rush of adrenaline is followed by a crash, and despite his fear Monroe struggled to stay alert. He tried to think of Patterson and imagined what the reaction would be among the rest of the snipers when they got the word that he was MIA. They wouldn't care. He had no faith that anyone would be looking for him. *What's one less nigger to those motherfuckers.* He wondered if even Patterson would volunteer for a SAR mission, so close to his DEROS. *I wouldn't if I were him.*

He recalled the helicopter, come to save him, whirling above him in a furor of wind and noise and gunfire, then falling away as the face of the gunner looked down at him. The rest was confused memories, Patterson yelling at him, the shots that killed the Vietnamese generals and the way they both went down. Gradually, he deduced that he had been shot, but how? By whom? Monroe's head cleared and he realized that he had been out-dueled. The sniper had found him, and hit him, at over nine hundred yards with Sadowski's Remington. A fraction truer and he would be dead.

Monroe thought of Sadowski, a cracker from Arkansas with a chip on his shoulder. He had a delicate voice and soft hands, feminine qualities that he veiled with a level of bloodthirstiness that disturbed even the veteran snipers. He had no friends, which was not unusual among snipers, but neither did he have enemies for he had enough sense to keep his mouth shut about most things. Sadowski tolerated Monroe, which qualified the two men to work together. They made a decent team, though Sadowski's kills were of dubious value. Ostensibly hunting VC tax collectors, he stalked the trails near villages, but he shot anything that moved. A kill wasn't official until it had been inspected and weapons or intelligence data collected. No coward, Sadowski was conscientious about checking the bodies of the people he shot, even if the only souvenir was a pack of cigarettes. He had forty-seven kills; he had hoped to reach one hundred.

"Two knots, right to left," whispered Monroe, reading the mirage in the spotter's scope. Sadowski ignored him; at one hundred yards the drop and the windage would have negligible effect on the point of impact. Monroe watched unimpressed as the face in his scope exploded, drilled through the nose by the Remington's heavy bullet.

"Hit."

They lay dog for five minutes, then relocated fifty yards away. The body baked on the trail for three more hours, undisturbed despite the cluster of hooches less than two hundred yards beyond. Finally, Sadowski crawled into the open to check his kill. Monroe covered him with the M-14, deadly accurate at such short range and capable of laying down a withering fire. If the range had been longer, they would have traded weapons.

Sadowski's hand was in his victim's pocket when the Soviet-made 7.62mm bullet passed through his groin. Monroe had never heard the sound of a Mosin Nagant before, but he knew it wasn't American. Sadowski flipped into a fetal ball and screamed. There had been no muzzle flash. Monroe froze, startled but knowledgeable enough to know that any movement might betray his own position. Sadowski cried out again, plaintive and fearful this time. He called Monroe's name.

With supernatural slowness, Monroe reached for the spotter's scope and brought it to his eye. At one hundred yards, the scope was powerful enough to reveal the most intimate view of a man's face. He had seen the faces of his victims before, but they were uninteresting to him, merely targets. Few bore any expression, for they did not know they were about to die. Faces in general meant little to Monroe; he would have had trouble describing his sister. As his own face revealed nothing of himself to others, he cared nothing about what the faces of others might reveal to him.

But what Monroe saw through the 20x spotter's scope shocked him. The fear bulged from Sadowski's eyes, zeroing in on the hide where Monroe waited, the nearest place of safety. Then they broke away, searching crazily along the far tree line where the shot originated, before returning like lasers to the hide, as if he could peer directly through the weeds at Monroe. Sadowski's lips quivered and Monroe heard his name again, floating across the paddy. *Look away*, thought Monroe. *Or he'll get us both. And shut the fuck up.* The VC sniper had gut-shot Sadowski on purpose, knowing the Americans worked in pairs. He waited now, counting on the dying fool's partner to come to his aid.

Monroe swung the scope toward the tree line, waiting for the muzzle blast of the shot that would finish off Sadowski. *Charlie would get tired, want to move on.* After a few minutes, however, he realized that this sniper was no amateur and Sadowski was no longer a target. He was bait. As Monroe waited for the sniper, the sniper waited for him. Monroe could only watch as Sadowski died; he was as good as dead already, soaked in his own blood. But snipers never left their partners, even if the living carried the dead. Sniper teams had disappeared, but no sniper had ever come back alone.

Sadowski lay on the trail, immobile, his legs paralyzed by the explosion in his crotch that had taken out his sciatic nerves. He quieted down, whimpering now as he groped for his balls, resigned to his inevitable bleed-out.

The sniper was patient. The sun peaked overhead and descended throughout the afternoon. As the shadows grew longer, Sadowski stopped calling for Monroe. He called for his mother. *How long will you wait?* thought Monroe. *And where are the people from the ville?* It was only a matter of time before they came to flush him out. The shadows grew deeper and Monroe's spotter's scope began to lose its effectiveness. He packed it away and slipped deeper into the weeds to sanitize the hide. If he was going to get to Sadowski, it would have to be at night, but the moon was already rising and the VC had begun to stir, no doubt tightening a ring around him. The sun set like a door slamming shut—and Monroe glided away into the jungle.

Monroe locked the truth about Sadowski deep within himself; not even the Intel pricks who interrogated him as if he were an enemy POW could crack him. They threatened him with a court-martial and he dared them to do it. *The white boy broke too quick a trail; he left me . . .* After a few days, Anderson paired Monroe with Patterson and they dropped the investigation.

Monroe thought of Patterson now. *Dumber than a box of rocks,* an expression his mother used. Monroe wished he had told Patterson about his mother. She was a drunk. What did Patterson care? Fear returned, and Monroe resumed his vigilance.

FIF⊤EEN

9th Infantry Division Headquarters
Dong Tam

E ighty-five men comprised Special Troops, HQ Command, 9th Infantry Division, most of them snipers, housed in two single-story hooches in a corner of the base camp reserved for the REMFs: the clerks & jerks, the grease monkeys and other personnel required to keep the division running. All of the barracks looked similar: set on concrete piers, topped with sheet metal roofs and surrounded by sandbags. Interior ceilings were open and the screened windows were placed high on the walls to facilitate airflow and venting of heat, and to minimize damage to the screens when the troops came home drunk or angry and looking for something to destroy after getting a Dear John letter at mail call. The CQ staffed a desk and a field phone in one corner of each building, assuring some measure of order when the barracks were occupied and security when they weren't. CQ was boring duty but safe, coveted by every grunt who might otherwise be out in the field.

There was no mistaking the sniper company hooches. Clean and quiet, nobody but snipers came near. The REMFs called the sniper barracks "Murder, Inc." The eerie silence struck Brady as he approached. Radio Vietnam was on the air, but the sound drifted from other barracks. He heard no orders or conversations, not even the sound of snoring. He could only hear the faint beating of helicopter blades at the division airstrip, a sound so omnipresent that nobody noticed the slight increase in air traffic this morning.

Brady stepped into the sniper hooch and stopped dead in his tracks as he presented himself to the Charge of Quarters.

Patterson stared with curiosity at the spectacle before him. Although Brady wore a uniform, it was clear that he was no soldier. His fatigues fit poorly. They were filthy and torn, and stained by salty tides of sweat. He wore hospital flip-flops on his feet. The least military aspect of Brady was his hair, which fell past his ears. It was not implausible that Brady had business there, for snipers were often involved in covert operations. PsychOps, Seals, CIA, LRRPs, Special Forces: they all had their share of odd characters who lived like animals and who turned up at base camps from time to time. Patterson had fifty weeks under his belt as an infantryman, and he knew that you did not fuck with these people.

"You need something?" he inquired. Patterson noted for the first time the man's swollen lips and eye; he was covered with cuts and scrapes.

Brady recognized Patterson at once. "I need to talk to you." He spoke gently, as if to demonstrate his harmlessness.

"Who are you?"

"I'm a reporter."

Patterson peered past Brady into the sunlight through the door. "Where's your escort? Snipers ain't s'posed to talk to reporters."

"Olivetti was busy. They let me come up here alone."

"Who's Olivetti?"

"PIO. My escort," said Brady smoothly, increasingly comfortable. He pressed on without further explanation. "What's your name?"

"Don't answer that!" The command originated behind Brady, who turned to find the sunlight blocked by Captain Anderson, standing in the door, his eyes focused on the shabby stranger in his Ops. Patterson sprang to attention. "Who are you?" demanded Anderson.

"Dan Brady. Freelance." He extended his press card, but Anderson ignored it.

"Where's your escort?"

"Busy," explained Brady, knowing that the con was up. Anderson was all business.

"Yeah? We'll see," said Anderson, who turned to Patterson. "Get your gear. We're going back to Christine on the next log bird. You and me."

Patterson thought to object. *I'm s'posed to be answering phones.* But he could see that Anderson was angry, so Patterson said only, "Yes, sir." He'd never worked with an officer before, and he wondered if Anderson was going with him as a way to apologize for breaking his promise to keep him out of combat until his DEROS.

"Come with me," ordered Anderson, grabbing Brady by the collar of his shirt. The newsman limped after Anderson, who strode purposefully, without regard for Brady's injuries.

"You guys got a big mission in progress?" asked Brady, wincing with each step.

"No questions," ordered Anderson. "And no answers." The conversation ended.

SIXTEEN

09:11

9th Infantry Division Headquarters
Dong Tam

B oettcher found Olivetti at his desk, hammering slowly on his cast iron Underwood, writing a hometown news release about a harmonica-playing cook who entertained the local orphans when not peeling potatoes. Olivetti snapped to attention and said, "I heard about Mr. Brady, sir. Some hooker must be laughing her ass off right now."

"Cut the crap, Olivetti. The Old Man's not too happy about this. The idea was to frustrate him, not kill him. General Vandermeer wants to know if you had anything to do with it."

"Not me, sir. I left him at the hotel in good shape."

Boettcher cocked his head suspiciously. "Good," he said. "If there's anything you aren't telling me, I don't want to know. Sometimes, the Old Man is a little too straight for his own good, if you know what I mean."

"No problem, Colonel. The general takes care of us, and we'll take care of him. If he needs any special favors, sir, you let me know."

"Count on it," replied Boettcher.

The door to the PIO office burst open. Captain Anderson stepped into the room, pushing Brady in front of him.

"Olivetti!" began Anderson, belatedly realizing that Boettcher was in the room. The general's chief of staff was not a popular man among the other division officers. He had stabbed too many men in the back and had ruined the careers of too many others to be trusted by those not yet touched by him. It mattered little that most of those who had been broken by Boettcher had been unsuitable deadwood; paranoia ran deep, even among the most competent officers. Upon seeing Boettcher, Anderson merely said politely, "Good morning, Colonel."

"What's going on?" replied Boettcher, seeing Brady, who limped gently to a battered metal chair and sat down. The march from the sniper compound had been rapid, and his swollen testicles were still painful. Pale and shaky, Brady held one hand against his temple as if to quell a migraine. A rainbow of color in his swollen lips and one eye that had turned purple punctuated his pallor.

"Found him in my hooch," explained Anderson. "No escort." He glanced once at Brady and turned to leave. "Keep the press away from my men, Olivetti. That is your job, isn't it?"

He was gone before Olivetti could respond. Brady repressed a grim smile over the irony of Anderson's parting comment. "I thought your job was to facilitate contact with the press," he said, in barely a whisper.

"What are you doing here?" said Boettcher. "You should be on your way back to Saigon."

"Your hospital staff tried to send me. But I had to find someone first." Brady's breath had finally returned and he glanced up at Olivetti, whose stare betrayed shock at the injuries Brady had sustained. "What's the matter, Olivetti? Never seen a hematoma before?"

Olivetti shrugged. "I've seen guys with their arms blown off look better than you."

"Olivetti," said Boettcher. "Give it a rest." He turned to Brady and asked, "Who were you looking for?"

"The sniper who shot General Cho."

Brady noted that Boettcher's eyes narrowed. Olivetti's widened. Perplexed, the enlisted man turned to his superior officer.

Boettcher spoke. "Brady, it seems that someone, probably your VC friends, are trying to use you for propaganda purposes. I suggest you go home to

Saigon and get yourself cleaned up."

Brady shook his head slowly. "The sniper was a Negro. And he shot General Cho in the throat."

"If you check with MACV," said Boettcher, "you'll find that General Cho was killed in combat when his helicopter was shot down."

"MACV," repeated Brady, chuckling without humor. "They are the last people I go to when I want to verify a story. Either they don't know what they're talking about, or they're lying. One is as likely as the other."

"Go home and write up your bullshit, Brady, but stay out of our way." The colonel walked stiffly from the room.

Brady grinned painfully. "Olivetti, did you notice that your boss didn't ask me a single question? You know why? Because he already knows all the answers."

"Well, I sure don't know what the hell is going on." Olivetti returned to his typewriter.

"Probably not," said Brady. "But you know the truth when you hear it. Truth has its own odor, and Boettcher damn near gagged on it."

"I don't smell anything except your clothes."

"You only smell what you're authorized to smell, is that it?" The newsman hiked up his pants irritably and the sudden movement made his head throb. "I got these clothes from the dead pile. You know what that is?"

Olivetti knew. He did not know whether to be outraged or heartbroken by the sight of a civilian dressed in the cast-off garments of wounded soldiers, tossed in a pile in the ER as men were stripped and prepped for surgery. Brady's clothes were beyond filthy, though they did not appear to be stiff with dried blood. It had taken some grisly searching to find a shirt and a pair of trousers filthy with nothing more than mud and sweat. Olivetti stared at Brady with a mixture of horror, disgust, and begrudging respect.

"I want to talk to Vandermeer," said Brady.

"You don't look like you're in any condition to do anything."

"Cut the crap. How do I get to him?"

"The Old Man's heading out right now." Olivetti pointed through the window to the helipad, fifty yards away, where the blades of the general's repaired helicopter had already blurred into a solid disk. "He'll be back by noon."

From the window, Brady watched as Vandermeer strode into the prop blast, his head ducked against the wind. Boettcher ran into view, racing to catch up with his commander. Brady grinned mirthlessly as Boettcher put his hand on the general's shoulder, then climbed into the chopper as Vandermeer motioned him aboard. The newsman could imagine the conversation. "They're talking about me right now, Olivetti. I'm a problem."

"Congratulations." Olivetti returned to his typewriter. He struck one key, then began searching for the next.

"Aren't you curious to know about General Cho?" asked Brady. "Who shot him? And why? And how I found out about it?"

Olivetti continued typing. Eventually, he said, "First, I never heard of General Cho. Second, I don't care who shot him; he's just another gook to me. And third, Colonel Boettcher says you're being played for a fool. I got more important stories to write, like this one about some shithead cook with a harmonica."

Brady laughed. "General Nguyen Cho was the Great Asian Hope of Vietnam. A real patriot. An ARVN general who didn't avoid a fight. He ran the delta with an iron fist. Took no prisoners. Not a one. The human rights nuts didn't much care for him, but the Pentagon, the CIA, they were planning to make him president someday. I interviewed him once, you know."

"Good for you. Now you can write his obituary."

"Maybe I will. I'll mention how he was shot by an American sniper because he was negotiating a peace settlement with the NVA."

Olivetti stopped pecking on his typewriter and looked up. For once, he had nothing to say.

Brady smirked. "Get the picture, Slick? No way in hell that MACV can let that one out of the bag."

"Nice story," said Olivetti, recovered. "But if the colonel says it never happened, then it never happened. You can't find a criminal if there ain't no crime." He resumed typing, but his mind was no longer on the hometown news release.

"Oh, I know the crime. And I think I've found the criminal," answered Brady.

Olivetti tried to ignore him, but he wondered what Vandermeer and Boettcher were saying to each other.

SEVEN‡EEN

Vandermeer frequently flew in the right seat on routine missions. He took the stick because he needed the airtime to maintain his rating, but mostly he flew for the sheer pleasure of it, and the sense of control. So little else responded the way he intended. Hueys were extremely powerful when empty, especially Reliable Six, the best-maintained ship in the fleet. Vandermeer pulled pitch and the aircraft leapt obediently into the air.

The maintenance shop had been up all night, sweating under clouds of tiny moths attracted to the spotlights in the sultry heat, to restore Reliable Six to airworthiness. There were holes in two hydraulic lines and the entire system had to be bled and recharged after replacing the damaged sections. The windshield had been replaced and the blood hosed out. Even the engine was new, the original turbine blades shredded beyond repair. Each bullet hole had been circled in white chalk, like a silhouette of a murder victim at a crime scene, and the crew chief had ordered new skin panels to replace those that had been punctured. Boettcher had countermanded that order, however. He directed the chief to leave the holes as they were, white circles and all. Few generals ever flew close enough to combat to acquire bullet holes in their aircraft, and Boettcher wanted the troops to see that their commander was not afraid to go wherever they did.

At three thousand feet, Vandermeer removed his radio headset and leaned back in his copilot's seat, signaling for Boettcher. Over the engine noise he yelled, "Ron, how much does Brady know?"

"I'm not sure, General. But he knows that General Cho was shot by one of our snipers. He's got some of the details correct, including the fact that the sniper was a Negro."

To Vandermeer's left, the pilot maintained a steady watch through the new windshield, deaf to the conversation. Through his headset, he monitored a dozen radio frequencies—troop communications as well as air traffic control, where there was any, but over the beat of the rotors, he could hear nothing of the officers' conversation. Likewise, the door gunners maintained their attention outward, barely aware that their division commander and his adjutant bellowed at each other only two feet away.

"I see." Vandermeer turned abruptly away and faced forward in his seat to think. He replaced his headset. Strangely, the radios were silent. He pressed the squelch key and the hiss confirmed that he was properly connected.

"Quiet day," muttered the pilot into his microphone.

"Radio discipline," said Vandermeer. "Something's up, and the troops know it." He lapsed into thought.

Boettcher tapped him on the shoulder, and Vandermeer pulled his headset from one ear.

"General, we need to get Brady out of our AO and we need to isolate the sniper who made it out with you."

"Where is the sniper now?"

"Headed to Firebase Christine, in accordance with the decision this morning to augment the force there with snipers and night vision scopes."

"And Monroe is still out there somewhere. I'd say they are both pretty isolated already."

"We have to do more than get Brady out of our hair, sir. We have to kill his story."

"He's a good correspondent, Ron. He has contacts all over this country. He's going to verify it, and I doubt that we can do much about it. Let MACV handle it. They're the ones who sanctioned the mission; they can deal with

Brady. He'll be so busy with them, he won't be back to bother us."

"Sir, as soon as it is revealed on the front page of the *New York Times* that a sniper from this division shot the most popular allied general in Vietnam while on an illegal mission, it won't matter who initiated the mission. You'll take the fall. You'll be a hero at the Pentagon, but Congress will never confirm your next star. Westmoreland and the bureaucrats will run for cover, and you'll be hanging out there, the renegade general fighting an unauthorized war in Cambodia. We'll be finished."

"What do you suggest?" asked Vandermeer.

"We can convince him that he's wrong, or we can kill him."

"Don't be ridiculous."

"I'm absolutely serious."

Vandermeer stared at his chief of staff as if he'd never seen him before. He knew Boettcher to be a man of many things, but he had never imagined that murder was one of them. "Ron, we aren't the only ones with a stake in this. I've already compromised my honor for MACV over this incident. I won't do it again. I think it is about time Lyons did his own dirty work, don't you?"

Boettcher smiled grimly and slowly nodded his head. *Honor means nothing anymore, except to a few old dinosaurs like you. Brady would destroy you in an instant if it weren't for men like me, and men as dissolute as Lyons.*

Vandermeer retreated into silence, replacing his headset and staring into the haze as they crossed the Mekong. Though ignorant of the substance of the conversation between the division commander and the chief of staff, the pilot could read the frustration on Boettcher's face as he leaned forward in his seat with his elbows on his knees. The pilot would fly his chopper into a mountain if Vandermeer ordered it, but Boettcher was a different story and there wasn't a warrant officer in the Army who didn't enjoy watching a full colonel pout. He triggered the talk switch on the aircraft yoke.

"Want the stick, General?"

"You keep it, Tony. Just get us to Binh Thuy ASAP." Vandermeer, too, seemed to sulk.

A tornado of dust rose from the VIP pad at Binh Thuy Air Force Base as Reliable Six settled on her skids. A blue staff car, "USAF" stenciled neatly on the driver and passenger doors, whisked Vandermeer away, while Boettcher waited with the aircrew on the boiling tarmac.

Like Vandermeer's HQ in Dong Tam, the HQ complex at Binh Thuy was built for speed, functionality, and safety. Cinder-block buildings huddled under the control tower, their communications facilitated by the wreath of antennas that sprouted from its roof. The runway ran off in either direction from the tower, eleven thousand feet long, enough to handle the biggest birds in the Air Force, even though the C-130s and Skyraiders that staged from Binh Thuy barely needed half that. The airport was busy twenty-four hours per day, and as Vandermeer stepped from his car a Skyraider, heavy with a max bomb load, roared past the complex. Vandermeer turned to watch as the wingman followed, his propeller thrashing the air in the struggle to get airborne in the lift-killing heat.

An air policeman escorted Vandermeer to the HQ command division and passed him off to a staff officer who then ushered him directly into the office of the wing commander. Colonel Roger Malloitte rose to greet him.

"General, I would have met you at the pad, but we got your inbound call so suddenly I couldn't extricate myself from ongoing briefings." The men shook hands. Officers in sister services rarely knew each other well, but Malloitte and Vandermeer had developed a mutual respect in the time they had worked together in the delta.

"Don't be ridiculous, Roger. I wasn't expecting a parade."

"What brings you here?" asked Malloitte, getting to the point. He knew that major generals didn't jump in their helicopters to drop in for unannounced social visits. Though he respected Vandermeer, he was not sure he was glad to see him.

"You've been following the Intel reports?"

"Yes, sir. Something's up. It may be nothing, but I've augmented our perimeter security." Because of the runway, Binh Thuy had an extremely long perimeter, protected by a relatively small security detachment. Although surrounded by billows of concertina and chain link fences, parts of the base were not even guarded except for periodic patrols inside the wire. Malloitte had no illusions about stopping a concerted attack anywhere along the remote portions of the perimeter, but with interior lines he could concentrate his forces quickly at the point of penetration. Though confident his airmen were up to the task, he knew the Army scoffed at any Air Force personnel who presumed to fight with a rifle. Malloitte wondered if Vandermeer had come there to offer reinforcements.

"We've got some vulnerable outposts," said Vandermeer. "I need tac air support tonight. Can you provide at least one gunship on CAP between 1800 and 0600 tomorrow?"

Malloitte puzzled. "Of course, General. Colonel Ingram has already coordinated that with us." Vandermeer nodded and slowly turned to shut the door to Malloitte's office. Malloitte started to get the picture. "You didn't fly all the way over here to ask for air support, sir."

"I've lost a soldier in Cambodia," said Vandermeer bluntly. "I want him back. And I need Air Force forward air controllers to keep an eye out for him."

Colonel Malloitte walked to the chart on his wall, similar to the one hanging in Vandermeer's briefing room, except this one was marked with navigation aids and pocked with runway symbols all over the delta. The Cambodian border was clearly marked. Without speaking, the colonel studied the map, imagining it in three dimensions, as he mentally cataloged every aircraft type and ordnance load airborne at that moment. He had no aircraft anywhere near the border, and with no battles brewing, they had made no plans to send any there. "Where is he?" asked Malloitte at last.

Vandermeer pointed just north of the Vinh Te Canal. "Here. We think."

"I can't cross the border, sir. But I'll route some of my guys along the canal. Can I tell them what they're looking for?"

"Yes," said Vandermeer. "But officially, my boy doesn't exist."

Malloitte nodded. The men shook hands. Vandermeer refused an escort back to his helicopter, leaving Malloitte to stare at his map, irritated that he would soon be putting his own resources at risk for a single soldier stupid enough to become marooned in enemy territory, thick with small arms capable of bringing down his slow-moving observation aircraft. *We'll see what we can see, General, but I'm not letting my guys go anywhere near that border. The poor bastard is probably dead, anyway.*

EIGHTEEN

Vandermeer spent the rest of the morning airborne, evaluating the developing situation and picking up wounded. From the scurrying of footsteps in the hallway, the HQ staff knew that Reliable Six was inbound. Colonel Ingram exited the communications center and marched briskly from the dusty compound into the waning afternoon sunlight as Vandermeer's black helicopter floated noisily onto the helipad.

From the PIO office, Brady watched Vandermeer and Ingram exchange salutes, while Boettcher dashed quickly away. The two men talked intensely as they strode past the MP bunker. Remaining at the aircraft, the pilots completed the engine shutdown checklist and conducted a careful postflight inspection. Then they settled in the deepening shade to wait. There would be no happy hour at the officers' club tonight.

In a sandbagged Quonset building, isolated from the rest of the command compound, Boettcher found Colonel Lyons at his desk, eating a turkey sandwich just delivered from the mess hall. They greeted each other with grudging cordiality, aware of the differences between their commanders, but bound by their pact.

"Brady knows about Cho," Boettcher announced. "I'm sure he's getting his information from the enemy. His VC contacts have been feeding him a line about Cho being in Cambodia to discuss an end to the war and that he was shot by an American sniper in an effort to sabotage the peace process."

"Sabotage, my ass. He probably *was* talking peace with General Le, but shooting Cho was just one of the serendipities of war. So at best, Brady only has half of his story right. We know he'll publish it anyway, so we can do one of two things: Tell him the whole truth, or eliminate him."

"He'll never believe it was dumb luck," added Boettcher.

"You were going to see to it that this story didn't get out of hand."

"General Vandermeer has refused to cooperate. He says it is about time that G-2 did some of their own dirty work."

"We won't do it, Colonel," said Lyons. "We might not be a bunch of honor-bound West Point boy scouts, but we are professional soldiers and we do not murder American civilians."

"Only American soldiers."

"Soldiers are expendable. If you want to uphold your part of the bargain, you're going to have to persuade the CIA to take care of the matter, or handle it yourself."

"Very well," said Boettcher, nodding his head slowly, thinking. "But I'd rather have the VC kill him for us."

"What are you saying?"

"The surviving sniper is headed to Firebase Christine tonight, part of a small detachment of reinforcements. The base is undermanned because the Ruff Puffs are mostly home for Tet. If Charlie tries to overrun them tonight, the only thing to stop them will be air support. I'll send Brady and one of my guys out there, but if Charlie overruns the place, we'll be rid of the sniper, plus Brady."

"You'll never make general, Ron, because you have no moral fiber. But if you ever want to come work for me, let me know." Lyons reached for his phone. "I'll make sure the air support is committed elsewhere."

Boettcher lowered his eyes and stared hard at Olivetti. "Look at me," he said. The colonel held Olivetti's attention so long that Olivetti began to fidget. Finally, Boettcher said, "Take him to Christine."

"Sir, they're gonna get hit tonight."

"Don't worry about that. Spooky will be on CAP. Charlie will never get within ten feet of the wire. But I have a job for you to do."

"What's that, sir?"

"You still ready to do whatever it takes to help the Old Man?"

"Yes, sir."

"The battlefield is a dangerous place, Olivetti, and Brady could get hurt if he's not careful. You get my drift?"

"Sir, are you telling me to kill him?"

"I'm telling you that I plucked your ass out of three feet of Mekong mud, and I can drop you right back in it. If you want to keep this comfortable job, son, I expect you to take care of awkward problems, no matter what it takes."

NINETEEN

9th Infantry Division Headquarters
Dong Tam

A n Air Force gunship checked in on the command frequency at 1815. "Rogue Two Zero, Rogue Two Zero, this is Spooky Eight Zero on CAP with forty thousand rounds of happiness, five miles east of your position, over."

Vandermeer listened as the American RTO at Firebase Christine performed a commo check and welcomed the gunship to the party. He could feel the lift in the RTO's spirits from knowing Spooky flew overhead like a guardian angel.

Colonel Boettcher entered the DTOC. He handed a turkey sandwich and a small carton of milk to Vandermeer, then unfolded a metal chair and seated himself next to his commander.

"Spooky is on station," said the general.

Another round of commo checks and sitreps passed across the radios. Even Brady sensed the tension through the airwaves. The communications were quick and whispered. Many calls were acknowledged simply with squelch breaks, the RTOs touching their transmitter keys twice to interrupt the radio's hiss.

Flight Ops for the 9th Aviation Battalion was sheltered in a lonely GP tent located adjacent to the airstrip. Sprouting antennae and surrounded by a berm of sandbags, the structure served as a terminal of sorts, staffed by a single pilot who monitored schedules, weather reports, aircraft maintenance status, and the radio telephone. Pilots pulled duty on a rotating basis, once per month, twenty-four miserable hours at a time. These men lived to fly, could juggle a collective, throttle, and cyclic control stick with aplomb, while monitoring three radios and an intercom and simultaneously scanning for friendly aircraft and enemy ground fire. They swaggered in their flight suits and boasted of their expertise in the air. They sneered at ground pounders and they hated the one day per month they were required to fly a desk. It was bad enough that someone else flew and perhaps destroyed their aircraft, but the physical conditions inside the Ops Center made everyone yearn for the fresh air of the cockpit, incoming ground fire notwithstanding.

Clouds of dust and spent fuel drifted through the tent with every takeoff; any effort to close the tent flaps turned the interior into an oven. The phone rang incessantly with calls from people the pilots didn't know who asked questions they couldn't answer; pissed-off infantrymen always packed the place looking for rides to Saigon for R&R or DEROS, and officers who stepped to the front of the line waving priority orders in their faces, demanding immediate transportation to some location that nobody ever heard of.

The duty officer had not slept or eaten for any of the twenty-two hours that he had been on duty. His eyes were bloodshot with exhaustion and dust and he could smell his own breath whenever he opened his mouth. He had stopped answering the phone; if it was important enough, the caller would come down personally and stand in line with the rest of the grunts and duffel bags and cargo and combat gear that spilled out of the Ops Center and onto the tarmac.

Flight operations had been haywire since dawn, when every available bird had been assigned to transport two companies of troops to Can Tho. The duty officer did not know that these troops were the strategic reserve, and he did not care. That deployment had been completed by noon, but the resulting backlog remained when Olivetti walked into the Ops Center, Brady in tow.

The last thing the duty officer needed was one more son of a bitch trying to get to Saigon. And Brady had Saigon written all over him.

Brady stepped over a pair of sleeping grunts on his way to the duty desk. "Anything going to Firebase Christine?" he asked, as he dropped his press card on the makeshift desk of ammo crates and plywood. The newsman scanned the rows of brutal faces, looking for anyone with a Remington or an M-14 or a starlight scope.

The warrant officer looked up as he grabbed the radio handset to relay a new set of destination coordinates to a departing flight. "Log bird," he told Brady.

The logistics birds, usually CH-46 Chinooks, carried food, mail, and ammo, routine flights to remote bases to shuttle personnel and resupply. Christine was a regular stop on the log bird route with two flights per week. But the log birds had been rescheduled twice today already to carry extra ammo and a team of snipers. The third flight of the day was cranking now, a UH-1 Huey with still more ammo and extra rations. The duty officer realized that something was going on at Firebase Christine, and equally clear that Brady knew more about it than he did. As always, rumor came first and the press came next. Nobody went to a shit hole like Christine just to interview the advisers there.

"I'll take it," said Brady.

Olivetti dropped a set of blanket travel orders on the makeshift desk.

The warrant officer looked through the door toward the tarmac and shrugged his shoulders. "There's your aircraft. Have a nice trip."

"Thanks," said Brady. He went out the door immediately, jogging gingerly toward the aircraft with the self-assurance of an experienced hitchhiker, waving his arm to signal his intention to board.

The grunts inside the Ops tent looked up at the duty officer, and then at Brady's figure in tattered fatigues and no hat, no pack, no weapon, shuffling across the runway like an ill-prepared adventure tourist, followed by Olivetti in full combat gear, including his M-16. Their eyes followed Brady into the sunlight before finally settling on each other. They shook their heads with bemused resignation and lapsed back into helpless waiting for their flight home.

TWENTY

Firebase Christine

A t Firebase Christine a premature dusk had fallen. The sun's rays fell obliquely across the treetops, which cast deepening shadows below. An hour of penumbral daylight remained.

The ARVN infantry, strung in a precarious line inside the rows of concertina wire, moved quietly into position, two men to a fighting hole. In the gun pits, crews prepared fleshette rounds, each like a giant shotgun shell capable of filling the air with thousands of lethal darts. The advisers strolled about, calming jittery nerves and keeping a discreet eye on the jungle, seventy-five yards away.

Each man placed his claymore mine. The small devices packed a wallop; 700 BBs suspended in a volatile batter of plastic explosive. The lethal mixture spread across the face of a convex steel plate, like an open-faced peanut butter sandwich. A cover, stamped with the warning "This Side Toward Enemy" protected the explosive from any accidental impacts. Prongs supported the mine, allowing soldiers to plant them in the ground like the small "KEEP OFF THE GRASS" signs in parks back home.

Gruff American voices fell to whispers as the twilight turned to night. "Don't talk," the advisers ordered, tucking the troops in for the night, bucking them up. The advisers spoke in infantile Vietnamese like toddlers with a precocious knowledge of military jargon and ribald curses.

"Stack your magazines."

"Lay out your grenades."

"Don't shoot anything you can't see, or you'll give away your position."

At 1800 hours, darkness set in, not gradually but instantly, as if someone had pulled the plug on the sun. The natural chatter of the jungle stopped too, as the bugs and bats and toads took note of the change, and then, as if on cue, the babbling and gibbering and croaking resumed. A whiff of fog began to develop, and the jungle turned utterly black. Dimly, the ARVN defenders heard noises: voices and the scrape of metal against metal. Or perhaps it was simply the Silent Men moving in the fog, reincarnating the sounds of their own battles, months before.

They were not imagining the noises, for no force of a thousand armed men can move into position in absolute silence. On the trail where Monroe lay hiding, an NCO moved among the resting troops, rousing them with whispered commands. The men ate another cold meal while they waited for the fog to settle in. They secured their packs, taking with them only weapons and ammunition. A few soldiers withdrew letters or charms and stuffed them in their pockets before stowing their packs in a neat row along the trail. Then, hidden under the veil of mist, they mustered quickly and headed for the boats that waited to ferry them across the canal. The same guard remained behind to watch their gear. Monroe observed that the guard was missing one arm.

Their departure was impressive, so many men moving with such efficiency and silence. As Monroe listened to them march away, he felt hunger more insistent than pain. And he knew he needed the food soon, to survive, to move, to make it out of this swampy shit hole. There was food in the packs the man had stowed on the trail, and the guard had something else he needed. Slowly, he withdrew his K-Bar knife from its sheath and crept forward through the fog.

Though trained in knife fighting, few snipers ever killed anyone with a blade. Monroe tried to recall the moves he had been taught: how to kill a man from behind, how to kill him face-to-face. The techniques were simple and brutal, nothing so dramatic as the quiet slicing of a man's throat with your hand over his mouth. That was good for the movies, but even a man with a severed jugular would thrash about until he bled to death. Monroe prepared to simply thrust the point of his heavy blade directly through the man's temple with one barbaric blow. If the blade penetrated deep enough, it would cut the brain stem and the man would crumple quietly to the ground, dead instantly. And if the blade missed its mark, the blow alone could render a man unconscious, easy prey for a second thrust to the heart.

Monroe could barely discern the guard in the darkness, but he considered that to be to his advantage. Moving as silently as the fog itself, Monroe maneuvered to within a yard of the one-armed soldier. As Monroe prepared to thrust the knife into the man's temple, another squad of soldiers appeared on the trail. They jogged along in dead quiet, one hand touching the shoulder of the man in front, led by an NCO with a red-filtered flashlight, the beam focused only on the trail in front of him. Monroe froze as the team moved by. If they saw him, they mistook him for one of their own, but in the gloom it was difficult to tell if they even saw the NVA guard as they passed by him.

The guard slung his AK-47 over his shoulder and opened his fly. He turned around to urinate, face-to-face with Monroe.

"*Ai do?*" cried the guard, reaching for his weapon. "Who's there?"

Too close to kill this man with a roundhouse thrust to the side of his head, Monroe thrust his blade upward under the man's chin, stapling his mouth shut and ripping through his sinus cavity. By the time the hilt slammed into the man's jaw, the point had passed through his brain and punctured the top of his skull. The force of Monroe's thrust lifted the guard into the air. The man was small, barely the size of an American ten-year-old, and Monroe held him aloft until his feet stopped twitching and his single arm went limp. Blood from his sinus cavity burst from his nose as Monroe lowered him to the ground. Trembling with exhaustion, Monroe lay next to his victim, listening, while the warm blood washed over his fist that still gripped the knife. He heard only his own panting and the sound of blood draining rapidly from the corpse's nose, like someone pouring water from a glass. He became aware of the man's smell, more pungent in death than life, his blood laced with the greasy stench of *nuc mam*. Monroe's stomach heaved.

Despite the blood groove on the blade, the knife was not easily withdrawn from the dead man's head. Unlike some men who romanticized their victims, Monroe felt only revulsion for the messy killing, the stinking corpse, and the slippery black blood that coated his hands like oil. He wanted only to get away. Quickly, he stripped the dead man of his AK-47 and his boots. Grabbing three packs from among those stacked along the trail, Monroe stepped silently back into the jungle.

In deep cover, he rested. He cleaned his bloody hands as well as he could on his filthy uniform, already stiff with his own dried blood and now soaked again with the blood of the man he had just killed. He removed his boots. Vietnamese feet were small, but large enough that Monroe managed to get his feet into the dead soldier's canvas boots. He cut the uppers to allow his toes to protrude, carefully leaving the sole intact. Next, he rummaged through the packs, searching by feel in the darkness for food. The packs were similar in what they contained: clean socks, rubberized ponchos, rope, first-aid kits, a paperback book or two, canteen, cleaning solvent, and food. This was not the gear of a ragtag guerrilla force, but of a well-equipped professional army. The food was contained in a metal tin: rice and dried fish. One pack had strips of salted meat, like jerky: dried rat. Monroe took it all, quickly stuffing a handful of rice into his mouth and swilling water as he consolidated the remaining provisions into a single pack, along with a first-aid kit and poncho. Then he buried his boots and the remaining gear as well as he could.

He made his way carefully back to the trail. Kneeling beside the man he had killed, he considered the soldier more compassionately than he had before. Poor fuck, thought Monroe. *Too bad you lost your arm instead of your leg. Otherwise, you'da been back in Hanoi tonight, sitting in your wheelchair.* Killing him had been relatively easy, but Monroe knew he didn't want to kill with a knife again.

Monroe listened for movement. Hearing none, he stepped onto the trail and walked slowly north, his new boot prints mixing with the thousands already there. He knew the enemy would find the dead soldier soon, and would follow the trail of large GI footprints into the brush. But there the trail would end.

Monroe held the AK-47 ready in case he should encounter an NVA squad resting along the trail. He had traveled only forty yards when he sniffed the pungent odor of a Vietnamese cigarette. Whoever smoked it, however, concealed the glowing tip, for Monroe could see nothing in the darkness. Perhaps it was simply another guard, standing watch over the packs of another platoon. Or perhaps it was a whole platoon. Monroe stepped silently into the jungle again, moving steadily north, seeking always the thickest vegetation.

And then he heard the rumble of gunfire to the east.

TWENTY-1

30.JANUARY.1968 > **18:37**

9th Infantry Division Headquarters
Dong Tam

A t the division airstrip, the aircraft commander pulled pitch as Brady and Olivetti jumped into the cargo bay behind him. The helicopter rose in a whirl of dust. Nose low, it raced just above the deck for several hundred yards, accelerating with each sweep of the rotor blade. When airspeed reached ninety knots, the pilot climbed hard and fast, leveling at fifteen hundred feet, just beyond small arms range. As they flew, the downwash churned warm breezes through the back of the helicopter.

Brady put his head back and did not look down. The undulating view from the open door and the reek of exhaust nauseated him. His headache persisted along with the pain in his ribs and groin, aggravated now by the low-level turbulence caused by thermal currents in the air. He groaned with each bump.

Olivetti heard nothing but the thunderous beat of the rotor blades. He sat quietly, holding his M-16 and staring at the setting sun. Even at altitude, the sun faded fast. The lights were on in Saigon, a glow to the east, while below, the river turned silver, then black as the navy PBRs sallied forth to enforce the nighttime curfew, their spotlights streaking across the water. Other aircraft spotted the sky. A dust-off bird passed below them with a load of wounded from an engagement farther west, and at twenty-five hundred feet a forward air controller flew lazy eights, vulture-like, looking for targets upon which to call in air support. Somewhere above flew Spooky 80, blacked out and hidden in the darkening sky.

The pilot reduced pitch and pulled the plug, spiralling earthward in a steep descent that threatened to pull Olivetti's stomach out through his mouth. The door gunner stood behind his M-60, cool, with nerves of a twenty-year-old, the wind sucking at his clothes, grooving on his good balance and utter lack of fear. At the last moment, Olivetti heard the turbine whine change pitch, and the chopper flared into a perfect hover. Olivetti jumped, with no small amount of help from the door gunner, who nearly threw him from the helicopter with a rough tug on his fatigue shirt. Brady landed next to him, his shirttail flapping in the rotor wash. Holding his helmet on his head with one hand and clutching his M-16 in the other, Olivetti led the way toward the command post.

"Where's your CO?" Olivetti queried of the first American he saw.

"Who are you?" In the twilight, Olivetti saw a man as tall as himself, with an M-16 and web gear loaded with extra magazines and grenades, ready for business.

"Specialist 4th class Olivetti, sir. Division PIO. General Vandermeer authorized Mr. Brady here to visit this firebase tonight. I'm here to keep him out of your way."

A scream cut through the darkness as one of the Popular Forces troops slumped into his foxhole, his oversized American helmet spinning like a top on the ground next to him. The thunder of a Remington from one of the towers almost immediately answered. Master Sergeant Wolfe ducked instinctively and jumped back into the command bunker with Olivetti. "We got a sniper war going on right now, Mister Whoever-the-Fuck-You-Are. Some son of a bitch out there has already shot four of our guys. If you want to run out there chasing your goddamn reporter, you go right ahead. I don't give a shit about you or him." Sergeant Wolfe turned and screamed toward one of the guard towers, "Somebody shoot that gook sniper!"

From inside the command post, the RTO called, "Cap'n! I've got Spooky 80 for you!"

Olivetti stepped into the CP. The RTO squatted in one corner, one hand clamped over his right ear. He held the handset of the PRC-25 against his other ear. "Spooky 80, this is Rogue 20. Request illumination, over." The enlisted man passed the handset to his commander, who spoke emphatically.

"Spooky 80, we have sporadic contact and sniper fire from enemy troops up and down our perimeter. Illuminate the area, and stand by for a fire mission, over."

"Copy. Wilco," came the reply in the unflappable tone that Air Force pilots equated with professionalism, and which they assumed during even the most extreme moments of stress.

The jungle lit up. Harsh light spewed from a magnesium flare that swung from its parachute, replacing the obscurity of darkness with eerie reality in silver and black. Shadows and perspectives changed constantly as the two-hundred-thousand candlelight flare swung to and fro in the night air. The flare lasted three minutes, barely an instant to the defenders at Firebase Christine who peered anxiously into the ghostly world beyond the muzzles of their guns.

Brady peeked outside. He could see the three guard towers, the tallest objects in the metallic landscape. He took advantage of the light to scurry along a row of foxholes to the nearest tower.

"Brady!" yelled Olivetti. "Where the hell you think you're going? "

Brady ignored him.

The jungle fell ominously silent, as even the insects were confused. The enemy froze in their tracks and ceased yelling commands. Through gaps in the trees, they scanned the sky for the gunship that had stolen the darkness, their only advantage.

The first flare died, and a pang of panic seized the now night-blinded defenders. The VC welcomed the darkness again. But a second flare burst and cast its garish light among the trees. The AC-47 turned immediately after releasing the flare. The baritone of its engines provided only a general indication of its position. Blacked out, the airplane was but a shadow among the stars.

"Spooky 80, fire mission!"

"This is Spooky 80, ready to copy," said the pilot in a drawn-out monotone. With fifty gunship missions under his belt, he had been beseeched by desperate men, men about to be overrun, too harried or exposed to properly identify their locations or the enemy's. Only firm control and precise communications had allowed him to fire his awesome weapons on target, sometimes so close to friendly troops that he could hear, over the radio, the dull drumming of his own bullets hitting the ground near the RTO.

"Spooky 80," replied the adviser, also calm. "Fire mission! Keep the illumination coming. We'll ID our position with yellow smoke. Saturate the area one hundred yards north of our position, over."

"Roger, Rogue. Pop smoke now."

In unison, a dozen men tossed hissing cylinders beyond the concertina wire. The colored smoke roiled thickly upward, black in the artificial light.

"Rogue, this is Spooky 80. We have your smoke. We are commencing our attack now."

Squad leaders ordered everyone into their holes. The ARVN troops curled up and pulled their helmets tight.

Brady stood on the tower ladder.

Above, Spooky 80 banked into its firing orbit.

"Hey," yelled Brady, as his head came level to the tower floor. "Any snipers here?"

"There's snipers everywhere," said someone. "Who the fuck are you?" The man spoke without taking his eyes from his starlight scope, spotting for his partner, who remained frozen and mute behind his Remington.

"I'm from Division. Looking for a sniper. Negro."

"Patterson's the only nigger we got. He's here somewhere. Now get the hell out of here. I'm busy."

In the flare light, Brady could see the watchtowers at each corner of the firebase, fifty yards apart. He started to run to the next tower, but Olivetti appeared out the shadows and grabbed him by the collar. "Get down, Brady! Spooky's about to unload!"

Three thousand feet above, the copilot lifted the red safety cover from the master arming switch and armed the three electric mini-guns in the cargo compartment of the AC-47. The Spooky pilot peered out the window through the round glass of a gun sight mounted beside his left shoulder. The sight was internally illuminated with a glowing red bull's-eye, the pipper, which he brought to bear on an area one hundred yards east of the drifting smoke.

Like the gun sight, the plane's electric gatling guns were fixed, bolted to the cargo bay floor. Only by banking and turning the entire aircraft could they be aimed. By flying at precisely 3,500 feet, at 110 knots, and at an angle of bank of 23 degrees, Spooky could deliver 6,000 rounds per minute onto his target. A split-second delay on the trigger or a half-degree error in the angle of bank, however, could deliver the gunship's ordnance upon friendly troops.

When the gunship's mini-guns came to life, their rate of fire was so rapid that the crack of each shot overlapped the next until the sound became a vicious howling, not the percussive rattle of a machine gun. A solid bridge of tracers raced from the muzzles, and inside the aircraft, spent cartridges sprayed into hoppers while the pilot concentrated on his gun sight, angle of bank, and airspeed.

Below, the volley sounded like heavy rain on a still pond as it shredded trees and drummed into the ground. The jungle shuddered; limbs fell, leaves disintegrated, and a sad breeze began to blow, carrying with it the gasps of dying men as audible as the screams that floated out of the darkness, part of the ventriloquism of war. Fog, residual moisture from obliterated plants, drifted from the impact zone.

The barrage ended.

Brady jumped to his feet before the stun wore off. His footsteps were the only noise, save the crackle of small fires among the trees and the belated plunge of branches.

The mini-guns growled again, somewhere above. At first, the men heard only the ominous whine of the guns, but then the bullets, which traveled slower than the speed of sound, pummeled the terrain ahead of them like a load of gravel dropped from a flying dump truck. And with each pass, the number of enemy dwindled.

The ARVN began to stir. A squad leader checked his men, counting heads. Radios hissed and orders were relayed. NCOs called for status reports while the grunts shouldered their weapons and stared into the drifting smoke.

Increasingly angry, Olivetti chased Brady through the shimmering light of successive flares toward the second tower. From the moment he had boarded Vandermeer's helicopter, a fury had been building within him. Olivetti had never experienced the delicious aftertaste of fear, when the adrenaline crash played with men's minds, converting horror to glory and pain to hubris. To him, war was not merely hell, it was a motherfucker, and Firebase Christine at that moment reminded him why he had vowed to do whatever it took to ensure that he never got this close to combat again. Division PIO was a skate job, a lifesaving job, and no civilian reporter was going to jeopardize Olivetti's best chance to survive the war. Then he noticed the drone of Spooky 80 leaving the AO, drifting away in the night.

"Spooky 80," called the RTO. "Keep up the illumination. We have another fire mission, over."

"Rogue, be advised that we have been directed back to CAP. Looks like a busy night ahead."

"Roger, Spooky, it's getting pretty busy right here. We have troops in contact. We have a fire mission, over."

"Stand by, Rogue." The tone was terse. The pilot contacted AF Liaison to confirm his mission. Troops in combat were the highest priority. Wolfe knew he would be back shortly, but he wanted fire support now, before the enemy could close the distance. If Charlie got inside the wire, even Spooky 80 could not shoot so close to his own troops. The fog was thickening, too. They needed the mini-guns now.

"Spooky 80," said Wolfe, taking the handset from his RTO. "This is the unit commander. I want fire support and I want it now! How copy!"

"Rogue, this is Spooky 80. Be advised, we have been directed to remain on CAP. We are not authorized to support you at this time. Good luck."

Wolfe threw down the handset. "Good luck, my ass." He ran to the north wall, where the assault would come. "Get me some goddamn flares!" he yelled as he exited the command bunker.

"Private Patterson, are you up here?"

"Who's asking?"

"My name's Brady. Are you Patterson?"

"Yeah." Patterson took his eyes from the night vision scope and looked down as Brady clambered into the watchtower. "What do you want?"

At the sound of Brady's voice, Captain Anderson looked behind him. He spotted Olivetti, then returned to the scope on his Remington.

"Pretty exposed position up here," said Brady.

"If you don't like it, go somewhere else," said Anderson. "Olivetti, get this reporter out of here."

"I hear you're the guy who shot General Cho yesterday." Brady climbed into the parapet and hunkered down inside the ring of sandbags. He directed his question to Patterson.

For several moments, neither sniper moved, their eyes glued to their scopes. Finally, Patterson turned and gave Brady a once-over, then returned to his business. "Never heard of him," said Patterson.

"He was an ARVN general. Very famous." Brady paused, then continued:

"He was shot yesterday in Cambodia by an American sniper, a black American sniper, according to my sources."

Patterson said nothing, his eyes glued to his scope.

"They tell me you are the only black sniper in the division."

"I didn't shoot nobody. I ain't got the nerves for it no more."

"Well, you got a pretty big price on your head for a sniper who doesn't shoot anyone. Charlie's giving you credit for General Cho, plus one of their own generals. And a girl. You didn't shoot a girl, I suppose. And her dog?"

"Nope."

"Olivetti, tell this asshole that if he doesn't get off my platform, I'll kick his ass off." Anderson spoke without moving his eye from the scope on his Remington. "We ain't got time for this shit."

"You heard the captain," said Patterson. "Now get away from me."

"Brady!" The call originated from the ground, and Brady leaned over the parapet. "Brady!" repeated Olivetti. "Get your ass outta there, or I'll take you back under arrest!"

"You're too late, Olivetti! I found my witness!"

"Hey!" Anderson whirled around and leveled his rifle at Brady. "We don't know what the hell you're talking about! Now you get off this platform, or the last thing you'll ever witness is a match grade bullet between your eyes!"

Olivetti was on the ladder, ready to step onto the watchtower landing, when an RPG-7 fishtailed out of the jungle and struck Anderson in the back. Instantly, the air filled with blood and internal organs, as the man disintegrated into an arc of gore spewed out across the firebase. The blast passed over Olivetti's head, except for a sliver of steel that passed through his chest, like a rabbit punch that left him gagging for breath and crumpled on the floor of the watchtower.

Brady took the full force of the sniper's viscera as Anderson came apart. It threw him to the floor, where he lay stunned, uncomprehending the sudden stark silence or the paste of entrails that smeared his face and hands and hair.

Under a collapsed pile of sandbags lay Patterson.

For a moment, everyone lay dazed, as confused as Brady, then taking inventory of their bodies, moving fingers and toes and waiting for pain to strike.

The rocket heralded the general assault, and across Firebase Christine, a crescendo of noise enveloped the base. Other rockets crisscrossed the firebase with vapor trails. Mortar rounds whistled in and exploded, shrapnel humming in the air. Small arms fire crackled in the trees. Tracers snapped overhead, a lethal swarm of AK-47 rounds streaking through the air. Expecting another attack from Spooky 80 above, with its bullets pulverizing every square inch of ground, the enemy commander, casualties mounting, no longer had the option to wait for the fog.

A trumpet sounded, eerie in the darkness, the signal to attack. Small men in khaki uniforms surged out of the trees, strangely silent, neither firing nor yelling. The defenders sensed their motion more than they saw them. The heavy *boom* of a sniper's Remington sent a starlight-guided bullet through the chest of the lead soldier, a sapper with a satchel full of explosives, while around him his comrades charged into the concertina wire he had been given the honor to destroy.

"Claymores!" yelled the American advisers, and the crack of detonations commenced, intermittent at first, then coalescing into an overwhelming roar. The mines blew gaps in the jungle, rending humans and plant life into voids of swirling smoke. Underlying it all, the brutal rattle of machine guns swept across the ground, tracers crossing in interlocking fields of fire.

A blizzard of projectiles cascaded over the doomed soldiers in the wire. Pitifully, they threw grenades and charged forward until a NATO round from an M-60 or a tiny .223 bullet from an M-16 or a claymore's BB or a swarm of fleshettes from a howitzer tore them apart and drove them to the ground screaming. It continued forever, ninety seconds, until the blasts slowed and tapered away. The machine guns stopped, glowing red in the darkness. The only remaining sounds were the cries of Vietnamese men calling for their mothers in Hanoi.

Uninjured, Brady was first to gather his senses. Amid the din of battle and despite the flying shrapnel that still peppered the remains of the watchtower, he took in the scene by the flickering light of the flares, still drifting, one after another, in their parachutes. Anderson was gone, except for his two legs, still joined at the waist. A bucket of blood now drained from them, pouring through the floorboards and saturating everything in the watchtower. Brady saw Olivetti sitting in one corner, holding his chest, an irritated look on his face. It was too dark to spot the rhythmic pumping of blood from a nick in his aorta.

Patterson still lay where he had fallen, and Brady first saw his eyes, wide and white, staring back at him in the darkness. "Motherfuck," said Patterson, and Brady heard him clearly despite the battle below.

Stragglers were in the wire now, and American voices gave commands to lower the muzzles of the 105s. Fleshette rounds swept the perimeter, like huge shotgun blasts clearing blackbirds from a telephone wire.

Brady crawled to Patterson and rolled him onto his back. His uniform was soaking wet.

"I have a wife," coughed Patterson, "and three kids." He wiped blood from his face as he spoke, his eyes bitter.

"Relax," said Brady, "you're gonna be OK." Brady had tended to wounded men before and he told them all they were going to be OK. Someone had told Brady the same thing when he had taken a round at Chosin. Everyone knew it was a bullshit statement, but everyone, even Brady, believed it when it was spoken to them. "You're gonna be OK."

"This ain't right."

"Where are you hit?" demanded Brady as he frisked Patterson down one side of his body and up the other.

"Man, I'm supposed to be answering the fuckin' phones."

"Patterson, for Christ's sake," persisted Brady, "you're OK. This isn't your blood." The newsman spoke calmly, matter-of-fact, while holding Patterson's hand. Patterson stopped babbling and slowly looked Brady in the eye. "You with me now?" asked Brady.

Patterson nodded.

"Help me with Olivetti."

The battle surged again as a wave of NVA rose from the wire, just beyond the berm that surrounded the firebase. While the first wave had died crossing the fields of fire, others had crawled under the plane of the fusillade to within twenty meters. Mortars now opened up from the jungle, ranging the outpost, then firing for effect. Shrapnel sang among the howitzer tubes, keeping heads down while men in the wire pulled the concertina apart with grappling hooks. They threw smoke grenades that mixed with the fog and the first squad of men came from nowhere as they tumbled upon the defenders in the darkness.

"In your holes!" ordered Wolfe. "Kill anything that moves outside your hole!" Ignoring his own orders, he raced for the command bunker, a huge target among the black-clad intruders scurrying now over the berm like shadowy ghosts in the gloom. He reached the command bunker and saw a shape running across the sandbags on the roof. Wolfe fired a three-round burst, then another, from his M-16 and the phantom leapt into the air with a scream, disappearing into the darkness. In the doorway, he yelled, "It's Wolfe! Gimme flares!" But there was silence within, the smell of cordite heavy and acrid in his nose, the telltale scent of grenades. Even in the darkness, the radio antennas above the roofline were a dead giveaway as to the bunker's function. He saw figures moving again and realized that sappers had come over the south berm also, scaling the muddy walls between the Punji stakes while the understrength company of Ruff Puffs fought the enemy to the north. They scurried about like mice now, loose in the interior of Christine, tossing satchel charges into the gun pits and bunkers.

Wolfe stepped away from the command bunker, following the sound of each burst from an AK-47, stalking the murky battlefield by ear, herding the fleeting figures toward the defenders' bunkers, or killing them himself should one run into him in the darkness.

"They inside the perimeter," said Patterson, alert to the different sounds of the battle, of AK-47 bursts below them. His M-14 was slippery with blood, but he tucked it under his arm, ready to shoot anyone coming up the ladder. "We gotta move. This ain't no place to be if they start throwing grenades up here."

Brady glanced at Olivetti, an unmoving figure in the darkness. "You lead," said Brady. As Patterson eased himself onto the platform's ladder, Brady grabbed Olivetti around the waist, dragging him after him in a clumsy embrace.

"I'm OK," said Olivetti, weak but clear, as Brady dropped him the last five feet to the ground.

The tower erupted into splinters as an AK-47 commenced firing a few feet away. Patterson fired at the sound of the weapon and was rewarded with the clatter of a gun hitting the ground. Patterson pulled the newsman by his shirt. "Stay with me." Olivetti struggled to his feet, but Brady grabbed him again, adrenaline augmenting his strength. They staggered in the darkness, tripping over bodies, until they ran headlong into three men in pith helmets, each group as surprised as the other. Patterson reacted first, however, executing a butt stroke with his rifle to one man's head, before snapping the barrel back in time to fire a point-blank bullet into another man's chest. Still, he sensed the presence of the third man, behind him now, raising his rifle toward his back. Then Brady released his grip on Olivetti and threw himself onto the man, clawing for the rifle like an animal. He found the man's face and drove his fingers deep into his eyes. The rifle fell from the screaming man's grasp as Brady now locked his elbow around the soldier's neck, jerking it again and again in an effort to snap it. But the man was strong, wrapping his own arms around Brady's throat. The two men froze in a rigid embrace, veins popping as they squeezed the life from each other. Patterson fell on him then, joining the struggle by twisting the man's head until Brady felt the vertebrae pop against his arm and the soldier fell limp. Brady released him then. The corpse fell chest-down on the ground, his face skyward.

They lay exhausted. Men around them screamed and threw grenades. Limbs, dirt, sandbags, and blood rained upon the dead and upon the living and upon those in between. The noise of the battle seemed muted, distant in the darkness, then passing nearby in a brief exchange. Finally the firing stopped. Patterson and Brady sat back-to-back in the darkness, AK-47s in their lap. Occasionally a scream interrupted the silence when two men found each other, only one of whom survived. A red flare sputtered in the fog, illuminating nothing, but turning the opaque fog the color of blood. Two hours later, the first streams of sunrise slowly warmed the upper layers of the fog, allowing a hint of light to filter to the steaming ground below.

Brady struggled to his knees and noticed Olivetti lying beside him, holding his chest with one hand, his M-16 with the other. Olivetti's eyes were alert, but he did not move except to lift his hand away from his chest to see if it was still bleeding, a pitiful look on his face. Olivetti carried a standard first-aid kit in his web gear, and Brady ripped opened the combat dressing. Patterson lifted Olivetti's head while Brady wrapped the bandage around Olivetti's torso. Brady took Olivetti's hand. "You're gonna make it," said the newsman. "You hear me, Olivetti?"

Olivetti smiled wanly. Patterson said, "You know this man?"

"He's my friend," Brady replied.

"He said you was under arrest."

"He's still my friend."

They sat in the swirling fog waiting for the daylight to penetrate further, unsure of what they might find.

"Hey, Patterson," said Brady, quiet and tired, but not a whisper. "What the hell happened with General Cho. I didn't come all the way out here just to save your worthless life, you know."

"You loyal," said Patterson. "You loyal to me and you loyal to this man, even though he says you under arrest. Why he tryin' to arrest you, man?"

"I'm loyal as a dog, Patterson."

Patterson said nothing for a moment, then muttered, "How'd you know about the dog?"

Brady turned. A shudder of excitement ran through him. This was the first real confirmation of any part of the story told to him in the alley in My Tho. "The girl lived long enough to tell her story."

Patterson bowed his head. "She died hard." Brady could barely hear him.

"What about the general?"

"My partner shot him."

Brady glanced up to the watchtower, where Anderson's remains still dripped through the bullet holes in the floorboards. "Your partner?"

"Not him," said Patterson. "Another one. He didn't make it neither."

"He's dead?" The disappointment in Brady's tone was obvious.

"MIA. Good as dead."

The newsman rocked back on his haunches, Vietnamese-style, his chin on his chest. *So the NVA was right,* he thought. *They really had wounded him. Probably killed him, only they didn't know it yet.* But Brady nevertheless had his witness, and he resolved to get the whole story from Patterson. "What were you doing in Cambodia?"

"Shooting generals," said Patterson, smirking mirthlessly at a response that might have been considered sardonic if they had been sitting at a bar at the EM Club.

"Hey, Brady."

The newsman recognized Olivetti's voice and turned. Patterson heard him, too.

"You should have minded your own business, Slick." Only then did Brady realize that Olivetti had raised the muzzle of his M-16 and his finger was on the trigger.

"No!" yelled Patterson. He slapped Olivetti's rifle away as Brady instinctively threw himself to the ground. As a dozen rounds from Olivetti's M-16 arced harmlessly over the firebase, Brady looked back to find Patterson standing over Olivetti, holding his weapon. Olivetti's eyes fluttered and closed.

"*Ai ban do?*" The call emanated from the gloom, difficult to locate. Patterson dropped to one knee and glanced at Brady, who pointed silently with his finger, his eyes wide and straining.

"Who fired that clip?" the man repeated, in English this time.

"Friendlies!" called Patterson. "Hold your fire." He recognized the voice.

"Stay put! I'll come to you. Don't shoot." A man emerged from the mist, scuttling quickly and low to the ground. He carried an M-16 in his right hand and a PRC-25 radio in the other. Bloodstained battle dressings wrapped his head and torso—he wore no shirt. A tattoo of a skull decorated his left arm below the elbow. "Sniper," he said when he recognized Patterson. He reached out his fist for a quick dap and, incredibly, he smiled.

"Sylvester," whispered Patterson. "Glad to see you, brother."

"He dead?" asked the soldier, nodding toward Olivetti.

"Not yet." Brady checked Olivetti's bandage, soggy with blood.

"What's the situation?" asked Patterson.

"Fuck if I know." A moan echoed quietly through the fog and they all tensed reflexively. "Charlie cleared out, I think, but there could be a hundred of those little fuckers inside the walls in this fog. I need you both on the perimeter right now. Follow me."

Patterson nodded and hopped to his feet.

"I'll stay with Olivetti," said Brady.

"No," said Sylvester, impatient. "I don't know what the fuck you're doing here, but this man is dead and you will be too if you don't get off your ass and grab a weapon."

"He'll make it if we can get medevac."

"There ain't gonna be no medevac," growled Sylvester softly, chewing his words as his patience ebbed. "The whole fucking country blew up last night. We got gooks sitting in the fuckin' living room at the American embassy in Saigon. We got no medevac, no air support, no nothing except fifteen scared shitless Ruff Puffs and us."

"I'm a civilian," Brady persisted. "I'm taking care of this man." He turned toward Olivetti and winced, pulled muscles in his neck reminding him of his struggle with the NVA soldier whose body now lay a few feet away. *Christ, what now,* he thought. Charlie in the embassy! The story of the war was unfolding in Saigon and he was stuck at Firebase Christine in the fog with a broken damn neck. Then he remembered Olivetti. "You don't need me," he said. "This battle's over."

"Fuck you," answered Sylvester, grabbing Patterson by his shirt and leading him to the berm.

"Where's Wolfe?" asked Patterson.

"Dead."

TWENTY-2

31.JANUARY.1968 > **04:03**

**Khet Prey Veng,
Cambodia**

The fog sidled thick among the bamboo and sycamore trunks, but withered in the moonlight just above the treetops. Monroe moved carefully, lest he weave back toward the trail. The rumble of battle was distinct, the explosions and rattle of machine guns rising and falling with the weak breeze that blew from east to west. He spotted flares beyond the horizon, illuminating the top of the fog layer eerily, the way the lights of Philadelphia would bounce off the underbelly of heavy clouds back home. The faint redolence of cordite wafted over the trees. He hoped the battle distracted the NVA trail watchers while he moved more quickly through the jungle.

Monroe heard the hideous whine of Spooky 80 and the intensity of the barrage diminished not long afterward. The fight did not end, however, but seemed only to ebb temporarily before surging back again, this time dominated by small arms fire, M-16s and AK-47s interrupted by grenades and more powerful satchel charges. At last the gunfire dribbled away, the last few desultory shots like the explosions of the last few kernels of popcorn at the bottom of the pan. He moved more carefully as silence returned to the jungle.

As dawn approached, the fog thickened slightly. Foot traffic on the trail increased, men moving faster and more noisily than before. Monroe stayed away from the path, but he could determine from the sounds of talking that traffic was moving in the opposite direction than it was the night before. There was movement in the forest ahead of him, people crashing through the trees making no effort to conceal themselves. Monroe froze in his tracks.

The sounds moved closer and Monroe readied his rifle, ready to spray anyone who might burst through the foliage and drifting fog. Shadowy forms drifted in the mist. Two soldiers lumbered into the jungle, a dead man in a poncho between them. They deposited the poncho on the ground and moved back to the trail, followed by other men with similar loads. Monroe dropped to one knee, then to his stomach, as the pile of corpses grew. Finally, the last remnants of the NVA battalion moved through and a pair of trail watchers moved in to cover the newly beaten path with living foliage. Expertly, they pulled branches and come-along vines across the fresh trail to the burial ground, hiding it completely as they backed their way out to the main path along the canal. In a week, the pile would be reduced to bones by an army of vultures, wild pigs, insects, and rats. And with the monsoon, this land would be underwater and even the bones would be washed away.

The jungle was never more silent, the wild creatures holding their breath in the presence of one hundred human dead stacked like lumber. Only Monroe moved, approaching the grisly pile reluctantly, yet compelled toward it by some ghastly fascination. Unlike the men Monroe had killed with a single bullet, these men were torn to shreds by shrapnel or fleshettes from the howitzers at Firebase Christine. They were not truly a pile of corpses as much as a salad of body parts: torsos, intestines, legs, and arms. Skulls blown apart like coconuts. Monroe stared at the chest-high pile and listened to the dripping blood.

The sun broke over the horizon and the fog thinned slightly, the sight too cruel even for the Silent Men. A shaft of light created a tiny rainbow as it filtered through the tendrils of mist. Nothing moved but the daylight, dancing across the luminous wounds. A sudden glint reflected back to Monroe's eyes. A shaving mirror had fallen from the pocket of one corpse and it lay twinkling on the ground.

Mirrors served the enemy better than radios, for wireless communications required batteries that died in sodden monsoons and were too heavy to lug down the Ho Chi Minh trail by the thousands. So Charlie signaled with mirrors, except in the presence of snipers, who tended to aim at them. He could probably find a dozen more mirrors in the bloody pockets of the dead men in front of him. But while the NVA signaled carefully across open rice paddies and rivers, ever vigilant to avoid bouncing a sunray upward where American aircraft might spot it, this was precisely what Monroe resolved to do.

He tried to move quickly and be gone, but revulsion held him back. The hair on Monroe's arms bristled as he crept up on them, men who would never see or hear him regardless of how much noise he made. But as he reached carefully for the mirror, a hand swatted him away, an arm reaching from the pile as if to slap his wrist for robbing the dead. Monroe recoiled, leaping backward and flailing at the air with his fists. He drew his knife reflexively and froze in a combat crouch. But there was no attacker, only the thinning fog shifting among the trees. The arm lay on the ground, attached to no one, the fingers reaching of their own accord toward the mirror. Monroe saw then that the entire pile was moving, writhing with rigor mortis, jaws closing, hands clenching, eyes opening, everything stiffening with the congealing of blood. Fear enveloped him, covered him, drawing back his nostrils and lips, revealing his teeth. He collapsed to his knees, adrenaline replaced by dawning hysteria as a sob burst from his chest. His lips trembled and he placed his forehead to the ground, rocking for several minutes back and forth on his knees.

He sat up at last, angry at his own timidity, his wild eyes riveted upon the mirror. With desperate willpower, he forced himself to approach the wriggling mass and pluck it from the ground.

TWEИTY-3

Firebase Christine

The dust-offs found precious few WIAs, for hand-to-hand combat was not like the indifferent nature of machine gun fire or shrapnel, where a projectile would just as likely hit an arm as it would cut a jugular. Hand-to-hand was personal—and final. The first chopper arrived at noon. The fog had cleared, but the battles at Soc Trang and Binh Thuy had kept the birds on the ground as the pilots themselves killed NVA sappers under the wings of their own aircraft. Eight grunts, still filthy from their fighting at the airfields, some covered in the blood of friends or enemies, sat on the floor of the inbound Huey, legs dangling, ready to un-ass. They had no packs, but they cinched their vests and helmet straps tight and everyone carried extra ammo and water. They were a mean bunch with bloodshot eyes and powder-stained faces. Among them, in crisp fatigues and a holstered sidearm, sat Colonel Lyons.

Vandermeer had been surprised when Lyons volunteered to lead the relief of Christine. Intel reeled from a night of ugly surprises throughout the delta. NVA invested Can Tho, as well as My Tho, Tra Vinh, Ben Tre, Vinh Long, Moc Hoa, and Tieu Can. Every airfield under Vandermeer's command had been mortared and most had been assaulted. Damage had been minor—thank God for the strategic reserve—but the perimeters of many bases had been penetrated, with Charlie roaming the runways and tossing satchel charges into any parked aircraft. The fog and low ceilings had hampered air support. *Goddamn the Air Force,* thought Vandermeer. Spooky had flown CAP all night—called off for whatever goddamn reason from Christine—where they flew in circles waiting for the fog to break, fearful of firing onto allied troops. G-2 ran around like headless chickens, with Lyons leading the circle jerk. Vandermeer surmised that Lyons wanted to redeem himself by exposing himself, however slightly, to danger. Men did strange things when humiliated. Vandermeer let him go.

Visibility on the ground improved, though the fog had merely risen into a thick ceiling at one hundred feet.

The pilot flew upriver above the clouds, navigating by dead reckoning and visual observation of the river through breaks in the undercast. Below him, barely ten feet from the skids, the fog lay so thick and immobile that he felt he could get out and walk on it. There was no conversation, as both pilot and copilot monitored the radios, talking to Firebase Christine, where Sylvester still handled the PRC-25 and directed the chopper with cool expertise. The pilot glanced at the fuel gauge, and quickly calculated their remaining loiter time. Five minutes.

The pilot thumbed his radio key. "Rogue 20, this is Dust-off 10. We're coming down. Vector me in by the sound of my engine. Can you hear me?"

"Roger!"

The normal LZ, the sandbar, was outside the perimeter, too far and too dangerous to carry wounded men. Charlie could still be out there.

Sylvester stood by with his compass open. "Dust-off, I hear you. Come north. Stand by for a vector." He shot a back-azimuth toward the sound of the helicopter. "Three four zero."

"Vector 340."

The helicopter came closer.

"Two nine zero," said the RTO.

The helicopter thundered somewhere overhead.

Dust-off 10 eased into the clouds. The medic crossed himself.

"You're drifting," warned Rogue 20. "Vector 140. Twenty feet."

The aircraft slipped sideways, Lyons appreciated the pilot's skill. The altimeter indicated fifty feet. The tension in the cockpit was electric. The pilot rolled off all power and bottomed the collective, allowing the helicopter to drop straight down, hitting firmly, but under control. The men un-assed immediately as Sylvester directed them to fighting positions around the perimeter. To the medic, he waved at four men lying nearby, Olivetti among them.

"Get them on board," he said, "but don't leave without me." He pointed to his wounds. "This is my third Heart." Three Purple Hearts meant an automatic ticket home, and Sylvester had every intention of holding the Army to that bargain. Lyons watched him, surprised by the leadership skills of young ruffians. *This one*, he thought, *is more at home here than he will be in Anytown, USA.*

"What happened last night?" he asked.

"Hell if I know, Colonel," replied Sylvester, curious that an officer of such rank would be so interested in the plight of a worthless firebase like Christine. "We had 'em dead until some son of a bitch called off Spooky and left us with no illumination and no air support. Fucking Ruffs ain't worth a shit, even when we have a full complement, and half of 'em were home with mama-san. Still there, probably. Charlie just snuck through the back door, and once he got into the compound all hell broke loose." Sylvester spat and added, "Fuckin' Air Force."

Lyons spotted Brady as he assisted the medic to lift Olivetti onto the dust-off. "You, on the chopper."

"Get the wounded out first, Colonel. I can wait." Brady was sure that his neck was broken, but he needed to talk with Patterson. He hid the pain as he stood up to face Lyons.

"Let's go," yelled the medic.

"Get on board," repeated Lyons. "Right now, Brady." He drew his sidearm.

Sylvester raised an eyebrow, but headed to the UH-1, the RPMs rising again with an increasing whine. Lyons followed, pushing Brady ahead of him. Brady looked wistfully back to Patterson, still manning his position on the wall, and waved. "I got my story, Colonel. I know all about General Cho."

"You don't know a damn thing."

The dust-off lifted off in a tornado of dust and disappeared back into the cloud bank.

The medevac billowed onto the hospital LZ at noon. Brady hopped from the bloody cargo deck and waved away the medics who rushed to assist him. A sprained neck was nothing to worry about and even a fractured vertebra wouldn't kill him. He didn't need a doctor to test for nerve damage or paralysis; he could move his fingers and toes and he had all the sensation he could stand. He watched the stretcher teams unload their cargo as Lyons disembarked next to him.

"What was Cho doing in Cambodia?" asked Brady.

This man has nine lives, thought Lyons. Whatever plans Boettcher had cooked up to eliminate Brady had backfired, and now someone had to talk to him. "We cannot verify where General Cho was when he was shot down, Brady. We have not recovered his body and the VC probably have it. This is all there is to your story. This bullshit about peace talks is propaganda, and your commie friends are playing you for a dupe. I would think very, very hard before you publish anything of that nature. You've already been made a fool of once."

Brady turned and glared at him.

"The CIA set you up last year because they didn't like your reporting. Now you're being set up by the VC," added Lyons. "Why do you think they chose you? 'Cause you're a sucker."

Brady said nothing about Patterson, although Lyons's suggestion of a setup nagged at him. "You may be right, Colonel." Brady sensed an opportunity to establish rapport. He had dealt with martinets like Lyons in a dozen other armies and he had discovered that a little humility was effective in winning them over. "I have to be careful."

Lyons nodded as the last of the wounded were whisked away. The Huey's RPMs began to climb again as the pilot received orders via radio for his next dust-off mission. Lyons led Brady away from the rising dust cloud, raising his voice against the clamor. "You're missing the biggest story of the war, Brady. Today is Tet, Vietnamese new year, and Charlie just sacked half the country last night while the ARVN went home to celebrate. Every reporter in the country is under fire today, filing the story that will win their Pulitzer. And you're missing it."

Brady had first heard of the Tet offensive from Sylvester, now Lyons. He followed the colonel to a jeep beside the helipad, where a driver waited. "Just how big is this offensive?"

"Massive. We underestimated it in a big way. Saigon is a combat zone. We're sending in troops wherever we can find them, but most of our own installations are under attack also." Lyons took the passenger seat of the jeep and offered no invitation for Brady to join him. He leaned closer to Brady and said quietly, "I'll tell you what, Brady. The story about Cho is a dead end for you personally and professionally, as well as a propaganda problem for me. You let this one go, and I'll give you the story that will get you back on the staff at the *Times*."

"What are you talking about?"

"This Tet offensive. The battle for Saigon. Charlie threw a lot of manpower into taking over the city and the government. President Thieu's offices and residence were both attacked. Thing is, the President isn't even in Saigon. You want to be the only reporter in the country to know where he is?"

"Of course," said Brady, curious but suspicious.

"I want you out of my hair." Lyons eyed him hard, as if to communicate that this was a no shit deal, and he wouldn't tolerate any double cross.

"I'm a whore like every other reporter in this war. Give me something worth chasing, and I'm gone."

"The President of South Vietnam is a couple of klicks down the road from here, under the protection of the 9th ARVN Division at My Tho," said Lyons. "He was never in Saigon. There's your scoop, Brady. Go get an interview."

There was a sort of Oriental deceit about Lyons, as there seemed to be with every Intel spook Brady encountered. But though Lyons strove for inscrutability, he had not mastered the art of gentle misdirection. The Vietnamese never told the whole truth and never told a bald-faced lie. But Lyons simply lied, except when he told the truth. Lyons had lied about Cho because the truth bore embarrassing consequences, and because verification would be difficult and because he thought he could get away with it. Brady considered what Lyons had told him about Thieu and tried to figure what Lyons might gain by sending Brady on a wild-goose chase to My Tho. This time, Lyons might be telling the truth.

The two men stared at each other until Brady smiled and offered Lyons a casual Boy Scout salute. Lyons nodded and drove away in a cloud of dust.

Sylvester waited for the stretcher cases to precede him, then walked to triage. His legs failed him as he walked through the door. He would awake twenty-four hours later, on a C-141 bound for the United States.

The stretchers entered the triage tent into a chamber of controlled horror. Other battles were in progress farther north, and casualties accumulated faster than the triage staff could handle. Medics and technicians scrambled among the wounded and dying, tending to them as they came off the choppers, bloody, screaming, still dressed in their battle gear, filthy tourniquets throttling raw stumps. Some men were conscious, apparently alert and unconcerned, clutching their bandages to their abdomens, lest their intestines fall out. One man coughed blood through a dirty tube that stuck from his throat, his tracheotomy performed with a bayonet and the shaft of a Bic pen. Dead men, grenades still clipped to their web gear, lay in a row along one side of the tent.

The triage officer, a female captain, evaluated each casualty as he came through the tent flap. She was hard core, with a decade of pain under her belt. She saved men and doomed them, dozens every hour, a woman able to sleep at night only with the help of too much booze.

"O.R., stat!" The stretcher bearers carried the first WIA directly to the operating room, where surgeons would stop the bleeding, sew up wounds, amputate whatever necessary, and stabilize the wounded man's condition. Lifesaving work only, nothing fancy. Just keep the guy alive long enough to get him to a real hospital in Japan or Okinawa or Hawaii.

Two men were ambulatory. They would live whether they got immediate surgery or not. The nurse sent them to the end of the line.

The stretcher bearers brought another body to her. She paused. Olivetti, she noted, was in one piece; pale, probably in shock. Almost automatically, she ordered him to a waiting operating room. Then she noticed the blood. Olivetti almost floated in it, wavelets sloshed around him and splashed onto the wooden floor. "Wait." The stretcher bearers stopped and she took his pulse, first his wrist, then his neck. Zero. She pulled his eyelids open and noted his pupils did not respond to the light. Even as she examined him, Olivetti seemed to turn color, the mottled pallor of gray, the promise of death from exsanguination. Emotionlessly, she tagged him "expectant," and motioned for him to be left with the others that lined the edge of the tent.

The stretcher bearer, a huge black medic with no small amount of medical knowledge himself, stared imploringly at the nurse. He felt she was always too quick to tag them, even too quick to pronounce men dead. He believed a lot of men had died in their body bags. "Captain," he said quietly.

"He's bled out," she said.

The medic squeezed Olivetti's arm. Enough blood pressure existed to keep the arteries from collapsing. They could still get an IV into him. "His veins are good, Captain."

Angry at the medic for contradicting her, and angry at the world for having to make the decisions she did, the woman grabbed a chest tube and pushed the medic aside. Almost brutally, she thrust the tube into Olivetti's lung. Six hundred ccs of frothy blood flooded out, pushed by air pressure trapped in the lung. Olivetti was simultaneously bleeding to death and drowning in his own blood. He gasped.

"Infuse him," she said.

"Yes, ma'am," he replied. Maybe she wasn't the Grim Reaper after all.

The medic checked Olivetti's dog tags for blood type and sent his partner to the refrigerator for plasma, and lots of it. As he knelt over Olivetti, the shadow of a man fell across him. He looked up.

"Is he going to make it?" asked Colonel Boettcher.

"Hard to say, sir."

Boettcher lowered himself to one knee and took Olivetti's hand. "Anything I can do? He's one of mine."

"Start CPR."

The other stretcher bearer returned with plasma in two plastic bags, each with a syringe. The medic inserted the first needle into Olivetti's arm and handed the bag to his assistant. "Squeeze the bag, brother. Hard as you can. We gotta fill this guy up." He inserted the other needles into other veins and the men pumped two liters of cold plasma into Olivetti while Boettcher pressed rhythmically upon his chest.

The black medic recognized Boettcher as Vandermeer's aide, and knew him to be a son of a bitch. He never thought he'd see the day that Boettcher would get as bloody tending casualties as the Old Man.

Olivetti's eyes fluttered open.

"Captain!" yelled the medic. "Get an O.R. ready!"

The nurse dashed to them and saw Olivetti's eyes open and close, and his body spasm. Unintelligible sounds came from his mouth. "My God," she said, as she ran to check on the operating rooms.

"Olivetti," said Boettcher. "It's me."

"Forget it, Colonel. He ain't gonna talk to you. And we gotta prep him."

"Colonel." Olivetti's voice was barely audible, a croak. He shivered so badly from the newly infused refrigerated blood that wavelets of blood sloshed back and forth in the stretcher.

"Hang on, son." Boettcher turned to the medic. "You're going to make it."

"Brady," said Olivetti.

Boettcher frowned, unsure that he had heard correctly. He put his ear close to Olivetti's mouth.

"Brady knows everything."

The nurse reappeared. "Get him up. Let's go." As Boettcher stood to assist, she said, "This is as far as you go, Colonel. I'll call you personally as soon as we know anything at all."

Numb, Boettcher watched Olivetti disappear into O.R. Number 1. Activity swirled around him. He recalled a prayer for Olivetti and thought to get the chaplain to his side in case he needed last rites. Most Italians were Catholic, he reasoned, realizing that he knew virtually nothing of a personal nature about the man.

As he drove back to HQ, Boettcher wondered, *Where the hell is Brady, and what does the son of a bitch know?*

TWENTY-4

10:00

**Khet Prey Veng,
Cambodia**

The fog cooked away by 1000, evaporated by a ferocious sun under a pale sky. A few feathers of cirrus lingered from some distant thunderstorm, and a solitary vulture hovered in the superheated updrafts. Monroe sought out the deepest shade he could find, but the jungle was ragged, a copse of wild rambutan trees and clumps of young bamboo claiming abandoned fields. The terrain was familiar, for he and Patterson had crossed it two nights before, feeling their way through the overgrown irrigation channels where moisture still seeped up from the water table. Vegetation grew thicker there, and Monroe crawled slowly toward it, remembering the water. Distances seemed greater by daylight, and he fought the temptation to run, moving six inches at a time, slowly, slowly. The excruciating pain of his concussion had abated, replaced now with the throb of dehydration. The sun reached its zenith at noon, just as Monroe slithered under the first branches of a mangrove tree and dropped exhausted into the tangle of shrubbery in the abandoned channel.

Protected from the sun and close to the shallow water table, the bottom of the ditch was muddy. Monroe scooped away a handful of muck and thrust his face into the hole, drinking the filthy water greedily. He told himself to be alert, to listen carefully for movement, for his back trail was not well covered. He would be easy to track, but the relief was too great as he sucked water from the ground as fast as the hole refilled.

His thirst sated, Monroe made no effort to move. He simply stopped drinking, wallowing facedown in the cool mud. Seduced by a canteenful of foul water, his thoughts ranged beyond concern for the enemy, his back trail, food, water, pain, and fear. He wondered about his mother again, and whether she was sober enough this week to take care of his thirteen-year-old sister. She was a good mother, sometimes. *She'd kick Charlie's ass,* he thought, and he began to cry.

The reality hit him then that he would not see her again. Lost snipers never came back; their MIA status was permanent. He had been fooling himself since the moment he dragged himself from the canal, determined to make his way back to the rally point now barely two thousand yards away. He had taken the mirror for the purpose of signaling the men who would be waiting for him there, except there would be no one to greet him. Monroe knew that now as he had known it all along, and the futility of it filled him with despair. He rolled onto his back and sobbed quietly, dry-eyed, too dehydrated to excrete tears. And as he cried he stuffed his mouth with the stolen rice and fish, the instinct to survive competing with the temptation to die.

The faint sounds of engines alerted him, UH-1s over the horizon. *Firebase Christine,* he thought. *They must have held.* But he knew no Hueys would return to a combat zone without something overhead. FACs would be in the air, probably checking Charlie's retreat and ready to call down air strikes on anything moving on the Vietnamese side of the border. Charlie was home free once he crossed the canal.

Monroe rolled onto his stomach and crawled cautiously to the edge of the ditch. He scanned eastward until he spotted it.

Cowpoke 20 flew his Cessna O-2 at two thousand feet above the Vinh Te Canal, close enough to attract small arms fire if Charlie was foolish enough to shoot, but high enough that it would take a lucky shot to bring him down. A dangerous game nevertheless; a hundred men could fire a thousand rounds in five seconds, and it only took one of them to take out the single engine that powered the tiny aircraft. But Charlie rarely fired at the Cowpokes, forward air controllers for the division, for the flimsy aircraft had more firepower at their disposal than all the artillery in the delta. First Lieutenant Lou Narvick had been assigned his call sign three months before. Since then, he had become increasingly aggressive in his flight patterns, almost disappointed that he had yet to experience the thrill of watching a tracer float by his wingtip. He searched now for the remains of the NVA battalion that had attacked Firebase Christine. Air Force Liaison held some fast movers on the ground at Binh Thuy and had a pair of Skyraiders circling on combat air patrol loaded with napalm and HE, just in case Cowpoke 20 spotted anything moving on the water. Also during his mission briefing, almost as an afterthought, the director of Ops had been told to keep alert for possible friendlies along the canal. *Must have been a wild night,* he thought, *if they've got troops scattered out this far.*

Narvick eased down to fifteen hundred feet.

Monroe noted the angle of the sun, although the angle of the aircraft above the horizon was more important. The plane flew low, increasing the danger that the reflected beam could be spotted by anyone on the ground. With luck, Charlie would assume the flash came from one of his own. But so would the FAC. If the pilot was foolish enough to investigate, however, Monroe resolved to show himself. No Negroes fought for the NVA. He eased himself from the shadows of his hide and aimed the reflected sunbeam at the tiny target just above the milky blue horizon.

Narvick had fixed his eyes upon the overgrowth along the edges of the Vinh Te Canal when the pinprick of light winked in his peripheral vision, a thousand yards into Cambodia. At first he imagined he had spotted a routine enemy signal, except the light followed him as he banked into a 180-degree turn. *Arrogant prick,* thought Narvick. He considered calling in Buggy 15 and Buggy 18, circling just beyond the horizon at fifteen thousand feet, two Skyraiders loaded with napalm, but instead he followed procedure and thumbed the microphone button on his yoke.

"Reliable Twelve, this is Cowpoke 20, over." He forced extra boredom into his voice in case Charlie was listening, just to let the little bastards know that some chump with a mirror wasn't going to get under his skin.

"Go ahead, Cowpoke 20. This is Reliable Twelve, over." The RTO at the fire support coordination center played along, laying on the boredom as thick as Narvick.

"Reliable, this is Cowpoke 20. I've got some gook flashing a mirror at me about half a klick west of grid coordinates 81142266. Am I cleared to nuke him, over?"

"Stand by, Cowpoke. I'm checking with ARVN." The RTO signaled for the fire support duty officer and the ARVN liaison officer. Bombing missions required the approval of all friendly forces, lest the allies mistake each other for the enemy. Unfortunately, the ARVN officers rarely gave authority to attack, figuring that the Americans couldn't differentiate between one Vietnamese and another and would just as soon kill them all. The Americans suspected the ARVN advisers were no better at identifying the enemy than they were and thus denied permission to attack anyone. The RTO explained the situation briefly and waited to relay the denial to Cowpoke 20.

Captain Thanh, the son of a Saigonese aristocrat, commissioned in the South Vietnamese Air Force by virtue of his midlevel connections, presented a proper appearance in his uniform. His servant shined his boots to a crisp shine every night. But his soldiering skills were a matter of ridicule among the American officers who staffed the division air support center. Thanh had earned the assignment as the Vietnamese air liaison officer because he knew important people and because he spoke English. That he knew nothing about airplanes never seemed relevant.

Thanh accepted the mission request from the RTO and turned to the huge map of the Division AO on the control center wall, where he pretended to plot the coordinates provided by Cowpoke 20. The map marked the locations of all friendly units, updated constantly in grease pencil by a pair of GIs to whom the dozen RTOs passed a steady stream of unit position reports. The RTOs reported troop locations as grid coordinates to ensure a minimal level of operational security. The grid coordinates were changeable, like a code, understood only by those with identical charts. Positions were never reported in the clear, to prevent the NVA from listening in and plotting an ambush.

"Denied," said Thanh. "Possible ARVN forces in the area."

The American RTOs winked at each other, for they knew there were no friendly troops anywhere near the spot reported by Cowpoke 20. There were nothing but NVA in Cambodia. Ironically, it was the right decision for the wrong reason: Cambodia remained off-limits.

"Cowpoke 20," purred the RTO. "Mission denied."

"Roger copy." Narvick had expected the denial. He banked right, homeward, glad to have the damned reflection out of his eyes.

Monroe dropped his head to the ground, convinced that his signals had served no purpose but to give away his position to the enemy. They would come after him soon. He considered his options: surrender or die, which for snipers were one and the same. What could he offer them, he wondered, that would be worth his life?

In the air support center, Captain Dale Freidlow watched his Vietnamese counterpart with the same amusement as did the enlisted RTOs. Something troubled him, however, and he reached into his pocket for the OD notepad that all of Vandermeer's staff carried. He reviewed what he had written at the morning staff meeting and reached for the phone. "Colonel Ingram," he ordered, and the switchboard operator put him through to the director of Ops. Freidlow spoke briefly, then hung up with a crisp, "Yes, sir!"

Captain Freidlow, though an Air Force liaison officer serving in an Army division that considered sister services to be sissies, received none of the ridicule of his Vietnamese counterpart. Freidlow had earned a Purple Heart and a DFC in an F-4 over Hanoi. Grounded now due to injuries, he commanded respect from the men in the control center as well as the jocks in the air.

"RTO! Get Cowpoke 20 for me." Freidlow slipped on a headset and checked his watch. Plenty of daylight left. He heard Cowpoke 20 respond to the RTO's call and Freidlow took over the conversation.

"Cowpoke 20, this is Reliable Twelve. Go to backup freq now."

Narvick lifted his eyebrows with interest and twisted the frequency dial on his radio. "Reliable, this is Cowpoke 20." The reserve frequency added another level of security to the conversation, and Narvick wondered what was up.

"Cowpoke 20, we have reason to believe that the signal you have received may be friendly. Can you investigate, over?"

"Reliable, this is Cowpoke 20. Request you check the coordinates I gave you, over." *It's in fucking Cambodia, you moron.*

"Cowpoke 20, we have reviewed the location carefully, and we request you investigate immediately."

Narvick nodded. *Well I'll be damned,* he thought. *Poor bastard must be CIA or something.* "Roger, Reliable. Stand by for ID."

"Cowpoke, this is Reliable. Don't get shot down."

Narvick broke squelch on his mike, indicating he had heard the message and understood. One MIA in Cambodia was bad enough; Division didn't want another one. The pucker factor had just gone way up.

Monroe barely heard the pathetic whine of the Cessna engine before the O-2 shot over him, rustling the rubbery leaves of the small banana trees that grew above the rogue undergrowth in the drainage canal where he lay. He fumbled for the mirror, but Cowpoke 20 passed him in a flash, banking high and hard into a second pass from the opposite direction. Narvick was scared now, and frustrated. He had seen no one in the fields or under the brush in the overgrown ditches, and the threat of ground fire was far too real at treetop level, even for a man yearning for the thrill of dodging tracers.

Monroe pulled himself back into the undergrowth and jumped to the opposite side of the ditch. As he crawled into the sunlight, the afternoon rays hit him in the eyes, which was good, for he could signal from deeper in the shadows. He found Cowpoke 20 as Narvick rolled out of his bank at fifteen hundred feet, and bounced his signal squarely off the O-2's windshield.

"Gotcha!" gasped Narvick, fighting the moderate G forces generated by his turn. *Now let's see who the fuck you are.* He pushed the nose down as Monroe's flash blinded him insistently. He heard popping sounds unlike anything he had heard on previous missions. He knew the sounds of bullets instinctively, however, as they punched little holes in his fuselage. And then he saw the tracers arcing past his wingtips, lazy green fireflies, silent, ballistic, slow as they approached but terrifyingly fast as they whipped by. Already at max throttle, he yanked on the yoke, fighting for altitude, as much as 175 knots would give him.

Cowpoke 20 leveled at twenty-five hundred feet, still too low, but approaching stall speed. The tracers were still with him, but not so close, behind him now as he raced back across the Vinh Te Canal.

"Reliable Twelve, this is Cowpoke 20."

"Go ahead, Cowpoke." Freidlow was still working the mike.

"Reliable Twelve, I just took a few rounds in the fuselage. Damage unknown. All systems normal. I am not declaring an emergency at this time. I am inbound, ETA 1330. How copy?"

"Cowpoke 20, Reliable Twelve. Copy all. Understand the signal was not friendly. Confirm."

"Reliable, whoever was signaling stayed with me, but the ground fire came from elsewhere. I think I surprised them, because they opened up on me late. They could have blasted me at treetop level, but I was in a turn at fifteen hundred feet before I saw any tracers. It was no ambush, over."

"Roger copy, Cowpoke. Report to flight ops for debriefing as soon as you shut down. Reliable Twelve out." Freidlow handed the headset and microphone back to the RTO and reached for the field phone.

TWENTY-5

13:09

9th Division Headquarters, Dong Tam

V andermeer kicked the metal trash can by his desk, sending it ricocheting against the walls, the contents spewing around the room. Unlike many of his best officers, who could let loose torrents of high-decibel obscenities when the situation called for it, Vandermeer had always managed to get his points across with a piercing look and a measured growl. But he yelled now, ripping Boettcher as if he were a West Point plebe, indifferent to who might hear through the office door.

"You sent Olivetti out there with instructions to kill Brady? For what? To save my ass? Well, my ass cost that kid his life, and Brady still got his goddamned story!"

Boettcher stood at attention in front of the general's desk. He had never seen Vandermeer so inflamed, spittle flying from his lips. "Olivetti's a good kid, sir. He'll pull through."

"They're all good kids." Vandermeer spoke without yelling, now only bitterness in his voice. "Olivetti died on the operating table thirty minutes ago."

I just left Olivetti thirty minutes ago, thought Boettcher. *How can you know already?* Boettcher prided himself on his back-channel networks. It bothered him that Vandermeer had a network of his own. *If Olivetti hadn't fucked up, you'd be thanking me, recommending him for a Bronze Star,* he thought. But the aide held his tongue. A knock on the door interrupted his thoughts.

"Come in!" barked Vandermeer, finished with the conversation.

Colonel Lyons stepped in. "General, I have news."

"Good." Vandermeer moved to his locker, where he reached for his web gear and flight helmet. "Ron, alert the crew to start cranking. I'll be along in a moment." To Lyons, he added, "What have you got, Colonel."

"Brady is out of our hair for the time being, sir, but there is a new development regarding the missing sniper."

Vandermeer stared at him in disbelief. "We have over sixty-five engagements ongoing right now in our AO and my G-2 is here to tell me about a missing sniper and a newspaper reporter. Is it too much to ask, Colonel, for a little combat intelligence?"

There was no suitable response, for the Intel community throughout the chain of command from MACV down to unit level had utterly failed to predict the intensity of the enemy offensive. Even now, the G-2 shop offered little besides recording the locations where attacks commenced and alerting Colonel Ingram of which units needed help. Ingram, in the DOC handling the defense, had been taking in the G-2's reports all day, using the information to slowly organize a series of counterattacks that would ultimately rout the enemy through the use of armor and close air support. Vandermeer felt useless and blind while his subordinates supervised the situation. He headed for the door, intent upon visiting the battleground himself, gathering his own intelligence while the spooks in G-2 sat on their asses and waited for phones to ring.

"Monroe is alive, sir."

Vandermeer stopped dead in his tracks and ran his fingers through his hair, pressing his palms against his temple, as if to keep his head from exploding.

"We received a signal about an hour ago," continued Lyons. "A FAC flying along the border checking for stragglers saw flashes from the ground, probably a signal mirror. It could have been a trap, but we don't think so."

"Why not?"

"While going to investigate, the FAC took a round through the floor a thousand yards from the signal at fifteen hundred feet altitude. If it was an ambush, they'd wait until he was directly overhead and hit him with everything they had. Charlie didn't want to shoot that O-2 down; they've got enough trouble right now without gunships coming in to cover a downed FAC pilot. They just want to be left alone right now. All of which leads us to believe that the person who signaled that chopper was Monroe."

"What are we doing about it?" asked Vandermeer.

"Colonel Ingram is putting together a SAR team. But I advised him that we have higher priorities right now than to go off trying to rescue a single soldier while enemy activity is at an unprecedented level."

"What would you know about enemy activity?"

Lyons accepted the rebuke. "General, I'll admit that the entire G-2 staff all the way to MACV has egg on our face right now. But you can't allow your dissatisfaction with me to cloud your judgment."

"Egg on your face and blood on your hands."

"Sir, it's only natural that you should feel guilty about Olivetti. But don't try to assuage your guilt by sending other men out on an ill-advised mission to rescue a man who can only complicate the situation."

"I *assuage* my guilt by flying too close to the enemy. What I want to know, Colonel, is how you *assuage* yours." Vandermeer stalked past his G-2 and walked out the door.

The division tactical operations center was noisy when Vandermeer entered, but calm. The radios reported sitreps, position reports, body counts, and calls for dust-off or fire support. Runners scurried in and out with messages or updated any of the huge maps that lined the walls. Thirty men operated in the DTOC under the command of Colonel Ingram, coordinating the efforts of Div Arty, G-3, Air Force, and Navy to accomplish missions as small as a Huey mail run and as large as the current division defense of the Tet attack. Vandermeer envied Ingram as he watched his G-3 preside over the business at hand. Ingram would have his star someday because he had the soul of a commander. He knew what he was about and overtook the will of others almost without effort, despite a gruff exterior that tolerated neither nonsense nor ego. Vandermeer had been that way once, though smoother and more polished. *Ops is straightforward,* he thought. *Men followed me because I knew where I was going.* He had not felt as sure of himself since.

Vandermeer was startled when the guard escorted two soldiers into the room behind him, both filthy enough to attract the stares of the men staffing the DTOC. Weapons were not permitted inside the room, but these men were armed, one with a Remington, the other with an M-14. Ingram spotted them instantly and quickly waved them into the map-walled conference room adjacent to his office. He approached Vandermeer and said, "Follow me, sir. These are the boys going to get our lost man back."

The room was small, barely ten feet square, crowded with two officers and the two heavily armed men. Vandermeer could smell the cordite on their uniforms. The blood had not yet begun to stink.

"Sit down," ordered Ingram. "When's the last time you had any sleep?"

"Twenty-four," said Revelle.

"Two days," said Patterson, although he wasn't sure. He spoke in a quiet deadpan while his eyes took in the room methodically, by habit, one object at a time. They settled on Vandermeer, held there when Patterson felt the general staring back at him. Vandermeer responded with a subtle nod and Patterson nodded back. No one caught it except Revelle, another sniper trained to observe the imperceptible.

"You'll catch a couple hours on the boat," said Ingram. He added, "I'm sorry about Captain Anderson."

The snipers nodded and glanced at Vandermeer, whose face turned to stone. No one had informed him that Anderson was dead.

Ingram got right to the point. "We have reason to believe that Private Monroe is alive somewhere north of the Vinh Te Canal. He apparently signaled a forward air controller at approximately this position, here." He plucked a pen from his pocket and touched the point to the map on the wall. "I want to know what you would do in this situation. Where is he going?"

"Rally point," said Patterson.

"Show me."

Patterson struggled to his feet and pointed to the spot on the map where they had crossed the canal two days before. "We was s'posed to meet back here."

"We'll insert you there and wait," said Ingram.

"Sir, if Charlie saw the signal, they'll be moving toward him," Revelle pointed out to Ingram. "How long ago was the signal?"

"Couple of hours. If Charlie spotted it, they'll know where Monroe was, but they don't know where he's going. We do." Ingram stared at the men. "This is a volunteer mission. We can't spare anyone to back you up. We're up to our ass in Viet Cong right now, but this man is one of ours. The Navy is willing to provide a PBR to get you upriver."

Patterson glanced at Revelle, who shrugged.

The brief silence was interrupted by a knock on the door. Colonel Lyons stepped into the briefing room and said with a stage whisper, "General, something urgent has come up." By his demeanor it was clear that the G-2 needed to speak to Vandermeer alone.

"What is it?" asked the general after excusing himself from Ingram's briefing. He spoke quietly in one corner of the DTOC, the conversation private amid the hubbub.

"MACV just sent orders for you, personally, to get to the 9th ARVN headquarters at My Tho with all possible haste, and to mobilize whatever forces are available to you to ensure the safety of President Thieu." Lyons handed the written order to Vandermeer. "We're holding a line open for you in my office."

"What the hell is this all about?"

"I wish I knew, sir."

For once, Vandermeer believed that his director of intelligence was as much in the dark as he was. He stifled an insult and followed Lyons to the secure telephone in the G-2's office. "This is General Vandermeer," he announced into the handset.

Lyons stood by, unable to hear anything except Vandermeer's steady breathing as the general listened to his instructions. Finally, he spoke: "Yes, sir." He then hung up the phone.

Ignoring Lyons, Vandermeer returned to the briefing room, almost walking into the snipers as they exited. To Colonel Ingram, he said, "Terry, I want every available combat unit sent to the ARVN 9th HQ on the double. Get 'em there any way you can."

"The reserves are committed, General."

"Send the headquarters company, and every cook and truck mechanic you can find. Tell the chaplain to draw a weapon. Extra ammo and C-rats. Nothing else. You stay here. Send them piecemeal if necessary. I want the first troops on the road in thirty minutes. I'll be in My Tho to meet 'em."

"What about the snipers?"

Vandermeer paused for only a moment. "Their mission doesn't change: go get Monroe."

Ingram nodded and wheeled away. No further questions were necessary for he and Vandermeer operated on the same wavelength, like dancers who know each other's moves by heart. He snared a master sergeant by the arm and delivered instructions quietly and earnestly as he escorted him to the door. Ingram then turned to his nearest RTO and said, "Get me the motor pool."

Lyons watched with grudging admiration. These were men of action and he could feel their relish for unambiguous orders. He wished that Intelligence were as well defined. "General," he said, "we have no idea what is going on at My Tho. Don't you think you should wait until the situation is more clear before you just drive in with the first convoy?"

"I don't have time to wait for the convoy, Colonel." As they stepped from the DTOC into the sunlight, Vandermeer whistled loudly to the MPs in the bunker guarding the entrance to the command compound. He thrust his hand in the air and circled his finger in a large circle. "Whatever those ARVN sons of bitches are up to, I'm gonna land right on top of 'em." On the chopper pad, Reliable Six's turbine began to whine.

TWENTY-6

The convoy to My Tho was small, but armed with enough firepower to deter an ambush by any group smaller than a battalion. Brady hitched a ride in the last deuce and a half, all three sandwiched between two APCs and led by an M-49 tank with a fleshette round chambered in its canon. Each APC sported a .50 caliber machine gun, and a machine gunner with an M-60 occupied the passenger seat of each truck. Land mines concerned them more than snipers, prompting the APCs to ride empty, the grunts electing to ride atop the vehicles, where an explosion might throw them clear. Brady felt relatively safe, but his body had started to stiffen twelve hours after his struggle with the sapper at Christine. Each jolt sent a spasm of pain through his neck. He was too tired to interview the men around him, even when they offered information about themselves. It always amazed him how men about to face combat, even men in the midst of combat, would want to tell a reporter about their hometown. Slowly, Brady realized who these soldiers were. Clean shaven with pressed uniforms and polished boots, they were utterly different than their bloodstained counterparts who had relieved the defenders at Firebase Christine. *REMFs*, he realized. Was the situation so desperate that the cooks and payroll clerks had been thrown into the breach?

Brady thought of his colleagues in Saigon. They would be in the thick of it, back at the bureau offices, if they were still alive. The uncertainty of the situation excited him as it always did. *When the shit hits the fan*, thought Brady, *the truth comes out.*

The convoy encountered no resistance, although Brady could hear the sound of rockets and small arms fire ahead. The convoy roared forward in ignorance, anticipating orders upon their arrival in My Tho. Brady realized that the war had been reduced to Napoleonic tactics: march to the sound of the guns. A helicopter gunship roared overhead, reminding him that he was living in the twentieth century. Thirty minutes later the convoy ground to a halt. The First Shirt ran down the line of vehicles yelling, "Everybody out!" They found themselves on the outskirts of town in a park by the river, a grassy square dominated by two giant banyan trees under which a pair of ARVN officers sat with their RTOs. Other ARVN troops hunkered down along the perimeter of the park. While the first sergeant herded his troops into a combat formation, Brady observed the company commander exchange salutes with an ARVN major. The major, realized Brady, would be the man he needed to talk to.

The company moved out, single file parallel to the river. Overhead, a gunship banked toward the city, then loosed a spread of rockets. The impact was close, two blocks away, and Brady could see smoke rising from numerous fires around town. Faintly, he detected the odor of burnt flesh. He found the major smoking a cigarette under the banyan trees. The ARVN officer eyed Brady coolly; he did not have time for American reporters.

"*Bao chi,*" said Brady, introducing himself as a reporter. He held out his press credentials, his only possession.

"I'm busy." The man spoke in distinct English with a haughtiness that marked him as an educated man.

"I have a message for President Thieu." Brady's breath was short as the pain in his neck now came in waves.

The man snapped his head around quickly to stare into Brady's face, twelve inches above his own. He saw the filth in Brady's hair and nostrils, the bloodshot eyes, and a uniform beyond foul. He did not know what to make of such a specter as Brady; the reporter was either a lunatic gone crazy in the war, or a man who had been through hell to deliver a message to the president. "What is your message?"

"I was sent here to deliver it personally."

"Who sent you?"

"Colonel Lyons, G-2 at Dong Tam."

The major had never heard of Lyons, but he saw that Brady had arrived with the soldiers from the 9th Infantry Division. He sucked his breath inward between his teeth, an expression of exasperation. "Wait." He turned to his RTO and spoke too quickly in Vietnamese for Brady to understand. The RTO raised HQ and handed the handset to the major. Again, he spoke quickly. He listened, spoke again, and returned the handset to his RTO. "What is your message? I will deliver it."

"I'll come with you."

"You will wait here."

Brady had his scoop; the president was here. "General Cho was killed yesterday in Cambodia while negotiating a peace treaty with the NVA."

The major's eyes opened wide, then narrowed to mere suspicious slits, accentuating the flat Asian features of his face. Again he spoke into the handset and waited for a response. Finally, he said, "Our commander was killed in combat when his helicopter flew too close to enemy ground fire. I would urge you to remember where you are and to keep such unsubstantiated accusations to yourself. Is there anything else you wish to communicate to President Thieu?"

Brady bowed. "I'm sorry, Major. I meant no offense." Painfully, he straightened his body, exhaustion starting to take hold. He needed transport to Saigon in order to file his story, but was not sure how best to get there. He could file by telephone, Brady knew, if he could find one. The phones were dubious in the best of times, but the hotels usually managed to eventually get him through. "I left some clothes and camera gear at a hotel on Rue des Chats Noirs two days ago. Is that part of the city safe?"

The major pointed. "Go that way. You might get there."

The newsman turned to go. He had walked only a few yards, however, when an American jeep roared up behind him, driven by a Vietnamese soldier accompanied by an ARVN colonel. "You!" called the colonel. "Are you Brady?"

Brady stopped. "Yes."

"You are here to meet with the President?"

"Yes."

The colonel looked him over and frowned. "Like that?" Brady started to reply, but the man waved him off. "Please get in."

They drove rapidly past the expressionless major under the banyan tree and through the streets of My Tho, jammed with military convoys and armored vehicles from the ARVN 9th Infantry Division. Most of the traffic was at a standstill, apparently waiting for instructions. Overhead, a pair of UH-1 gunships wheeled to attack a target somewhere behind them. The jeep crossed a narrow canal via an arched, one-lane bridge with cast concrete dragons guarding each corner. Across the canal was the 9th ARVN Infantry Division headquarters, where ARVN MPs raised the counterweighted barricade to allow the jeep to pass through.

"I am Colonel Nahn, attaché to the President," said the colonel.

"Dan Brady." He almost added 'New York Times' after his name, but sensed that it would make no difference. "Where are we going?"

"You shall see soon enough."

Inside the division compound, Brady was surprised to see two American M-48 tanks and a half dozen armored personnel carriers, all bearing the markings of the US 9th Infantry Division. American troops reclined in the shade of their vehicles while their commanders conferred in the sun, under the 90mm muzzle of one of the tanks. Colonel Nahn's jeep passed between the tanks, covering the GIs with a fresh layer of dust before halting in front of a two-story building with distinctly civilian architecture.

"Follow me," ordered the colonel, hopping from the jeep even before it had come to a complete stop.

Dating back to the pre–World War days of French dominion over Vietnam, the building originally served as a hotel. It had once included flowerpots and tiny balconies with louvered windows and doors. But age and war had taken their toll, and the bright pastels on the stucco walls had faded to the color of dust, the tile roof patched with corrugated steel and bristling with a massive cluster of radio antennae. The most charming aspect of the building now was that its solid walls were sturdy enough to withstand bullets and shrapnel, and thus afford a level of protection to its occupants.

An ARVN guard saluted with formality as the colonel entered. Brady felt the guard's curious and scornful stare as he followed the colonel through the door.

They entered the hotel foyer, which to Brady's amazement, was air conditioned. Chandeliers had been replaced by rows of neon lights that burned all day, for the original louvered doors designed for light and airflow had been closed and sandbagged. Another pair of MPs, American this time, checked the colonel's credentials and security badge. "He is with me," vouched Nahn, and the unsmiling MP nodded with his head for them to proceed. They passed through the foyer into a dimly lit hallway, typical of hotels worldwide, doors on either side. More American MPs guarded one door, one of whom Brady recognized. He nodded at the kid from Davenport, wondering what the hell he and all the other GIs were doing there. The other MP, a sergeant, examined Nahn's badge and said, "Go ahead, sir." Davenport stepped aside and smiled nervously at Brady as the newsman entered the presidential suite.

The room was out of context with the rest of the building. Brady first noticed that a thick yellow carpet with red stripes, the colors of the Republic of Vietnam flag, covered the tile floor. Vietnamese paintings and tapestries hung from freshly painted walls. Unlike the foyer, this room still had its chandelier. Closed doors led to other rooms within the suite. An ARVN soldier performed the duties of a butler, preparing drinks in the modern kitchen that served as a bar. Across the living room, French doors opened onto a balcony, but here reality returned. Two more American MPs, armed with M-16s and wearing helmets and flak jackets, stood guard. Brady realized the hotel abutted a river, for beyond the balcony an American PBR patrolled an endless expanse of brown water.

In the kitchen were two men. Though Brady had never met President Thieu, he recognized him immediately. The president of Vietnam was almost as familiar to Americans as their own president. A growing number of Americans who opposed the war, including members of Congress, hotly debated Thieu's legitimacy. Brady also recognized the other man in the room. General Vandermeer seemed as shocked to see Brady as Brady was to see him.

"Mr. President," said Nahn. "I have the newsman, Mr. Brady."

Thieu extended his hand. "So," he began, "you have news of General Cho."

"Yes, sir." A perfunctory handshake; the president clearly intended to avoid pleasantries. "I have reason to believe that he was negotiating with the NVA to end the war."

"This is communist propaganda, Mr. Brady. General Cho was my friend and a loyal and brave commander. A cavalier accusation to the contrary by a member of the press would be most irresponsible. The reason that I am here today, in the bosom of the 9th Infantry Division, is because at this time of national peril, there is no safer place for the President of Vietnam." The accent betrayed a knowledge of English, French, and Vietnamese. He clipped his words with authority.

"Mr. President, do you mind if I ask why General Vandermeer is here?"

Thieu glanced at Vandermeer in surprise. "Do you know each other?"

"Yes," said Vandermeer. "Mr. Brady has been visiting my command for the last couple of days. He seems to turn up in the most unusual places."

Thieu nodded and turned back to Brady. "With the extremely inopportune death of General Cho, both MACV and I agreed that it was advisable to have someone with the authority and experience of General Vandermeer to step in to assure my safety and coordinate the defense of My Tho. Although we have several qualified candidates within the Army of Vietnam, it is not so easy to simply appoint someone to a division command while in the midst of a battle such as the one now being fought throughout the country."

"I see." Brady drew a breath to ask another question, but Thieu cut him off.

"Thank you for coming, Mr. Brady. Please remember what I have told you about General Cho. Do not dishonor him." The president turned to his attaché. "Please ensure Mr. Brady's safety and see if you can get him some decent clothes."

Colonel Nahn bowed and motioned for Brady to follow him. The meeting had lasted less than a minute.

"Mr. President," said Vandermeer, "I would suggest that you minimize any contact with the press. Your presence here is classified and the less people know about it, the safer you will be."

"Ordinarily, you would be quite right," replied Thieu. "But these are not ordinary circumstances."

"All the more reason to be careful, sir."

"The Viet Cong know precisely where I am, General."

Vandermeer suspected Thieu was correct, even though he himself had not been aware of the president's location until he had been summoned to My Tho within the last hour. He said nothing, waiting for Thieu to elaborate.

"General Cho told them." Thieu saw the surprise on Vandermeer's face and smiled. "I envy your American naiveté.. You are all so honorable and straightforward. It is a character unique to powerful countries and powerful people who can simply forgo the deceit that the rest of the world lives by."

"My own Intelligence Department finds my naiveté aggravating," said Vandermeer, his voice testy. "And I admit that I find the Vietnamese character difficult to understand. So I would appreciate it if you would simply tell me what the hell is going on."

Thieu took a seat in an exquisite wicker chair with a high back and large armrests, as imperial as a throne. "General Cho was not negotiating a peace treaty. He was planning my assassination. His loyalty was not to the NVA, nor to the Republic of Vietnam, but only to himself. With me out of the way, he planned a coup."

"How do you know this?"

"When we learned that one of your snipers had shot him in Cambodia, we arrested several of his lieutenants. There are others still commanding units of this division whose loyalty is questionable. That is why I asked MACV to send you here. These traitors might be willing to shoot me, but they would never be so foolish as to kill an American general. I feel much safer with you in this room and American soldiers outside."

Vandermeer stood in the French door, staring across the river. *That son of a bitch, Cho,* he thought. In the event that Saigon was threatened, the ARVN Ops Plan for the security of the president called for him to be evacuated to the 9th ARVN Infantry Division HQ, where he would be immune from any attack short of a full-scale combined arms assault using armor and artillery and air support. With the American 9th Infantry Division just down the road at Dong Tam, there was no more impregnable place in Vietnam. So Cho had cut some sort of deal with the NVA to ensure that the Tet attacks in Saigon posed a serious enough threat to warrant activation of the Ops Plan. The president had been delivered directly into the protective custody of the ARVN 9th Infantry Division, where Cho and his lieutenants could quietly assassinate him. If Monroe had not shot him, Cho would probably be the president by now. "Mr. President, the enemy may know you are here, but I still don't understand why you would want to advertise your location."

"Advertise?"

"The interview you just gave to Dan Brady. By tomorrow night it will be headline news that the President of South Vietnam has evacuated Saigon and is under US protection in My Tho."

Thieu laughed. "I feel safer all the time, General, under the protection of a man as honorable and naive as you. You may recall that President Diem was secretly under American protection when he was murdered in a previous coup. Perhaps if the world knows that you are responsible for my safety, the US government will be less inclined to forsake me."

The attaché escorted Brady through the lobby of the old hotel and into the sweltering sunlight. "I am a presidential attaché," explained Nahn. "not a quartermaster. I'm afraid I will have to hand you off to the quartermaster for this division in order to find some fresh clothes."

"Don't worry about it, Colonel. I doubt that any ARVN division would have anything big enough to fit an American anyway." Brady bowed slightly. "Actually, these clothes seem to give me a certain disgusting credibility. I am extremely grateful for your courtesy. If you don't mind, I think I'll find a place out here to prepare my copy before I forget anything."

"You may use our phones to call in your report, but I will have to see it first."

Out of habit, Brady patted his pockets for his pen and pad. "Of course," he said.

Nahn handed him a pen and a green notebook small enough to fit in Brady's shirt pocket. The black pen had "U.S. GOVERNMENT" stenciled on it. Brady nodded and headed for a spot in the shade behind the silent American tank. He heard a whump in the distance. Smoke rose above the town several blocks away. Nahn retreated into the air-conditioned hotel.

Brady scribbled as fast as he could, recording every word he could remember in a stream of jumbled prose. He sat in the shade among a group of American soldiers who watched him quietly, or played nervously with their weapons. Brady was aware of them as he wrote, expecting questions or volunteered information about themselves. They were quiet.

Every instinct he had developed in twenty years as a reporter told Brady that his meeting with Thieu was a smokescreen designed to deflect the truth about Cho. Any story big enough to escalate to the president was bigger than a minor leak about the president's location. Brady, convinced now that Cho had died in Cambodia, needed proof, and he knew where to get it. Casually, Brady got to his feet and ambled across the sun-blasted compound. Approaching the barricade, he held out his press credentials. *"Bao chi,"* he said wearily. "I was with Colonel Nahn." The guard shrugged and let him cross the arched bridge into the labyrinth of My Tho.

The streets of My Tho were not deserted. A steady stream of refugees, most on foot, mixed with a few Lambretta scooters and honking Renaults, fled from the fires and explosions. Most carried what few possessions they might have gathered in bundles or suitcases. Brady saw many families sitting on street corners with nowhere to go, crying children watched over by stonefaced parents. It was not a tide of people, and Brady could walk against the flow without effort. He attracted many stares, but not a soul engaged him.

He reached a corner, however, where there were no more refugees. Smoke wafted through the empty streets and the impacts of the rockets could be felt through the ground where he stood. A body in black pajamas lay in the intersection. Beyond the corpse stood an old hotel, colonial French, its doors closed, a spray of shrapnel gouged across the wood. Brady crossed the intersection at a dead run, his hands in the air, hoping that any snipers would appreciate his peaceful intent. He did not yell *"bao chi!,"* for it would only be confusing in the silence and he imagined that anyone watching was dangerous enough without adding confusion to his predicament. He reached the door at full speed and threw himself against it, crashing into the lobby. There was no power and the hotel's interior was dark, hot and still. Brady rolled away from the doorway and lay silent for a moment.

"Hello!" he yelled. He got to his feet. *"Chao anh!"* he called in Vietnamese, but out of context, the formal greeting was nonsensical. Brady suspected that the owner had VC ties, for someone had notified the local cadre of his presence when he had checked in there two days before. But VC or not, it was unlikely that the hotel was abandoned for the man was a capitalist too with a family to feed, and business owners would defend their livelihoods with their lives. Brady banged on the bell on the registration desk. "Hey! Anybody home?"

The desk clerk observed Brady's approach from behind the screen of beads that separated the desk from the living quarters. Brady spotted him only when the muzzle of an AK-47 pushed a row of beads aside.

"What do you want?" The man's English had drastically improved.

"Do you remember me?" asked Brady.

"Yes," said the clerk, matter-of-factly. Brady recognized his eyes, sad and luminous.

"I want to meet with the NVA officer who saved my life."

The desk clerk stared at Brady for another minute, paralyzed with suspicion and indecision.

"I have information for him about an American sniper."

Another man stepped though the curtain, also armed with an AK-47, indistinguishable from a million other Vietnamese: rubber sandals and loose cotton clothes. The Vietnamese exchanged quick words. The man stared him down for a moment, then gestured across the registration desk with a brusque wave. Most Americans would have interpreted the wave as "goodbye." In Vietnam it meant, "Follow me." Brady understood.

The man led Brady through a warren of filthy alleys, even through occupied dwellings, to get from one narrow passageway to another. He made no effort to disguise his route or to cover Brady's eyes. *Wherever we're going,* thought Brady, *they don't plan to be there long.* It also occurred to him that he was hopelessly lost and would never find his way back again, and so posed no threat. Or perhaps they would simply hear him out, then kill him. He struggled along through the tiny alleys, dodging bicycles and laundry, pain shooting through him every time he used his neck muscles to duck under a doorway or clothesline.

They approached a hovel similar to the others. The man threw aside a canvas door and ushered Brady inside. The single room was illuminated by a kerosene lantern set upon an upturned wooden crate. A military bedroll lay on the plywood floor with two NVA packs stacked in a corner. The only furniture was an incongruous wooden stool intricately carved in the shape of a dragon from a single block of wood. On the stool, smoking a Marlboro, sat the man who had first told him of General Cho's death. In his lap he cradled an American Remington.

"What do you want?" said the man.

Brady noticed the gun. "I was at Firebase Christine, where one particular sniper caused a lot of problems for the defenders. I would think such weapons are wasted in the narrow confines of these alleys. "

The man studied him for a moment. "You have an uncommon command of tactics, Mr. Brady. Most reporters would not even notice my gun."

The target, Brady realized, *is Thieu. How did they know he was here?* "The President is inaccessible. The ARVN will level this town before anyone goes near him."

Dac offered a cigarette to Brady. "You know that he is here, then." Dac spoke calmly, as if in casual conversation despite a spray of automatic gunfire from an AK-47, somewhere beyond the door.

An explosion rattled the flimsy building and a helicopter thundered overhead at low level, the blades slapping the air as the pilot banked hard to avoid small arms fire. "You blew it," said Brady, competing with Dac to remain cool as the action intensified outside. "You're taking terrible losses. "

Dac nodded. "The Americans are fools. They are destroying the entire city with rockets and bombs, merely to oust a couple of hundred Viet Cong fighters. They will kill hundreds of civilians and create thousands of refugees. We underestimated their fear."

"What about Thieu?" asked Brady, seeking to confirm what he already knew. "Is he the target?"

"As you said, we blew it. I will have to shoot him some other day."

"Then you better get the hell out of here, because this place is going to be burned to a cinder in about five minutes." Brady's calm began to evaporate as the explosions crept closer.

Dac exhaled a lungful of smoke, then tossed the butt of his cigarette onto the dirt floor. "Why are you here?"

"You challenged me to confirm your story about the sniper who shot General Cho. I've done that. But I need one more piece of proof. You show me Cho's body and I'll blow the lid off this war for you."

"What about the sniper?" asked Dac, leaning forward. "Have you found the man who shot him?"

"The man who shot him never returned from the mission. But he's not important. Here's the thing . . ."

"He is important to me, Mr. Brady. How do you know he is dead?"

"I found his partner. He's the black man you saw." Brady added, "He shot the dog."

"Not the woman?"

"No."

"Thank you, Mr. Brady. You can go now." Dac stood up, as if to dismiss Brady.

"Go? No, I must see Cho's body before I put my career on the line. Either I see it, or I don't print it."

"Mr. Brady, the woman was my wife. The man who killed her is now also dead. I have no further interest in General Cho, or you or your story, or the war. Soon enough, I shall die, too."

Brady rose slowly to his feet, understanding now the game Dac had played. Despite his years in Asia, he was no better than most Americans at seeing through the deceit that concealed the fundamental nature of war-torn Vietnamese. By American standards, Brady had been duped, but in Vietnam, honor and deceit were not necessarily antithetical. *"Toi rat dau long khi nghe tin chi ay chet,"* said Brady. His expression of condolence was an unusual courtesy in Vietnam, taking Dac slightly aback.

"My wife was pregnant when that sniper shot her." Dac's nostrils flared. He gripped the stock of his Remington so tightly that his knuckles popped audibly.

Another barrage of rockets streaked into the maze of flammable homes. A whoosh erupted nearby and the sound of screaming carried across the rooftops. Smoke began filtering into the room. The men sat facing each other as the smoke thickened. Brady could hear scurrying feet outside and the guide who had brought him there peeked inside.

"Your death today won't honor your wife," said Brady quietly. "She died for this country, for peace."

"Don't try to shame me."

"Take me to General Cho's body. If I verify what you have told me, my articles will hasten the end of the war."

Brady heard the crackling of fire and realized that the roof was burning. Large embers floated down around them like snowflakes. Dac stood motionless, glaring at Brady.

"In my country you would be considered a traitor."

"Democracy permits a depraved press and capitalism encourages it. We don't consider it treason."

Dac snorted. He spoke in Vietnamese to the man who had delivered Brady. Then turning to Brady he said, "We will show you Cho's body."

TWENTY-7

Brady never imagined that thirty minutes after meeting Dac he would be in a cab bound for the Cambodian border. He could have refused. Dac would have guaranteed his safety back to Saigon, since he had sufficiently verified his story to publish even without Cho's body. But every reporter in Vietnam angled for a chance to see the war from the enemy side, naively frustrated that the NVA had not rolled out the red carpet. Didn't the gooks understand how helpful the press could be? But for Brady, less naive than most, the prospect of traveling with the NVA scared him. He had seen American firepower at work and could not imagine the horror of watching a canister of napalm tumbling toward him from the wing of an A-1 Skyraider. And he was still not confident that the verbal orders of some VC sniper would carry any weight among hard core NVA grunts in Cambodia. But he was going to do what no American reporter had yet done in Vietnam: travel with Charlie.

So he found himself shuffling along with Dac, mixing with the refugees, the Remington field-stripped and stuffed in a bundle of clothes. Overhead wheeled a pair of Cobras and a PsyOps Huey, broadcasting warnings to the civilian population to evacuate their homes. One Cobra loosed a volley of white phosphorous to mark an enemy strongpoint while the backup covered his break. Then the second gunship rolled in and blasted the now burning target with high-explosive rounds, sending flaming debris flying into other flimsy neighborhoods and destroying the entire block where Dac and Brady had met only minutes before. Only then did the ground troops move in, one block at a time, to root out any remaining VC. There were no prisoners. Civilians foolish enough to remain in their homes burned to death with the enemy.

They moved away from the river into alleys increasingly narrow while soot from the burning city sifted down upon them. Dac knew the network of unpaved passages like the back of his hand, dodging left, then right from one alleyway to another. He stopped and looked back for Brady. Gasping for breath and slowed by the throbbing pain in his neck, the newsman stumbled up behind him and leaned against the concrete wall that lined the alley. Dac pointed around the corner. A tiny Renault waited, a taxi identical to the hundreds that filled street in cities all over Vietnam. "He is waiting for us," explained Dac. They approached the cab from behind, and sensing all clear, Dac opened the passenger door and jumped inside. Brady crawled into the rear seat. The taxi moved away slowly, picking up speed as it turned onto a main thoroughfare. The road led north. Moments later they headed west on Highway 1, the main drag between Saigon and Can Tho.

The road was heavy with military vehicles and a surprising number of civilians, fleeing the carnage only a few miles behind them in Saigon or My Tho. They stopped at checkpoints every few miles, where ARVN MPs backed up by Chieu Hoi turncoats—ex–Viet Cong foot soldiers who could recognize old comrades—searched every vehicle. But Dac and the driver had genuine identity cards and they both spoke English. Dac appeared too old to be a draft dodger or deserter, and an American in the backseat assured them of easy passage. They reached the Mekong just north of Vinh Long.

Security was tight. Civilian vehicles lined the street approaching the ferry, their priority hopelessly low behind the ARVN trucks and personnel carriers that rolled onto the huge ferry barge under the barrels of police carbines. To the consternation of a dozen other taxis, Dac directed his driver to proceed straight down the avenue, bypassing the waiting civilian traffic.

To Brady, he said, "Tell them you are *bao chi*, you have the rank of Major."

A guard stepped angrily in front of the taxi, slamming his fist on the hood. *"Ngung lai! Xe thuong dan di ra phia sua!"* he screamed, pointing back toward the rear of the line.

Brady stuck his head out the rear window. *"Bao chi!"* He flashed his press credentials. "This card authorizes me the rank of major. It is critical I cross the river now!"

The driver translated almost as fast as Brady spoke and casually held a pair of twenty-dollar bills out the window. The ARVN guard had struggled with a dozen well-heeled Saigonese that day who imagined a few dollars could excuse them from the war. He took satisfaction in pointing his rifle up their noses and sending them to the rear with the rest of the refugees. But he had not encountered a reporter or any civilian with true authority and was momentarily nonplussed. A jeep rolled up behind the taxi then, leading another column of ARVN trucks. Any effort to turn the taxi now would create gridlock in the street, choked with parked vehicles on all sides. The guard slipped his hand over the bribe and waved the taxi through. Angry civilians in motionless vehicles, witnessing the preferential treatment, honked their horns in protest, but the guard pocketed his cash and waved on the ARVN convoy behind the *bao chi*.

Surrounded by troop carriers full of ARVN troops, the men sat in the Renault without speaking, the Vietnamese smoking Salem cigarettes while Brady lay in the backseat, avoiding any movement that might send a jolt of pain up his neck. Too tired to be afraid, he welcomed the sleep hovering over him. Sleep merely teased him, however, as he wondered whether he had crossed the line from being an observer to becoming a participant in the drama he sought to report. Reporters faced this conundrum every day and he knew that journalists who had manipulated situations to suit their stories had won more than one Pulitzer. Brady realized he was Dac's ticket home, that no VC would be able to travel freely now without hiding in plain sight. What better cover than as an interpreter for an American correspondent? He wondered if Dac would desert him when they crossed the border.

The ferry fought the current for thirty minutes, leaving an oil slick in its wake to be flushed into the South China Sea. The captain ignored the wooden junks but kept a watchful eye on the endless column of cargo ships headed upriver to Phnom Penh. Ferry accidents were common because no one controlled the traffic on the river. People died by the hundreds but rarely did anyone report it unless Americans were among the drowned. Boats did not even stop to pick up survivors, except for the US Navy, who dropped them off at the nearest shore before returning to their business of searching for contraband. The Navy patrolled elsewhere today, leaving river traffic to fend for itself.

The cab headed south and west to cross the Mekong's Nine Dragons, the Cuu Long, so named for the multiple channels that spread out across the delta before reaching the South China Sea. The flat landscape, a sea of pale green shoots, formed perfectly square rice paddies. The war came here too, but troops on either side did not congregate sufficiently to warrant attack by bombs or artillery. VC tax collectors prowled this battlefield while snipers took them out one at a time. The farmers took care of their paddies and the rice continued to grow. The ARVN convoy passed through in a hurry, the cab trailing audaciously in its wake.

Brady struggled to sit upright in the backseat, minimizing the pain by balancing his head atop his spine and using as few muscles in his neck as possible. The driver tapped Dac on the shoulder and nodded toward the backseat.

"How were you injured?" asked Dac.

"I killed one of your comrades with my bare hands at Firebase Christine. He was a tough son of a bitch."

Dac laughed. "I like American expressions. 'Son of a bitch.' 'No shit.' 'Fuck you.' Very difficult to translate."

Even Brady smiled. "You speak better English than half the grunts in the US Army."

The driver hissed, inhaling through clenched teeth to attract Dac's attention. "Can Tho," he said, pointing ahead.

Can Tho was the major metropolis of the delta, known to Americans because of the large air base there, but home to half a million Vietnamese. Huddled on the south side of the Bassac River, this gateway to the delta and guardian of the main navigation channel to Phnom Penh dedicated itself to commerce and war with acres of warehouses and shops and docks and banks, with sandbag bunkers on every street corner. The rice crop of Vietnam passed through Can Tho and the ARVN maintained a heavy and visible presence.

Security tightened as the Renault rolled through the checkpoint at the vehicular ferry. Civilian traffic backed up the other way, but plenty of room remained on the southbound ferry even with the ARVN convoy. Nevertheless, the guards watched closely.

"Pay no attention to the guards," said Dac. " But don't look away if they look at you."

An ARVN soldier motioned for the vehicle ahead of them to proceed to the ferry, then waved the Renault forward. He studied the two men in the front seat carefully before turning his eyes upon Brady, alert now in the backseat. Because of the air base just west of the city, it was not unusual for Americans to travel by taxi in Can Tho but Americans had been scarce today, occupied on their own military bases coping with the Viet Cong. Brady's disheveled appearance aroused the guard's curiosity.

"Name!"

"Chung toi la phong vien tu Saigon, " said Dac, explaining Brady's credentials.

"Im di, " growled the guard. "Shut up." He returned to Brady. "Name!"

"Brady. I'm a reporter. *Bao chi.*" Brady forced his voice to remain calm while he turned his head to face the man, betraying no trace of the pain shooting through his neck.

"Get out."

"No!" Dac's warning was quiet, but urgent. If they exited the car they would be searched. Brady spotted the grip of a .38 pistol in Dac's pocket, and watched in alarm as Dac's hand reached for it. He thought, too, of the Remington wrapped in clothing in the trunk.

"Bao chi!" yelled Brady, flashing his press credentials. *"Bao chi! BAO CHI!"*

The ARVN soldier lowered his weapon, aiming the M-1 carbine at Brady's forehead. The commotion, however, had attracted the attention of the sergeant in command, who sauntered over to the Renault and gave each passenger the once-over. The driver stared straight ahead, gripping the steering wheel with white knuckles. Dac, however, glowered with indignation. He spoke to the sergeant in rapid Vietnamese: "Mr. Brady is a famous correspondent. Important people in Saigon have directed me to escort him to Can Tho so we can kiss his ass while he writes lies about things he does not understand. You will save yourself a lot of trouble if you let this idiot get on the ferry."

Brady understood none of it. The newsman waved his press card at the sergeant and repeated, *"Bao chi!"*

With a shrug, the sergeant waved them through. He touched Dac on the shoulder as the car passed by, thus transferring his evil spirits to the mouthy man with important friends. Brady recognized the traditional gesture, but sank back into his seat, his chest pounding, too relieved to be amused by it. He had never considered this trip a joyride, but he realized now how serious a thing it was to travel with the enemy. If Dac had started shooting, a dozen rifles would have riddled the cab and everyone inside. And if he survived, how would he explain his efforts to help enemy soldiers evade a government checkpoint? Brady understood that he was no longer simply an observer of war; he had become actively involved. He thought, *I am a traitor.*

Refugees were about in Can Tho, most heading north toward the river hoping to catch the ferry out of town. The VC had occupied the city overnight and still controlled many neighborhoods. Only the heavy security at the ferry terminals had prevented the enemy from sealing the city. The bodies of a dozen uniformed NVA testified to the effort they had made to take the landing. Most lay now on the sidewalk, still bleeding into the gutters. One corpse lay in the street, crushed as flat as plywood by the endless convoys of reinforcements that had crossed the river to secure the town. After a few more hours in the sun, the body would dehydrate and become stiff enough to prop up like a cardboard cutout. The taxi rolled over it with only the slightest bump.

The ARVN convoy continued south toward the fighting after docking in Can Tho. Dac directed his driver west, Route 91 to Chau Doc. In the back of the last troop truck a grim ARVN soldier waved goodbye.

They passed another checkpoint at Can Tho Airfield, where a billow of black smoke rose from within a revetment. The facility remained otherwise quiet, except for the stream of helicopters that arrived to be refueled and rearmed and sent back into the air. The taxi passed unmolested, for Americans like Brady were common here, only a few miles from the huge US air base at Binh Thuy. There, the fighting continued. Yet even here, the helicopters rearmed under fire, the mechanics and administrative REMFs holding the lines and savagely gunning down any enemy soldier who made it onto the tarmac. Tracers overflew the highway.

The taxi swerved to miss a pair of VC bodies sprawled in the road. Yet another roadblock appeared ahead. The driver slowed, anticipating another argument, another bribe, another bluff. They were surrounded, not by ARVN police, but by NVA regulars. *"Ngung lai!"* yelled Dac, and the taxi halted in its tracks.

The soldiers yanked open the doors, screaming at the occupants.

"Get out," instructed Dac. "Remain calm."

"Bao chi!" yelled Brady, reaching for his credentials.

"Quiet!" Dac hissed. "Keep your hands out of your pockets. I will handle this."

Brady froze, careful to keep his hands in sight.

Dac talked, fast and loud. Brady understood nothing, but was relieved that the troops seemed inclined to listen before simply shooting them on the spot. Dac talked on, until one of the soldiers signaled for a sergeant to come forward. Together, Dac and the sergeant approached Brady. "Show him your press credentials," said Dac.

Brady reached slowly into his pocket and handed the card to the man. Brady could see that he could not read it. Dac continued to talk. An observation helicopter swooped overhead, banking hard to come around again.

"*Di!*" ordered the soldier. He shouted an order to his men, who scrambled into the weeds along the roadside as the O6-H "Loach" completed its acrobatic turn and leveled off. Though unarmed, he had the entire squadron of gunships on his radio if he needed them. Dac and Brady dived into the Renault and the little car roared away in a whirlpool of dust. The Loach leveled out just above them. Brady leaned out the window, showing his American face, and waved. The pilot waved back and returned to the NVA behind them, targets all.

The rattling car and the wind roaring through the open windows made conversation difficult. The landscape remained flat, but dry enough now for sugarcane and bananas. Ten miles from Binh Thuy, the war could have been on another continent. They passed occasional villages of tin-roofed shacks and some sturdier buildings with altars for the spirits. There were people in the fields with children herding water buffalo, picturesque images of what Americans imagined Southeast Asia to be. The bucolic scenes had enchanted Brady when he first arrived in Vietnam, but he ignored them now.

"What did you say to them?" asked Brady, shouting above the wind noise. "What made them believe that you are one of them?"

"We have our passwords," Dac responded. "We were fortunate that they are professional soldiers. The local VC would have shot the car to pieces."

Professional or not, thought Brady, the NVA and VC were getting slaughtered. Every stop seemed more dangerous than the next. A flicker of doubt crept into his mind about going behind enemy lines. The weight of American firepower awed him when he observed it outgoing. He had developed an admiration for Dac, and for all of the VC fighters who survived everything thrown at them. *How much longer can they do it,* he wondered. They were losing this battle and the days ahead would be very difficult. Brady wondered if any of them would survive, including himself.

As they approached Chau Doc, an ARVN security checkpoint waved the Renault to a halt. The guards were alert, having spotted the oncoming car a mile away on the flat, endless straightaway. A wooden barrier blocked the road, heavy enough to rip the roof off the car if the driver tried to run through it. So the Renault coasted to a careful stop.

Two soldiers marched to either side of the vehicle and peered in, squinting in the fading light. As he had done before, Brady displayed his press card and said the words, *"Bao chi."*

Though corrupt, the 9th ARVN Division was not incompetent. The soldier ordered Brady from the vehicle. "Where is your unit?" he demanded.

"Bao chi." said Brady. "I am a reporter."

"That is a lie. You are wearing a uniform of the 9th US Infantry Division," said the man, pointing at the division insignia on the shoulder of his shirt. "You are a deserter."

Brady had not bathed or changed clothes since scavenging the dead pile in the hospital and he still wore sandals on his feet. *"Bao chi,"* he repeated, but he knew these soldiers would never believe him. He handed over his press credential.

"And I am Ho Chi Minh," said the soldier, earning a contemptuous laugh from the other guard. He tore the press card in half. "No Americans in Chau Doc. Too dangerous. You wait here for ARVN convoy to go back Can Tho." He added, *"Bao chi,"* in mock respect.

Still suspicious, the other guard directed the driver to exit the car and open the trunk. Dac nodded for the driver to do as he was told. As he opened his door, the driver casually handed the soldier a five-dollar bill, but made no effort to get out of his seat. A pistol shot interrupted the delta sunset. On the opposite side of the car, the other ARVN sentry crumpled. Dac then reversed his aim, firing under the driver's chin to claim the remaining soldier, who doubled over with an involuntary cough, his stomach imploded by the bullet. The driver jumped from the car and quickly frisked the bodies while Dac grabbed their radio.

As the driver retrieved his five dollars, the ARVN guard groaned and retched up a stomachful of blood. *"Thang nay con song!"* called the driver, "This one is still alive!" While the wounded man gagged and struggled to breathe, the driver lifted his wallet from his pocket.

Brady rolled the soldier over and tore open his shirt to reveal an insignificant hole, blood oozing out rhythmically, thick and slippery as oil. The wounded man's pack lay by the barrier, and Brady reached for it, though he knew that any bandage he might find would merely slow the inevitable. Without medical care, gut-shot men did not last long. But as Brady rummaged in the pack, Dac kicked it away.

"Do not waste your time," said Dac.

Brady looked up to see Dac lower the barrel of his .38 toward the wounded man's face.

"No!" yelled Brady. "You can't do that!"

"Then you do it." Dac proffered his handgun to Brady, grip first.

"I'm a journalist," said Brady, as if his status as an observer excused him from murder.

"You are with us or you are with them," said Dac. "If this man lives, every policeman in Chau Doc will be looking for you. They will find you and they will kill all three of us." Dac thrust the revolver at Brady. "Now kill him. Be quick about it."

"You kill him."

"You want us to trust you, but you do not want to demonstrate your trustworthiness. You must do this, or we will leave you." Dac dropped the gun at Brady's feet and motioned for the driver to open the trunk. The driver tossed in the guards' weapons and radios, then slammed the lid shut. He got behind the wheel and the engine sputtered to life.

"Wait!" Brady needed time. He scanned the road east and west: an arrow of rutted pavement, motionless except for the heat waves shimmering. A thousand acres of flooded paddies surrounded them, the water pink in the tropical sunset, while a sole family of peasants toiled a half-mile distant, indifferent to the common report of gunshots. No wind, just the heat, and the only sound was the sputter of the Renault engine, impatient.

The prospect of having to explain his situation to other ARVN troops convinced Brady that he did not want to be left here. If the ARVN held him, he might never file his story about Cho's assassination, or the NVA would pass it on to another reporter. Brady lifted the weapon from the dirt. *He'll be dead in an hour whether I shoot him or not,* he reasoned. The wounded man looked up at him as Brady brought the muzzle to bear. "Look away," said Brady, unnerved by the man's stare. The soldier obliged him, and Brady pumped another bullet into the man's heart.

Chau Doc had never been a beautiful city, ugly since the day the Vinh Te Canal transformed it from a simple cluster of thatched-roofed dwellings to a bustling French trading center on the Cambodian border. Always a brazen and bloodthirsty place, it had become the Wild West of Vietnam as the war stuffed it full of refugees, one hundred thousand indigents roaming the streets, all traumatized by their ordeal, desperate. A heavy ARVN presence prevented anarchy, yet the city survived on crime. The Army of Vietnam rounded up the pickpockets and psychopaths when it could, but they ignored the criminals who greased the wheels that kept the city alive: smugglers. In addition to the contraband smuggled across the Vinh Te Canal, they smuggled the NVA, one platoon at a time, and any effort to stop that would mean real combat. Nobody wanted that.

But combat had found them anyway. Chau Doc had been overwhelmed within minutes as the NVA swarmed across the canal and into town. The ARVN troops had withdrawn or disappeared and the town belonged to the enemy, save a few Navy Seals and Nung mercenaries who had taken to the streets rather than hole up in their fortified compounds. Gunfire echoed throughout the town, though large portions of Chau Doc remained quiescent under VC control.

Chau Doc was not the kind of town that shut down because of an enemy invasion. Many in town welcomed the NVA and brazenly collaborated with them, or at least tolerated them the same way they tolerated the Americans. In any other town, the men who ran the government were rounded up and executed by VC death squads, but bureaucrats operated the government in Chau Doc, men well known to the enemy for their willingness to look the other way while smugglers haggled over contraband of all kinds: Cambodian cattle, Thai marijuana, Laotian lumber, and North Vietnamese troops. In the wake of the Tet invasion, the restaurants and canal-side bars in Chau Doc popularized by Americans now became meeting places for local officials who came out of the woodwork to meet with the new authorities passing through.

Brady sat conspicuously at a cafe along the bank of the Vinh Te Canal. There was no decor; no lanterns or candles or fake potted plants. Hot and dim, a few bare bulbs muted by a covering of dust illuminated its interior. The back door opened to the canal. A few feet of dirt separated the building from the water, and here the proprietor set up some rickety tables. Whatever al fresco ambience there might have been was destroyed by the men who staggered to the canal to urinate when they drank too much Ba me Ba, and by the drifting garbage or occasional bloated corpse that bumped along the banks. The patrons who frequented this spot did so not for the evening breezes and moonlight, but for the privacy.

Although a place where people made a point not to notice who might be among them, Brady nevertheless attracted the attention of other patrons. Filthy with three days of his own meaty sweat and his borrowed uniform stiff with Olivetti's dried blood, Brady looked like Death and smelled it. The Vietnamese men stared with expressionless faces and communicated among themselves with head nods and glances toward the grotesque American. They were not NVA, but Viet Cong, dressed in loose cotton garb with rubber-soled sandals on their feet. But they left Brady alone, for he had arrived with Dac. It relieved him to see that Dac carried some weight among them. So Brady sat by himself, his hands folded on the table, fighting exhaustion and pain while Dac made arrangements with the proprietor for transportation across the canal. Brady still sat with his hands folded, sound asleep, when Dac returned ten minutes later.

TWE꞉TY-8

17:32

**9th Infantry Headquarters,
Dong Tam**

M ore than most army divisions, the 9th Infantry worked closely with the
Navy, using naval vessels to ferry troops from one AO to another in
the delta much the way other divisions used helicopters. Vandermeer had
directed the construction of a concrete jetty to facilitate the boarding of
troops. A sturdy structure, it was nevertheless sinking slowly into the river
because the engineers had never been able to find bedrock under the delta
silt upon which to rest the pilings. But they expected it to last through the
war, and when a Navy armored troop carrier pulled alongside, the most
dangerous part of boarding for an infantryman was avoiding the gauntlet of
razor wire strung along both sides of the dock. The wire hung deep into the
water, too, an effective barrier to discourage any sapper who might imagine
swimming underneath and planting his charge. Those foolish enough to try
had either drowned or bled to death in the underwater coils; they bobbed to
the surface from time to time.

Patterson waited on the dock with Revelle, both watching the Cambodian
sunset illuminate the underside of a bank of cumulus clouds at eight
thousand feet. Sampans and junks plied the river, rushing to get home before
the American Swifts enforced curfew. A large freighter plied the center of
the channel, beating its way to Phnom Penh, silent except for the large wake
that splashed against the dock, sinking it another millimeter into the mud.
Neither man spoke.

Most snipers traveled the river in patrol boats sometime during their tour, but infrequently enough so that they found the boats far more interesting than helicopters. Revelle spotted the PBR's bow wave from a half mile away, coming fast. He nudged Patterson, and both snipers watched intently as the heavily armed vessel approached. The boat was nothing more than a fiberglass cabin cruiser, purchased by the Navy from its civilian manufacturer and retrofitted with some heavy firepower and two Army FM transceivers. Powered by two 220 horsepower General Motors truck diesels that drove a pair of Jacuzzi jet pumps, the thirty-one-foot craft were the fastest movers on the river, despite the extra weight of twin .50s forward and a single .50 aft and a double load of ammo and a crew of four.

The skipper plowed to within thirty feet of the dock before he swung the helm hard over and killed the engines, throwing a large wake against the concrete pier before settling the boat gently alongside, its diesels chugging smugly, a maneuver requiring intimate knowledge of the boat's engines, the currents, and the river swells. The skipper seemed bored with his own proficiency.

"You the boys headin' upriver?"

"I reckon," said Revelle.

"Come aboard, then." The skipper gave the boat a hint of throttle to keep her tight to the dock while Patterson and Revelle clambered in. Then he let her drift away with the current before hitting the throttle again, smoothly accelerating to the middle of the river. "Clear your weapons!" he ordered. The gunners fore and aft drew back the heavy bolts on their .50 caliber machine guns and fired quick bursts into the water. The boat moved faster with yet more throttle, the skipper riding the river wakes and swells to "get on step," to ride high on its planing hull, despite the heavy load.

The skipper had little to say. A petty officer first class with fifteen years of plowing the oceans in frigates and oilers, he had extended his tour in Vietnam because he preferred having his own boat, even at thirty-one feet long, to bunking with five hundred men on any ship of the line. He had tattoos on both arms—a lion on one, a woman on the other—and he wore no discernable uniform: an OD T-shirt and flak vest over Navy denims. He'd seen everything and snipers did not impress him. So he kept his mouth shut as his head swiveled back and forth like radar, his eyes fierce as bullet holes, fixed a thousand yards upriver, the limit of his boat's killing range.

Patterson hunkered down on a coil of rope under the barrel of the aft gun and turned on the radio while Revelle found a spot amidships where he could sit with his back against the gunwales. The coxswain watched as Patterson checked his radio. "What net you on?" Patterson asked.

"RIVSEC," said the coxswain, a bare-chested kid in a flak jacket, his Spam-colored skin glowing even in the deepening darkness. "All the players are on the same push. Our call sign is Seal Baby Zero Two."

Patterson set the channel. *Ain't no players but you an' me, Sylvester.*

The crew had little to say to their passengers after that. Patterson watched the river turn black and glassy except for the white rooster tails generated by the jet pumps. Revelle painted his face with a cammo stick until he blended into the shadows like a bat, despite the rising moon that shed plenty of light upon the river. They passed Outpost Foxtrot in silence except for a position report radioed by the coxswain. Foxtrot was a landmark known well to the snipers, a shell-pocked chimney 150 feet in the air that brooded over the river, all that remained of a cement factory destroyed by the war. *Foxtrot*, thought Patterson. *Three hours to go.*

The snipers dozed until the PBR passed Firebase Christine, the faint scent of cordite still thick enough in the air to attract their attention simultaneously. They stayed awake after that, watching the black shoreline for the entrance to the Vinh Te Canal.

The skipper reduced throttle and steered gently to port. The engine RPMs dropped to a quiet gurgle as the boat edged closer to shore. "Man your stations," growled the skipper as the gunners swung their .50 caliber guns inland and the coxswain laid an M-60 machine gun across the gunwale. The boat drifted in, almost brushing the mangrove branches that encroached into the water like spiders' feet. Then the skipper hit the throttle and moved away, drifting in again one hundred yards downstream. The snipers went over the side on the third feint, while the PBR moved on, faking two more insertions before drifting back into the current and disappearing in the darkness to wait.

The warm water reached up to his waist and Patterson struggled to keep his weapon and the radio dry. They made too much noise struggling through the mangroves, and the snipers lay dog for thirty minutes when they finally reached the shore. They heard nothing, only the rippling water behind them and the mangrove leaves moving in the occasional breeze. Revelle moved out at last, pulling himself forward six inches at a time, quiet as a snail and only slightly faster. The thick mangroves gave way immediately to silty dry soil and scrub brush, difficult terrain in which to cover their trail. They could not stand erect, for there was adequate moonlight to illuminate their silhouette against the flat landscape and any trail watchers would have been alerted by the PBR. So Patterson crawled directly behind his partner, touching Revelle's boot with his hand, creating one trail for two men.

They had crawled inland for barely twenty minutes when Patterson felt Revelle's body freeze, a spasm too severe to be intentional. Both men snapped their weapons into their hands and lay dog again, every hair on their body vibrating like a tuning fork, listening for any human sound. Finally, Revelle slid back to Patterson. He put his lips to his partner's ear and whispered no louder than a gentle breath.

"Bodies. They dumped 'em along the trail."

"How many?"

"Two."

Patterson pointed the way. They skirted the corpses carefully, heedful of booby traps, but grimly pleased that the trailside had been trampled and bloodied enough that their passage would be unnoticed. The rally point was close, with sunrise still five hours away. Plenty of time.

Five hundred yards to the south, Monroe was also on the move, crawling as slowly as Patterson.

TWENTY-9

The tiny sampan crossed the Vinh Te Canal in less than two minutes. But the cramped boat prohibited any movement and Brady was so stiff he could barely step onto shore. Greeted by a contingent of soldiers with only the silhouette of their pith helmets visible in the darkness, one man stepped forward and spoke briefly with Dac. *"Di!"* he said, and the squad moved out, pushing Brady along in front of them.

The trail followed the canal briefly, then turned inland through dense undergrowth. Soon, however, stars appeared and the trees gave way to open croplands, abandoned to the war. Brady stumbled forward in his sandals until they came finally to a building. Despite the darkness, Brady could make it out to be a pagoda. Nearby stood another structure, a house with a covered veranda. The leader called a halt and the squad stopped in their tracks. Brady noted their proficiency.

Dac led Brady into the building. The house had been the home of a plantation owner, now dead or departed. Brady could see that the building served as a headquarters of some kind, with briefing tables in the living room and bedrolls laid out under maps along the walls. Dimly lit bulbs hung from wires strung across the ceiling. Blackout curtains covered the windows.

A dozen men slept on the floor in an orderly row along the walls. One man stood at a large table, frowning at a map of the Mekong Delta, not unlike that which hung in Vandermeer's war room at Dong Tam. Older than the others, Brady guessed him to be in command, although he wore no rank, only a sleeveless T-shirt and uniform trousers.

Dac spoke and the man glowered at Brady through bloodshot eyes. He uttered a few sharp words, but Dac responded in kind, handing over the ID cards of the dead ARVN soldiers killed at the security checkpoint. Brady imagined that this officer had suffered a defeat only twenty-four hours ago at Firebase Christine and had enough on his mind without an American journalist to worry about.

The man turned to Brady and spoke. *"Bao chi?"*

"Yes," said Brady, bowing slightly.

"You killed ARVN soldiers?"

"One."

"So you are a traitor?"

"No. I am a journalist. Noncombatant."

The officer ignored Brady and studied the names on the ARVN ID cards instead. "I'm sure the family of Tran Dai Thu will be glad to know their son was killed by a noncombatant."

"Don't insult me. I am here to help you."

The officer looked Brady over and sneered. "You are dressed like the Dust of Life. And you want to help us? I think it is you who wants help." He motioned to a young soldier by the door and spoke quickly. The boy snapped to attention, then scurried out of the room. "I am Colonel Nguyen Chi Ninh. I am ordered to show you the corpse of General Cho. And because I am a soldier I will follow my orders."

Dac led Brady outside, where two men in black pajamas dozed on the relatively cool veranda. "My brothers in the NLF," said Dac, distinguishing between the professional army of North Vietnam and the guerrilla fighters of the South. "They are here for consultations. You do not need to know who they are." Dac escorted Brady to a vacant spot and directed him to wait while he disappeared into the kitchen. The men from the National Liberation Front did not stir.

A soldier emerged from the house bearing a bowl of rice, which he placed on the deck in front of Brady, indicating for the American to eat.

"*Cam on,*" said Brady, thanking him.

Dac returned, carrying a combat pack and his rifle. As Brady shoveled the rice into his mouth with his fingers, Dac rummaged through his pack for the cleaning kit for his rifle—some dirty swabs, a toothbrush, and a small bottle of lightweight machine oil. Expertly, he broke the gun into its component pieces and laid them out on the floor.

"Where are we?" asked Brady as he swallowed the last of his rice.

"Near the Cambodian border."

"Which side?"

Dac glanced sideways. "Where do you think?"

"Colonel Ninh said he was following orders to assist me. Whose orders? Yours?"

"Yes, mine."

"Who are you?"

"A sniper," said Dac modestly. He added, "And the political commissar for the NLF in the delta. The NVA have their own commissars, but I have been fighting this war for a long time and I have gained some respect among our comrades from the North. They are barbarians, but they know I can fight as well as talk."

"How does a sniper become a commissar in the NLF?"

"It's the other way around. I joined the movement because of my wife. I met her while attending university in Paris. I was a rich playboy. I cared nothing about the hopeless politics of my country. She was the nationalist. So I joined the cause. Because I was educated, my responsibilities were to lead classes on Marxism and the history of the revolution. It is a long story."

"It's going to be a long night."

"Not so long." Dac pointed at a pair of soldiers. In the bright moonlight, Brady could see them digging in the overgrown field near the carcass of a crumpled and burned helicopter. "General Cho will join us shortly." Dac returned to cleaning the Remington.

The thought of performing some sort of battlefield autopsy on Cho's decomposing corpse unnerved Brady. He imagined that he had seen the worst the war could throw at him—burned infants, headless torsos, mutilated victims of torture. Neither fascinated nor disgusted by blood or guts, he imagined that the smell of a four-day corpse was enough to bring any man to his knees. But despite his training as a newsman, Brady had never developed an interest in the dead in any personal way. Once they were gone, they were gone. Watching Dac, Brady asked, "So what's with the gun? You shoot anyone who falls asleep at your lectures?"

Dac seemed not to understand that Brady was joking. "My comrades listen when I speak because they know I have killed twenty-five Americans and many more ARVN puppets. This weapon is my legitimacy."

"It's an American weapon."

"When I joined the NLF, they handed me a Mosin Nagant 7.62mm rifle with a 3.5 power scope. It weighed more than I did. The Russians gave us many of these worthless weapons, left over from Stalingrad or Leningrad, with burned-out bores and cockeyed optics. But very few Vietnamese have experience with weapons, and it is difficult enough to teach a man to fire an idiot's gun like a Kalashnikov. But I hunted game with my father, in the U Minh forest. I killed a panther once, when I was a boy. So the Mosin Nagant was a proper weapon for me as well as for a commissar.

"One day I was sleeping when I was awakened by the sound of a Remington. An American sniper had killed one of our guards, about two hundred yards from my position. I knew the sniper would come to collect the victim's weapon, so I waited. And then I shot him. And I took his Remington. I have killed a lot of men with this gun, but I am almost out of ammunition. Do you think Jane Fonda would send me some?"

Dac's mention of Fonda surprised Brady. Although he sympathized with the sentiments of those who would simply forsake South Vietnam and bring home the troops, the silly teenagers and the addled professors who presumed to speak for the peace movement embarrassed him. He realized now that their antics gave moral support to the communists even to the lowest levels of command. Only hours before, Brady had betrayed his country by shooting a wounded soldier, yet he still condemned the protesters for the pain they caused American grunts and the strength they gave to the enemy. He understood his own hypocrisy.

Dac grunted with a humorless huff. Brady assumed he was amused by his own joke, but Dac surprised him.

"Americans think communists are cruel and that we sacrifice our soldiers with cold calculation."

"It seems that way sometimes," said Brady, wondering where the conversation was going next.

"The man who owned this rifle was sacrificed as cruelly as any soldier can be. His partner watched him bleed to death."

Brady stared at the Remington, avoiding Dac's eyes for he sensed a good story. Stories from the heart came voluntarily, never coaxed out in an interview, and Brady knew that eye contact was as challenging as a question.

"I shot him low. It was a cruel thing, I know. But American snipers work in teams and I knew another sniper was watching. I wanted them both, so I wounded the sniper who showed himself and waited for his partner to come to his aid. But he never came, despite the pitiful cries of his partner. I could feel him searching for me, waiting for me to fire again. We were both too clever. He crawled away in the night, but I remember his name. His partner called him many times: Monroe."

The name hit Brady hard enough to make his head snap up. "Monroe? Are you sure?"

Dac was puzzled by Brady's apparent alarm. "I am ashamed of the way

I killed that man, Mr. Brady. I have heard the cries many times in my dreams."

"Monroe is the name of the sniper that killed your wife," said Brady.

Dac shot a glance at Brady, but the sudden blaze in his eye faded away quickly. Brady could not imagine what he thought.

Two soldiers, now approaching the house, dragged something behind them. Brady bolted up.

"Khien xac nay vao chua di," instructed Dac, and the men pulled a bloated corpse across the courtyard to the empty pagoda. "You can use this in there," explained Dac. "We will cover the door to prevent any light from escaping." He handed Brady a flashlight.

Brady ducked through the tomblike doorway, expecting Dac to follow, but a rubber poncho draped across the opening, leaving the newsman alone in the black chamber. He fumbled with the flashlight until it flicked on, revealing an igloo-like room with circular walls and a domed ceiling that peaked about seven feet above the floor. The Buddha had been removed, but the altar remained. There lay the corpse, bluish in the yellow beam of the flashlight, stiff and bloated. The smell of necrosis filled the room, though it was not yet overwhelming. Nevertheless, Brady tucked his nose into the crook of his elbow, even though his own clothes had the stink of death upon them.

He stepped closer to the body, almost expecting it to move. The unventilated room had cooked all day in the sun like an oven. Breathing the air hurt. Perspiration leaked from every pore; Brady could almost hear it dripping onto the dirt floor. The light roamed over the corpse, from head to toe. The body wore an American Nomex flight suit, practically brand-new, stretched tight as a balloon as the decomposing body expanded inside of it. Brady saw the name tag: CHO. Two stars were embroidered on the collar and the patch of the 9th ARVN Division sewn on the shoulder. Brady focused the light on the man's face, and saw it bore a resemblance to the man he had interviewed so long ago, though disfigured by swelling and decomposition. The body, Brady was convinced, was that of General Cho.

The beam of light settled on Cho's neck. The left half of the throat, torn away, revealed the vertebrae of the neck surrounded by meaty pulp covered by a green sheen, like meat left too long without refrigeration. It was a large wound caused by a small bullet, but Brady had seen the handiwork of the 5.56mm M-16 and he had no doubt that the heavier, high-powered round of a Remington would wreak equal devastation. He played the light over the body, seeking other wounds, but did not find holes in the uniform or bloodstains. Instinct told him that there was no point in unzipping the flight suit for a closer examination. The wound corroborated Dac's story. The evidence was not conclusive—nothing ever was—but it was clear to Brady that no preparation had been made for his arrival and that the body had been dug up as it had been buried and that it had been buried as it had fallen. Brady had verified that Cho died in Cambodia. The only question remained why.

Brady turned off the flashlight and swept aside the poncho curtain, gulping in the humid but fresh night air. Dac ordered his men into the chamber to rebury Cho's body.

"I believe you," said Brady.

Dac seemed not to listen, but instead held up a pair of American combat boots. "You said the sniper was dead," said Dac. "But he has killed one of our guards and taken his footwear to disguise his tracks. We found these. Or maybe he's a black ghost, Mr. Brady?" There was anger in Dac's voice.

Stunned by Dac's information, Brady obediently accepted Monroe's boots and stared straight at Dac. "I didn't know." *MIA,* thought Brady. *Good as dead.*

"He is very strong and very clever, but he is somewhere on this side of the canal. We will track him at first light. If we take him alive, you will ask him questions. And then I will kill him." Dac's voice was flat, monotonic, dehumanized by the venom in his heart.

"Dac, let me take him back with me. His testimony would be devastating, a huge propaganda coup for your side."

"I will hand you his heart, nothing else." Dac turned and climbed the steps to the veranda, where he found a spot next to his sleeping comrades in the NLF. He lay on his back, eyes open, the Remington held in his arms.

Brady awoke to the sound of running, not in panic, but in order. He lay on the veranda, facing toward the courtyard, where three platoons of soldiers formed in rows as the first hint of dawn lightened the sky above the sycamore trees. Slowly, he sat up and put his bare feet into Monroe's boots. After two days in sandals, the American boots felt good enough to make him momentarily forget the lingering pain in his neck.

Colonel Ninh stepped onto the veranda, dressed now in combat fatigues of the NVA, red officer's insignia on his collar. "Get up," he ordered. "You have a job to do, just like the rest of us."

Brady stumbled to his feet. "Thank you for your cooperation, Colonel. You are a gentleman."

Ninh stopped, his eyes as cold as those of a *cham quap,* the deadliest snake in the jungle. In Vietnam, laughter did not always signify humor, and Ninh laughed now. "Gentlemen start wars. They do not fight them." He walked away to organize his troops.

They moved out while the night shadows reached deep into the undergrowth. Brady was impressed by the troops' discipline as they strung themselves into a line, two hundred men abreast. Dac explained. "The line is anchored at the canal. We know the sniper is moving north. So we will face our line north and swing the trap shut like a giant door, squeezing everything before it up against the canal."

Brady placed himself in the middle of the line and followed behind them as the soldiers moved carefully forward through the trees and across open rice paddies, flushing their quarry like a wounded tiger. He found himself wondering what sort of man they were hunting. Clearly gifted, he had eluded capture for two days in territory teeming with the enemy. His wounds were apparently not severe, although combat wounds were always filthy, always serious if not treated. *He's got to be at the end of his rope*, thought Brady. Was he the kind of man who would fight when cornered? Or was he pragmatic enough to understand when it was time to surrender? Brady knew one thing for certain: just getting close enough to urge him to surrender would be very dangerous.

TH_TRTY

**Khet Prey Veng,
Cambodia**

Dawn broke clear, the fog mysteriously absent. The temperature reached 95 degrees at 0800 and continued to rise. Monroe stirred in his hide, desperate for water and hungry again. His head ached from dehydration, replacing the pain from his wound. Groggy, he checked his AK-47 and stared up at the spinning sun.

He heard noises, men behind him moving noisily through the forest. NVA soldiers debouched from the trees beyond the fields, NCOs barking orders to keep the men in formation, as they moved on line toward him. Spaced five yards apart, the NVA swept the ground ahead of them, slowly closing the distance between themselves and the canal. Monroe estimated the range to be seven hundred yards. The distance he had crawled in six hours the night before, the enemy would cross in twenty minutes. Ahead of the troop line, a solitary soldier walked through the field, glancing occasionally toward him, but never staring directly toward Monroe's hide. Monroe recognized the man's weapon, the heavy wooden stock with the telescopic sight, and realized that this was the sniper who had been at the side of General Cho when Monroe's bullet had blown him out of his chair. *Black pajamas*, thought Monroe, *I think you found me* . . . Monroe shouldered this weapon, but his head began spinning again. He put the gun down and lay his head on the stock, waiting for it to clear.

One hundred and fifty yards from Monroe where the trail split toward the water, Patterson waited with Revelle. Deep in their hide, they too spotted the NVA. Patterson swung the spotter's scope and instinctively measured the mirages over the baking fields to calculate wind speed. Revelle moved the scope on his Remington from man to man, seeking officers. Both men understood that not only were the NVA squeezing Monroe toward the canal, but they were themselves now also caught in the trap.

Patterson grabbed the radio, already set with the frequency to the Navy PBR. "Seal Baby, this is Batman. We may need you soon. Stand by, over."

"Roger, Daddy-O. We're ready when you are." The Navy was never particular about radio protocol.

Brady stepped from the jungle into the open field twenty paces behind the line of soldiers. Colonel Ninh walked beside him, issuing orders to runners who scurried behind the line. The newsman watched in fascination as the northern end of the line reached the Bassac River and swung toward the canal, two hundred troops abreast marching with parade ground precision across drainage ditches, clumps of jungle, and dry rice paddies. The Duke of Wellington could not have controlled his formations any better at Waterloo. The movement was eerily silent except for the officers, who shouted a few commands, but led mostly with arm movements.

Sweeping through jungle and hedgerows since dawn, the NVA had tightened the noose with each step toward the water. They had found nothing so far—no trace of the sniper since he had discarded his boots. With the canal now less than half a mile away, Brady worried that Cho's killer had somehow slipped through the cordon. "Colonel Ninh," he asked, "what will you do if we reach the canal and there is still no sign of him?"

"You mean if he escapes?"

Brady nodded.

"Then we shall have no need of you, will we?"

Brady glanced back at him, but Ninh paid no attention, his eyes scanning the open terrain with his binoculars. In the distance, Brady could make out Dac moving slowly through the weeds, head down, reading the ground for any human footprint or damaged stalk of grass that might betray the passage of a man. He stopped. Squatting flat-footed, his head barely above the wild rice and brambles, Dac stared at one of the tiny oases of trees and undergrowth that dotted the landscape. Then he turned and jogged quickly to the line of soldiers behind him, where he reported to Colonel Ninh.

"No o trong dam cay dang kia," said Dac, pointing to a copse of trees.

Brady understood none of the Vietnamese, but he knew by Dac's confident manner and his pointing finger that the man they sought was less than two hundred yards away. "Is he there?" asked Brady. "How do you know?"

"I will ask the questions," said Ninh, though he spoke in English for Brady's benefit.

"I found his trail. He should have walked through the field, but perhaps the moon was too bright for him last night. He crawled. The grass is bent toward the trees, but there is no trail coming out. He is in there. I am sure of it."

Patterson slapped Revelle on the arm and pointed across the field.

"Got him," muttered Revelle, shouldering his weapon. Colonel Ninh's collar insignia were unmistakable and the crosshairs were trained now on Ninh's head. "What's the range?"

"Five hundred. Wind left, one knot. Don't shoot yet."

The NVA advance halted. The snipers watched through their scopes, confused, as Ninh used hand signals to order everyone to kneel on one knee. Pointing at Brady, Ninh said, "Go, *bao chi,* and persuade this man to surrender. We do not want to scare him by getting too close. And if he does start shooting, I prefer that he shoot you rather than any of my men. Now hurry, while you still have some idea where he is."

Brady offered a grim nod and stepped forward, jogging through the line of kneeling men toward the trees where Dac had pointed. Brady wondered again how a man could survive as long as he had, wounded and exhausted. Adrenaline was an amazing chemical and he hoped that it was as effective in making the sniper think clearly as it was in simply keeping him on his feet. He prayed to God that Monroe would see that he was an American; he had to get the sniper's attention before he simply shot him dead at one hundred yards.

"Who the fuck is that?" asked Revelle.

Patterson recognized Brady from Firebase Christine, but said nothing, not comprehending why the civilian would now appear here.

The snipers watched as Brady lumbered through the field, gasping for breath in the scorching heat, sweat streaming from his face. Fifty yards from the hide he stopped. Bent at the waist, hands on his knees, Brady paused to catch his breath. "I'm an American!" he yelled, still bent over. "Don't shoot!" He sank to his knees.

"What the fuck?" said Revelle. "Do we shoot this round-eye or what?"

"Wait," cautioned Patterson. "Don't shoot till the Navy gets here."

Brady staggered to his feet. "I'm here to help you! I'm a reporter! If you surrender to me, the NVA will let me take you home!"

There was no response.

"You have my word!" yelled Brady. "Let me help you!"

Silence. Brady stepped forward slowly, self-consciously raising his hands, almost expecting a bullet. The trees were close now. "I need you for a witness," said Brady, speaking to the bushes, loud but not screaming. "If you'll testify to shooting General Cho, they'll let us go. It's your only hope."

Still the newsman heard nothing, but he could almost feel the muzzle of Monroe's rifle against his chest. Brady's heart raced as he pushed aside a branch and stepped into the thicket. Still nothing. *He could be standing right next to me,* thought Brady. His skin crawled and he felt chilly in the hundred-degree heat, waiting for a knife thrust or a bullet or simply a club over the head. *Where the fuck are you?* he thought. "Come on!" implored Brady. "Let's go home!" The newsman took a step deeper into the undergrowth.

Brady saw him, an apparition so sudden that the newsman nearly tripped over him. Monroe lay in the weeds, covered with leaves and dead grass, invisible from any distance greater than a few feet. The newsman saw only Monroe's head, as if decapitated, laying upon the stock of his AK-47, unconscious.

Brady knelt beside him and carefully nudged Monroe's shoulder. Receiving no response, he removed the AK-47, jumping back in panic when Monroe groaned slightly. Realizing that Monroe was alive, Brady dashed into the open field. Brandishing the rifle over his head, he signaled with his hands for Ninh to move his troops forward. "He's alive!" Brady yelled.

Ninh spotted Brady at the same time as his troops, and he ordered everyone to their feet. With hand signals, Ninh motioned for his flanks to move forward. *"Ngung ban lai!"* he ordered. "Hold your fire!"

A squad from the northern flank moved onto the trail, rifles at port arms, running quickly to secure their prisoner. Patterson and Revelle hunkered deep into their hide as the NVA shuffled past, looking up only as the last man went by.

Revelle whispered, "We're too late, Patterson. Let's get the fuck outta here."

"Where you want to go?" The river was to their back and the arrival of the Navy would only draw attention to themselves. Revelle did not respond, but re-zeroed his crosshair on Ninh. Vaguely, both men understood that command of the mission had passed to Patterson. Although he did not carry the Remington, his head was cooler, his decisions more battlefield savvy. Revelle felt a sense of relief, Patterson a sense of unease that a white man now waited for him to make decisions for them both. In fact, Patterson did not know what to do, only that it was safest to remain where they were, undetected. "Wait," he ordered.

The NVA swarmed across the field, yet maintained their disciplined line. The snipers were impressed that some squads assigned themselves to perimeter guard, while others surrounded the clump of trees where Brady pointed. Dac ran to join the newsman and both men disappeared into the thicket, followed by a squad of soldiers. Ninh remained distant, watching the action with his binoculars. Minutes passed. Finally, a lead soldier stepped into the sunlight, followed by six men carrying a poncho, three on each side. With his spotter's scope, Patterson could not see who they carried, but he was obviously large by Vietnamese standards; his feet protruded from the makeshift litter. But he wore NVA boots.

"Who is it?" asked Revelle. "Is it Monroe?"

"Yeah. It's him." Patterson stared at the boots, the tips cut squarely off and the man's toes protruding. Not even the NVA would intentionally issue footwear so ill-fitting. The toes were too filthy to determine their color, but they were certainly American.

"Where are we taking him?"

"There is a hospital two kilometers from here," said Dac. The band moved out, six bearers and four guards, two in front, two bringing up the rear.

The trail paralleled the river. They crossed the border almost immediately, stepping over a fallen timber across the trail with a hand-lettered sign: CAMBODIA. No geographical feature justified the border. One side looked like the other, rice paddies and nipa palms. Perversely, the sign was written in French, unreadable to any of the men around him, though they all knew what it meant. A sanctuary. The bearers relaxed and began to talk. The guards slung their rifles. Dac assigned one man to stay behind as a trail watcher, easy duty on the Cambodian side of the border. The man sauntered into the weeds to urinate before lighting a cigarette and settling into the shade of a rambutan tree, its hairy fruit stripped from its limbs months before. The others moved on.

TH꞉RTY-1

Khet Prey Veng,
Cambodia

C olonel Ninh stayed with his men. The American sniper became a political issue now, propaganda bait, and Dac was responsible for the political aspects of the war. Ninh, grateful to be rid of him and the American, considered himself a soldier with a war to fight. Dac was full of communist bullshit that meant nothing to the men under his command. *Snipers were cowards afraid of showing themselves,* thought Ninh, *and the two of them deserved each other.* So the colonel concealed his men where shade was available, and sent his troops back to bivouac one platoon at a time. The others smoked and awaited the order to move out, while watching the skies for American aircraft.

"They're leavin'," whispered Revelle as the last of Ninh's troops marched away. "Let's call the Navy and *di di* out of here."

Patterson broke squelch on the radio and muttered into the handset. "Seal Baby, this is Batman. We're moving north one klick. Can you follow, over?"

After a brief pause, the answer came back. "Roger, Batman. If you got the money, we got the time."

"What the fuck are you thinking?" said Revelle. "We ain't following them gooks."

"We're following Monroe."

"Monroe's dead. Just like us if we go after him."

"They wouldn't carry him off if he was dead." Patterson matter-of-factly began sterilizing the hide and sheathed his spotter's scope. Revelle said nothing. Both men knew the fate of any sniper captured by the North Vietnamese. They would coax him back to life, only to kill him slowly. An American patrol would find him strung up in a tree someday, his testicles in his mouth, a grisly message to GIs and commanders alike. "I'll shoot him myself," said Patterson.

"We'll never get the chance," responded Revelle, intense despite his whisper.

"He's my partner."

"I'm your partner."

"Then what if it was you out there?"

Revelle glowered at Patterson, the muscles in his jaw clenched and throbbing while Patterson slung the spotting lens over his shoulder and hefted his pack.

"I'll lead," stated Patterson. "Grab the radio." There was no argument, no anger. Patterson had simply taken command, his course irrevocably set, with or without Revelle.

Revelle remained motionless as Patterson began moving slowly away from him through the thickets along the water's edge. *Fuckin' niggers,* he thought. *If it was me out there, you'd already be back in the fuckin' boat.* But Revelle also knew that Patterson had put him in an impossible position. He could not go back alone. If Patterson died, he would be accused of cowardice, as had been Monroe when he left his partner behind. And if Patterson made it back, with or without Monroe, the humiliation would be even worse. So Revelle capped his lens and flipped on the safety. He stowed his extra ammo in his pack and fluffed the foliage where he had lain. *Fuckin' Christ, I can't believe we're goin' to do this.* He moved out quietly in trail, steaming with anger at Patterson, at Monroe, at himself, determined to kill as many people as he could before the day was over.

They traveled all day, slowly, one deliberate step after another, each carefully considered and placed. Where the vegetation thinned they crawled, passing over the same corpses they had encountered the night before, laying dog for fifteen minutes when their passage disturbed a swarm of flies that lifted like a smoke signal over the bodies and settled back down again like a blanket. Patterson spotted the trail watcher dozing at the border, and froze again, becoming part of the terrain. With slow-motion hand signals, the sniper team argued about whether to kill the man, Revelle eager to break the man's neck with his bare hands. But Patterson overruled him, wading into the river to give the watcher a wide berth and coming ashore again behind him. They never saw the sign indicating the Cambodian border, not that it would have made any difference.

They stayed in the mangroves and riverside weeds, keeping between the trail and river. Slowly, they moved, covering in twelve hours what Monroe's bearers covered in thirty minutes. At dusk, however, their cover ended, the overgrown riverbank giving way to an open field that extended to the water's edge, where two men stood at the end of a wooden pier that extended deep into the river. Patterson motioned slowly for Revelle to join him. Wordlessly, Revelle shouldered the Remington and glassed the pier while Patterson unsheathed his spotter's scope.

"Two gooks," whispered Revelle. "AK-47s and NVA uniforms. They're just smokin' and chillin' out."

"It's Cambodia," replied Patterson. "They got nothin' to worry 'bout here." He studied the heatwaves in his scope. They boiled straight up: dead calm. "Fifty meters. No wind."

"Nothing to worry about," repeated Revelle, adjusting the elevation on his scope to zero. "Nothin' to worry about." He sounded almost happy.

Patterson swung his scope inland, across fields of rice paddies, overgrown now with waist-high grass and wild rice. Four hundred yards down range stood a home, as abandoned as the fields, but not unoccupied. Similar to the farmhouse where Monroe had shot General Cho, this building, too, had belonged to gentlemen farmers before the war, Frenchmen who had lived well when the fields were filled with crops. A wide veranda faced the river, shading the interior of the house even now as the sun set low in the west. The roof was tile, still sound, though Patterson could see that the doors and windows were gone, blown out in some forgotten firefight or stolen by vandals or otherwise claimed by the routine destruction of war. Patterson did not know the purpose of the building, but he did know Monroe was inside, for standing on the veranda, Dan Brady stared east toward the river.

As always, the Mekong Delta sunset came quickly. The snipers lay still for an hour, while guards on the pier were relieved. Dim light shone from the windows of the building. Through the evening chorus of crickets and cicadas, Patterson thought he could detect the hum of a generator. They would cross the trail now, while the moon remained below the horizon and before the natural cacophony of the evening settled down for the night. Crossings were dangerous, but the guards could not see the trail from the pier, even if they were alert. Invisible in the shadows, the overhanging trees buried it in darkness; the snipers could walk across standing up. This they would do, slow and silent, for walking was quieter than crawling, and faster. Patterson crossed first, slipping smoothly into the overgrowth on the far side of the trail. Both men lay still for ten minutes before Revelle followed, walking backward in a crouch, groping in the darkness for the powdery trail and wiping away his footprints with his hands. They pushed deeper into the thickets and waited for the moon.

The quarter moon rose red just above the trees behind them, shedding enough light to travel by. Patterson stayed in the treeline that marked the southern edge of the field. They covered fifty yards per hour. At midnight, the smell of *nuc mam* reached them, powerful and wretched. The enemy was awake, cooking a midnight meal. Patterson retreated to the densest thickets, where Revelle used his hands in the darkness to find Patterson's head. He whispered directly into Patterson's ear, his lips brushing against it.

"It's now or never. They might move him again in the morning."

"We don't know what this place is," whispered Patterson. "Could be a hundred gooks in there. If they move him, we'll take 'em out on the trail. If not, we'll figure this place out in the daylight and snatch him tomorrow night."

Revelle sank back into the darkness, unhappy again, but he knew this was not the time to argue. Both men got comfortable, lying on their stomachs, shoulders touching in the darkness. Revelle broke squelch on the radio, twice to signal sitrep normal. Seal Baby responded with two breaks of their own. All senses were alert for scraps of enemy conversation, the odor of their cooking, and for silhouettes in the dim electric light. But the sultry night turned tranquil and the snipers heard neither moving troops nor sounds of weapons maintenance. The insects fell silent and the bats swooped in the moonlight.

TH:RTY-2

T he building was a hospital, occupied by men in various stages of anguish, a dozen in each room except the kitchen, where the doctor did his work. Not a brain surgeon, but competent enough for what he did, he had received his medical training in India. He worked fast and dirty. He boiled his instruments and did without anesthesia or competent staff except one, a middle-aged woman with no medical skills but the stern nature of a parent who could silence a screaming man with a look and a touch. She ran the facility with the rigid authority granted to nurses by soldiers in every army, and she was unimpressed by Dac's credentials or his prisoner.

"My prisoner is important to the cause," said Dac. "I need a room where he can receive care and be guarded. His presence here is classified."

"You want a room for him, alone?" she asked, incredulous.

"Yes."

The bearers lowered Monroe to the floor so the woman could examine him. She squeezed his skin to check his hydration and placed the palm of her hand against his forehead. Tilting his head to one side to examine the infected gash on his head, she asked, "Does he have any wounds other than this?"

Dac said nothing.

She hissed with disgust. Turning toward what had been the living room, she pointed at two dozen men lying on the floor, their heads against the wall, feet toward the center of the room, those that had legs. "All of my rooms are full. Should I lay these men in the dirt outside so they can die slowly of infection or heat stroke, or would you prefer to simply kill them quickly, with your fancy gun, perhaps." She pointed at Dac's Remington. "You won't even need your telescopic site."

The eyes of ten men focused on Dac, the others unconscious or delirious with pain. Dac turned away, but pulled the nurse aside by her arm. "You are drunk with the adoration of your patients. Put him where you will, but beware that your ego does not interfere with your duty. If he dies, so will you."

"Thank you, General." Meek, her exaggeration of his rank sufficiently expressed her contempt. With a toss of her head, she motioned for the bearers to deposit Monroe on the floor, among the rest of her patients, occupying a space previously held by a man now dead. "Take off his clothes. Bathe him in cold water to reduce the fever. We have no medicines here. He will live or die on his own." She walked away to tend to the next surgery, while Brady helped strip the filthy fatigues from Monroe's body.

Throughout the day, Brady sponged Monroe with a clean rag he scrounged from a pile outside the kitchen operating room. The field hospital lacked drugs, but it put the walking wounded to work tending cauldrons of boiling water, one for washing clothes, one for the surgeon's tools, one for dishes and field gear. They kept the wards shipshape and clean, even the floors mopped daily with more scalding water. The wounded, consumed with their own despair, paid no attention to the American among them. Monroe lapsed in and out of delirium, lying naked on the floor in a pool of his own sweat, as the afternoon sun pushed the room temperature above one hundred degrees. The humidity sautéed them all, stunting any evaporation that might have a cooling effect on men's fevers. Exhausted, Brady stood up stiffly and staggered to the marginally cooler veranda.

"Will he live?" asked Dac.

"In American hospitals, they pack fevers in ice."

"Then perhaps we should give him some ice cream." The sarcasm in Dac's voice betrayed his continuing irritation over his treatment by the nurse.

"Dac, I'm sorry about your wife."

Dac turned to stare at him. "Don't ask me to give him up. I will not do it."

"He is a living witness to a war crime. His testimony could change everything. Honor your wife by winning the war, not by murdering the man who killed her."

"Are you married, Brady?"

"No."

"Then you have never been in love. And no man is capable of hatred until he has experienced love. So you cannot understand how I hate this man."

The cirrus thickened, blotting out the stars; the night turned black as ink. The snipers had been awake for forty-eight hours, alert as owls. Adrenaline could carry a man for days, but in the quiet darkness that enveloped them, even fear succumbed to exhaustion. Patterson fought the urge to sleep, reminding himself that the Freaky Flukey stood there in the dark right next to them, waiting, just waiting for him to doze off. He'd seen it a hundred times.

He slowed his breathing to control his thoughts, but they surged from his brain in a relentless stream of consciousness. He cursed himself for being foolish, for not holding the captain to his promise. *I'm s'posed to be answering the phone. Monroe ain't my business no more. Lord, Jesus,* he prayed, *why did you make me stupid?* Monroe, he knew, would not have come after him if the situation had been reversed. Who was Monroe anyway, but another cagey nigger with an attitude, like half the angry brothers Patterson had known in Vietnam? Except Monroe wasn't angry about racism. *Hell,* thought Patterson, *inside his black skin, he as white as any peckerwood in 'Nam.* Patterson did not understand Monroe's anger, or the hatred of white men, or even the lament of other black men. Sometimes Patterson was grateful for his ignorance.

But Patterson could not shake the gathering swell of doom that had been growing inside him since the day he had met Monroe. Despite his lack of learning, Patterson could read other human beings. A primitive soul, he could smell goodness or evil instinctively. Monroe carried the scent of both as well as the scent of other things that Patterson could not fathom. He had the spirit, the juju, to make things happen. Without even being aware of it, Monroe left in his wake a trail of passion that left men changed. Dimly, Patterson knew that he might have only one opportunity to do something great in his life, and that would be to save one man who could actually make a difference in the world. God dispensed neither justice nor mercy, Patterson now knew, but he prayed at least for purpose, a reason for the sorrow. If God existed, He had something special in mind for Monroe.

Patterson thought of the women in his life, his wife and three daughters. No, even if they knew Monroe, they would not understand why he had accepted this mission. Women didn't believe in greatness. They believed in having a job, fixing the screen door, and coming home alive. Patterson foresaw his own death then and found himself crying, sniffling in the darkness, hating Monroe for the terror in his heart and for the explanation his family would never receive. *Baby, I'm so sorry.*

Revelle touched his arm. "Patterson, shut up."

Patterson wiped his eyes and calmed his breathing, conscious of every breath he drew. He prayed for dawn and wished it might never come.

TH:RTY-3

**Khet Prey Veng,
Cambodia**

T he fog arrived on schedule, but thinner than usual, as a push of ocean air destabilized the shallow atmospheric inversion that persisted during the dry season. Still thick enough to limit visibility to one hundred yards, it obscured the pier on the river, and draped the hospital in a wispy veil. Dawn found the NVA asleep, save the few guards and those undeterred by the restless spirits of the Silent Men. One such man was Dac. A true Marxist believer, he had long ago forsaken the spirituality of his Buddhist ancestors as well as the animism of his soldiers. He relished inspecting his troops on foggy mornings, to emerge from the mist like a spirit himself, comfortable among the dead. Dac considered himself superior to the men he commanded, a sin he admitted regularly during self-criticism sessions with his superiors and peers, most of whom felt the same way. Yet he loved the average soldier for his stoicism and strength. He had no illusions about their commitment to the Party, but enlightenment would come later, after they won the war.

Dac checked the slumbering ward, where Brady slept, sitting against the wall next to the unconscious Monroe. He was surprised when Brady opened his eyes and winked at him. Turning from the doorway, Dac crossed the veranda and descended a few wooden stairs to the ground, his Remington tucked casually under his arm. He would have gone unarmed, but he liked the way the men respected the American rifle.

The trail to the pier lay along the far hedgerow, across the field from Patterson and Revelle. But the field was only fifty yards wide, long and narrow, and Dac made his passage toward the water clearly visible to the American snipers. Both men noted his rifle. Revelle's crosshair remained centered on Dac's ear for several minutes, until Dac finally faded back into the fog, somewhere near the river.

"Comrades!" called Dac as he approached the sleepy soldiers on the pier. *"Chao cac dong chi!"*

"Ai do. Ngung lai!" challenged one guard, more alert than the other.

"Dong chi Dac va Nguoi Lang Thinh," replied Dac, identifying himself as he emerged from the fog. "Comrade Dac and the Silent Men."

The guard relaxed and both men now stood at attention, staring past Dac into the mist as Dac stepped onto the wooden pier. *"Hay tu nhien,"* he ordered, putting them at ease. He chatted with them briefly, careful to praise their alertness and reflect upon the honor they brought to their mothers. In Vietnam there was no greater shame than the loss of *tin*, to bring discredit upon one's family. Dac had seen a thousand men die to avoid losing face. Only the fanatics died for the Cause. *In this way,* thought Dac, *we are similar to the Americans, who die as gallantly as we do, despite having no Cause at all.*

After assuring the guards that their relief would be along soon, Dac returned to the trail, intending to visit the trail watcher they had left at the border. If all remained quiet, he would recall him to join the rest of his unit. But as the trail entered the riverside jungle, Dac paused, bothered by something he could not identify, as if the Silent Men were whispering to him. The path was dry and dusty during the day, covered by thousands of NVA boot prints that firmed up slightly under the morning mist. He stood still among the boot marks, studying them, waiting for them to tell him what was out of order. But no answer came, so Dac shrugged his shoulders and proceeded, chiding himself for his paranoia. As he walked, Dac looked behind him as if the Silent Men were calling him back, and then he saw what he had not seen before—his own footprints. Normally unnoticeable among the tableau of other footprints, Dac's prints stood out clearly in an area swept clean of any telltale passage.

Dac returned to the spot where he had stood and saw that a pristine swath had crossed the trail from one side to the other, as if a huge snail had bridged the path, smoothing it in his wake. Following the crossing cautiously, Dac stepped into the jungle, seeking what he hoped he would not find. On all fours, he pushed the jungle growth away, his nose inches from the ground. He found the first boot print almost immediately. The distinctly American herringbone tread pattern headed in the direction of the hospital.

The hair on Dac's neck stood on end, and his body flushed with sweat. Were they watching him even now? How many were there? Barely a squad of able-bodied men guarded the hospital. A surprise assault by a small team of skilled attackers could wipe them out in seconds. But Dac knew what these men came for—the sniper. How had they found him here?

Dac retreated quickly, forcing as much composure into his demeanor as possible, wondering how many weapons were already trained on him. He glanced toward the hospital and saw the fog lifting rapidly as the sun climbed higher in the sky. *Why haven't they attacked*, he wondered. Fog was the attackers' ally. But fog could be his ally also, and he realized that the mist was still thick enough to conceal his actions. Back at the pier, Dac moved his two men quietly into the grass, where they would act as a blocking force, trapping the Americans between the hospital and the river. But the problem remained: how to warn his troops.

Without a radio, it was imperative that he return to the hospital as quickly as possible. The idea of retracing his steps terrified him. The Americans hid in the hedgerow—he knew it—and the paths from the river to the hospital lay in the shade of the trees on either side of the field. He wondered why they had not killed him already. His only option, Dac decided, was to *tron trong anh sang*, to "hide in sunlight." Lacking time to crawl the entire length of the field, he would simply walk to the hospital, calmly and without urgency, just another soldier heading in for some breakfast. For whatever reason, the Americans had not yet initiated their attack, and Dac was determined not to give them any reason to do so now.

Brady listened to Dac's footsteps descend the stairs from the veranda, then drifted back to a semi-sleep, grateful for the early-morning window of time when the ward cooled enough for him to stop sweating. A gentle kick from the NVA guard awakened him. The man spoke no English, but he pointed to Monroe, who lay awake, staring without comprehension at the room, the ceiling, the men around him, and the soldier's AK-47. The newsman flinched with surprise, drawing Monroe's attention.

"Don't move!" said Brady. "Lie still." He spun around, scanning the ward. "Nurse!"

Nurse Thao appeared from the kitchen, wiping blood from her hands on a sterile towel. Looking down at Monroe, contemptuous of his minor wound and amused by the silly American *bao chi* who expected her to tend to a headache when she had amputations to worry about, she said in English, "Water." Expressionless, she returned to the kitchen.

Brady pointed to the guard's canteen and mimed the act of drinking. Reluctantly, the guard offered it to him. Monroe struggled to sit up, then drank the man's water gratefully.

"What's your name?" asked Brady.

"Who are you?" Monroe's voice was a coarse whisper.

"Dan Brady. American. I'm here to get you home."

Monroe grabbed his head, which now resumed throbbing. "Where am I?"

The English conversation had attracted the attention of several other patients who now eyed the two Americans with callous curiosity. "Listen to me," said Brady. "Don't flip out on me. Just sit here and listen."

Monroe nodded and stared at his lap, holding his exploding head in his hands.

"You're in an NVA hospital somewhere in Cambodia. Don't worry; you're going to be OK. They've promised me that you can go home as long as you cooperate."

Monroe snorted, then coughed, each exhalation seeming to burst the nerve endings in his skull. "They're going to kill us."

"No. We know you shot General Cho. You have to tell us why and who ordered it. Then you go home and we all watch as the boys in the Pentagon try to explain you away. The gooks see you as a propaganda tool. It's the American brass that want you dead, not the NVA."

"Who the fuck is General Cho?"

Dac stepped into the grass as the last vestiges of the fog evaporated into the now sweltering sunshine. He was of average height by Vietnamese standards, short enough that the grass rose almost to his crotch, and Revelle spotted him at one hundred yards, moving casually, his rifle in the crook of his right arm, tucked up under his armpit. But for his pith helmet, Dac gave the impression of a man flushing quail.

"Don't shoot," said Patterson. "Our cover is blown soon as you pull the trigger."

"Look at this little fucker. Like he ain't got a care in the world."

Patterson already had his scope on Dac and he, too, had noticed Dac's bored demeanor. But with the more powerful spotter's scope, Patterson could also see the features of Dac's face. "His head is down, but his eyes ain't looking at the ground. He's lookin' at the trees."

"You think he knows we're here?"

"If he's looking for us, he's got the biggest balls of any gook I ever saw."

Revelle lowered the elevation on the Remington to zero. The target would pass within twenty-five yards.

Dac was conscious of the sound of his breathing and of the thump of each heartbeat and the high-pitched hum of his brain activity. If there were other sounds, like the flitting of grasshoppers that bolted away from each footstep, he couldn't hear them. He tried to dispel his terror with thoughts of happier days. But he could not remember the face of his infant son, and though he missed his wife, he could not bring himself to focus on her memory while the muzzles of American rifles followed his every step. His eyes refused to stare straight ahead, darting from hedgerow to hedgerow, left to right, right to left, wondering where the shot would come from that would take his life.

The fog had lifted to a thin overcast, and now this too started to burn away. As the sun began dappling the field and beaming between the leaves of the sycamores, a sudden reflection winked from the overgrown hedgerow to his left. Reflexively, Dac jerked his head toward it. At barely fifty yards, he could see through gaps in the veil of foliage, and there he saw something round, out of place among tree limbs and leaves. Without thinking, he dropped to the ground.

"What the fuck?" whispered Patterson, angry and fearful. "He spotted us! What did you do?"

"Nothing," Revelle lied, cursing himself. He had glanced up when a shaft of sunlight penetrated the overhead cover, allowing the muzzle of his weapon to point slightly upward. The round lens on the Redfield telescopic sight was deep-set to avoid glare, but not so deep that a sight pointed at the sun wouldn't reflect a smattering of photons, enough to attract attention in an area of deep shadow. An amateur's error. "I know where he is," said Revelle. "We can take him with a grenade."

"That one ain't no fool. He's crawling already. He could be anywhere out there."

"Well, what the fuck we gonna do, Patterson? We gotta do somethin'."

Patterson reached into his pack for a grenade, which he stuffed into the large thigh pocket of his fatigues. He placed his M-14 on the ground by Revelle's left foot. Withdrawing his K-Bar knife from the sheath on his boot, he quickly dipped under the dense curtain of vines and tree limbs that comprised the hedgerow and slipped into the field of grass.

Oh Christ, cursed Revelle as he reached for the radio.

The force of gravity seemed insufficient to Dac as he dove to the ground, planting his face into the soil and grasping desperately to the stalks of grass as if he were afraid he might bounce above them. Immediately he began crawling, pushing with his feet and elbows while keeping his head hard against the ground, worrying that his ass might rise above the grass or that the grass itself would betray his movements as he crushed it beneath him. The precious Remington, now an encumbrance, dragged along the ground with one elbow looped through the sling. He remembered that he had one round in the chamber and five more in the magazine. In the event of an attack, the bolt action rifle would be useless. I have found their cover, he thought. *They will attack now.* He crawled faster, expecting grenades.

Patterson stood a foot taller than Dac and eighty pounds heavier. The grass that could conceal Dac could only partially hide a man as large as Patterson, but at one hundred yards it would take an eagle's eye to spot a skilled sniper in two and a half feet of grass. Crawling without his M-14, Patterson moved fast, pausing frequently to listen, then shuttling forward, hoping to surprise his quarry at close range, very close range, where he could bring a knife to bear faster than a rifle. He pushed with his feet and elbows, almost swimming across the ground in six-inch increments, for that was as far as he could see. He stopped and rested, controlling his breathing so he could listen. The rustling sounds of a man dragging himself through the grass came to him, ahead and to his left. The man was fast, and Patterson had failed to cut him off. It would be a race now, two men crawling, one chasing the other.

Patterson knew that he could not catch him, and each yard closer to the hospital would bring him closer to being spotted. A grenade would stop the man, but the explosion would alert the NVA to the American presence. But Patterson reached for his grenade anyway, careful not to pull the pin. Listening carefully to Dac's passage through the grass, Patterson heaved the unarmed MK2 toward the sound.

The grenade landed directly in front of Dac. He heard the thump of its impact and knew instinctively what it was. He wheeled away, then lay as flat as he could, waiting for the explosion and the rain of shrapnel that he hoped would pass over him. Involuntarily, Dac quaked with each second that he waited. Five seconds passed, then ten. *Could it be a dud? Where had it come from?* He waited still more seconds to see if other grenades would follow. He dared not breathe for fear that any sound would invite another "Western Pineapple" to fall from the sky. The field fell silent, even the grasshoppers confused.

But Patterson kept moving. An inch at a time, boa-like, he closed the distance on Dac.

Dac quivered with uncertainty. To try to run would bring a fusillade of bullets from the treeline, barely twenty-five yards away. To call out a warning would invite more grenades, and at one hundred yards he wondered if anyone would hear him anyway. Yet someone had seen him, or heard him, or somehow detected him well enough to drop a grenade almost on his head. That person, Dac realized, was in the field with him. Very slowly, Dac brought his rifle to his shoulder. The muzzle, however, disappeared into the grass and Dac had a momentary sense of panic that whoever was out there might grab the barrel and yank the rifle right out of his hands. He pulled the rifle in close, the muzzle just inches beyond his nose. *Move*, he commanded himself.

With excruciating wariness, Dac turned again toward the hospital. He became aware of the heat, the sun beating upon his back. His pores opened. Each bead of sweat seemed to pop audibly from his skin, penetrating the absolute silence and announcing his location. Each blade of grass broke with a snap as he crawled over it. He imagined that he heard men breathing, just out of sight.

Patterson lay still as a stone, absorbing heat from the sun as perspiration trickled steadily into his eyes and behind his ears. He had stopped moving because his prey had stopped moving. Both men now simply listened, each waiting for the other to move. Patterson felt confident, however, that he had maneuvered himself between the enemy sniper and his destination. It was a waiting game now. The sun already approached its zenith and darkness, for once, favored the Americans. The man would have to move soon, and when he did Patterson would be waiting for him. So Patterson conserved his strength and strained his ears while staring at his hand grenade, six inches from his nose.

The grenade lay on its side where it had landed. Dac froze, his eyes riveted upon the nasty object, likely to explode at any moment or upon the slightest touch. The Chinese grenades provided to the NVA were so prone to failure that anyone foolish enough to do so could collect them after a battle in baskets, like American Easter eggs. But American grenades were almost always reliable so he studied it with some curiosity, despite his fear. Then he spotted the pin, still in place, and realized that this was no dud. Had the enemy tossed it intentionally unarmed? Were they toying with him? Or were they even more terrified than he, too rattled to remember to pull the pin? *These men are professionals,* he reasoned. *They don't forget to pull the pin on a grenade.* Dac considered pulling the pin himself and throwing the grenade toward the trees to alert his guards. But he realized that as soon as he blew the Americans' cover, they would stand up and shoot him. His best course of action, therefore, was to remain absolutely silent and use the grenade against the men stalking him. They would make a noise soon, and when they did, he would respond with their own Pineapple. Slowly, he reached for it.

Patterson struck like a cobra, grabbing Dac's hand and lunging through the grass, burying the K-Bar blade into Dac's chest like a fang. He withdrew the heavy blade and rammed it home again, surprised by the ease with which it penetrated the rib cage and the lungs. Dac screamed once, weak and reedy, until Patterson slammed his palm over Dac's mouth. The men rolled in the grass, Dac thrashing wildly while Patterson withdrew his knife for another thrust. Dac's other hand still gripped his rifle and he struggled to bring it to bear as Patterson's final thrust ripped though Dac's shallow abdomen, the point of the K-Bar imbedding itself in one of Dac's vertebrae. Dac pulled the trigger then, the sound as much a shock to Patterson as the impact of the bullet that ripped through his knee, splintering the bones of his lower leg. He recoiled in agony.

Still concealed in the hide, Revelle swung the muzzle of his Remington toward the sound of the gunshot. He dared not think what the shot meant, although he knew that Patterson had no weapon but his knife. *Stupid fuckin' nigger,* he thought. *I told you we shoulda* di di'*d last night.* He considered leaving, quietly fading into the bush, but he just wouldn't. *Stupid fuckin' nigger.* He reached for the radio. "Seal Baby, Seal Baby, this is Batman. We need you now."

He heard Seal Baby's acknowledgment as Dac rose from the weeds. Staggering forward, he waved one hand over his head while grasping with the other hand the blade of Patterson's knife, still protruding from his abdomen. Through his Redfield scope, Revelle could see blood frothing into the air from Dac's mouth as he tried to bleat out a warning, but he had no air with which to power his vocal cords. What air had been in his lungs had escaped through the lacerations inflicted by Patterson's K-Bar. If he didn't bleed to death from the damage to his spleen and liver, he would suffocate soon enough.

The gunshot, however, had attracted the attention of men at the hospital. Two guards ran to the veranda railing, unlimbering their AK-47s. Another pointed at Dac and dashed into the field to assist him. Revelle assessed the threats and determined that the wounded man was an asset—the enemy would expend effort to protect him rather than try to subdue Revelle. So Revelle raised his sights to the veranda, where both guards had now shouldered their weapons, seeking a target.

Revelle centered the crosshairs on the forehead of one guard and focused on his breathing as he slowly squeezed the trigger. As soon as the Remington bucked Revelle knew the shot was good, so in tune with his weapon was he that he could almost watch the bullet leave the thick semivarminter barrel. The man took the bullet in the head, flipping head over heels like a rag doll, through an open window into the hospital ward. He landed in a heap atop several wounded men, twitching with short-circuited nerves, another member of the "dancing dead." His pith helmet rolled across the floor, stopping at Brady's feet as the belated report of Revelle's shot rolled into the room.

Brady leapt to his feet. Equally shocked by the sudden chaos, Monroe's guard turned his attention to his dead comrade and the wounded men. The entire ward erupted in yelling as the least severely injured men scrambled away from the windows or tried to protect their stumps and other wounds from the pandemonium that raged around them. Unlike the confused men in the ward, however, Monroe recognized immediately the sound of the Remington. Forcing his throbbing head to clear, he staggered to his feet and threw himself into the guard. He grabbed the AK-47 with one hand and with the other rammed his fingers deep into the man's eyes. Screaming, the soldier released his grip on his weapon, whereupon Monroe killed him with it, a three-shot burst to the sternum. With a wild spray of bullets through the room, Monroe bolted through the shattered window onto the veranda. There he encountered the remaining sentry, recovered enough from the shock of the attack to turn his weapon on Monroe. Before he could pull the trigger, however, the base of the man's skull exploded, followed by the familiar rumble of the Remington. Monroe leapt over the railing onto the ground. Like a rabbit he ran into the vast field, zigzagging, knowing that an American sniper was there to cover his back. Spotting Monroe, Revelle worked the bolt as fast as he could, hurling round after round into the hospital, stoking the chaos and taking out anyone with a weapon. At one hundred yards he did not miss. Then as Revelle jacked in another round, Brady dashed howling onto the veranda, beseeching Monroe to stop. Revelle smiled grimly as he drew a bead on the strange white man. *Goodbye, buddy, whoever the fuck you are.* But as Revelle pulled the trigger, Brady vaulted the veranda railing. The 173 grain bullet struck Brady in the ankle, shattering the intricate anatomy, and blowing Monroe's boot across the porch with Brady's foot still in it.

The Remington fired again and Monroe saw the foliage rustle with the shock wave one hundred yards away. He ran toward it. Only a smattering of shots followed him, as Revelle's deadly accuracy effectively suppressed any return fire.

Then Monroe spotted Dac and the Vietnamese soldier who had gone to aid him. Even at sixty yards, he could see bloody vomit spewing from Dac's mouth and the knife still stuck in his gut. But the other man was dangerous, already on one knee, his weapon raised, ready to shoot the naked black American soldier running toward him. Monroe swept the muzzle of his AK-47 across the man's chest and pulled the trigger. The magazine was empty. Before Monroe could react, however, the man's uniform seemed to inflate as a bullet passed through him, bringing with it a volume of organs and blood that filled his shirt. He pitched face forward into the grass. Behind him, kneeling on his good knee, was Patterson, Dac's Remington in his hands.

Monroe raced past Dac, now slumped to his knees, to gather Patterson into his arms. "Get to the water," gasped Patterson as Monroe held him upright. The Remington boomed again. "Revelle's in the trees." Monroe put his shoulder under Patterson's arm and lifted him to his feet, Patterson's bloody leg dragging, useless. The Remington had suppressed any fire from the hospital and only desultory shots chased them. Given Revelle's terrifying accuracy, the limited numbers of armed soldiers, the loss of leadership, and the general bedlam within the hospital, there would be no pursuit.

Revelle grabbed the flare gun and fired through the canopy. "Seal Baby," he screamed into the radio, "where the fuck are you?"

But Dac's two-man blocking force now loosed a fusillade from the opposite end of the field. Moving quickly up field at the first sound of gunfire, they closed to within fifty yards of Monroe and Patterson. Three rounds from an AK-47 struck Patterson, stitched across his chest. Patterson went down hard. In a desperate lunge for help, he grabbed Monroe's arm, dragging him down as more bullets flew overhead.

A new sound overwhelmed the battlefield. Seal Baby arrived, its twin .50s laying a blanket of fire across the entire battlefield. The aft .50 joined in, as did the coxswain with an M-60 amidships, adding ten rounds per second to the PBR's firepower. An eerie hum settled in over the grass, the whine of a thousand bullets three feet above the ground, like locusts mowing down everything in their path. And back in his hide, Revelle fired the Remington, the deep booms coming as fast as he could work the bolt. His work done, Revelle abandoned the radio and his gear, all except the guns. With the Remington in one hand and the M-14 in the other, he emerged from the treeline to assist Patterson. Despite the mayhem around him, Monroe heard the big gun go silent.

Caught from behind, the two-man blocking force never knew what hit them, the .50 caliber slugs that slammed into their backs rending them into offal. The curtain of heavy projectiles descended upon the battlefield indiscriminately, tearing apart the hospital and the wounded men inside. Nurse Thao died at the operating table, along with the doctor and the patient.

"We'll make it!" screamed Monroe. "Revelle's coming! Just hang on, man. Hang on!"

"I can't breathe," gasped Patterson, oxygenated blood coating his teeth and spraying with each word. Both of his punctured lungs filled with blood, and what didn't drain from the entry wound flooded out through his mouth. "I'm supposed to be answering the fuckin' phones." An enormous tear rolled down his cheek.

"I'll carry you!" screamed Monroe as he struggled to lift Patterson into his arms.

"You ain't never gonna carry nobody but yourself, Monroe." Patterson's head dropped to the ground. "Let me be," he coughed, blood flying. He snatched the hand grenade from the ground and held it close to his chest. "Go on, nigger. Run!" He pulled the pin and shoved Dac's rifle into Monroe's hand.

Whatever emotions cascaded through Monroe at that second, only one took command: the will to survive. Screaming with despair, Monroe grabbed the Remington and turned away, nearly colliding with Revelle, who had now made it across the field. Only one thought remained in Monroe's mind.

"Get to the boat!" he yelled, heading toward the shore

"What about Patterson?" Revelle turned where Monroe pointed, but glanced backward toward where his partner lay.

"He's dead!" Monroe pushed Revelle forward and the two snipers dashed the final yards to the pier, where the PBR now waited. Enveloped in smoke from its own guns, Seal Baby poured such a volume of fire into the field that the tracers, ricocheting wildly, created a red veil across the field, killing everything it touched. Both men threw themselves off the pier, crazed with determination to reach the thundering boat. The skipper nudged the PBR forward and sideways, while the coxswain dropped his smoking M-60 to extend his arm to Monroe, then Revelle. Their hands touched and the skipper shoved the throttles forward. The little boat roared for open water, spewing lead in its wake. Amid the overwhelming wail of the guns, Monroe heard one sound as he clung to the gunwale. The puny roar of Patterson's grenade would resonate forever in his ears.

TH!RTY-4

**Khet Prey Veng,
Cambodia**

Two kilometers from the hospital, Colonel Ninh first heard the singular boom of Revelle's rifle while his troops conducted the daily security sweep of the field around the pagoda. It concerned him, but his focus remained on recovering the remnants of his slaughtered battalions, men who staggered into camp piecemeal as they retreated from one battle or another: Firebase Christine, Can Tho, Vinh Long Airfield, My Tho. Even in Chau Doc, the tide had turned against the NVA. But NVA and VC alike recognized the drawl of an American .50 caliber machine gun as heavy with meaning, a signature sound on any battlefield in Vietnam. When Ninh heard the Navy PBR open up, he did what commanders had done since gunpowder had been added to the technology of war. He marched to the sound of the guns.

The battle had been brief, however, the surviving Americans gone twenty minutes before the first squad of Ninh's men arrived. They found the remains of the hospital smoldering, its floors awash in blood and the remains of the medical staff strewn about the kitchen, where a headless corpse still lay on the makeshift operating table. The smell of cordite saturated the air and the least dazed survivors poked about the grounds looking for anyone still breathing. By the time Ninh arrived, his men had established a makeshift infirmary in the shade of a large tree where unskilled men performed crude medical triage, their expertise learned the hard way. Ninh surveyed the row of mangled men and wondered what other disasters the Americans had prepared for him. A captain and two soldiers approached carrying the body of Dac and laid him gently on the ground.

"Chinh tri bo," mumbled one of the men respectfully. "The commissar."

Colonel Ninh glanced down, but his attention returned to the living. An unconscious man caught his attention. He knelt on one knee next to Brady and put his hand on Brady's chest to feel for a pulse. *Lieu co the phuc hoi duoc khong?"* he asked. "Will he live?" Ninh saw that his foot was gone, the bleeding staunched by a bloody tourniquet.

"Until the infection kills him, Colonel. We have no medicines, certainly none to spare on an American."

"He came here to assist us."

"His assistance has been very beneficial as you can see, Colonel."

"Prepare a litter and detail three men to take him to the CIA compound in Chau Doc."

"Sir," protested the captain, "Chau Doc is dangerous for us now, and our men are exhausted. We owe this man nothing."

"He is an American newspaper reporter, Captain, and sympathetic to our cause. He will win this war for us." Ninh hated himself for thinking like a commissar, calculating and soulless. He glanced again at Dac's corpse and felt no pity. *Commissar, for once I can act with honor without sacrificing strategy.* Colonel Ninh walked away as the captain signaled for a litter.

Monroe had vague memories of his return to Division, the smell of hot brass in the boat and the sound of Patterson's grenade. The fever kicked in on the run down river and Monroe remembered the shakes as they took Sadowski's rifle from him and loaded him onto a stretcher in the back of a waiting ambulance. A gaggle of officers had been there to greet him, just watching, really; he recalled gold Major's leaves on their collars. Where was Revelle, he wondered, lost in the hubbub or already gone to debrief the mission? Then the doctors took over.

Consciousness came and went during the rough ride to the 3rd Surgical Hospital in the back of an Army ambulance, a model left over from Korea, hardly used in Vietnam, where the real ambulances were the dust-off helicopters. At Intake, his wounds did not warrant immediate treatment so they triaged him to the end of the line with a blanket to control the fever-driven chills. Six hours later the doctors prepped him for surgery. They cleaned his wound carefully, marveling at how close the graze was to puncturing the three membranes that protected his brain. Honing their plastic surgery skills in preparation for the day they would enter private practice, they sewed him up and noted on his chart—*gunshot wound struck cranial bridging vein causing Venus tear resulting in subdermal hematoma, patient stable.* Monroe was then assigned to the surgery ward with a simple post-op prescription: antibiotics and a bath.

The next morning, Monroe came to.

The duty nurse spotted him as she made her rounds, administering medications. "Good morning." She spoke quietly, professionally, without any annoying cheerfulness. "You feel OK?"

Monroe nodded. An artillery shell rolled around inside his skull.

A doctor came by later. He checked Monroe's stitches and shined a light into his eyes before jotting his findings on the chart, which he stashed away in a slot at the end of the bed. With a brief word to the nurse, he was on to the next patient in less than two minutes.

The nurse snapped her fingers and signaled to a black male orderly. "Remove his catheter."

The orderly was all business, plucking the catheter from Monroe's penis as if he were pulling the pin on a grenade. Monroe yelped.

Monroe dozed in his bed when he was roused by a subtle change in the pervading gloom. There was an expectancy in the air. Men were awake. Faster, quicker breaths replaced the soporific sound of drug-induced slumber.

Monroe saw by the shadows that it was afternoon. The clock on the wall said 1600. Others clock watched, too.

"Four o'clock." The soldier in the adjacent bed spoke softly. "Quiet," he said, "in the afternoon. Meds come at four."

Expectancy turned to curiosity, then resentment as a full bird colonel entered the ward, his presence interfering with the efficient distribution of painkillers. Colonel Boettcher strode purposefully to Monroe's bed, ignoring the stares of the other wounded men. He pulled up a chair and sat down.

"Private Monroe," he said quietly, "do you know who I am?"

Monroe looked him over, not raising his throbbing head from his pillow. "No, sir."

"My name is Colonel Ron Boettcher, Chief of Staff."

Monroe did not know what staff this colonel professed to be the chief of, but he said nothing, glancing toward the nurses station where the Demerol cart was being loaded.

"I work for General Vandermeer." Boettcher saw Monroe's focus return to him with the mention of Vandermeer's name. "I'm here to thank you for a tremendous job. We're very proud of you, son. My staff is preparing a couple of awards for your heroism. You'll be able to wear them, although the citation will remain classified. You understand that you may never discuss what happened to you, don't you?"

"What about Patterson?" Tears welled up in Monroe's eyes as he recalled for the first time since his rescue how Patterson had died. *What does this motherfucker want with me*, he thought, as a sob snagged in his throat.

"I'm sorry," said Boettcher. "Private Patterson will receive his awards posthumously." He paused for a few awkward moments as a trail of individual tears rolled down Monroe's cheek and soaked into the pillow. "Monroe, Patterson was a good soldier, but I'm here to talk about you right now."

Monroe managed a deep breath.

"Your application to the US Military Academy Prep School has been approved," said Boettcher. "Do you understand what I'm saying?"

"What application?" answered Monroe, his eyes staring indifferently toward the ceiling.

"You applied for virtually every MOS and volunteer assignment in the army, Private. Except Infantry, of course. Do you recall your application to West Point?"

"No, sir."

Boettcher shook his head slowly from side to side, disgusted that he had approved such a coveted application for a man who didn't even remember applying for it. "The Prep School is not the same as West Point, Monroe. You do not have the necessary academic background to succeed there. However, the Army is always looking for potential leaders and we believe you can be an officer if you apply yourself. Your assignment is to attend academic classes at Fort Belvoir, Virginia, for a year where you will be schooled in the math and English that you failed to get in high school. If you do well, you'll be admitted to West Point, where after fours years of study, you will be commissioned as a lieutenant in the Army." Boettcher paused to make sure that Monroe understood what he was saying. "Your other option," he continued, "is to return to combat in a couple of weeks after your wounds heal."

Monroe placed his hands against his temples to make the pain subside.

Boettcher said, "Do you understand what I'm offering you, Private?"

"Yes, sir."

"Do you want to go to the Prep School?"

Monroe simply turned his eyes upon Boettcher, as if the answer was so obvious as to not warrant a verbal response.

"OK, then." Boettcher lowered his voice and moved closer to Monroe. "Here's the catch: your mission was classified and you may never, under any circumstances, discuss it with anyone even after you leave the Army. If you do, I will personally escort you to prison. But if you keep your mouth shut, you could be a general someday."

The two men locked eyes until the pain welled up again in Monroe's head and he looked for the med cart. Boettcher stood up. "Good luck, Monroe." He placed a set of orders on the nightstand next to the metal cot and quietly walked away as the nurse finally made her rounds.

With effort, Monroe leaned over to open the drawer to the nightstand. He placed his orders to the Prep School next to the only other object in the drawer. He had surrendered Sadowski's Remington to Revelle, but in the commotion nobody had noticed that he had field stripped the bolt. It lay now in his drawer, more than a souvenir. He thumbed the bolt and heard the cart roll his way. Looking up, he noticed General Vandermeer huddled with Boettcher in the distant hall wall, nodding, listening. He caught the general's eye, held it longer than he intended, then looked away.

GLOSSARY

AFN	Armed Forces Network; the military radio station in Vietnam
AO	area of operations
Arclight raid	B-52 bomber attack
ARVN	Army of Vietnam
BOQ	bachelor officers quarters
brigadier general	1 star
BX	base exchange
C&C	command and control
CAP	combat air patrol
Charlie	The Viet Cong; from "Victor Charlie," the phonetic alphabet for "VC"
CIB	combat infantry badge; awarded only after participation in actual combat
CIC	combat information center
CINC	commander in chief
CO	commanding officer
CQ	charge of quarters
DEROS	date of return from overseas; the date your tour of duty ended, the day you went home
deuce and a half	ten-wheeled truck with 2 1/2 ton capacity
E&E	escape and evade
First Shirt	first sergeant
FNG	fucking new guy; the latest replacement
G-2	Division Intelligence
G-3	Division Operations
HE	high explosive, the most common and most deadly type of artillery round
Huey	UH-1 helicopter, used primarily for carrying cargo or up to ten troops

JP4	fuel used in the UH-1 helicopter (Jet Propellant #4)
KIA	killed in action
lieutenant general	three stars
LZ	landing zone
MACV	military assistance command, Vietnam
major general	two stars
MP	military police
NVA	North Vietnamese Army
OD	olive drab
PBR	patrol boat, river
PIO	Public Information Office
POL	petroleum, oil, and lubricants
PSP	pierced steel planking, 2' by 8' slabs of sheet metal with holes in it, hooked together to form a hard surface on soft ground suitable for aircraft runways
REMF	rear echelon motherfucker
RTO	radio telephone perator
Ruff Puff	Regional Popular Forces, the South Vietnamese militia
sitrep	situation report
Slick	helicopter, specifically an unarmed UH-1
SOP	standard operating procedure
squelch	normal hiss on a radio between transmissions
UH-1	most common helicopter in Vietnam (See Huey)
VC	Viet Cong
WIA	wounded in action
Willie Pete	white phosphorous
XO	executive officer

ACKNOWLEDGMENTS

Few novels spring intact from the mind of the author. In writing The Silent Men, I have benefited from the knowledge, experiences, and moral support of numerous people. Dale Freidig, Lou Novak, Pete Rose, David Cargill, and Kim Pham have generously offered invaluable technical advice. I also want to thank Debra Cafiero, who believed in this story before anyone else, and my wife, Amy Solomon, who not only tolerated my hours at the computer but also had just the right suggestions to help me overcome frequent bouts of writer's block.

In addition, my research has been greatly informed by the eloquence of other writers. The following bibliography is a partial list of authors deserving credit for some of the ideas that have inspired me.

Anson, Robert, *War News* (New York: Simon & Schuster, 1989).

Boa Ninh, *The Sorrow of War* (London: Minerva, 1994).

Gilbert, Adrian, *Sniper* (London: Sidgwick & Jackson, 1994).

Henderson, Charles, *Marine Sniper* (Briarcliff Manor, NY: Stein and Day, 1986).

Herr, Michael, *Dispatches* (New York: Alfred Knopf, 1977).

Marcinko, Richard, *Rogue Warrior* (New York: Pocket Books, 1992).

Mason, Robert, *Chickenhawk* (New York: Viking Press, 1983).

O'Brien, Tim, *The Things They Carried* (New York: Penguin Books, 1990).

Page, Tim, and Pimlott, John, *Nam, The Vietnam Experience 1965-75* (New York: Mallard Press, 1989).

Parrish, Robert, *Combat Recon* (New York: St Martin's Press, 1991).

Sasser, Charles, and Roberts, Craig, *One Shot One Kill* (New York: Pocket Books, 1990).

Terry, Wallace, *Bloods* (New York: Ballantine Books, 1984).

Ward, Joseph, *Dear Mom: A Sniper's Vietnam* (New York: Ballantine Books, 1991).

Wolff, Tobias, *In Pharaoh's Army* (New York: Alfred Knopf, 1994).